# THIS IS MOSTRIM

~ ~ ~

## THE EXILE

MARK CASSIDY

**Copyright © Mark Cassidy, 2025**
First Published in Ireland, in 2025, in co-operation with
Choice Publishing, Drogheda, County Louth, Republic of Ireland.
www.choicepublishing.ie

Paperback ISBN: 978-1-917242-28-8

The moral right of the author has been asserted.

All rights reserved. No part of this publication may be reproduced, stored in a retrieval system, transmitted in any form, or by any means, electronic, mechanical, photocopying, recording or otherwise, without the prior permission of the copyright holder.

# TITLES IN THIS COLLECTION

*This Is Mostrim – The Famine*

*This Is Mostrim – The Exile*

*This Is Mostrim – The Homecoming*

To James, Michael and Kathleen

Also

Remembering all those who have had to flee their homeland.

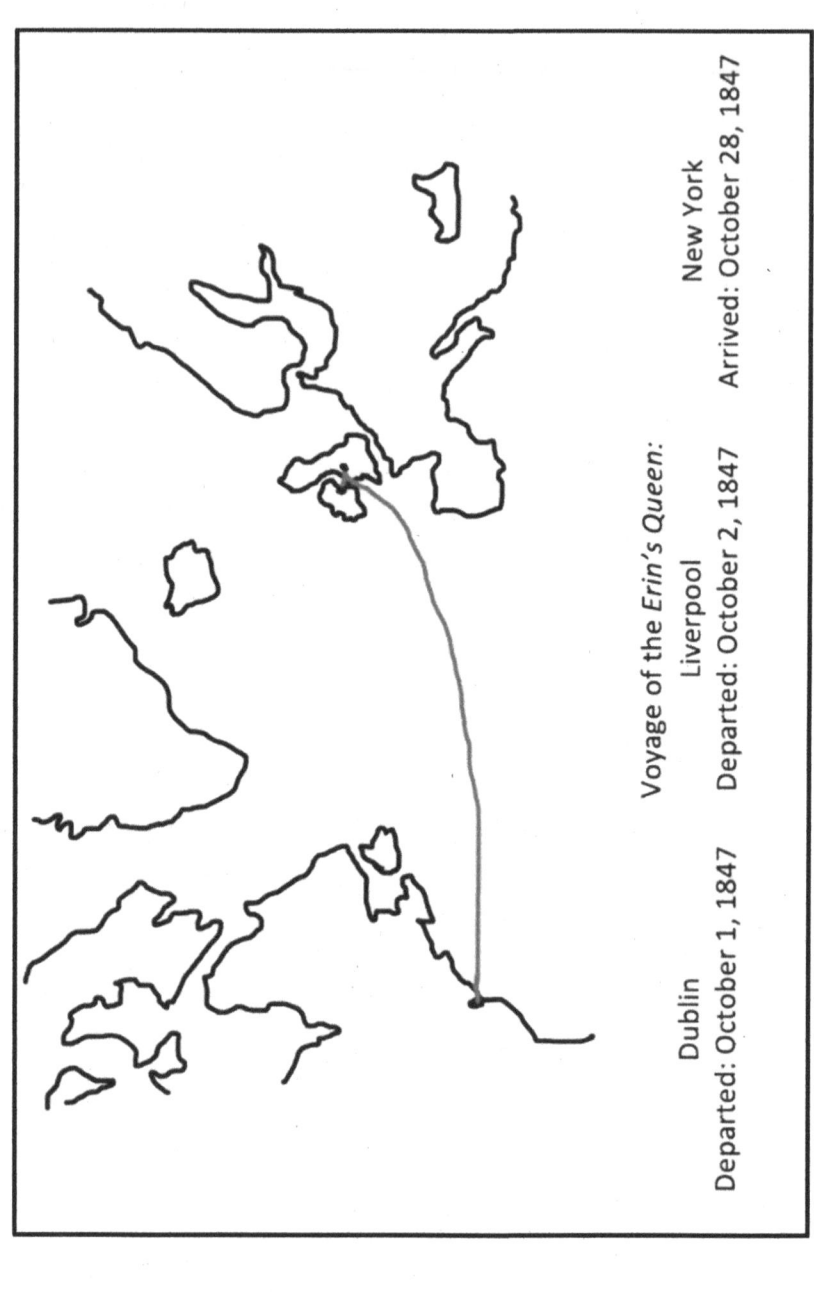

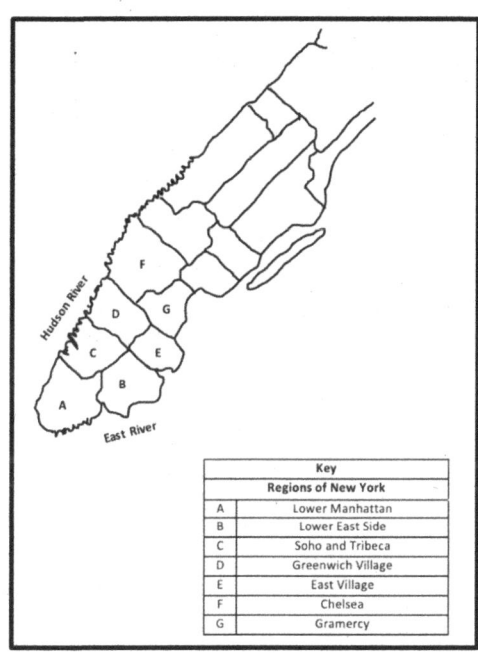

| Key | |
|---|---|
| Regions of New York | |
| A | Lower Manhattan |
| B | Lower East Side |
| C | Soho and Tribeca |
| D | Greenwich Village |
| E | East Village |
| F | Chelsea |
| G | Gramercy |

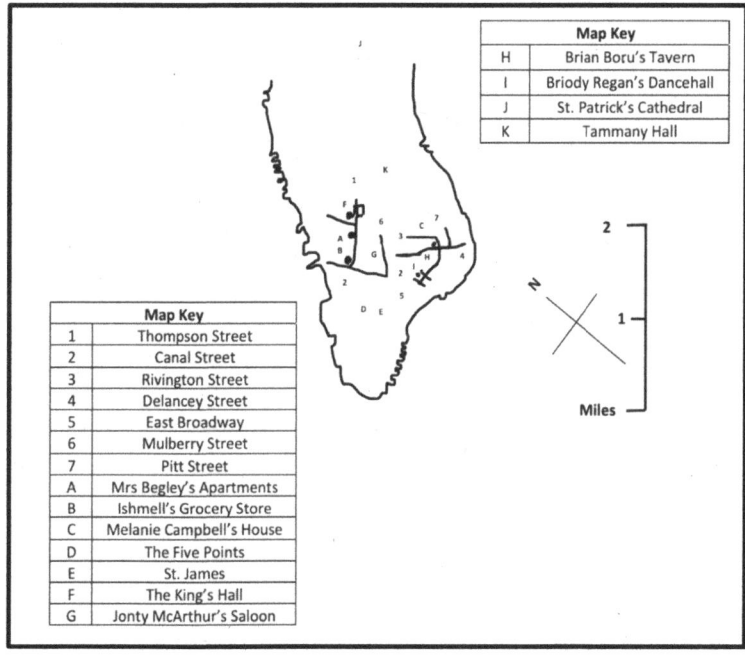

| Map Key | |
|---|---|
| H | Brian Boru's Tavern |
| I | Briody Regan's Dancehall |
| J | St. Patrick's Cathedral |
| K | Tammany Hall |

| Map Key | |
|---|---|
| 1 | Thompson Street |
| 2 | Canal Street |
| 3 | Rivington Street |
| 4 | Delancey Street |
| 5 | East Broadway |
| 6 | Mulberry Street |
| 7 | Pitt Street |
| A | Mrs Begley's Apartments |
| B | Ishmell's Grocery Store |
| C | Melanie Campbell's House |
| D | The Five Points |
| E | St. James |
| F | The King's Hall |
| G | Jonty McArthur's Saloon |

## One – New York in the Fall

All eyes were on Jim Gorman. He rested the letter on his knee. He smoothed out the corners – an old habit stretching back to our hedge-school days. He scratched his chin. Silence reigned once more. The heated exchanges that threatened the reading were abandoned for the moment. The letter wasn't finished. He stared out at the garden. He needed the break too. No doubt what he had just learned shook him to the core. I followed his gaze.

Outside, a pumpkin-head swung in the wind. It reminded me of the very first night in this house – and only our second on the American mainland. Three years gone past in the blink of an eye. *I bpreabadh na sul,* as Mickser would say. It still feels weird to hear Irish being spoken in a different land. Still, I suppose, time waits for nobody. Ina Begley came to mind. I pictured her sullen face beneath a headscarf. It was at Halloween also, in 1847, when we met for the first time. A loud bang broke the silence, a stark reminder that the world outside was getting on with the business of the night.

Jim's gaze returned to matters at hand. Six flushed faces waited patiently, the heat of the lamplight pulsing on our cheeks.

'After that, we've got to go back,' I said, as nicely as I could manage.

I didn't want another argument.

'Yes, *we* do,' said Father Murtagh, 'but not you, Joseph. We've had this out already. If it was just yourself, I'd have you on board in a heartbeat. But your job is here now – not in Ireland. In America, with Melanie.'

I stretched myself to ease the tension. I really didn't want to go back on the attack. Jim yawned loudly and picked up the letter with his good arm.

'Lads, can I finish this first before ye start at it again.'

His plea fell on deaf ears. The row was back in full swing.

'This changes everything now, Father, and you know it,' I pointed out.

'I told you already, your best option is to go west and claim some land. You're a family man now, with more to think about than charging off back to Ireland. You've fought the good fight, Joseph, and I commend you on it. But you just can't do what you want anymore. You have to put Melanie and the child first. It's not an option. You know I'm right.'

'So, your suggestion is to forget about Shay Gorman and Constance Ryan – not to mention justice for poor Turk? Run off to Oklahoma and claim ground? Merciful hour! Well, I'm not going to shame myself in the sight of God by staking out a plot of Indian land and taking it from them, just like the English did to us. I won't support their annihilation, the poor little buggers, because I know what it's like to be on the receiving end. Did you not hear what Jim just said – we've been pardoned. They can't touch us. I'm free to go back if I want.'

'I'm not saying that at all,' explained Father Murtagh. 'But a man trying to do right by his family doesn't head in the direction of a famine. If you feel so strongly about Oklahoma and the Indians, then don't go. There's always Youngstown. Go to Ohio instead and forget about Ireland now. Go out there, man, and stake your claim. Be a new American and a true American, just like the pamphlet says.'

'You're not listening, Padre. I don't have a choice. This McKeon girl has left things that way. None of us have a choice, if it comes to down to it. We must return and at least try to put things right.'

I felt even worse after hearing myself say it. And so did Jim, judging by his face. Until that moment, they were just a few scrawled sentences his wife had written six weeks earlier; sentences which had only just reached us by mail. But the seriousness of these new developments was already beginning to sink in. Jim's eyes scanned the paper once more. He repeated the words slowly – the lines which determined his son's innocence once and for all, the lines which proved we were no longer wanted men, the lines which would take us back over the Atlantic Ocean towards disease and hunger and British oppression. His lips moved again, churning out more fantastic news, as the padre and I entered into another ceasefire.

*Astonishing new development... proving Shay's innocence .... Annie McKeon, former handmaid to Viscount de Bromley.... a public statement under oath from information confided in her by an ex-lover, a Miss Sheila McAndrew.... pillow-talk... a set-up leading to Shay's imprisonment and transportation to the colonies.... police now seeking the whereabouts of Walter Pollach in England and other leading managerial figures of the one-time Cranley House.... Constance Ryan, against her will.... drugged, kidnapped and sold as a bride....Shaun Burke and Viscount de Bromley to be questioned by police.... Constance still missing... Sugrue Gang receives full pardon... police in crash speak up on their behalf...*

'One of the policemen did the decent thing, admitting Peter Hogan's evidence was given under duress,' said Jim, dropping the pages and addressing me directly.

'Duress? More like bloody torture,' I returned. 'The peelers are every bit as bad as the politicians who put them there.'

'They spoke up for us as well,' continued Jim. 'Apparently, those on duty at the paddy-wagon crash gave a glowing account of our kindness towards them.'

'You see, there's decency in all walks of life,' added the padre.

'All Sugrue's doing,' I declared. 'I wouldn't piss on them if they were on fire. He was good to them – treated them with care and respect. The soldier in him, I suppose. The authorities *had* to throw out the charges. It was either that or admit collusion in the whole stinking affair.'

It felt like one of those detective stories you'd read in the *New York Tribune* – like the end of a fairytale. And yet, the words were as painful as they were sweet. At least the confession that Walter Pollach had made to Jim was now public knowledge – no longer a *convenient excuse*, as the chief constable in Mostrim once called it.

'Shaddup, you guys, and don't be so truculent all the time,' said Breda Nayle. 'Letta man continue.'

It always made me smile, that sing-song city accent. Her intervention ended the argument – for now.

'He's reading already,' she snapped.

'Thank you, Breda,' said Jim, before drawing the pages closer with his free hand.

His voice creaked with emotion as he read on.

'*Maria Edgeworth died almost six months ago. Her death divided the parish. Some, even among the Catholic community, speak highly of her. Others blame her kind for the plight of the people and the anarchy in the countryside. And then there are the rest. The situation has become so bad the vast majority of afflicted souls would hardly notice if their own mothers were dead, let alone Maria Edgeworth.*'

Jim paused briefly and looked to his audience. This news was hard on him. It was hard on most of us. It told on the faces. It was hard on Charles Langley too – the Iron Man of Oxford, as the padre had begun to call him. Any human who could crawl out from under a hundred-weight of collapsed ballast without so much as a scratch deserves to be called an iron man. His ginger head was a study of concentration. The youngsters sat impatiently, waiting for the letter to end. Maria Edgeworth didn't mean a thing to them. I could barely make out Mickser Burrows sitting at the far wall. Dusk was setting and Jim reached over and turned up the wick of an oil lamp, then continued Mairead's tidings.

*'Ireland has adopted a new national flag. A tricolour of green, white and orange will represent Catholics, Protestants and peace between them.'*

'Jeb Turling can take down the old green flag in his loft now,' I quipped, in a private yarn with Jim, 'the one with the gold harp.'

'I think we both know how likely that is to happen,' he replied, before returning to the letter. 'That's it all, folks, apart from a bit of small talk that you fellas wouldn't be interested in.'

Jim placed the letter on the table and gave it another ironing with his fist. He fixed his elbow in its sling. The sight of it brought back my shame. If I had been with him, instead of trying to recover Mickser's money, I know it would never have happened. Jeremiah felt it worst of all. Every time he thought of Bartholomew he felt sick. Survivor guilt – that's what the padre calls it. He has a name for every ache and pain, and a pill for every ill. He also said it was the real reason I wanted to go back – because, since the funeral, I couldn't bear to be around Melanie. Imagine to say something like that and us not long married. The cheek of him. He was talking through his hat. It was time for the hard decisions.

'Small talk. You mean romantic talk,' teased Breda, 'we gals love that kindda shit.'

'Breda, a lady doesn't use such turn of phrase,' Father Murtagh pointed out.

'Sorry, Pops,' she said, and smiled coyly.

Father Murtagh took a stand. He looked nervous.

'Right, the talking is over and done with. It's time to lay your cards on the table. Who wants to start the ball rolling? Charles? Jeremiah?'

'As long as it's not Mickser,' said Jim, 'we all know what happened the last time he laid his cards on the table.'

'Cheap shot, Jim Gorman,' replied Mickser. 'There isn't much you can do with a gun stuck in your face.'

'Joseph, perhaps,' added the padre. 'Maybe he's finally come to his senses?'

I looked away. I had no desire to rekindle the argument. The padre's grand plan for me was Youngstown, Ohio. A job in the steel mills. He was set on Youngstown because he never warmed to the idea of taking pot luck on a pan of gold in Sutter's Mill. And he knew he couldn't talk me into grabbing land from the redskins. I'd seen enough land-grabbing in the old country to do me a lifetime.

In the days following the explosion on the railroad I was all for Ohio. But after Mairead's latest letter, this changed again – especially as I was no more a fugitive of the majestic, imperial, despicable Queen Victoria's law. It was time to do the decent thing. And the decent thing to me – Joseph Jabber Farrell – was to return to Ireland to right some of the wrongs highlighted in that very letter.

Charles Langley stroked the red hair around his mouth, a tell-tale sign that he was about to speak. I seized the moment instead.

'I've been listening to the same bullshite since we started living in Thompson Street – go out and stake your claim to be a true American and not some deadbeat, as Breda would say, the like you'd find hanging around the city ghettos. I never minded being classed a deadbeat, as long as I could be classed an Irishman and a Mostrim man as well. When I stepped onto the *Erin's Queen* I did not leave Ireland and Mostrim behind – *we* did not leave Ireland and Mostrim behind. We carry Ireland and Mostrim everywhere we go. We *are* Ireland and we *are* Mostrim. And while I'm here, three thousand miles away, this is Ireland and this is Mostrim. America was only ever meant to be temporary – for me at least. That's how I see it anyway. My job is in the old country and I say we go back.'

Father Murtagh sighed heavily and looked towards the heavens.

'We *are* going back, at least some of us. But Joseph, listen to me, you *can't* come with us. It's not an option. And I'm not discussing it any longer. As I said already – if you were a single man, there wouldn't be a problem.'

'I'm sorry to burst your bubble, Father, but I know my catechism. I studied for the priesthood too,' I snapped. 'And I won't turn my back on the gifts of the Holy Spirit I received at Confirmation. One of those gifts is fortitude. When I see injustice I like to think I have the fortitude to put it right. So, I'm going back to Ireland and that's an end to it.'

I felt it was time to play the padre at his own game.

'I know all that,' he answered. 'And I commend you for it. But surely you know that the Spirit does not give fortitude to be acted on alone, but to be used in conjunction with the other gifts. Therefore, have the depth of wisdom and knowledge to understand how Melanie will feel if you take off for Ireland. Use the counsel given from above to choose the correct path – not the path of a single man, but the correct path of a husband and father. Have the reverence and fear in the Lord to do the right thing, Joseph.'

'Nobody asked if I'd like to come along,' declared Breda, straightening in her chair. 'Actually, I've grown quite incandescent to the idea of running off with a rustic bellwethe', and experiencing his antediluvian world.'

Despite Jim Gorman's jibes about my seminarial education, I hadn't the faintest idea what she was on about. But the padre seemed to find it amusing.

'Do you know what they do to girls who kiss priests in Ireland,' warned Mickser, trying desperately to hold in the laughing.

Mickser could never keep a straight face – except, of course, at the Spieler. The swelling, especially on his left side, had gone down a lot. But the deep cut on his head still needed to be dressed daily.

'That's enough out of you,' said Father Murtagh. 'Thank you, Breda. We all know you're a brave little soldier with the best intentions in the world but, believe me, Ireland is no place for a girl to go on holiday. Sorry, to go on vacation.'

'You don't scare me, Pops, with you' melodramatic warnings. And for you' information, Mickse', I didn't kiss a priest in Ireland, I kissed a priest in Thompson Street.'

'It's very decent of you to offer,' said Jim, 'but let's get real for a moment. Breda, you can't possibly come with us. We can't let you leave your poor mother here by herself. You're all she's got in the world.'

Jeremiah's gaze dropped to the floor when he heard this.

'James is right,' continued Father Murtagh, 'and besides your mother, we can't bring a defenceless young woman to a place where anarchy, not to mention famine, is raging even more now than it did when we were leaving.'

Jeremiah nodded his head slowly. His heart was sinking fast.

'Don't get the wrong idea,' said Jim, 'you're educated, you're smart. And above all else, you're a gutsy little cailin. That's a gutsy little *broad* in your language, Breda.'

'I'm no defenceless young woman,' snapped Breda. 'I can be as pugnacious as the best of them.'

There was another silence then. Jim looked at Jeremiah. He had been young once too. And he remembered what young love felt like. He didn't want Jeremiah to resent him when they got back to Ireland. They had too much to do besides him pining for a girl.

Suddenly it occurred to Jim – why should he play the villain, when someone else could fill the part.

'I'll tell you what, Breda, have a chat with your mother,' he suggested. 'Then you'll understand what I'm talking about.'

Jim turned towards me then.

'I'm afraid I have to agree with the padre,' he said. 'I'm sorry old pal, we've had a great run. But this is where we need to part company. Father Murtagh was right, your job is in America now. Whether it's Oklahoma, California, Ohio, or wherever, you'll take your new family and our good wishes with you. The blessings of God on you, Jabber. You made a promise to Bartholomew's sister and you must stand by it now.'

It was hard to hear that – especially from Jim Gorman. It was as if we'd been through a war together. Ever since the paddy-wagon crash in August, 1847, I'd spent some part of every day in his company. Every single day for the past three years and three months – whether hiding in haybarns or beneath a dead man's bed, under the tarpaulin of a barge boat or in the bedroom of a Dublin whorehouse – Jim Gorman and I had found ourselves very much inseparable.

'Well, what about my mother, Jim? I promised her on her deathbed I'd keep you fellas out of harm's way.'

Jim left his seat and walked across the room. He placed a hand on my shoulder. I would have preferred if he had drawn out and flattened me.

'You've kept your promise to your mother, Jabber, and more than that. She would be very proud of all you have done for us. The fact is she's not the only one who's proud of you. The last thing Sugrue said to me before I boarded the *Erin's Queen* was, and I quote: "I've seen the best of Jabber Farrell since our trouble began. We owe him a huge debt of gratitude." Now, you've done your duty by us. It's time to do your duty by Melanie.'

I could feel the hairs rising on the back of my neck. But I didn't look at him. I looked out the window instead. The pumpkin-head was swinging even more now. The wind must have been getting stronger. I knew what they were thinking – the game was finally up. Jim and Father Murtagh would be returning to Ireland, but without me.

'Now,' continued Jim, returning to matters at hand, 'as the padre has already said, it's time for the rest of you fellas to put your cards on the table. Tie up your loose ends over the next few hours. We meet back here – Father Murtagh's living room – after dark. I'm afraid that's all the time we have. Barnsie and his boys won't rest until they have us, so pardon me for hurrying you all up. After tonight, we won't all be together in the same room again. Some of you will remain in America. The rest of us will be leaving New York behind. Regrettably, after three great years, our time here is over.'

'Three years – it hasn't been that long,' lamented the padre.

'Yes, Father,' I said, trying to get back in his good books, 'it has – three years, almost to the day, since we stepped off the *Erin's Queen* and onto American soil. I remember every detail as if it was this morning.'

## Two – The Erin's Queen

Jim Gorman was always a rock of sense. Even while growing up, in our carefree days, he could forever be relied upon to do the right thing. I put it down to a nervous streak in him. His reliability, however, also got me in heaps of trouble. Having Jim to worry about every little tittle-tattle meant I was usually free to act the eejit. Whenever he was around I'd play the clown as much as possible. And not just in Ireland. From the moment we set sail, it was great fun to see him fussing about the place like an auld mother hen.

Before the ship had even reached first stop at Liverpool, I decided to escape the boredom of the *Silver Star* lounge. I employed one of the crew to take me on a sightseeing tour. We climbed to the mainsail summit. Father Murtagh still refers to it in his letters; the disgust on Jim's face as he looked up at me peering out to sea through a telescope from the crow's nest.

'It's unheard of for a first-class passenger to climb to the top of the sails,' Jim fumed, 'if you don't like being a gentleman that's fine, but at least act the part until we get to America.'

'Take heed to what Jim's saying,' added Father Murtagh, 'one false move and we're all done for here.'

It was expected that the *Erin's Queen* would make the American shoreline in about a month, excluding the Liverpool stopover – where us fugitives waited an anxious twelve hours while more passengers and goods were loaded. Every movement of every peeler was watched carefully. We pulled out of dock at midnight, October 2, with four hundred and fifty passengers and a crew of forty on board, according to the skipper – a Captain McKenzie. A huge sense of relief washed over me as we left Liverpool behind, Father Murtagh stressing the importance of sticking to the plan while he sussed out the newcomers on the first-class landing.

Father Murtagh seemed to know a lot about ships. He said the conditions aboard British ships were far worse than on their American counterparts. They were known in the papers as coffin ships. Jim and I found this hard to believe. The *Erin's Queen* was a British ship. Yet all we had encountered thus far were luxurious meeting areas, sumptuous meals and hot water. It was a service the like of which us boys never thought existed – cool drinking water was even supplied at service stations throughout the upper decks! The lounge had every sort of beverage under the sun and the dining hall was lively, even if Jim found most of its inhabitants to be insufferable bores. That's when Father Murtagh became most on edge – when we had to *interact*, as he put it, with the public. He was a nervous wreck, constantly looking over his shoulder and questioning everything. Anyone would swear there was a hundred-pounds bounty *on his head*, and not ours. His fussing was drawing attention, if you ask me.

Jim spent most of the first two days sitting up on deck. The wooden benches were nice in the sun. At one stage we totted up the expenses and how much money was left. Three first-class silver standard tickets had cost forty-five pounds; the rent on a horse and carriage for two days was five pounds; four suits with shoes and top hats – not forgetting four masks – cost ten pounds; and other expenses had come to under four pounds.

'If *they* cost fifteen pounds each, merciful hour, how much are the gold standard,' I said, staring at my ticket.

I looked around the first-class landing. I went from man to man – every last one of them had long, bushy side-bourns. I pointed this out to Jim.

'Who would they remind you of,' he asked.

'Mister Blythe, counsellor for the Crown in Longford,' I said, and Jim nodded.

'The auld bollox,' he continued, 'with his m'lawd, m'lawd.'

We eavesdropped on the crew's instructions. They were being organised for a job in steerage by a fella in a dragoon hat.

'Four quarts of water, not a drop more,' he ordered. 'You bring the rice, and you two fellows take care of the tea. Two ounces, per person. Not a pinch more. Wear your facemasks at all times. There could be all sorts of diseases down there. And Nigel, if you spot a rat today, don't freak out. There's a good chap.'

Then some more crewmen arrived from behind a *staff only* door and they scattered in all directions.

Jim had also left ten pounds for Sugrue and Jeb Turling. He spoke at length about Lady Jane Teale – and her generous, life-saving gift. We whispered a prayer for the good lady. Then, while in the process of counting out twenty-four pounds and ten shillings, his collar was seized unceremoniously.

'What in God's name do you think you're doing,' growled Father Murtagh. 'Put that money away this instant. God bless us, this is worse than the stunt Joseph pulled with the crow's nest. You don't see the gentlemen of first-class counting their money out in public.'

'Jim's been accused of many things, Father,' I said, 'but being a first-class gentleman certainly isn't one of them.'

It was only meant as a joke, but Father Murtagh didn't see the funny side. He said he was disappointed with Jim, that he had come to expect more from him.

On the third evening, after the sun had made magnificent yellow and orange streaks on the horizon, I noticed something strange. It was something that made me mad. Father Murtagh, dressed in his vestments – his usual green overcoat nowhere to be seen – was stood on the forecastle. He was talking to one of the crew. I knew it was the forecastle because of the briefing the genial Captain McKenzie had given us on the way to Liverpool. The crew member – a sailor – darted into a small cabin and returned, before himself and Father Murtagh descended an iron ladder that led to the lower deck. I scuttled along the rail as they continued to the cast-iron gates separating steerage from the rest of the ship's world. The sailor produced a key and opened the gates, letting Father Murtagh through. He then locked up and returned to the forecastle. So much for preserving a low profile, I thought, before going back to my cabin.

In keeping with the shared spaces, our rooms were adorned in elegance. And if this was only silver standard, I dread to think what the penthouses were like. Everything smelled so new and fresh. Crisp bedsheets dressed mattresses that were so comfortable they made my back feel strange. There were *two* basins for shaving – just in case you didn't feel like waiting your turn. There was a constant supply of water for washing. The soap trays were always full. A string dangled from the ceiling. Pull it once and, moments later, house-service was knocking at your door. In the communal washroom, a bath could be had by simply instructing the domestic staff – who would then prepare it from boiled kettles. Most impressive of all were the candles – none of those stinking tallow type that smoked the place out of it. These were the new oil candles that featured only a year or so before in the *Freeman's Journal* – spermaceti candles. They really were the last word in lighting. Their plaited wicks eliminated the need for constant trimming and they didn't soften up, even in the warmest of weathers.

The next morning, as we readied ourselves for breakfast, I questioned a tired-looking Father Murtagh on his exploits in the hull of the ship.

'So, it's unheard of, is it, for the first-class gentlemen to climb the mainsail?'

'James said that,' he retorted, 'not I.'

'Well excuse me, Father, but how is wandering off down to steerage helping us be gentlemen?'

Father Murtagh was only getting into bed as Jim and I were dressing ourselves for the dining hall.

'I'll explain later, Joseph. I'm just too tired to talk right now.'

'No, you won't. You'll explain right now. You had no problem chastising me over my little tour to the top of the ship. Now it's you that's wandering around the place like some sort of stray ass.'

He looked about ready to pass out. However, before he slid between his comfortable white sheets, he muttered something about being up all night with a cholera patient. The Last Rites had been administered and the funeral service was just over.

'A funeral! On a ship? Pull the other one.'

'Take a look for yourself, down by the stern. The sharks are still following us.'

'Sharks?'

'Yeah, our loss is their gain,' he said, before his head hit the pillow.

I was amazed by this.

'You have to be codding me, Father. What sort of a funeral would allow the like of that?'

The only reply was an assortment of irregular snores, so I ran up on deck and back to the stern. Sure enough, three good-sized sharks tailed the ship, their dorsal fins weaving back and forth. I made for the dining hall before I got sick, and stomped across to where Jim Gorman was enjoying a hearty plate of eggs and bacon.

'They threw a dead body overboard this morning – threw it to the sharks. They're actually still following the ship.'

Jim looked up from his breakfast and shrugged his shoulders.

'At least it was a dead one.'

I can take a joke like the next man, but I don't like anyone – even a good friend like Jim Gorman – mocking the dear departed.

'What? How can you sit there, making fun of such a thing? Is that the way the Catholic religion is heading – we'll end up cannibals yet.'

Jim put down his knife and fork.

'I wasn't making fun,' he explained. 'What are they supposed to do, keep the body in steerage until it contaminates and stinks everyone out of it? We can't dig a six-foot hole in the hull of the ship. It's easy for us upper-deck passengers, with all our sensibilities, to frown upon the barbarity of it all.'

'Yeah, well, they could show a little more respect. The body is the temple of the Holy Spirit.'

'We're in the middle of the ocean, Jabber, or haven't you noticed. Dead bodies have nowhere to go but in the water.'

I was waiting for a fuller explanation. But Jim just returned to his plate of bacon and eggs. I suppose, when he put it so simply, I couldn't help feeling slightly foolish and very naïve.

It had been the funeral of a Corkonian, a boy known as Timmy O'Sullivan. They wrapped him in white cloth. Four men held him on the railing. His mother looked on, comforting her daughter. The keening was low key – both women embarrassed in the midst of so many strangers – as the body was sprinkled with holy water and dropped respectfully over the edge.

It marked the beginning of Father Murtagh's ministry aboard the ship. In steerage every day, he comforted and prayed with the poor. They prayed for big things and small, but mostly that their ship would not sink or be hit by lightning. Those in residence below deck were a nervous and superstitious lot. Until Father

Murtagh arrived, the scaremongers among them were having a field day. They had so many at their wits' end. Striking icebergs was high on the list of imminent disasters. Stories of storms that never happened were retold every time the ship staggered between the waves, sending the icy brine down the hatches and into their compartments. Mondays were of particular concern. An old Connemara man admitted that even the thoughts of a storm on a Monday were enough to cause palpitations.

'Judgement Day is set for a Monday,' he forecasted.

'They forgot to teach us that in the seminary,' said Father Murtagh, and he smiled in an attempt to ease the nerves of those gathered around him.

'As long as the new wind-measuring machine, the one invented by Beaufort the Irishman, doesn't stir too much on a Monday, we'll all be the happier for it, Father.'

'And what harm if it does,' replied Father Murtagh, 'won't we be in America all the quicker for it.'

Fair play to the good father, he knew how to make a silk purse from a sow's ear.

It was tense in the dining hall – especially in the evenings, when it was crowded. We'd get dressed up in our suits, like our wealthy travel companions, and put on as many airs and graces as we could think up. Jim called them our Earl-of-Grantham suits. Father Murtagh finally admitted that we'd started the journey a bit too uptight; we had to relax more, especially in the meeting areas. He had assumed a new identity. Father Gerard Dolan, a name coined in haste to facilitate a funeral in steerage, soon became famous in the higher echelons of the ship too. He strolled around, his Missal tucked snuggly in his wide sleeves, wandering as freely between the ship's divisions as Captain McKenzie and his company.

After a week or so, however, that fame almost caught up on him. As the laid-back Father Dolan melted into the comfort of his seat and read through a list of after-dinner drinks, he turned as sour as the cream he had just enjoyed with his mashed potatoes. His face contorted in horror. In a single moment, his eyes bulged with anxiety.

'Are you alright, Father,' asked Jim. 'Is it the spuds?'

He grabbed both our arms at the same time.

'The table next us,' he whispered. 'The newspaper. Don't look now.'

I hate it when someone tells you *not to look now*, because it's always the first thing you do. A group of ladies sat at the table that Father Murtagh was talking about. One of their company – a beautiful, dusky, brown-haired girl, in a bonnet tied with a bow – was reading a newspaper. Everything seemed to be orderly. Then I looked a second time. I still couldn't see anything wrong.

'Is it their dresses,' I asked. 'Because those big hula dresses are all the go with these uppity women.'

I winked at Jim as I continued.

'Not that you'd notice, Father, but a lot of the material is in the, ahem, bottom half.'

Father Murtagh was fit to bust me when I said that.

'I don't care about their dresses,' he seethed. 'The newspaper. Read what's on the newspaper.'

I tried to look over the girl's shoulder. One of her tablemates, a much older redheaded lady – who just happened to be facing us – cut me with a dirty look.

'Can we help you,' she snapped.

She had the most unusual accent – the way she said *heealpp*. I almost took it for some other language. I was caught rightly now, so there was no point in being sheepish about it. I rose to my feet instinctively, much to Father Murtagh's dismay.

'Excuse my intrusion,' I said, taking the old lady's gloved hand and pressing it against my lips. 'I couldn't help but notice your friend is perusing.'

Dropping the old lady's arm, I turned to the beautiful, brown-haired, girl.

'Would you be so kind as to lend us the newspaper at your convenience,' I asked. 'The good Father Dolan would like to see how loaves and fishes are floating on the stock exchange.'

Despite the attempted humour, my heart was beating fast; I could feel the thumping. Then the old redhead burst into laughter. This prompted the four younger girls, including the brown-haired beauty with the newspaper, to break out in titters.

'Marie-Claire,' said the redhead, and the newspaper was offered at once.

I bowed, as was customary with men of our standing. Then I winked at Marie-Claire as I took the newspaper from her beautifully-manicured fingers.

'Not to mention the price of altar wine,' I added, and the redhead led another chorus of guffaws.

I knew Father Murtagh was annoyed with me. But he had to stay quiet. The dining hall was my terrain now, affording me all the protection I needed from his disapproval. Jim Gorman enjoyed my acting. As I unfurled the week-old copy of the *London Times* at our table, Jim congratulated me on my stage presence.

'I wouldn't mind if Marie-Claire came with the newspaper,' I whispered.

Father Murtagh got straight down to business. It was still open on the page. He pointed to the article and looked around.

WANTED MEN AT LARGE, screamed the heading. *Warning to all passenger ship captains and crews operating from Ireland since the beginning of September. You may be unwittingly transporting three very dangerous criminals, wanted in connection to atrocities against Her*

Majesty's police force at Edgeworthstown, in the county of Longford, Ireland. The names of these felons are Patrick Sugrue, James Gorman and Joseph Farrell, known collectively as the Sugrue Gang. If found aboard, these persons should be securely detained, where a £1000 reward can be claimed upon their arrests.* Underneath was a crude drawing – so bad it made me feel safe – of each of our faces.

'At least they upped the bounty,' I said.

'What?'

'The bounty – the price on our heads. The reward. We were only worth a hundred at the time of our escape.'

'Whisht,' said Father Murtagh, looking around suspiciously. 'I don't want to hear another word.'

We sat in silence for a long time. The girls must have thought we had fallen out. I watched Father Murtagh's eyes darting about the place. You could hear the panic in his breathing.

'I'm sorry for the delay. I meant to get back to you sooner, but something came up in the kitchen.'

It was the waitress who had given us a drinks menu some time earlier.

I ordered a beer – one of those strong German beers I saw some of the older fellas dipping their whiskers into on the first night of the journey. Jim had a brandy to warm up the October night.

'And yourself, Your Reverence?'

She finally broke Father Murtagh's attention.

'I meant to call back sooner. Would you like a drink now?'

He looked her up and down.

'It's me, the waitress. I was here earlier, remember?'

Father Murtagh was acting strange. He took a hold of her sleeve.

'Excuse me, but where do you get your uniforms?'

The waitress looked puzzled.

'*Uniforms?*'

'Yes, those uniforms.'

'From the manager of the catering staff, I guess,' said the waitress.

'And they're all the same? What I mean is they've all got those white frilly bits on the neck and hem?'

'Yes, Your Reverence. I think so. Well, all the waitress ones have, at any rate.'

'Great. Any chance I could meet this manager of the catering staff? I'd like to get my hands on one of those uniforms,' said Father Murtagh. 'And I'll have a crème-de-monte for now, thank you.'

'Sure,' she said, hastily gathering the drinks menus and throwing a cautious backward glance as she retreated to the kitchen.

'Father, are you alright,' asked Jim, trying to stifle a smirk.

'There's nothing you want to tell us, Father,' I chanced saying.

'There is,' he replied. 'I need one of those uniforms. I must have it.'

'You're nearly there as it is, Father,' Jim pointed out. 'But for the white frills it looks just like your own habit – if you don't mind me saying so.'

'Precisely, James. That's exactly what I was thinking. All we have to do is get one of those uniforms – one big enough to fit Joseph.'

Father Murtagh put a finger under my name on the page in front of him.

'It's the only answer I can think of to this particular problem.'

'Now hold on there, Father,' I said. 'If you want to dress up in women's clothes then, by all means, suit yourself. But you're not getting me into some waitressing number, not in a million years.'

'Oh, I don't know, Jabber,' quipped Jim, 'lose a couple of pounds around the waist and I think you'd look smashing in it.'

'This is not up for discussion. You fellas enjoy your drinks. I'm away to find the catering manager.'

'Sit down, Father, and enjoy your own drink. Because it's not happening. I'm not getting into a dress and that's final.'

Jim told me to quieten down and the old redhead smiled over and gave a suggestive pout.

But there was no talking to him. Father Murtagh was already heading for the *kitchen staff only* door.

## Three – Brendan the Navigator

Twenty-four hours later I was walking the ship's decks in a woman's dress. That's how I viewed it. Father Murtagh, of course, had a different opinion. As far as he was concerned, it was something that had to be undertaken to ensure my safe passage to America. The article in the *London Times* had frightened the life out of him. Jim Gorman already had an alias. His name was John Brown. Lady Jane Teale's letter meant he could prove it. And Father Murtagh had his alias in Father Gerard Dolan, even though he was sure nobody was going to track him to America over a stolen chalice. It may have been a gold and silver, diamond-encrusted, chalice. It may also have been a sacrilegious act to steal the chalice in the first place. Nonetheless, the one thing – the only thing – the Brits were hesitant to interfere with in Ireland at that present time was the concern of the Catholic Church. They wouldn't be sending a posse of lawmen on the trail of a renegade priest.

I was a totally different matter. As far as Father Murtagh was concerned, I was utterly exposed. I had no proof of identity should charges be laid at my door. Something had to be done to correct this. Hence the woman's dress – or waitress's uniform. The ship's catering staff manager was sought out in a hurry. Father Murtagh used all his tact to procure the largest possible uniform. He needled out the frilly bits and sliced it down the front, transforming it into a cassock. He even had the exact number of buttons down the front – with thirty-three buttonholes to match.

Thus, I became Father Joseph – a deacon out of Maynooth seminary. With a borrowed green stole tied up in a cincture, and a gleaming pectoral cross, I really looked the part.

Father Murtagh took great care in explaining to all who were interested – and even those who weren't – that he was instructing Father Joseph, on his way to fulfilling a late ministry. We would sit through dinner talking shop, more loudly than we ought to, using the full range of religious jargon. I had a better memory than I realised – needing very little briefing on ecclesiastical terminology studied all those years ago. Words like *cruets* and *ciborium* flowed from my lips. Other diners, those in the vicinity, endured us with a respectful silence. Many silver-standard passengers were of Protestant or Anglican persuasion. Some were curious and would look for insights into this strange new world. Others would offer a stare of objection at the high-pitched tone of our deliberations. Father Murtagh was happy with the ruse. He was patient and honest with all public inquiries, except on one occasion when the inquirer became a little too intimate.

'Why, pray tell, would two priests be headed for New York with all the trouble at home,' probed the nosey auld bag, a sheepskin tippet pulled up around her shoulders. 'It just doesn't make …'

'I'm glad you asked,' interjected Father Murtagh. 'Saint John, chapter four, verse forty-four, springs immediately to mind – one is never a prophet in one's own land. The auspices are excellent that my colleague, Joseph, will make a fine priest in the new country.'

The sheepskin-tippet woman tightened her brow.

'Auspices, what on earth are you rambling about?'

'My dear lady, reading the auspices was one of the oldest traditions known to the priests of ancient Rome. It included examining the entrails of birds to see if a certain date or situation would have a favourable outcome. And it's making a comeback.

We cut one open only last week. The auspices have declared that Joseph here will make an indelible mark in his ministry.'

Scrunching up her nose at the thought of birds' entrails, the woman abandoned her line of questioning and took into a drink. Father Murtagh was certainly ready for whatever the snobs had to throw at him.

Another evening, a pushy little English ex-commander made the observation that this Catholic Church must have a hefty war chest, to be sending its foot soldiers to America on such luxurious tickets. Father Murtagh deflected this comment away to safety by explaining that himself and Joseph were merely answering the Lord's call to go out into His vineyard and toil until nightfall.

Once he put on his dinner-jacket, Jim Gorman was transformed into John Brown. Despite his rock-solid alias, the people of silver standard made him uneasy. Therefore, he talked as little as possible. Jim was never comfortable, not even on the night we dined as guests of the skipper. Captain McKenzie had heard about the funeral – the first fatality of his entire watch – and he sent one of his crew to our cabin with an invite to dinner. He wanted to thank Father Murtagh formally for carrying out the funeral in such a dignified and sensitive manner. We had already met the captain for a walking tour of the ship. That was nice. But this was different. This time we got to stay at the very top deck – the lions' and lionesses' den – for a significantly longer look, and a chance to rub shoulders with the filthy rich.

I won't forget that day in a hurry. It was exciting and terrifying at the same time – only a few steps up a staircase, but a world apart from what we were used to. The rooms were small but the style was breathtaking. Gold standard really did mean the best of the best. The first place we visited was the gaming room. A chandelier, similar to the one in the main hall of Cranley House, lit up the ceiling. Decorative sconces hung from the walls and matching candelabras illuminated the grand piano. There was an old fellow, fingering the rim of his stove-pipe hat, playing a game at the card table. He looked under pressure – the sleeves of his shirt pulled up and his weskit open.

'That's nice. I bet it's deerskin,' said Jim.

'What's that,' I replied.

'His shirt. It's nice to see a bit of style.'

'It's dear, alright,' agreed Father Murtagh, 'I bet it's antelope.'

A clack of balls turned my attention towards the billiard table. I was surprised to see a long-haired fella in a fringed tunic. His hair was straight and shiny, split in two perfect halves and bound up in a neat band. He wore moccasin shoes – the height of comfort. After each shot he surveyed the room suspiciously. He played against a scruffy-looking brute – well, scruffy-looking by first-class standards – in a billycock hat which he refused to part with, even when bent across the table. A reefer jacket, hanging close by, must have belonged to him.

'Imagine trying to play billiards on a stormy sea,' said Father Murtagh.

'The stormier the better, especially if I was playing Billy Bowlegs over there,' I replied, as the Indian sunk another ball and straightened up triumphantly.

Jim returned with drinks and the door swung open. In walked two crewmen. I remembered their faces from when they brought the rations down to steerage. Even when off-duty, they dressed alike – breeches tucked into their long boots, and stylish peacoats. They headed straight for the back of the room, where a dainty cove in a grey cutaway suit and red braces guffawed as he dealt cards at a table with a *vingt-et-un* sign.

As we sipped our drinks a bell went off and the barkeep announced that the steakhouse was now open.

'Settle, Father,' I said, 'there's no rush.'

'On the contrary, Joseph, gather up your pint. Let's not keep the captain waiting. It was good of him to ask us in the first place.'

Father Murtagh didn't have to worry. Captain McKenzie was nowhere to be seen. A doorman asked for our names and if we had a reservation. As soon as he saw the collars, he dispensed with his formalities and guided us to a table in the centre of the steakhouse. It was another magnificent room. There were large bowls of fruit – with pineapples, no less – sitting on every table. On the wall opposite the entrance, a buckskinned cowboy tipped his hat and smiled while his brown colt reared.

'I hope you don't mind,' the doorman said cordially, 'but this is what we like to call Captain McKenzie's table. He sends his unreserved apologies, as his attention has been called upon. He shan't be long, but asks if you would proceed without him.'

He gave us menus, even though Father Murtagh told him we would prefer to wait until the good captain arrived. I noticed that worried look on Jim's face again. There was a crowd across from us. They all sat in their serapes, despite the warmth of the room and the coat hangers provided.

'That must be Billy Bowlegs' family,' I said, to see if I could get Jim smiling.

I had a look at the menu. For luncheon there was consommé fermier and egg a l'argenteuil. I hadn't a notion what that meant.

'Would sirs like something from the buffet,' asked the doorman, who was now doubling up as a waiter.

I looked at the buffet list. Corned ox tongue or Virginia and Cumberland pie. What, in heaven's name, was a galantine of chicken. Potted shrimp or Norwegian anchovies – surely they didn't have to go all that way to catch a bite to eat!

'Or would sirs like to see the cheeseboard,' continued the doorman.

'Yes, a nice bit of cheese would be grand,' said Father Murtagh.

'Very well. We've got Cheshire, Stilton Blue, Gorgonzola, Edam, Roquefort and Camembert.'

All of us, including Father Murtagh, stared at the doorman in amazement. I can only speak for myself – I had never heard of any of them.

'Any ordinary cheese?'

The doorman looked at Jim as if he had asked a hard question. I didn't care if he brought us cheese or not. All I wanted was the pineapple sitting in the fruit bowl. Up until that day, I had never tasted pineapple.

'Forget about the cheese,' said Father Murtagh. 'We'll have a drink while we wait for Captain McKenzie.'

'Very well, sir. A beer is it? Would you like an iced Coors, a pitcher of Munich or a pils from Amsterdam?'

Father Murtagh's face said it all. By now, we were just fed up with this fella and his fancy carry on.

'Surprise us,' I said, taking the bull by the horns. 'Bring down something we can blow the froth off.'

But that was as much waitering as the doorman was prepared to do. He slapped his heels together and stood ram-rod straight, clicking his fingers in the direction of the bar.

'What's eating you,' I asked Jim.

'I hope everything's above board, if you pardon the pun,' he answered, dipping his fingers in a water jar and hastily running them through his sandy hair.

'What do you mean?'

'I hope the captain's invite is genuine, and that he isn't just having us here for a reason,' said Jim. 'Remember that ship yesterday morning? Maybe he found something out about us?'

So that was the reason for Jim's long face. A passing frigate, the day before, still had him in a panic. At the time, Jim ran in and boarded up our cabin door.

'They're here for us, they're here for us,' he was shouting.

Father Murtagh had to calm him down. I unblocked the door while explaining that locking yourself in a ship's dormitory was a pointless exercise. It turns out the frigate was just unloading its American mail and newspapers for Captain McKenzie's passengers. But the whole experience had Jim in a sweat. His mood darkened further when he bought a copy of the *North Star*, checking its *Lost and Found* section only to discover the same wanted notice as was in the *London Times* which Marie-Claire had given us.

'Sacre bleu, les garcons d'Irlande.'

The voice came from directly behind me; I recognised the gumbo at once. It was the redhaired lady from a few nights before. My heart raced as I turned to look at Marie-Claire. But disappointment was my lot. And as jolly as the old redhead could be, she was no substitute for my dusky belle. A senior gentleman accompanied her – the monocle he used to scan the newspaper now dangling on its chain from his breast pocket.

We were properly introduced. The redhead's name was Cherie. She was travelling home to New Orleans after a holiday in England. The gentleman's name was Albert. He spoke with an English accent.

'You know, Reverend, I really gotta hand it to you. I thought you was kiddin' the other night.'

'About what,' asked Father Murtagh.

'About Joseph and the woman's dress. Why he fills that little black number just fine and dandy.'

'Oh yes,' said Father Murtagh, laughing along, 'I didn't know what you were getting at for a minute. I was only joking about the waitress's uniform, Cherie, as well you might know. Joseph is a priest, you see. He left his robes behind the other night.'

I was getting annoyed at the way they were talking about me while I was seated in their company.

'Such a shame. Marie-Claire is going to be one very disappointed young lady. Let's just say she was looking forward to seeing more of *Father* Joseph.'

You could have knocked me down with a feather when I heard it. I was about to declare to the whole room that I'm not a fully-fledged priest, only a deacon, when Father Murtagh got in before me.

'The joy we get from our vow of chastity makes up for the Marie-Claires of this world,' chirped the former curate of Mostrim.

Cherie put on a pained look before continuing.

'The priesthood is the tough life and make no mistake – le vie difficile.'

Before I could get in a line of my own, the doors swung again and in walked the agreeable Captain McKenzie. After retiring his stripes for the night, he looked different in a reefer jacket. We all stood up and he shook our hands in turn, apologising for the lateness of his arrival. He even took a moment to shake hands with Cherie and Albert.

'Une parle vu francois,' he asked Albert.

Albert shook his head.

'Jai t'aime, mon Cherie. That's all the French you'll ever need to know,' said the silver-tongued captain, as she giggled like a schoolgirl and patted her blushing face with a napkin.

Then he excused himself and went to shake hands with the Bowlegs family, their serapes still snuggled about their shoulders.

The steakhouse was filling up. Ladies walked by – reticules on one gloved arm and men on the other – in big hula dresses, just like the beautiful green one Cherie was wearing. I still called them that, even though Father Murtagh told me not too.

'They're *crinoline* dresses,' he stressed, 'and a man of your station should know that. We must brush up on your first-class vocabulary, Joseph.'

*My station* – did you ever know the like. So, he taught me a few handy phrases to get by as a gentleman. *Poor bull* meant bad eating or hard times. Dusky girls like Marie-Claire were known to more distinguished folk as *creoles*. And the great unwashed of steerage were, well, the glitterati hadn't got around to renaming them yet. I was right about Billy Bowlegs, the long-haired youth in the moccasin shoes. When the billiards was over, he nestled in among the serapes.

But the focal point of attention was the captain. They couldn't get enough of him. Diners from other tables would come over to chat him up. Some were clearly showing off – speaking of events which transpired earlier on the port side of deck, and the rush of adrenalin they had experienced while standing on the railings of the bow as the jack staff flapped about their faces. It soon became clear that Captain McKenzie's briefing on marine transport was not exclusive to us boys from Mostrim.

But as far as the captain was concerned, Father Murtagh was the star of the show. He asked him all about the funeral in steerage. Then he asked him all about his life as a priest. The captain said he had a keen interest because his mother had been an Irish Catholic, God rest her soul. And, despite being brought up as a member of the Lutheran Church, he always had a soft spot for his dear old mother's faith.

'I was only seven when she died. Even so, I happen to think some of her beliefs rubbed off on me. I wouldn't be as religious as some on the ship, especially my passengers below deck, but you would not catch Captain Brendy McKenzie leaving port without first whispering a little prayer to Saint Erasmus of Formia.'

'The patron saint of sailors,' said Father Murtagh.

'Correct, Saint Elmo's fire, the very man,' replied the captain, 'that's all my mother's doing. You know your job, Father.'

'Did you say your name is Brendy – as in Brendan?'

'I did for sure,' affirmed the captain. 'And that's my mother's doing too – after her dear old man.'

Father Murtagh was delighted with this.

'With a name like that you just had to be a sailor, nay, the captain of sailors.'

Captain Mckenzie was made up with this sort of talk.

'Did you ever hear of Brendan the Navigator,' continued Father Murtagh, and with all his naying he was beginning to sound like a first-class horse.

The captain confessed that he had to plead ignorance.

'He was a sixth-century Irish monk, who founded a monastery at Clonfert in County Galway. Legend has it he also found America.'

'I didn't know it was lost,' I said to Jim, and Father Murtagh threw me a side glance before returning his attention on the captain.

'Yes, he was the first to *discover* America – in a boat no bigger than a currach. It was no accident, your mother calling you Brendan.'

Father Murtagh leaned in as if to divulge a terrific secret.

'It was God's Will.'

Captain McKenzie was beaming when he heard this. He lifted Jim's pint and inspected the glass. Then he called across the barkeep.

'These are the wrong glasses,' declared the captain, 'I told the maitre d'hotel about this before.'

'Pardon me, Captain, but aren't we heading *towards* America,' said the barkeep.

'I understand that, but these gentlemen are not American. And neither are those people there,' he replied, gesturing towards the serape-wearing family.

'Very well, sir, but will you inform the maitre…'

'I'll leave word for him, don't you worry,' agreed the captain, before the barkeep fetched a tray to bring away our drinks.

'Hey, I wasn't finished that,' I said, much to the captain's amusement.

'Don't worry. The chap will be back to you in a moment with a proper pint in a proper pint glass. You see, the imperial pint is one fifth again bigger than the pint across the pond. That's why they use the American glass for the sailing over, and the imperial glass on the way back. I insist they always use the bigger glass for our first-class passengers, but they change whenever they get my back turned.'

Then it was the captain's turn to lean in as if to divulge his terrific secret.

'They know only too well that if they use the smaller measures, they'll have more drink for themselves when we arrive. Once the quota hasn't been reached, I allow my staff to party away the surplus at the journey's end.'

Father Murtagh and Captain McKenzie were getting along famously now. Jim and I sat there like dummies, wondering when our drinks would be restored. For something to do, I started re-reading the menu. Veal and ham pie sounded delicious. The barkeep returned with a tray of drinks. A waiter came with him; pencil and paper were at the ready.

Jim ordered mutton chops. I wanted to order the veal but I lost my nerve. It just didn't seem right – Maisie Rourke and her little one starved to death and me talking out loud about veal and ham pies. In the end I ordered mutton chops too – because they came with mashed, fried, and baked jacket potatoes. Father Murtagh and Captain McKenzie were so engrossed in each other's company, the waiter went away a second time.

'When I heard about it, I could have cried,' said the captain. 'I did my training aboard the *Jeanie Johnston*. Great little ship – we didn't lose a single passenger in all my time with her, thanks mostly to the efforts of a Doctor Nicholas Donavon. And after him came a fellow called Blennerhassett. Two fabulous doctors – very thorough and caring. We sailed her over and back to Quebec, under the stewardship of the stout-hearted Captain John Munn.'

'How long did it take you to make the trip to Quebec,' asked Father Murtagh, still titillated by all the seafaring tales.

'How long is a piece of string,' answered Captain McKenzie. 'It was all down to the weather. Depending on the strength of the winds and currents, not to mention storms, most voyages took between four and six weeks. Our record was twenty-seven days.'

'And your longest journey,' inquired Father Murtagh.

'Seventy-four long days,' confessed the captain, 'and we spent three of those being thrown around like a little ball. The calm came after the storm – we hit doldrums and barely moved for two weeks.'

Jim and I listened in. I was quite content – as long as I didn't have to pretend, or talk about priestly things.

'And what about this man here,' said the captain, after ordering something French. 'Isn't he a brave chap to be following the vocation at his stage of life.'

'We'll get the zucchetto on him yet,' answered Father Murtagh, and he must have known by the way I looked that I could have swung for him.

I had my fill of religious jargon; I just couldn't take any more.

'Who's your man on the horse,' I said, changing the subject and forcing their attention to the wall.

'That's Kit Carson,' answered the captain, 'Napoleon of the Plains. He's the most famous scout alive. Wait until I tell you a good one about him and...'

Jim looked at me and smiled. Father Murtagh and Captain McKenzie were off again, nineteen to the dozen.

'Nice move,' he said.

'Shut your mouth,' I replied, 'and eat your praties.'

## Four – The Priest and the Midwife

'Once a hand is put to the plough there can be no turning back.'

Those were the words of Father Murtagh as he stretched out an arm for the water and wine – which I delivered right on cue. His biblical message was certainly true in my case. Gone were my lazy morning lie-ins, not to mention lounging about the upper decks until midday with Jim Gorman. As a fully-fledged deacon – and Father Murtagh's next-in-command – I had to be up early, assisting at mass below decks. The passengers of steerage would kill you for their daily mass. And not just mass, but whatever passed for religion as they saw it – an odd mixture of dogmatic devotion and superstitious fanaticism. As the only two holy men aboard the *Erin's Queen*, they doted on us like we were the beatified. They battled each other for our attention.

There's an old saying: to be a good liar one must have a good memory. With this in mind, there was certainly no turning back from the plough of religious responsibility I had been firmly yoked up to. Father Murtagh's – or should I say Father Gerard Dolan's – cover story was another case in point. The morning after our dinner with the captain, a quick check of the *New York Herald* uncovered our worst fears. Not only was the *London Times'* advertisement regarding the Sugrue Gang plastered all over page five, but in the paper's *Missing Friends* section there was also a notice concerning the whereabouts of a Catholic priest – Father Hugo Donaghy, a former curate of the Down and Connor diocese. This sent Father Murtagh haywire with suspicion and heaped even more emphasis on the importance of his false alias. If they were putting a notice in the American newspapers concerning a priest from Down and Connor, then what was to stop them printing one about a priest from Ardagh and Clonmacnoise.

'You're an Aughnacliffe man, Father Dolan. Well then, you have to know Father Austin Reilly, the parish priest of Gowna. Sure, Gowna's only the other end of the parish from yis,' said an old fella, in between puffing on his pipe. 'I must write back and tell them I met Father Gerard Dolan on my way out.'

'They wouldn't know me,' answered Father Murtagh. 'I never ministered in the parish. I went straight in as a chaplain to the army.'

'Oh, you're a padre. I thought you said you were a curate in one of the parishes in Longford. Was it Mostrim you said?'

'A padre is right,' agreed Father Murtagh, blowing his cheeks out in relief. 'I was assigned to Mostrim but took the army instead.'

After that, Father Murtagh became affectionately known to the steerage population simply as *padre*. I was his constant companion on his twice-daily trips through the cast-iron gates. I'll always remember my maiden voyage down into the belly of the ship. There was a horrible burning smell. The smoke made me cough. It made my eyes water. I thought they were burning tar.

The padre was great with the people in steerage. He was made up with them. He organized ceilis – or hooleys, as some liked to call them – and quizzes, to pass the time and encourage their spirits. The surroundings were cramped beyond belief; filth and dirt piled up everywhere. When despair set in, their stout-hearted man of God implored them to channel their bruised and battered attentions on holding out until the next hooley. These hooleys – consisting mainly of a fiddle and a drum and a lot of singing and dancing – were meant to be a weekend thing. But they became nightly as the journey progressed. And then there were the cancelled hooleys, four nights in all, as a mark of respect to those whose bodies had just been committed to sea.

On the nineteenth day of the voyage, Father Murtagh delivered a baby. To be fair to Captain McKenzie, he scoured the ship for a medic. Amazingly, there wasn't one doctor – or a nurse – in the first-class compartments. When I say delivered, I mean the padre helped another woman out. He was by no means proficient in the skills of midwifery. And he hated the sight of blood. But he couldn't get out of it – the pregnant woman and her helper wouldn't let him. They considered it imperative that the padre's hands be the first to touch the child, to guide the little fella into this world. And so, the padre and the helping woman carefully removed the pregnant lady from her bunk. They helped her all the way up to the captain's quarters – where a supply of hot water, clean towels, and as much peace and quiet as the ship would permit awaited them.

I soon found out how a padre's Sunday-morning absence could have profound consequences for his understudy. The people had no one to say mass. They circled me before I could retreat to the upper decks. They blocked the roped banister and congregated on the steps beneath the low ceiling. I was trapped!

'Please, Father,' begged this one lady who was well on in age, 'please say mass for us. I haven't missed a Sunday mass that I can ever remember.'

'It would be good for the journey,' said another, 'our safety in this big sea.'

'Merciful hour, I can't say mass, even if I wanted to,' I tried to explain. 'I'm only a deacon. I'm not ordained yet. I can't consecrate the bread and wine.'

I thought I was away scot-free after that. But with their long faces and loud sighs, not to mention the dirty looks I received, I felt sorry for them. Something important hit home that day – all these people had was their God. I relented and told them I'd say the mass but I couldn't give out Holy Communion; I hadn't the power. Well the smiles and good cheer made it all worthwhile. So I said the mass. The first reading was chapter four from *Galatians* and was particularly suited to the morning that was in it – *when the time had come, God sent forth his Son, born of a Woman, born under the law, to redeem those who were under the law, that we might receive the adoption as sons.* The Gospel was Saint Luke. At chapter seventeen, verse twenty-one, I homed in on the line: *The Kingdom of God is within.* I used this in my homily. I asked my spellbound audience what this could mean. Obviously, I wasn't expecting an answer. I went on to say what I thought it meant. The power to build God's kingdom is within each and every one of us. The power to do the right thing – the kind thing, the merciful thing, the generous thing – is within our capabilities. By making those choices we get so much more in return – happiness, strength, peace of mind. You could have heard a pin fall as I broke for what would have been the liturgy of the Eucharist.

After mass, I stayed a while chatting with the people. They brought Rosary beads and holy relics, and I blessed them all. Some brought small children and I blessed them too. They sat me down and made me have tea. Some of them even told me a bit about themselves. I didn't envy them – steerage was worse than I had ever imagined. The stuffy, cramped, environment was a breathing ground for sickness and disease. There were many large families confined to single six-feet bunks, a wooden panel the only separation and privacy from the next bed. Up to ten or twelve people – often times three generations of the same family – sharing a straw mattress, their few belongings wrapped up in sacks or cardboard suitcases. Small families sharing with complete strangers or children travelling alone as postage mail. One young fella of about ten years didn't even know the person collecting him in New York. All he had was a name written on a piece of wood – a name that he couldn't read. He would become an indentured labourer for a period of five years to work off the price of the passage.

'*Five years.* For the price of a ticket!'

'It cost a hundred guineas, Father.'

It was still only a little over five pounds, no matter what way you say it, in exchange for five hard years on a farm. Slavery in its purist form. I didn't bother saying so. There was no point. The boy was happy, so why ruin it on him.

There were no bathrooms or restrooms – as some of the crew called them – or water closets with the sort of luxury we enjoyed in silver standard. Old coal buckets, one for each berth, were what they had instead. There were lids on the buckets so that, when the ship took a rise or dip, pee and excrement did not end up all over the family bedspread. There was no steakhouse. In fact, there was no eating house of any description. There weren't even tables and chairs. In steerage, they ate their daily rations of bread, rice, and oatmeal in the bunks where they slept. They had water and gruel for supper, and they were very glad of it.

The burning had started again. My eyes watered and I couldn't catch my breath.

'We're sorry, Father,' said the woman who had never missed mass, 'we burn bitumen to keep away the disease. Here, let me share my water with you.'

'No,' I said, 'but thank you. Spare your water for yourself.'

God knows, she had little enough of it.

'What disease,' I asked.

'The typhus,' she answered, 'it's a terrible nuisance altogether.'

The padre was all for letting mother and baby sleep. He made for the door of Captain McKenzie's cabin, but the old lady stopped him in his tracks.

'What about the christening, Padre?'

'Oh, we can do that again,' said Father Murtagh. 'The man who made time made plenty of it.'

He smiled, but she remained stone-faced.

'What about now, Padre? The child won't thrive until he has his baptism.'

'What? You mean *right now?*'

She didn't answer, just kept a hard, hopeful, stare on him.

'Get the basin and a towel and we'll do it so,' he said, uncorking his holy water bottle. 'You obviously wouldn't agree that patience is a virtue.'

'Thank you kindly, Padre.'

She smiled at long last.

'What name did you decide on,' he asked, as he tilted the new baby's head back and dribbled some holy water onto his wisp of hair.

The young Galway woman looked dumbfounded in the captain's bed linen.

'Ainm do leanbh,' said the old woman, cheerily resuming her duties. 'She doesn't have the language, Padre.'

There proceeded a conversation in Irish. Then the old woman turned to Father Murtagh and asked his name.

'Father Mur... ahem, Father Gerard Dolan,' he answered, remembering his own new name in the nick of time.

'Gerard so, Padre. She wants to call her baby after yourself, if that be alright. God bless you and all belong to you.'

Father Murtagh completed the baptism and welcomed Gearoid Seosamh Seoige into the Christian community. The Seosamh was a nod to his right-hand man – the Irish word for Joe. After all the deaths, the christening was a source of great joy to the people in steerage. They kicked up an awful fuss with a fiddle and a couple of bottles of brew.

'We better bless those in quarantine,' said the padre, pulling me aside before I could get my hands on a jar of malt.

There was a rattle from the gates above. A shout declared the deck open for one hour, and the berths emptied out. I watched the delight on the faces of my congregation as they rushed for the stairs. A sailor opened the door into quarantine. A frightful-looking boy peered out. It was hard to guess his age, such was the damage done by the ravages of disease.

'Typhus,' whispered the padre, before sprinkling a generous amount of holy water in the boy's direction.

There was a woman lying in a dark corner, unfit to lift her head from the rags she used for a pillow. Instinctively, I made my way over to give her some water. The sailor with the keys halted my progress.

'Sorry, no contact,' said the sailor, 'a bad dose of dysentery. She could infect the lot of us.'

I felt so sorry for these poor unfortunes as memories of the workhouse black room returned to my mind.

'No wonder the Brits call them coffin ships,' I growled at the padre as the sailor locked up, 'the sharks won't have long to wait for their next feed.'

Jim Gorman was out on deck sunning himself when the exodus from steerage came rushing towards him. He watched as the last of them poured through the cast-iron gates. Mothers, looking older than they should have, shook their bedspreads into the sea and aired cardigans on the railings. Men, who should have been in the prime of their lives, stripped off to their waists to feel the warmth of the sun on their emaciated shoulders. Children ran about the boards, using the skirts of hairy-chinned grannies to hide from each other. And all the while, as they celebrated life for an hour a day, the masters and mistresses of the universe looked down from their gold-standard ivory towers and bristled with indignation.

That was when Jim first confessed his fears, while pointing out the man with the grey fedora.

'It was the hat drew me,' Jim later explained. 'It just didn't belong in third-class.'

A neat ginger beard framed his mouth. He had arms and legs like giant matchsticks. The whistle went, calling the passengers back into steerage.

'You're gone as paranoid as the padre,' I replied.

'Who's the padre,' he asked, inspecting the knuckles of his little hands – a sure sign that Jim's nerves were at him.

'That's what they call Father Murtagh below in steerage now. Practically everyone on the ship has a new hat,' I pointed out. 'People buy new hats when they're going on long journeys, or on holidays.'

'Or when they're running away from a famine?'

'Correct, Jim, when they're running away from a famine.'

'It's not just the hat, it's the way he was looking at me,' continued Jim. 'He was looking at me for a reason – as if he knew me, or knew something about me.'

'Ah here, I thought Father Murtagh was bad, making me traipse about in a black dress. You'll be making a habit and wearing it next.'

'I'm serious, Jabber. And it's not the first time I got him looking at me. The other day, I caught him staring through the bars of the iron gate. As I approached, he emptied his pipe and went back below. There's something more to that fella than meets the eye.'

'You think he's one of Giles's men? Or perhaps Pollach sent him – bought the bugger a ticket in steerage – so he could spy on us for a month while stinking to high heaven? If either of those two bastards even suspected we were on board this ship, we'd never have got as far as Lambay Island.'

'What if he has seen the advert in the papers and cottoned on? What if he's looking to cash in on the reward?'

'That's ridiculous, Jim. Those poor people down in steerage can barely write their names in Irish, let alone peruse the *London Times* at their leisure – that's if they had the price of a *London Times*. Your head is all over the place.'

'I can still hear the seminary in you,' said Jim.

'What do you mean by that?'

'*Peruse*. Now that's not a word you'd hear in the hedge school. It's the result of a good priestly education.'

'As my dear mother used to say, Jim, education is no load to carry.'

Early next day we awoke to all the upheaval. The corridors of silver standard were alive with the noise of running and racing. I went up on deck. I looked over at gold-standard landing. They were already up and dressed, waving at a boat being rowed towards the *Erin's Queen*. Land had been spotted – the American shoreline was visible in the far-off distance. The rowing boat was very small for taking all who waited. A lady with a bandbox pushed her way through the crewmen's cordon. She attempted the ladder, only to be hauled back by a sailor. After some loud exchanges, a crewman went down into the rowing boat. He returned to the ship with a cardboard box, opened it, and distributed facemasks among his colleagues and the gold-standard passengers. Then the rowing boat took off again, without so much as bringing one passenger ashore.

The harbour was dotted with waiting ships. The excitement seemed even greater among the people of steerage. They hugged and kissed and jumped around in joyous celebration beyond the still-locked iron gates. Then members of the crew appeared and ushered us back to our respective quarters. We were asked to stay in our rooms and await further instructions. Father Murtagh collected up our belongings. I told him not to forget my trousers – my days of going around in a waitress's uniform were about to end. And so we waited…and waited…and waited.

The *Erin's Queen* halted at half past seven on the morning of Thursday, the twenty-eighth day of October, eighteen hundred and forty-seven. She anchored. She bobbed on the water for the rest of that day. She rocked all her passengers to sleep that night. At dawn the next day, I was fed up of staying in my room and awaiting further instructions. I was walking on an empty deck when I heard a whistle from portside. It was an Irishman from the *Caledonia Star* – the ship that was stalled alongside.

'What's happening with you fellas,' he asked, examining his stove-pipe for dents before returning his gaze. 'We've been here waiting for nine whole days.'

'*Nine days*,' I exclaimed, 'what on earth is going on?'

'We're all being quarantined,' explained the Irishman, 'it's a government thing. The bastards think we've all got the plague.'

'As if we weren't long enough out here,' I said, looking back in the direction of the ocean.

'Well I don't give a shite,' returned the Irishman, 'if *we're* not moving today, I'm going to swim for it. And the American government can do whatever they like.'

'Good on you,' I shouted, before making haste with the news. 'But wait for the tide or you'll end up back where you started – next parish, Bundoran.'

## Five – Polling Day in the New World

That whole day again, and all the next day – Saturday, the thirtieth – we waited patiently and nervously. Father Murtagh busied himself in steerage, where the passengers were more upbeat after Captain McKenzie's orders to hand out a large quantity of food – the leftover rations – now that the journey was over. He threw in a few dozen bottles of wine for good measure. The padre eased their worries, keeping my news about the *Caledonia Star's* nine-day wait firmly to himself. He said mass and administered Holy Communion to those unable to attend. By then, there were about two dozen in sick bay and ten quarantined. The lock-up was still empty – the passengers had behaved impeccably throughout the month.

I arrived with more treats from the captain's cupboards. This buoyed their spirits further. Another child travelling alone chewed a toffee contentedly and told me she didn't care if we never got off the ship. An old woman coughed into her handkerchief, turning it red. I whispered a prayer and remembered my mother, pretending not to notice.

Up on deck, Jim Gorman walked constantly – trying to rid his body of nervous energy. He circled the ship from bow to stern, stopping each time at the iron gates of steerage. He had survived the journey. This was supposed to be the easy bit. He told me he was crazy for the feel of dry land under his boots. But no such luck. Night time found us back in our bunks once more.

'This can't be happening,' said Jim, agreeing to join myself and the padre for a brandy in an effort to while away a sleepless night.

First light on Sunday, the last day of October, brought fresh hope. We were awoken by the crew's sailors, with instructions to get our baggage and follow them. Along with others from silver standard, we were led into an area penned off with chains. There was a steady flow of people from the gold-standard compartment to the most upper deck, where more sailors ushered them along to a gangplank at the stern. At first, I wandered where their luggage was. Captain McKenzie stood next to the baggage handlers, thanking the passengers as they disembarked. Albert held the hem of Cherie's gown as she prepared to depart. There was no sign of Marie-Claire and the rest of her crinoline-wearing friends. Not that she'd be interested in my attentions if she could see me then – going about the place in a black frock.

At the end of the gangplank was a ferryboat, taking the passengers. There were people already aboard. I recognised one as the Irishman in the stove-pipe hat from the *Caledonia Star*. When the gold-standard passengers were all safely aboard, it was our turn. A crewman took Jim's suitcases, to stack on a smaller vessel.

'You guys are travelling light,' he joked, shaking the second suitcase.

As he was leaving the *Erin's Queen*, Father Murtagh turned to Captain McKenzie and asked about the passengers in steerage.

'Don't worry, Father Dolan,' replied the captain, 'they will be looked after in due course. You have my word.'

This put Father Murtagh's mind at ease.

'I had my swimming trunks on and me ready to jump in,' joked the Irishman with the stove-pipe, coming over and offering a lump of tobacco, 'just as the ferry came for us.'

When I looked back towards the ship, Marie-Claire and her friends stood in the silver standard waiting pen. I was hoping she'd make it onto our ferry. But the boat was almost full and she was a long way back in the queue.

'Now, there's a picture if ever I saw one – a sight that would make a deacon very blue indeed,' quipped the padre, following my hungry gaze.

'You're not supposed to be staring at women,' I snapped.

'And why not? I may be a priest, but I'm still a man.'

The ferryboat was soon overcrowded and heading for the New York docks. A scruffy-looking seaman – whom I presumed, by the gimp of him, to be in charge of the operation – started into a speech.

'Every man aboard take heed. Today is voting day in the city of New York. A new mayor will be elected. Ted Ireland is in the running. Only for Ted Ireland you would be waiting on those ships out there until kingdom come. Ted Ireland is the reason you have been freed from quarantine today. He is one of our own – his parents hail from County Cork. We do things differently in this city – we stick together and look after our own. Ted Ireland represents the Society of Saint Tammany and the proud sons of Erin.'

Most of the first-class passengers looked away in silence. One well-to-do gentleman, a fella who had complained to Captain McKenzie about having to board the same ferry as the silver-standard people, refused to hold his tongue.

'What an utter load of nonsense,' he shouted back, 'you have made a dog's dinner of your own country and now you want to make a mess of New York into the bargain.'

The scruffy-looking seaman wasn't going to argue. He wasn't there to argue. But by the way he eyed the protestor, you could tell he was annoyed.

'Show your loyalty to the old country and your appreciation to Ted Ireland. Go into the city's voting booths and make your mark for the Democratic political party. When you get off this ferry, the good folk of Tammany will be there to assist you. Feel free to avail of our hospitality. God bless you and God bless Ireland.'

And with that the gentleman protestor was at it again.

'Unbelievable,' said Jim, smiling and rubbing his hands together. 'In Ireland, you're not allowed vote without land. In America, they're encouraging you to vote even before you set foot on land. That's what I call democracy. Now I know I'm in America.'

As we disembarked the ferryboat, I took note of the men on the quays – loading and unloading the ships' cargoes.

'Reminds me of Dublin,' I said to Jim.

'Yeah,' he agreed, 'just like the quays on the Liffey. I wonder is there a Winetavern Street whorehouse anywhere close by.'

'I hope so,' I replied, 'after eyeing up Marie-Claire for the past month I feel like the brown bull of Cooley.'

Some of them were only boys – strong looking, but boys nonetheless. They worked the line with black men, who looked neither young nor old. Everyone was moving at top speed. They didn't talk to each other. Most of the black men had rope necklaces with pieces of wood attached. On the wood were numbers. One of them looked up when he saw us staring. He diverted his gaze and kept moving.

'It's strange to be back on dry land,' remarked the padre.

Father Murtagh was right. It *was* strange – and hard to believe the voyage was over. A crude-looking quayside stall sold cholera masks for two cents. That was strange too – there would be no more pounds, shillings and pence. From now on we'd be dealing in dollars and cents. The woman behind the stall caught me looking and held up a mask.

'Protect yourself,' she said, 'New York is walking with it.'

I didn't answer or venture over. Cholera was the least of my worries.

We were lined up in double file and marched to the *Hudson Bay Registry Office* building, where we waited patiently for our names to be recorded in huge ledgers. Two clerks sat at either end of a long desk, while the smell of polish reminded me of the pay room at Cranley House. When it came to his turn, Jim Gorman said his name was John Brown. He held out Lady Jane Teale's letter confidently. However, nobody wanted to see the letter. They weren't looking for proof. His name was recorded in a spidery scribble and that was that – John Brown had been inducted into the new world and was moved along the line towards the door marked *incoming*.

In the yard outside the registry office, we were received by a young fella in a red vest with the initials *GOP* written across it. He steered us in the direction of a waiting trailer.

'A boarding house for the weary travellers,' he said in a weird accent, pushing away a flop of blonde hair before taking one of Jim's empty suitcases.

A half-naked man charged at the young fella, who abandoned the suitcase and just about made his escape.

'I'll break yer bastarding back, I swear to God I will,' roared the half-naked man. 'Forgive the language, Reverends. Follow me guys, and I'll look after yis.'

He pulled on a dirty white vest over his bulging, hairy, belly. A large blue badge pinned to it read: *Vote Number 1 – Ireland*.

'After all, a vote for Ireland is a vote for America, isn't that right, Yer Reverence,' he quipped, before giving me a big, head-turning wink. 'Will yis jump in, guys, and make yer marks. Yis look like yis could do with a bit of grub and a few wee pints, all courtesy of Mister Ted Ireland.'

We looked at Father Murtagh for the next move.

'Well, I suppose,' stammered the padre, 'when in Rome…'

'I'm Jack Muldoon. But they call me Malarkey. I'm one of Ted

Ireland's voting men. He's running and we're tailing. Ya can ride up top with me, Reverend.'

The padre got into the front and I followed Jim Gorman onto the half-full trailer. After Jack Muldoon, or Malarkey – or whatever he was called – coaxed some more *Erin's Queen* passengers on board, he swung the trailer door shut and away with him up to drive the horses.

'I beg yer pardon, Reverend, but ya don't want to get mixed up with those port runner guys – the guys in the red vests. They've a bad name for starting guys on the wrong footing. Stick with me and I'll see yis right. I know by the cut of youse guys, yer used to better handling than the shanties those port runners are rubbing shoulders with.'

That's when Jim saw the man in the fedora hat again. He was stepping off a ferryboat – him and half the poor of Ireland. I could see why Jim would be wary of him. He seemed different from the wretches around him. It was the way he carried himself that set him apart. There was a confidence in his step. The rest of third-class staggered onto the pier, half-dazed from their trials at sea. But this slip of a man with his neat ginger beard glided along, as if without a care in the world.

'Look at his portmanteau,' said Jim, ruffled by the ginger's swagger. 'Pure leather. That's not natural for steerage.'

'Merciful hour, will you give it up, Jim,' I replied. 'The man is entitled to carry his clothes in a leather portmanteau if he likes. It's probably belonging to a dear old auntie of his, or maybe it was given to him as a going-away present.'

'Going-away present indeed,' countered Jim. 'There's a famine on, in case you've forgotten.'

The little ginger man didn't see us. He made his way into the registry office as we were being driven off in the opposite direction.

Jack Muldoon was all business. He couldn't sit still for a minute – shaking his reins for more speed or waving at other traffic to get out of the road. He told the padre that the smartest place to find level-pulling democrats is right at source – the boat in the harbour. Father Murtagh said he'd never seen so many horse-drawn carriages in the same street before. He admitted he was dizzy looking out from his perch. He wondered at how Jack Muldoon could steer his horses with such accuracy, zig-zagging in and out of laneways and avenues and between groups of people.

'I'll give ya a couple of wee tips, Yer Reverence – just because ye're fresh off the boat – to keep in mind for yer congregation. If yer Irish and want to get on in this land make sure to join Fitzpatrick's union. Throw yer dime in the Hibernian tin each week – making sure it causes a good rattle. Don't say mass too early on a Sunday morning. And tell yer flock to sink their few beers below in McArthur's bar. Observe these rituals well – encouraging others to do likewise – and everything else will just fall into place.'

'You're not suggesting I endorse a public house from the altar,' asked the padre.

'Ah now, ye can leave yer sensibilities beyond at the registration office. It's America yer in now, Yer Reverence. And in America endorsements are everything, whether they come from the altar or not.'

Muldoon stopped his horses and told Father Murtagh to sit tight for a wee while. He jumped out and ran into a polling station, returning with a bundle of loose papers. He opened the trailer and asked a young fella his name and age.

'Patrick O'Shaughnessy,' said the boy, 'sir, I'm fourteen.'

'Not today yer not,' replied Muldoon. 'For today yer ...'

He then looked at the name on the top sheet.

'Yer Tom Rodgers. And yer nineteen years old, from

Washington Square. Yer number two thousand and thirty-nine on the draft.'

Handing the page to Patrick O'Shaughnessy, Muldoon told him to return to the trailer when he was done and that the voting wasn't finished by a long way. He examined the other sheets before handing one to each of the trailer's male occupants. Jim Gorman's new name was Sean O'Rourke.

'Where's *our* voting papers,' asked Father Murtagh, including me in his protestation.

'Well,' said Muldoon, embarrassed for once, 'I wouldn't like to be the cause of holy men indulging in, well, anything that could be described as unfitting of the habit.'

'Show me one of those sheets,' demanded Father Murtagh, taking off his collar and handing it to Muldoon. 'Come on, Father Joe, take up your page. There's a time and a place for everything. God will understand if we throw our weight behind the cause.'

Muldoon practically wetted himself as he watched Father Murtagh ascend the steps, under the guise of Thomas Brogan, to make his mark for Ted Ireland. Then he drove his happy little gathering around New York, stopping another dozen or so times. The procedure was always the same – he would race into the polling booths, come out armed with twenty-three election sheets, and send in his trailer of voters to make their marks. I went from Paul O'Shea to Timothy Lyons, then Patrick O'Boyle to Seamus Hughes. As Pa Culloty, I turned up at a polling station only to find that three Pa Cullotys had already voted there that morning. By mid-afternoon – between exhaustion and excitement – we barely knew our *own* names.

It wasn't just the Irish immigrants who were rounded up. Behind a voting blind opposite Father Murtagh, a tall blonde boy awkwardly forged an X on the ballot paper beside the name of Ted Ireland. He looked anxiously at the padre, then said something in a strange language. It made Jack Muldoon laugh when Father Murtagh regaled us with the story.

'Ah that's the beauty of election time, Yer Reverence, prejudice goes out the window. Tammany Hall isn't fussy where she plucks them from – so long as there's enough of them to see Ted Ireland home.'

At one stage we met a rather dapper man in a black suit and top hat. He was handing out pamphlets from his perch outside a polling-station door. Muldoon was wildly excited by him, clasping his hand several times during their conversation.

'Who's he,' asked Father Murtagh, when we had set off again.

'The one and only William Tweed,' chirped Muldoon. 'The most dynamic prospect out of Tammany since Andrew Jackson ran for the big one.'

'You keep mentioning this Tammany, what is it?'

Muldoon shook his head in disbelief.

'Yer joking, right? *Tammany*. As in Tammany Hall. On Fourteenth Street. The seat of Irish political power in this great city since the late seventeen eighties. It might have been named for a Lenape Indian chief, but we've got a firm grip of her now.'

At one point, Muldoon pulled up outside a polling station amid a stand-off. Members of the Native American Party were blocking the entrance on a truckload of Ted Ireland supporters. A bell was rung several times before a man stood on a wooden platform and read from a scroll, warning all present to be wary of the Irish invaders, that they were striving to make America into a Papal state, and would stop at nothing until they had driven the real founders of the country from their rightful positions.

'At least they have a proper stage, not like the rickety old barrels they use at home,' Jim pointed out.

'Yeah, Pius Mooney would love it here,' I said.

'Pass no remarks on them guys,' shouted Jack Muldoon, 'they're just the Know-Nothings, letting us know how they got their name.'

When he heard this, the man on the stage was irate.

'Malarkey, you ill-reared bastard. Your curs done our man out of office; redrawing constituency lines and leaving him at the mercy of the Swedes and Poles.'

'Go on, ya Swallowtail,' growled Muldoon, 'the sooner ye waspy fuckers are dumped out of American politics, the better it'll be for all of us.'

Muldoon was mad. He made a rush at the entrance, swinging his big fists in all directions. A punch-up broke out. Jim, the padre and I stood by, not knowing what to do. There wasn't much point in joining a free-for-all when we didn't know who the Swallowtails were – or the Democrats, for that matter, apart from Muldoon. Then there was the sound of whistles; Malarkey retreated to the safety of his trailer.

'Where have we seen this before,' I said, as we watched the policemen baton-charge the brawlers.

'Ah here, I didn't come three thousand miles on the *Erin's Queen* to take up where I left off,' quipped Jim. 'It's nourishment I'm looking for, not punishment.'

'I do hope common sense will prevail,' said Father Murtagh, resuming his perch next the box-seat.

Muldoon's mood had soured. Wiping away blood from his nostrils, he apologised to *yer reverences* for losing his temper.

'No matter what, we won't be intimidated from doing our civic duty. Get in there guys,' he ordered, stopping outside yet another voting establishment, 'the machine won't work unless ye do yer bit.'

'What machine is that,' I asked, but nobody was listening.

After a while, Muldoon lightened up again. He pulled his

horses to a halt outside a public house called *McArthur's Saloon*, before unhinging the trailer door.

'This is hardly a polling station,' said the man next to Jim.

Muldoon strutted into the saloon and returned with a roll of white tickets. He tore one off and handed it to the padre. He passed the rest into the trailer. We all got one, even the females among us.

'Thirsty work, this voting business,' Muldoon said with a grin. 'It's time to wet yer whistles, courtesy of the bauld Ted Ireland. Ye greenhorns need to get connected, ya know – a job and a place to stay. Jonty McArthur will sort ye out. Just say ye're friends of Malarkey and everything else will fall into yer laps.'

He helped Father Murtagh down by the hand – the way you'd help a woman – before bowing respectfully. Then he bade us farewell, shook the reins and sped off through the city streets.

It was bedlam inside the saloon – even noisier than the street – for the time of day.

'Does anybody work in America,' I asked.

'Maybe their Public Work schemes finish earlier than ours,' remarked Jim.

'It's Sunday,' the padre pointed out, 'or are you losing the run of yourselves?'

We dodged our way through the crowd. At the counter, two barkeeps were going full pelt. There wasn't a hope of placing an order, never mind getting a drink. I looked to the rear. The rest of Muldoon's trailer were at our backs – talk about the blind leading the blind.

'Pints for Malarkey's men, compliments of Mister Ted Ireland,' announced a grey-haired gentleman, a tray of drinks in his hands.

It was like he had appeared out of nowhere, ten perfectly-poured pints at the ready.

'Come on now and take them off before I fall down with the weight of this tray. You can put your tickets on the counter.'

'Not for me, thank you,' said Father Murtagh.

'An Irishman who doesn't drink; I have it all now,' replied the grey-haired gentleman.

'He drinks alright, just not porter,' I said. 'He's partial to a drop of red wine of a Sunday.'

My joke seemed to go unnoticed.

'The clergy was always the same – expensive tastes. And I suppose you'll be looking for the short glass too?'

I had forgotten all about *my* habit.

'Oh, not at all,' I replied. 'I'd drink porter out of a sore dog's hole.'

'Language,' snapped the padre, 'must I keep reminding you?'

The grey-haired gentleman's face broke into a hearty laugh.

'Jonty McArthur, at your service,' he declared, leaving down the tray to shake my hand. 'Where are you from in the old country, Father?'

I was about to answer when one of the barkeeps came over for a private word, breaking Mister McArthur's concentration.

'No more credit for Burrows, the degenerate gobshite. All he's doing is going next door and spending it in the Spieler with Elsa. That casino will be his downfall. It's chicken one day and bones the next for that guy. Close off his tab,' he ordered the barkeep, before returning to us.

'You wouldn't have any idea of a good place to stay around here,' asked Jim.

'The Points,' returned Mister McArthur.

'Oh, the pints are grand,' said Jim, taking a gulp from his glass. 'You can tell this Ted Ireland fella that we're mighty grateful.'

'Stick with the Points and you won't go wrong.'

'Now, do you hear that,' I said to the padre. 'Spoken like a true professional.'

'Not the pints of stout, the *Five Points*,' explained Mister McArthur. 'It's the name of a district, not far from here. They'll see you right. The rents are low. You can get a comfortable apartment for two or three dollars per month. We've got to stick together boys, that's the golden rule in a city like New York. It's the only way to keep the machine ticking. Siege mentality is your only man. You'll figure it out soon enough.'

Before Jim Gorman could question him further, Mister McArthur scurried behind his counter. Another tray of pints arrived, as a rousing rendition of *Garryowen* broke through the wall of noise.

'Keep up, guys – time for a shot. It's America ye're in now,' quipped Mister McArthur, uncorking a whiskey and toppling it into a series of small glasses. 'And in America, we like to do things bigger and better.'

A well-dressed man emerged from the crowd. Strangely, he wore a straw hat. It certainly did nothing to compliment his beautiful coat. He was followed by another man with dubious-looking headgear – a fella with long curly hair and a black skullcap perched on top.

'Jonty, I want to talk to you. What's the story with my credit? Your boys are saying I'm at my limit. Is my word not good enough for you, all of a sudden?'

'Settle, Mickser,' said Mister McArthur. 'It's only for your own good. I don't want Missus Burrows in here chastising me again.'

'I told you before not to heed her. I'll deal with the queer one. But if you pull my credit, who's going to deal with me?'

'Steady on, I say. Maybe your Jew friend here will bankroll you? They're the money men in this town. Don't take me for no mug, Mickser.'

And that ended the subject. This Mickser lad lifted two pints from our tray, handing one to the man with the skullcap. There was an inscription sewed into the sleeve of his beautiful coat.

'Herringbone,' whispered Jim.

'Might be his name,' I whispered back.

'Those are Malarkey's drinks,' said Mister McArthur. 'You can leave your money on the counter.'

The very mention of Malarkey seemed to cheer Mickser up.

'How is the auld bollox,' he said with a smile, 'running around like a headless goose, no doubt. I guess, the day that's in it and all. These bucks must be fresh off the boat, if they're Malarkey's men?'

Mister McArthur ignored the question, instead asking the man with the skullcap – a man called Abraham – all about his family and how they were getting on with the new synagogue.

'Don't mention the synagogue in front of the priests,' said Abraham, lifting his pint in salutation. 'They're still ribbing us over Calvary. Let's hear it for Ted Ireland instead. I voted for him first thing this morning.'

'What's he on about,' I said, absentmindedly. 'What's Calvary?'

'The crucifixion of our Lord Jesus Christ,' whispered the padre.

'Where did he get his habit,' asked Abraham, 'at a jumble-sale?'

He was forward for a stranger – too forward for my liking. We all toasted Ted Ireland then.

'Why would a Jew vote for the Irish,' quipped the padre.

'Why would a Jew vote at all,' interjected Mister McArthur. 'They're running this city as it is – and they've the deadlines to prove it.'

'Hush now, Jonty. You guys aren't shy when it comes to mob

rule either,' Abraham pointed out.

'We provide the muscle, but you guys have the smarts,' replied Mister McArthur.

'Yesterday I was Jewish and tomorrow I will be Jewish again. But today I am an Irishman,' declared Abraham. 'A proud Irishman, who's trying to keep his shop door open.'

'What do you mean by that,' asked Jim.

'Regardless of what Jonty says, I couldn't get a drink – let alone my trading licence renewed – this side of the bridge without the Irish say-so.'

'Welcome to the club,' said Mister McArthur. 'I'm a Red Leg – well, descended from them. My crowd was sent to Hell or Barbados by Oliver Cromwell. They ended up being worked to death in the plantations of Montser...'

Something had broken Mister McArthur's concentration again. He jumped up and pushed his way across the floor, taking a drink from the counter and spilling it into a bucket. He seized an Indian by the shoulder and dragged him into the crowd. He reappeared, had stern words with one of his barkeeps, then returned to us.

'I told that young guy, when I hired him, not to serve that redskin.'

'Begod and he used to drink here all the time,' said Mickser. 'Is it because he's an Apache?'

'It is not,' replied Mister McArthur, 'I couldn't give a continental if he's an Apache or not. I've no problem with any of the Indians. But I warned that guy about playing with knives in this house, and all he did was laugh in my face.'

'Getting back to your Montserrat, the Irish themselves are no saints when it comes to carrying people across the water against their will. Didn't they join the nobles in Nantes out of the proceeds,' said Abraham.

'And what would you Jews know about saints, ye that killed

the greatest saint of them all,' answered Mister McArthur. 'Isn't that right, Mickser?'

I could tell that Mickser was fed up with the pair of them.

'Where are you bucks from,' he asked, ignoring Mister McArthur completely.

'Longford,' replied Jim, before Father Murtagh had time to think.

'Where's that?'

'In the middle of Ireland – in Leinster,' added Jim.

'*He's* from Leinster,' stressed the padre. 'The rest of us are from down south.'

'You don't sound like you're from the south,' said Mickser to the padre. 'Leinster? Ara, all I know about that dump is that the king of Leinster sold Ireland down the river for his own ends. It was them bucks who brought Strongbow in around the place.'

'That was almost seven hundred years ago,' I snapped, 'what do you want *us* to do, get down on bended knee and beg your forgiveness? And where are you from, Mister Herringbone?'

'Mister *who*,' answered Mickser.

'Your coat sleeve. Is that not your name?'

Mickser inspected his coat until he came across the nametag.

'The man who owns this coat is dead,' he growled. 'I'm from Galway.'

'You don't sound like you're from Galway,' remarked the padre.

'I'm here a lifetime. When did you bucks get here?'

'Sailed in on Thursday,' said Jim Gorman, 'courtesy of the *Erin's Queen.*'

'Oh, the Virgin Mary brought ye,' said Mickser, winking at Abraham.

'No, the *Erin's Queen,*' repeated Jim.

'The same thing,' said Mickser. 'The Virgin Mary *is* Erin's queen.'

'I thought it was Victoria.'

If this was Abraham's attempt at humour, nobody was laughing.

'We're looking for lodgings. Would you fellas know of anywhere handy? Mister McArthur suggested somewhere called the Five Points.'

'You're kidding me, right? You'd want to be well connected going down there, or at least making sure your shirt tail's hanging out. Isn't that right, *Mister McArthur*,' said Mickser, smirking at Jonty.

'What are you on about,' replied Jim, 'shirt tail hanging out?'

'Guys, enough with this *mister* business, call me Jonty from now on,' said Mister McArthur.

He leaned over and squeezed my shoulder.

'Pity this man's shirt tail isn't hanging out. The Parlour Mob could do with muscle like that.'

'I'm not in the habit of wearing shirts,' I replied.

'Nobody wants to live in the Five Points no more. Even the shanties and blacks are leaving the Points,' Mickser explained. 'And I'll tell you why – the Points is a first-degree shithole. Where did you bucks say yous were from? Longford? There's a woman who rents out apartments over on the West Docks – only a short walk from here. I'm nearly sure she's a Longford woman. She'll be the one to look after yous bucks.'

'A short walk, my ass,' said Jonty, obviously not happy with Mickser's less than favourable opinion of the Points.

'You didn't know any O'Nuallains when you were growing up in Galway,' Jim asked.

This Mickser fella put a big hairy hand across his mouth and eyed us with suspicion.

'That's Nolan, right – unless they're Connemara people.'

'They'd be descendants of the MacCarthy Mors, high kings in the south,' added the padre, trying to keep a straight face.

Mickser looked up and shook his head.

'You gotta be shitting me. You crazy Longford bastards. High kings, mar dhea. What do I look like – a simpleton? Jonty, you're not seriously sending these bumpkins down to the Points?'

'And why not? It was good enough for you, until you got up in the world.'

'Ara, come on, Jonty,' said Mickser, 'even the Jews had to get out.'

'Kicked out, more like,' muttered Jonty.

'I was a victim of circumstance,' explained Abraham. 'The best move I ever made. King Henry Square is a nice alternative.'

'It's Daniel O'Connell Square now, and don't you forget it. Didn't you drink lots of free Irish porter at its renaming,' Jonty pointed out.

They exploded into laughter while we looked on. It was obviously a joke among themselves.

'A public house in America must cost a pretty penny,' I said to Jonty.

'It's a *saloon*, my friend,' he replied with a chuckle. 'And it's inherited. I'm third-generation Irish. My family got a head-start due to Cromwell's holiday.'

'*Cromwell's holiday?*'

'The McArthurs of Drog-heeda, is that how you guys say it?'

'Drogheda,' replied Father Murtagh.

'Anyway, County Louth at any rate. Cromwell sent them on a permanent holiday to the Caribbean – an island called Montserrat – where they remained in slavery for many years.'

'What a bastard,' I snarled, before remembering that I was supposed to be a priest.

'Father Joseph,' exclaimed the padre.

'I beg your pardon,' I said, 'that was uncalled for.'

Jonty McArthur collected the empty glasses and got his tray ready once more.

'West Docks indeed! What's wrong with you, Mickser? That Elsa girl next door has your head gone astray. Never trust a gambler, guys. Take my advice – live in the Points, pray at Saint Pat's, drink my beer – and you can't go wrong.'

## Six – Ted Ireland

Father Murtagh eventually asked the standout question of the day – who is this Ted Ireland we had spent all day travelling around Manhattan voting for. Mister McArthur – Jonty – was only too happy to fill us in.

Ted Ireland was born in the middle of the Atlantic Ocean, the first and only child of Delia and Eamonn Murphy.

'Just like Gearoid Seosamh Seoige,' I added.

'Who,' asked Mickser.

'Never mind,' said the padre.

'Are you guys finished, or maybe ye'd like to tell it,' grunted Jonty. 'Well, Delia and Eamonn Murphy boarded a ship at the Cove in their native County Cork.'

When Jonty mentioned the Cove, I looked at Jim Gorman. I knew what he was thinking. The last place they imprisoned Shay was the Cove – or Cobh, or Queenstown as it had been recently renamed after Victoria's visit – before he was sent on to Tazmania.

'The story goes that two Murphys got on the ship and two Murphys got off the ship. But they weren't the same two Murphys. Well, at least one of them wasn't. Delia took her time on the gangplank, a large bump under her shawl. Alas, her husband would never see that bump come to fruition. As his wife panged in childbirth, Eamonn Murphy lay at the bottom of the deep Atlantic. He died of pneumonia. His body had given up while fleeing the shortage of ninety-two and he departed this life one day before his son's arrival. Delia named the boy Edward after his father and paternal grandfather. *Eamon O Murchu* – Edward Murphy – is the name enrolled in the Hudson Bay Registry Office. But it was a name which was to go on a transformation – not an uncommon thing for an Irish name back then.'

'Is that the same Hudson Bay Registry Office where we were this morning,' asked the padre.

'The one and only,' answered Mickser, before Jonty continued.

'Naturally, Delia's plight as a single mother came to the attention of the Irish-American community in New York. She chose not to enter a home for unmarried mothers or give her son up for adoption. Instead, Delia and little Edward were looked after with fondness by the parishioners of Saint James's – a small Lower East Side parish of about sixteen thousand worshippers. That's where the Murphy family's association with Tammany Hall started. The machine set up contributions to financially help women like Delia, who couldn't work on a full-time basis.'

Muldoon was back again. He was looking for more tickets. Jonty went behind the bar and started counting. He got as far as seven or eight before closing the book and handing it over.

'Here, Malarkey, you sort it out yourself. I'm busy here.'

'Good man Jonty,' said Muldoon, 'ye're looking after my lot, fair dues.'

Seeing as Malarkey had disrupted him, Jonty filled another tray of pints before resuming his story.

'Young Edward was sent to the Jesuit Boys' Primary, then to the Christian Brothers' De La Salle High School in Lower Manhattan. It was on induction day in the Jesuit Primary when the first transformation of his name took place. Edward was shy and quiet. When asked his name and where he came from, all the headmaster could make out were the hushed tones of *Edward* and *Ireland*. Therefore, he was registered in the school roll-book as Edward Ireland. Later, this was shortened by his high-school peers to Eddie Ireland. His first sweetheart insisted on calling him Teddy and, as his interest in politics grew stronger, he decided to shorten his Christian name and keep the Ireland – as it was good for business. Thus, Ted Ireland is the name that appears on the ballot paper today.'

Jonty went on to tell us why Ted Ireland was Irish-America's dream politician – once he grew in confidence.

'He always professed to be the best man to look after the Irish community *in* New York because he was raised by the Irish community *of* New York. His voting manifesto is: *Look after your city as you would look after your village.* The slogan really does tick all the boxes – tipping its hat to the homestead left behind while hinting at a future full of promise in a new, energetic, metropolis.'

'You should have Malarkey's job,' said Abraham.

'No, he should have Ted Ireland's job,' quipped Mickser.

I had to agree. Jonty could talk a better game than most – and he wasn't finished yet.

'When Ted first came to politics, he was determined that benevolence and Tammany would be interwoven and thrive under his guiding hand. Their Saint Vincent de Paul Society is particularly close to his heart. Back then, some thirty-five years ago now, it was said that there were two types of Irish-American politician – the *neighbourhooder* and the *lodginghouser*. Ted Ireland belonged in the former camp. He was a great neighbourhooder. Ted either knew his electorate by name, or he knew of them. He was the man on the street in his constituency. His bitter rival is the Native American Party, nicknamed the Know-Nothings. Ted hates their policies and everything they stand for. The Know-Nothings want a halt put to immigration, a two-decade waiting period for citizenship, and a restriction on any foreign-born person holding public office. In short, the Know-Nothings want the Ted Irelands of this world ground down like dust and scattered to the four winds.'

'We met them today outside one of the polling stations,' said the padre.

'Meet and beat – that's the way to deal with those bastards,' replied Mickser, 'oh, excuse me, Fathers.'

'As long as the ships keep coming,' continued Jonty, 'Ted Ireland knows not only is he important to the Irish-American voice, but that his position is being consolidated all the time. Still, he's not one to take chances. Before this election even began, he sent an envoy to Boston and enlisted the help of Barney McGinniskin – the first Irish-born policeman in America. It was pure gold. He had Barney's image in the *New York Tribune,* above a story on his life and times. Barney was pointing at a map of America with a speech bubble that read: *Vote Democrat, Vote Irish.*'

'Pure genius,' admitted Abraham, 'invoking the spirit of the immigrant in one four-word caption.'

'A nun follows his canvass trail wherever it shall lead,' Jonty pointed out. 'Her name is Sister Concepta. She hands out leaflets on shelters and soup kitchens in the city. She speaks of religious retreats for women. She donates Rosary beads, prayer books and miniature bottles of holy water.'

A voice from the crowd halted Jonty McArthur's tale.

'Padre, Padre,' exclaimed the voice.

My heart skipped a beat.

'Father Dolan. Is it yourself?'

Father Murtagh looked around. He didn't recognise the pipe-smoker. But I knew him instantly from the steerage compartment of the *Erin's Queen.* He was the man from Gowna – the one who had been asking about Father Austin Reilly, the parish priest of Colmcille. He must have gone voting with Malarkey, along with the man who was with him.

'Father Dolan, this is a neighbour of mine from back home. He met me off the ship. Dukey, this is the priest I was telling you about. Fancy seeing him again – and in the first public house we set foot in. It wouldn't happen in Gowna, never mind a place the like of New York. This man was known simply as *padre* on the way over. He said masses and funerals and done baptisms and all sorts. And he organised dances too. He was great gas altogether.'

Father Murtagh's cheeks burned with embarrassment. Jonty and Mickser exchanged fleeting glances. I was hoping they wouldn't involve me. I covered my habit as best I could. The old codger was only getting started.

'Dukey, you wouldn't believe it – Father Dolan is from Aughnacliffe. Imagine that,' he said, and slapped the padre on the back once more.

You could tell that Dukey didn't care for sentiment as much as his old pipe-smoking neighbour.

'What part,' he muttered suspiciously.

Father Murtagh remained silent. But Dukey wasn't to be ignored.

'What part,' he repeated loudly, 'of Aughnacliffe are you from?'

The padre wasn't going to get away without answering, that much was for sure.

'A place called the Hill of Molly. We didn't stay long,' said Father Murtagh.

The old pipe-smoker nearly shit himself with excitement.

'The Hill of Molly,' he gushed. 'Dukey, your family farmed land up there since God was a gossan.'

Dukey was beginning to get on our nerves. He stared at the padre for ages.

'They did,' he muttered eventually. 'There were never any Dolans lived at the Hill of Molly. That much I can guarantee.'

'As I said, we didn't stay for long,' explained the padre. 'I was only four or five when we left – can't even remember the place.'

The stare continued. Father Murtagh's blushes were contagious. I could feel my cheeks beginning to redden. There was an awkward, horrible, silence.

'Is that right,' said Dukey, and he took a sip of his pint. 'If you say so.'

We turned back to the counter, away from Dukey and the pipe-smoker. Thankfully, Jonty, Mickser and Abraham had had the good sense to let it play out. But their eyes burned holes in my back. Had we left Ireland at all. Here we were – three-thousand miles away from the place – and everyone still knew everything about everybody else.

## Seven – Looking for Lodgings

Father Murtagh decided it was better to tell the truth. After all, Jonty McArthur needn't have received us so hospitably. Therefore, a bit of respect wouldn't go astray. Being caught out in lies was one thing, but to be wearing the working attire of the Catholic Church while being caught out in lies was something else. It highly embarrassed the padre and he believed the only way to make amends was to come clean.

'Say no more,' said Jonty. 'Please, I couldn't give a continental. You don't owe me any explanation. Guys, we've seen it all around here. That's the beauty of a place like New York. You can get on a ship in the old country as one person, and get off again a completely new man – with a new name and new hope. It's a fresh start. Leave the skeletons back in the Emerald Isle.'

Despite this unexpected vote of confidence, Jonty McArthur still felt it necessary to get Jack Muldoon back on the job. He came down the next morning, his sandy hair tossed and his eyes bulging from the drink. He still had that awful vest on, although the blue Ted Ireland badge was missing.

'Will you dress yourself, Malarkey,' said Jonty, 'it's not below in the Imperial you are now.'

Jonty liked to dig Muldoon about his frequent visits to the Imperial Hotel, a British-run establishment over in Chelsea, where a busty English barmaid by the name of Dolly strutted her stuff. Muldoon threw a lazy glance across the bar in Jonty's direction before turning his attention to us.

'How are my friends from Longford – the far-downers, as my

dear old mother would call ye.'

'What are you talking about? *Far-downers?* Have you gone mad, Malarkey,' snapped Jonty.

'My late mother, God rest her soul, that's what she used to call anyone from Dublin or the surrounding areas – the far-downers.'

We looked at each other blankly.

'Far-downers,' said Father Murtagh, 'I've never heard such a term.'

'Oh come on guys, ye're kidding me, right?'

'Well, it's logical when you think about it,' explained the padre. 'Dublin is far *and* down from Derry. But Longford is not a surrounding area, it's in the Midlands.'

'Ye've never heard of the far-downers,' said Muldoon. 'Don't get cute, Yer Reverence. It's a famous pet name. Just like people from Derry are known, affectionately I might add, as muckers.'

Then he looked at me all serious.

'Even a mucker like me knows that much.'

Muldoon may have been nursing a massive hangover – and he was arguably insane – but he was still selling himself much too short. A mucker like him knew a fair bit. In fact, he was a wealth of knowledge on the New York Irish. He went on to tell his audience that he knew some far-downers who worked on the railway. They were Midlanders too, or so they told Muldoon – Offaly and Westmeath men.

'They even have their own language, some crazy regional shit they speak when they want some discretion. They taught me a few words. Let's see now…'

'What about somewhere to live first,' asked the padre. 'We'd be very interested in settling into a nice Catholic community.'

'Well, Saint Joseph's was the original Irish parish in New York. It's situated in Greenwich Village and has almost ten thousand members. Saint Stephen's is a wee bit bigger, but it's out in Hell's Kitchen.'

'Hell's kitchen,' exclaimed the padre, 'what sort of a name is that?'

'I assure Yer Reverence,' continued Muldoon, 'it sounds like a tough neighbourhood, but it's actually not too bad – and very Irish.'

Jonty McArthur started knotting the ends of his bar-towel when he heard this.

'Ah, those boys don't want to be trudging all the way out to Hell's Kitchen. Surely they can be accommodated somewhere more local, so they can come in here and avail of my knowledge any time they feel the need.'

'I catch yer drift, Jonty,' said Muldoon, 'I guess there's no point in venturing too far uptown.'

Muldoon then reeled off a number of prominent Irish suburbs close to Jonty's saloon – Water Street, Hudson Avenue, Vinegar Hill.

'Vinegar Hill,' shouted Jim, 'Sugrue would love the sound of that. It would take him right back to ninety-eight and the fighting in Wexford.'

'Sugrue,' said Muldoon, 'is he one of the guys ye met in here the first night?'

Padre threw a quick glance in my direction. It was plain that someone had been telling Muldoon the story of our brush with the Gowna men.

'No. Just an old warrior we left back in God's country,' Jim said ruefully.

'On second thoughts, forget I mentioned Vinegar Hill. It's a bit of a shanty town.'

'What about something closer, like Chelsea or the West Village,' suggested Jonty.

'No way. That's dockside territory,' warned Muldoon, 'ye can forget about any of the neighbourhoods along the West Side, the longshoremen would have yere guts for garters if they caught ye squatting up there. That's a closed shop, I'm afraid.'

'We're not looking to *squat* anywhere,' said Jim, showing Muldoon a fistful of pound notes, 'we're looking to rent. We like to pay our way.'

Muldoon acknowledged the neat bundle of Queen Victorias with a nod.

'I understand ye completely. The Gas House District along the East River is nice. We might take a stroll up there for a look. Then there's the Old Fourth Ward, but it's a wee bit ethnically mixed – Germans, Poles, Italians, Swedes, Africans, Chinese, Spaniards. But, if ye don't mind sharing... it's first up best dressed in the Ward.'

'Look, all we want is a nice, peaceful, Irish community,' Jim pointed out, 'not some multicoloured swap-shop. There has to be somewhere nearby?'

'That would be Thompson Street, just south of Washington Square,' declared Muldoon. 'It's even called after an Irish guy – a soldier from the days of the revolution.'

'Well,' said Jim, gathering up the pound notes, 'let's get our arses down there quick-smart.'

'As luck would have it, I've a hunch there's a Longford woman on Thompson Street with a couple of apartments to rent,' continued Muldoon, his memory becoming clearer as Jim Gorman folded the notes into his big purse. 'The young lady gets better looking every time I see her.'

'Who,' asked the padre, 'the Longford woman on Thompson Street?'

'No, Yer Reverence, Queen Victoria on those British pound notes.'

When we got to Thompson Street, Father Murtagh removed his collar and buried it in his pocket.

'Knowing our luck, this woman will know us from the ship as well,' he griped.

'She might be related to the Gowna men,' I quipped.

'I don't want to hear about those fellows again,' he returned, a face on him that would turn milk sour.

Jim Gorman's paranoia must have been spreading – I knew the Gowna men had embarrassed Father Murtagh, but it was only then I realised just how much the whole episode had shaken him. Suddenly, everybody in New York City knew about the stealing of Canon Reidy's prized chalice. But at least the Gowna men's nosiness had put an end to my days as a man of the cloth – particularly as that cloth happened to be a woman's serving uniform from the *Erin's Queen* ocean carrier.

Muldoon's hunch that a Longford woman on Thompson Street had a couple of apartments to rent proved correct – almost. She had rooms to rent for sure. But when confronted with the allegation that she hailed from Longford, she was appalled.

'Longford, how are you,' she growled. 'I'm from Longwood in the county of Meath, the same as my father and mother before me. You won't find anything but royal blood flowing through Ina Begley's veins. I'll tell you that for nothing, sonny.'

This Missus Begley seemed a total disciplinarian – for want of a better word. When she moved off towards the lawn, Muldoon reckoned the city was full of this type of Irishwoman; her bark was worse than her bite. She returned with a pumpkin-head from her garden tree. Muldoon insisted on helping her take down another from between two intersecting branches.

'I didn't ask for your help, sonny,' she rasped, 'what was it you wanted anyway?'

'Missus Begley, pardon me for the intrusion. These fine gentlemen have come all the way from Longford in Ireland. They have no accommodation. I was informed, only this morning, that a lovely lady from Longford – which turns out to be Longwood and for which I apologise – on Thompson Street has rooms for renting.'

Missus Begley momentarily forgot the second lantern she had been reaching for. She eyed us up suspiciously.

'Ye're a sorry-looking bunch,' she said, 'I thought youse were a street gang – with the cut of ye. Rooms, my eye – I have fully furnished apartments for letting.'

Muldoon laughed so much Missus Begley told him to *can it* – whatever that meant.

'What makes you think I'd trust a pup like you – in a dirty vest – and a few famine runaways, fresh off the boat with itchy feet? The last crowd of stowaways I had here bolted before they paid their rent.'

I knew Muldoon had a right to take up Jonty's offer of a fresh linen shirt.

'I assure you, madam, we are only here in good faith. And if this young pup's assurances need any backing, maybe my boss's assurances will put yer mind at ease on the matter.'

'And who might your boss be, sonny?'

'*Ted Ireland*, that's who,' Muldoon replied confidently.

As Missus Begley's brow relaxed and her face settled into something approaching friendliness, Jim Gorman produced a handful of pound notes.

'We're not looking to short-change anyone, missus,' he said. 'We far-downers like to pay our way.'

'Now what will I do with this one,' said Muldoon, picking up another pumpkin as Missus Begley showed us into her porch.

'Ted Ireland you say,' she chirped while smiling over, 'and

how is Mister Ireland these days, *Mister Muldoon?* I believe he's well on his way to another term and the counting only half done.'

'Well on his way, madam. And I'll be telling him all about the wonderful Missus Begley when I get back to the office.'

'Oh shucks,' she said, her cheeks glowing.

The Thompson Street area was nice. It was massively different from what any of us fellas were used to, but that was to be expected. Muldoon told us it could be territorial, but no more than the other areas of the city. Despite the obvious Irish presence, it housed a lot of black people. It had some European settlers too. Therefore, it was cut up or *deadlined* – as our new neighbours would say. Even though he acted the clown, Muldoon was obviously a deep thinker. He reckoned that because of the defined notions our ancestors had between parish and neighbourhood, the new Irish – or what Missus Begley termed the *famine runaways* – thought about city space in parochial terms.

'No matter where y'are in the city,' Muldoon concluded, 'y'are only a short walk away from a chapel or a public house.'

And so, our new residence afforded us a measure of comfort we never thought possible of such a built-up environment. Father Murtagh loved that he could see a church steeple from the new bedroom window. It reminded him of God's presence in our lives. The toll of its bell reminded Jim Gorman of our reliance on time and of Sugrue – especially those days when Sugrue had used the bells of Saint Mary's as a signal for lunchtime on the Public Works scheme in Cranley estate. And the occasional sighting of one of its priests and his big happy red face reminded me that McArthur's Saloon was only a five-minute walk in two separate directions.

Mickser Burrows, who lived in the same neighbourhood as Missus Begley and her apartments, was the first person we met upon arrival. He disliked her and called her an *auld rap*. He warned us to be weary of her. Missus Begley didn't like Mickser

Burrows either, confiding in the padre that he was a half-itinerant heathen with the manners of a pig.

'Only for his good wife,' she maintained, 'he'd be lying under a bush and the arse out of his trousers. She's a living saint, is what she is.'

Missus Begley only said that Missus Burrows was a living saint because she hailed from Oldcastle, in her native County Meath.

In fairness to him, Mickser never brought up the awkward situation with the Gowna men – not even once. He must have known we weren't who we claimed to be, especially when we ditched our habits. But he never mentioned it.

For a fella brought up in the wilds of west Galway, Mickser was full of surprises. He showed us how to be city gents – how to walk downtown with a certain swagger. If it wasn't for the straw hat, he could have been mistaken for one of those deeply-tanned, athletic types from Nolita – the gentlemen who talked with their hands. Mickser could always be seen puffing on a cigarette, and he loved getting his shoes shined at the corner of Canal. He taught us how to weed the backwardness – the *rural Ireland*, as he called it – out of our bones. Soon, we didn't even notice that all the boys on Thompson Street wore shoes, or that the girls went by our porch to church in white gloves.

Behind Mickser's life of debauchery, lay an ambitious man. He was always plotting and planning. His head was full of dreams and aspirations. He told us not to get too comfortable in our new surroundings, that *out west* was where the real money was to be made.

'Once I gather enough dollars together, I'm going panning for gold in Californay. Ara, there's a fortune waiting for anyone who makes it past the Indians.'

Mickser had been living in New York for years with no danger whatsoever of gathering enough dollars for his trip to California. Everything he gathered got scattered on the double again, either in McArthur's Saloon or the Spieler next door. But I really liked Mickser Burrows. He was a stand-up type of guy – as Jonty would put it. Only for him and his antics, Jim and the padre would have driven me clean crazy back then.

Defrocking himself was supposed to calm Father Murtagh down. Instead, all it did was wind him to the last. He believed that the Gowna men were out to get us. He thought Jim Gorman's ginger-bearded man from steerage was out to get us. He even stopped going to Jonty's with the rest of us – claiming it was awash with nosey Irish ne'er-do-wells; as far as the padre was concerned, we were sitting ducks for an arrest.

Jim Gorman lived by a golden rule – *better safe than sorry*. He took this to an extreme. New York was a long way from Ireland. But many of the British newspapers ending up in the city contained a *please copy* request, and the *London Times* had both myself and Jim listed as wanted men. More often than not, the American newspaper companies were willing to comply and lift this information. Jim's attitude was that every journalist in the Empire State was out to get him. He bought the *Tribune* daily, scanning it meticulously. He bought the *Punch,* the *Tomahawk,* the *Catholic Herald,* and *Bentley's Miscellany* too. There were more newspapers in his apartment than in the New York Municipal Library. Jim needed to settle down. He needed to relax and have a bit of a laugh below in Jonty's. He needed to blend in. And, most of all, he needed to remain Mister John Brown – attending New York on the business of his master, Lord Edward Teale.

## Eight – The Italian Parade

Mickser's good wife was a hardy slip of a woman. He talked her down as a nag and a dominator, but she must have done her nagging and her dominating behind closed doors. The padre thought her rather refined. Jim and I went along with this view. When drawn on the subject of her husband's wayward streak, all Missus Burrows wished to say was that *Michael is partial to the sup and fond of a card game*. She would say it softly, with a smile, as if she secretly found some sort of perverse pleasure in it. But the smile was only a front – Missus Burrows hated drink as much as she hated the British. She blamed it for keeping her down at heel.

'Why wouldn't she seem refined,' said Mickser, 'when she has that auld rap of a Begley one doing her growling for her. Nil aon phointe madra a bheith agat agus tu fein ag tafann.'

Missus Burrows was a frequent visitor to Ina Begley's house. She didn't even have to knock, just walk in unannounced. Her presence brought out the better side of Missus Begley. She was the only one allowed to call her *Ina*, and the only one who could squeeze a laugh out of the dear old lady.

As for Missus Burrows herself, nobody actually knew her first name. Mickser claimed he didn't even know; he called her *Missus* to her face and *the queer one* behind her back. And despite being her senior by a considerable distance, Ina Begley only ever referred to her as *Missus Burrows*. I always wondered about her first name.

'That woman will do no Purgatory,' Ina would say, 'not after putting up with that drunken, lazy, lump. She'll go straight to

Heaven.'

But Ina was no fool – she never said anything derogatory about Mickser in front of Missus Burrows.

There was a communal porch at the front of our apartment block. That's what Ina Begley and Muldoon called them – apartment *blocks*. It had a lovely low swing – a simple tile attached to a rafter by two lengths of rope. When it wasn't too cold, I developed a habit for swinging. The evening before Thanksgiving, Ina was sitting outside, drinking lemonade with Missus Burrows. She suffered an outburst of kindness – no doubt on account of the company – and brought me across a nice, cool, drink. Missus Burrows followed behind, peeping out from under her headscarf.

'The idolaters are at it again,' said Ina.

I asked her what she meant.

'The Italians – they're on their way with their statues and hymn books.'

I stopped swinging when I heard this. Jonty McArthur had been talking about the Italians, how their parades were something that had to be experienced. He told us there was one coming up on the Wednesday night before Thanksgiving, and to make sure not to miss it. He lauded it as a fantastic spectacle and said that's the beauty of a place like New York – you get to see how the other half lives.

'Where is it,' I asked, interrupting the women's prattle while trying not to sound too eager.

'Coming this way any minute now,' barked Ina. 'It's a terror to be bullied off your own streets by a crowd of blow-ins.'

I hopped down from the tile and summoned the boys. Soon, the whole of Thompson Street was out front as the parade inched closer. All seemed to gather at once. There wasn't a dog or a child left indoors. The leaders carried a sign – *Thanksgiving Parade in Honour of Saint Rocco*. Another banner, some way back, read: *Festa*

*Rocco*. Those marching behind the two pole-carriers were singing hymns. The singers bowed their heads as they filed past the church. Some of the Italian children looked up and smiled, but their parents stared ahead determinedly. Several holy statuettes were held aloft. The procession meandered its way around the bend and into Canal Street. Father Murtagh broke into spontaneous applause. A fancy-looking dude, leaning on a lamppost, took a gulp from a brown bottle and spat it at the padre's shoes. Women looked on with sullen expressions and folded arms. An old lady emptied her bucket out on the ground before the leaders. There was a sense of foreboding in the air, like on a fair day in Ireland when the peelers would show. It was hard to know what to expect. I was glad as the tail end of the parade traipsed by.

'A crowd of crows,' said Ina Begley.

This remark forced Missus Burrows into the titters.

'It's a murder of crows, Missus Begley,' I remarked.

'You and that priest's education,' said Jim.

'I'll *murder* you if you don't quit annoying me,' growled Ina.

'Come on,' said Jim, 'let's go with them for the crack.'

We followed the *Festa Rocco* parade around the corner to where Mickser's friend, Abraham, had a shop – *Ishmel's Grocery Store* – on the ground floor of a tenement building. It wasn't like the tenements in Dublin – the two up, two downs. This monstrosity housed thirty or forty families. Ishmel's had a little altar with a green, white, and red flag. Abraham wasn't about the place. But someone who looked like him stood in the shop doorway, smiling and clapping. Compared with Thompson Street, the mood was light-hearted. The spectators were talking excitedly. They cheered as the marching bands blew bugles and beat drums. Tables of food lined Canal Street. When I saw all the pizzas and pastas, cheeses and meat dishes, I couldn't help but think of the people of Mostrim and what they would have made of it all. The cold weather meant nothing to children as they scoffed ice cream to their hearts' content. There were lots of altars – decorated with statues and pictures of the Holy Family and other saints. Many of the buildings had green, white, and red bunting streamed across their facades. The procession halted at a large altar in the middle of Canal. Prayers were recited in a strange language. The padre said it was Italian. We joined in the Latin versions of the *Our Father* and the *Hail Mary*. Strangely, it was all done by ordinary people. There were no priests, unless they were in disguise – like Father Murtagh.

'Maybe you should get into your little black dress and say mass,' quipped Jim.

I didn't appreciate the wisecrack. It was just as well the padre hadn't heard him. He was busy looking at the tables.

'Easy known it's an Italian festival,' said Father Murtagh, 'good nourishing food everywhere.'

The padre was fascinated by the whole affair – especially at how lay-driven the celebration had been. In an effort to find out more, he set off among the altars and tables, talking to people who had marched in the parade. After a while, a straw hat floated through the crowd, following the padre in our direction. It was Mickser Burrows, chewing on a piece of tobacco.

'Imagine that,' he declared, standing with his thumbs in the lapels of his Herringbone, 'all these nicely laid-out tables and not a drink to be had on any of them.'

Mostly, Mickser was your regular city slicker. However, an odd time he reminded me of a fella you'd meet herding cattle at the butt of Cairn Hill. This was one of those times.

'I was told they don't contaminate the sacredness of Saint Rocco by bringing alcohol onto the streets. Instead, they drink wine in the privacy of their homes,' the padre informed us, as Mickser lobbed a big brown spit onto the pavement.

'Come on,' I said, 'we'll go down to Jonty's for a few before closing time.'

Mickser's face lit up.

'Now you're talking, gosuir,' he said, rubbing his hands together, 'all those meatballs have left me with an awful thirst.'

## Nine – Going to Saint Pat's

The time had come for Father Murtagh to take stock. His first port of call was the original seat of the Diocese of New York and the focal point of everything Irish in the city – Saint Patrick's Cathedral on Lower East Side's Mulberry Street. He asked me to come along, and I'm glad I went in the end. Outside, on the huge iron gates, the banners celebrating fifty years in existence were still flying high. They were dated May 1845 – some two and a half years previously. On entering the building, the splendour of the centre aisle hit me like a slap in the face. If anyone thought Saint Mel's Cathedral in Longford was fancy, Saint Pat's left it in the ha'penny place. A young priest passed by on his way to the altar. Father Murtagh seized his opportunity and asked if he would hear confessions.

'Certainly,' said the young priest, 'come this way. We won't bother with the confessional, if you don't mind. Is the sacristy alright for you?'

Father Murtagh followed the young priest up the long aisle. I politely declined an invitation to join them. I didn't like the idea of looking a priest in the eye while telling him I visited a knocking-shop in Dublin. There's comfort in the darkness of a confession box. So I hung around and looked at the pictures. And boy, were they something to behold.

'Wait 'til the others get a look at this.'

The murals depicting the Stations of the Cross were stunning.

'Michelangelo, eat your heart out.'

An old woman looked up from her Rosary beads.

'First sign of madness,' she said, before bowing her head to continue her prayers.

She gave me a bit of a start.

'Excuse me,' I said, 'sorry for the interruption.'

'Talking to yourself,' explained the old woman, in a clearly foreign accent, 'is the first sign of madness, they say.'

Then she gave out a smile.

'What a place,' I said.

'You are new to this country, yes?'

'How can you tell?'

'Because you sound Irish and you answer my question with a new question. You did not see the beauty of Saint Patrick's yet? This is your first time, no?'

'Yes, I'm new to this city. I got talked into coming here today.'

'Very good, no?'

'Yes, very impressive,' I admitted. 'You sound like an out-of-towner yourself.'

The old woman made a face and repeated *out-of-towner* to herself.

'You're not an American either,' I said.

'No, no,' she replied.

'And you're not Irish. I can get that from your voice.'

'I am from Poland. Missus Kerinsky is my name.'

'Please to meet you. Joseph Farrell at your service.'

We shook hands. I suddenly realised I had never shaken hands with an old woman before – or any woman for that matter. It felt weird.

'But people call me Jabber.'

'I like Joseph the most.'

She pointed to a stained-glass window – a bearded man in a brown robe and a Child on his shoulder. Under his sandals the inscription read: *Saint Joseph Most Chaste Spouse, Pray for Us.*

'Do you come here often?'

What a line – like something you'd say to a young one below in Jonty's snug. Thankfully, Missus Kerinsky didn't pick up on it.

'I come here all the time now,' she said. 'Since my husband die, I do not like to walk too much in the city. My Polish church is much too far from my home in West Side Docks. My old bones would not be able.'

'The West Side Docks. Forgive me, but isn't Saint Anthony's near the West Side Docks?'

Missus Kerinsky turned her nose up at the question. I hoped I hadn't said anything to upset her. Just in case, I apologised then. So much for trying to impress her with what the padre had told me about the churches in the area.

'No, no, this is okay,' she said. 'You are right. Saint Anthony's is very near. But I do not want to go to Italian church. They are all… what is the word… showmen – bunch of showmen – saying prayers out loud in street like a show.'

The poor auld Italians, I thought, they're getting it from all sides – the Irish first, and now the Poles.

'I suppose you're right, Missus. But don't be too hard on the Italians. After all, let those who have not sinned cast the first stone.'

'You sound like priest,' said old Missus Kerinsky.

All I could do was laugh.

'And what does a priest sound like,' I asked.

'There, what you have said. It sounds like my son Tomasc, and he is priest.'

'That's interesting. Maybe I could pass for a priest. But,

unfortunately, I can't confess to being one. My father was a great man for Scripture, he used to read it to us after supper. Where is your son ministering?'

'His parish is in Albany.'

'Ah that's grand. He's not far away so,' I said, and me not knowing Albany from a cow's shite.

'I come here and pray for him every day. That he will have his dream of becoming bishop one day. But, as you say unfortunately, this is not very possible. In America, the Irish, how do you say, dominate the church very strong. In this city, seventy per cent of all priests are Irish descent. And most of bishops are Irish-American also. I am afraid to say if you are not from one Holy Irish Apostolic Catholic Church you will not get far in this country, no?'

'Nil desperandum, Missus Kerinsky. Trust in God. I'll sit down beside you and we'll say a little prayer for Tomasc, that if God sees fit He may make your son a bishop. And if not, I'm sure he's a good priest. Isn't that all the Lord asks of anybody, to be the best that they can be?'

I pretended not to notice, but Missus Kerinsky was eyeing me suspiciously.

'You sure you are not priest?'

'An altar boy,' I admitted, 'many moons ago. I was expelled from my duties when the parish priest caught me drinking his wine.'

Missus Kerinsky laughed loudly and, remembering where we were, quickly excused herself.

'I was not meaning to say anything wrong about your country,' she explained. 'It is just so difficult for Polish priest to get on.'

'I understand entirely, Missus Kerinsky.'

We shook hands again – twice in the same day!

'Now if you'll excuses me, I shall bid you good day and let you get back to your Rosary. I won't forget your son in my prayers.'

I wondered around the cathedral, waiting for the padre. He must have had an awful heap of sins. Eventually he arrived back. A crowd was gathering for mass, so we decided to stay. The padre was bursting with excitement after his long chat. The cathedral's newest addition had just given him the lowdown on the way the church was being run in America.

'You didn't tell him you're a priest,' I whispered, as we knelt into the pew behind Missus Kerinsky.

Father Murtagh laughed at the question.

'Us curates have a universal understanding,' he answered. 'I didn't have to tell him. It's like telepathy, or something.'

'Do you know what, you're full of shite – you and your telepathy.'

Before mass, there was a Saint Vincent de Paul collection for Irish famine relief. A wooden plate was passed along. I looked around as the plate came our way. The fear descended like a cold mist. The padre had no money either – why hadn't we just gone home after confession. Missus Kerinsky threw in a coin, then turned with the plate. She handed it to me. I stood like a dummy. Eventually she turned away again. I passed the plate like a hot spud. But there were no side glances; the other mass-goers didn't even notice – they didn't care. Father Murtagh tapped the bottom of the plate as he passed it on. The coins jumped and made a racket. Trust the clergy for the dirty tricks! The young curate didn't care either. He didn't read the penniless from the pulpit after all. That was a practise belonging to a land three thousand miles across the ocean.

On our return to Thompson Street, Father Murtagh told Jim and Mickser all about the exciting new world he discovered at Saint Pat's. He praised the dynamic young curate, who captivated his congregation with talk of a new devotional revolution that had spread from the blackness of a famine and was now taking root on American shores. He praised the congregation, who had mixed freely during and after mass – man and woman, rich and poor – with no separate sections for the sexes or the financially embarrassed. The hum of post-mass conversation was a throwback to a happier time in Ireland. The padre talked of Calvary, the adjoining burial ground – a cemetery catering for paupers and unfortunates – and for the parishioners' vision and determination in handing on the faith and erecting such a palace of divine worship.

'What do you mean by unfortunates,' asked Mickser.

'Out-of-wedlock and suicide cases. In Ireland, these creations of God are buried aside – the church has no place for them in consecrated ground. And the children of the famine end up in the ceallurach,' explained Father Murtagh, as memories strayed back to Turk and his grave by a lonely brook.

The padre also spoke about confession. It wasn't treated with the same severity as in the old country – the non-judgemental manner of the young curate made the padre feel at ease. You could tell Father Murtagh longed for the chance to strut his stuff in a place like Saint Pat's, with no meddling parish priest watching over his shoulder or waiting for him to go wrong. All in all, the padre was most impressed by his first trip to Saint Patrick's Cathedral and encouraged the others to join him the following Sunday.

'I'm not going to any church,' snapped Jim Gorman, 'I've had my fill of being talked down to by men like Canon Reidy.'

'You can't abandon your religion over a few old bullies,' said Father Murtagh.

'I've news for you, Father,' replied Jim. 'I abandoned my religion the day I saw my boy transported to the four winds for something he didn't do. I abandoned it when Constance Ryan went missing from Cranley House and when they found Maisie Rourke and her girl – or what remained of them – curled up in a blanket in Lisnageeragh Lane. What kind of God would stand by and allow such things?'

'Don't say that, Jim. We have no right to question God's ways,' warned Father Murtagh, 'because God's ways are not man's ways.'

'Well, *Padre*, good luck to you and your Saint Pat's. I want no part of it anymore.'

Jim was flushed with anger. He got up from the table and went out to the porch for a swing.

We went to church the following Sunday without Jim Gorman. Mickser Burrows came along – out of curiosity. It had been years since he'd set foot in Saint Pat's.

'Did Jonty not tell me you're a Protestant,' I said.

'And what has that got to do with anything,' replied Mickser. 'Didn't I live in the Points for ten years. Well then, I'm as much Catholic as the rest of ye. Where do you think I perfected my Irish?'

'Sorry Mickser, I didn't mean any...'

'I *am* a Protestant, Jabber. But when I left Ireland, I left all that bigotry behind me. I don't go to church often but, when I do, I go to meet God – not a priest or a parson.'

Sometimes Mickser could really surprise me. There was a lot more to him than met the eye.

The large stone wall outside the cathedral reminded me of the old days.

'Sugrue would have loved going to mass at Saint Patrick's,' I said to the padre. 'There's great sitting space on that wall.'

'It certainly looks more comfortable than the one in Mostrim,' replied Father Murtagh. 'Canon Reidy used to give out, saying it would have been more in Sugrue's line to be sitting inside.'

'This Sugrue buck, he must have been an awful gangster by the way ye go on about him. It's a pity ye didn't bring him with ye to America,' said Mickser.

'And it's a pity you couldn't have got Jim to change his mind,' I said to the padre.

'No, Joseph, you can't force a thing like that. James Gorman has to find his own way back to God. And he will, I pray, with time.'

The young curate who had heard Father Murtagh's confession wasn't saying the mass we attended. An older priest came out with a half-dozen servers, all impeccably decked out in white and red. He certainly wasn't as laidback as his young colleague – getting stuck into the nitty-gritty of several political issues in his sermon. He encouraged his flock to have nothing to do with radical unions. *The scourge of working-life in the city*, he called them. He delved into the history which fuelled diasporic nationalism in Irish-American enclaves – the migration experience and integration into social, political, and religious organisations. I was wondering what all this had to do with the celebration of the Blessed Sacrament, when he began shouting about the ongoing depredations of British colonialism, including the persistence of nativism and anti-Catholicism in this supposed new world.

'I'd be for it if he knew I'm a proddy boots,' whispered Mickser.

'We must never allow these people to succeed in destroying God's temple. And I have it on good authority that they intend to destroy it – this very building. An offensive is planned for next Wednesday evening, after we've taken to the streets to profess our faith. What are we going to do – sit back and allow this to happen? I appeal to every able-bodied man here present to make a stand on the steps outside. Bring your brothers and your uncles and your fathers and your sons. Protect our cherished Saint Patrick's with whatever force is necessary. Yes, you heard me correctly, with *whatever force* it takes to repel this attack.'

The congregation became unsettled when it heard of the nativist threat to burn down the lovely cathedral. It was quickly agreed that we must lend our support. Even Mickser said that if he was back in time from seeing a man about a dog, he would be sure to help out.

After the final blessing, we lit candles at the large shrine in the side-aisle. All sorts of accents could be heard – including most of the counties of Ireland. We got talking to an old woman who was looking for matches. She reminisced about her beautiful homeland in Waterford. Her only wish was that her old eyes could behold the beach in Tramore, where she spent her girlhood, one last time before being closed by the Lord. I felt sad. Despite the recent horrors of the famine, there was still a yearning for home in the heart of this elderly immigrant. I thought of Missus Kerinsky and looked about. I wondered was she anywhere around.

Later, the padre talked up the whole *mass-at-Saint-Pat's* experience once more. Jim lay on the porch seat – Mickser's straw hat across his face – pretending to be asleep. But I knew he was listening to every word.

'It would do you good to go and take a look,' I said.

'We have to go down again this Wednesday to help out at the Corpus Christi procession. Mickser is coming too, if he's home in time. We could do with all the help we can get, Jim,' added Father Murtagh.

Jim lifted the hat from his eyes.

'What on earth are you talking about,' he said in a croaky voice, as if he really had been asleep. '*Help?* For a Corpus Christi parade? Are you having me on? And as for Mickser, is he not a Protestant?'

Then Father Murtagh told him all about the priest's altar plea for men to defend the cathedral and parade from the nativists. Jim Gorman shook his head in disbelief.

'Nativists? You mean the British,' he said.

'Not just the British, their cronies as well,' explained the padre.

'Boys, but there's no getting away from them – they've their nibs stuck everywhere. Let's face it, they've made our lives a misery on the far side of the Atlantic and they'll go on doing the same over here. Just how am I supposed to help with that?'

'You could start by taking a stand for Saint Pat's,' replied Father Murtagh. 'After mass, I lit two candles; one for Shay – a light to guide him home – and one for you, James. We mustn't lose faith in the goodness of God.'

Jim stretched out on his porch seat and repositioned Mickser's straw hat. It hid the tear that rolled down his temple and into his sandy hair – almost.

## Ten – The Dance

Father Murtagh's ministry continued in the streets of Lower Manhattan and on the docks of the East River, much as it had done during his exile in Dublin. The only real difference was the clothes he chose to wear. The padre's paranoia with the newspapers meant that he no longer wore his vestments in public. After his humiliation at the hands of the Gowna men, he had had enough. The first thing he stored away in our new wardrobe in Thompson Street was his dear old cassock. He kept his stole in his pocket, putting it on to hear confessions or when giving the Last Rites.

'Why do you do it,' I asked him, before we parted company. 'Why do you feel the need? You've no obligation to the people of New York, just like you had no obligation to the people of Dublin. What compels you to go out day after day?'

'You studied the Bible when you were in Maynooth seminary,' he replied. 'Well then, you should remember verse nine, chapter four, of the Gospel according to Saint John: *I must work the works of Him who sent Me while it is day; the night is coming when no one can work.* That applies not only to Jesus, but to all of us.'

I understood what the padre was saying. And boy, did he work hard. He would return in the evenings completely exhausted, keeping me awake for hours with his snoring. But I never complained – not once. As far as I was concerned, Father Murtagh was doing something I hadn't the strength to do. It took a few years of my life to find that out. It was a hard road – maybe the hardest. But the padre didn't see it like that. To him, building the Father's kingdom was an honour, not a hardship. Dispensing

God's graces and blessings on His people was a total pleasure. In time, Father Murtagh got to know the sailors arriving from South America, Africa, and the Indies. A Jamaican seaman he befriended gave the padre a monkey as a present.

Alas, after months of rooming with me at Thompson Street, the padre felt it was time to seek a more appropriate dwelling. He was quick to point out that this was by no means my fault. But laymen live different lives to the foot-soldiers of God.

'A bachelor's nocturnal lamentations have no business echoing in the ears of the anointed,' quipped the padre, sending Jonty's clientele into raptures.

'Were you spanking the monkey,' asked Mickser.

'Indeed, he was not. Joseph would never lift his hand against a defenceless animal,' replied the padre, before I could open my mouth. 'I'm referring to something entirely different.'

The padre's wanderlust did not take him far. He found a small place next to Abraham's corner shop – at the turn for Canal. The one-bedroom apartment and small patch of grass was enough for Father Murtagh. Together with Charlie – the monkey from Jamaica, he was as happy as a pig in muck. Charlie was no trouble. He wasn't a fussy eater – dining on nuts, biscuits, and bread – and only pooed in the sand tray provided. He was more easily trained than a pup, and sometimes displayed remarkable intelligence.

We were frequent visitors to Father Murtagh's new pad. On our maiden voyage, Charlie – who had been hiding behind a chair – sprang out and climbed up my back. He gave me a fair shock.

'Where did you get the chimpanzee,' Jim asked.

'He's not a chimpanzee, he's a capuchin. Boys, meet Charlie. Charlie, the Mostrim boys. I got him from one of the sailors at the Lower East Side. Charlie's from Jamaica.'

'A capuchin? As in the monks,' I enquired.

'Yes, Joseph, very good. As in the monks. I think he likes you fellows. The new landlady was here yesterday and I couldn't get him out from behind his chair.'

'And she allows you keep a monkey,' asked Jim.

'She allows dogs, doesn't she? What's the difference then? A pet is a pet,' explained the padre.

We had mighty fun with Charlie the monkey. Himself and Ina Begley had one thing in common – they could both walk all over me. Jim tantalised him with nuts. He'd hold them aloft between his fingers and, as soon as Charlie would make a grab, pull his hand away at the last second. This made Charlie turn his head to one side and stick out his tongue.

We complemented the padre on his fine place.

'Come on and I'll show you the rest,' he said.

He brought us on the grand tour. Jim was swinging the monkey in mid-air, pretending to let him fall and then catching him on the way down. The living room was Father Murtagh's pride and joy.

'Listen to that, Jim,' I said, 'the *living room*. The swanky talk from the padre – getting all Americanized on us.'

But Jim wasn't listening. He was looking out the window.

'That's what my new landlady calls it,' said the padre, slightly embarrassed, 'the living room.'

Jim dropped the monkey and bolted for the door. He ran into the garden and tried to hurdle the picket fence. His trailing foot clipped the railing and sent him sprawling. He was frantic. He raced out into the street.

'Where's he gone? Where's he gone?'

'Where's *who* gone,' I shouted after him.

'Don't let him get away.'

'Relax, will you,' said Father Murtagh. 'What are you talking about? Don't let who get away? You're making no sense, James.'

'The ginger man,' yelled Jim, 'he was here. Did ye not see him?'

'Okay,' said the padre. 'Take it easy. Let's go back into the house and discuss whatever is troubling you over a nice hot, *calm*, cup of tea.'

'I'm not messing.'

'I know that, and neither am I,' insisted the padre, 'but there's no one out here, James.'

If this was a joke, then Jim was as good an actor as ever I saw. He was extremely wound up. We had another look around. Eventually he agreed to go back inside. Then he explained what had just happened. While Father Murtagh had been showing us his new curtains, Jim spotted the thin man with the ginger beard – the man from the steerage of the *Erin's Queen* – spying across the fence.

'Hardly spying,' I said, 'that might be a bit dramatic.'

'Yes, *spying*,' rasped Jim, 'he was standing by the lamppost. As soon as I copped him, he took off.'

'You're taking the piss,' I said. 'How come we didn't see anyone?'

I knew Jim's carry-on would flare up the padre's paranoia all over again – and him only getting back to normal after the Gowna men's interrogation.

'How can you be so sure it was the same man? There are loads of fellows with ginger beards,' the padre pointed out. 'After all, this is New York – one of the biggest cities in the world.'

'Come on, Father,' begged Jim, 'don't take me for an eejit. I know it was the man from the ship.'

'Okay. Let's say, just for argument sake, this was the same man. Why would he be spying on us?'

'Well, that's fairly straightforward. There are still hundred-pound bounties on our heads. Just because we're not in Ireland doesn't mean they can't be claimed. A reward that big can travel a very long distance.'

It was time somebody brought some sense to this situation. So, I laid it on the line – for both of them.

'Jim, you're far too irrational. Ever since the ship – that notice in the newspaper – you've been like a hen with a hot egg. And you're not much better, Father. Ye'd both want to smarten yourselves up.'

'You think I'm seeing things. And you,' Jim said, turning towards me, 'you think I've gone off my rocker as well. Even though you've seen the ginger man for yourself.'

I had said my piece and there was no point in arguing further.

'I don't believe this,' continued Jim. 'I thought you fellas were supposed to be on my side. Instead, ye think I'm a mental case.'

'Nobody thinks that, Jim,' I answered, as the padre attempted to put a cup of tea in his shaking hand.

'Leave off,' he growled, and headed for the comfort of the porch swing.

Down in the saloon, all the talk was about James W. Marshall and his recent discovery at Sutter's Mill. The incident had Mickser Burrows going out of his mind with excitement.

'I'm definitely going. As soon as I get the price of my own and the queer one's passage and tie up a few loose ends, then I'm away to Californiay,' he chirped, as he signalled to Jonty for another pint of beer.

'What about you, Jabber,' said Jonty, 'can you see yourself panning for gold in the company of Mickser Burrows?'

I wasn't paying him much attention. Two girls had entered the snug section of Jonty's – a rare enough occurrence. I could see them through the gap, where the empty bottles were stored. After pulling Mickser's drink, Jonty moved onto my shoulder.

'There's nothing wrong with your eyesight, sonny,' he whispered.

He snapped me out of my trance.

'What's that?'

'I said there's nothing wrong with the peepers. Two fine broads and that's for sure.'

'What are you on about, Jonty?'

'Ah now, you can't fool an old guy like me. I've seen that look in a man's eye too many times. A whiskey glass and a woman's ass – wars were started over less. Oh, excuse me, Father Murtagh.'

'No need to apologise, Jonathan. You're among friends and I'm on sabbatical,' said the padre, taking a twirl to show off his new civilian clothes. 'And that goes for you too, Joseph. No need for the red face. After all, God made Eve as a companion for Adam.'

But I couldn't help my embarrassment. I wasn't used to being corralled into talking about the fairer sex in public, especially in front of a man of the cloth.

'Those girls want service,' said Mickser, as they stared back through the gap.

'Let them stew for a moment,' quipped Jonty.

'Bogod, it's strange to see young women entering a licensed shop on their own. Are you going to serve them at all, Jonty?'

'They're not on their own, Jabber,' returned Jonty. 'There's a pair of them in it.'

'You know what I mean – unaccompanied by *suitable male folk*.'

'Listen here now. This is McArthur's big city saloon, not some membership club for gentlemen – the like you'd find above in the West Village. Of course I'll serve them – with a broad smile. If I didn't give them a few looseners before they go dancing, the other public houses around here would only delight in taking my business. Their money is as good in my pocket as the next man's.'

The padre nodded his head in agreement.

'What dancing are you talking about,' I asked, trying to sound casual.

'The Galway County dance is on tonight in the Arms Hotel.'

'And what makes you think those girls would be interested in going there, Jonty?'

'Ah now, Jabber. What do you take me for?'

Jonty then moved his head towards mine and tapped on his temples.

'It's my business to know these things,' he whispered. 'And I'll let you in on a very badly kept secret around here, young Jabber. If I was single like you, it would be my business to know these things *too* – and my business to attend these things. Because that's where single guys go to meet girls like them… and greet girls like them… and, if you play your hand right, court girls like them.'

'How do you propose he gain entry? Joseph's not a Galway man,' Father Murtagh pointed out.

Jonty McArthur threw his eyes skyward.

'Oh the Lord save us,' he cried, and blew out his cheeks. 'You dudes really take the cake. This is New York, not some one-horse village in Longford. As I told you guys already, around here, you can be pretty much anything you want to be. You want to be a Galway man – nobody's going to stop you. There are no excuses. You can go to any county dance in New York that takes your fancy. You can go to all thirty-two of them if you really want. Get the picture? Now, excuse me guys, I'm off to the snug. I have two nice young ladies to take care off.'

'America really is the land of the free,' I said. 'Imagine telling them at home that a woman can just walk into a public house and order a drink, no questions asked.'

'They'll be wearing trousers next,' said the padre.

'And voting,' added Jim.

'Ye have great imaginations,' said Mickser. 'Those things will never happen – not in a million years.'

After Jonty's little speech there was no holding me back. Every Saturday night was spent at whatever county dance was being held in the Arms Hotel. At the beginning, I used to go alone. The odd time I wouldn't get in. If someone from the old country was collecting, I could be refused at the door. The tone of my voice would give it away that I wasn't from Kerry or Mayo or whatever county the dance was in aid of. I was surprised at how traditional and clannish those shindigs could be. Mind you, they may have been traditional and clannish, but they were far from backward. The latest fashions were on view – and the latest crazes. Yodelling was the newest thing sweeping across America. You could find the finest Alpine yodellers on a county-dance stage. Not to mention the best banjo players from darkest Africa. After much practice – and some mentoring from Jonty – I could get my tongue around most Irish accents. The northern lilt still deserted me. After a while, Father Murtagh would come along – if only for a change of scene.

It soon became clear that these New York county dances were as much about business as they were about drinking and waltzing a young one around the floor. They were places where connected Irishmen hired and fired. These captains of industry ran associations known as *county societies* – they sponsored the dances as well as other functions. With a strict door policy and often a background check, these county societies were intent on keeping particular jobs within their own county circles. Consequently, Kerry men were known to run the paper-handlers trade. Donegal men were associated with construction and tunnel work. Clare men were said to control the Lower Side Docks. It was all about pride of place – and a well-timed backhander to sweeten the deal.

But the system was far from watertight. Like anything else, the county societies could be infiltrated once one got to know of the cracks in the system. I secured a job painting houses by simply adjusting my speech to suit the Jacks. My background-check question was something concerning Sackville Street. I looked the Dublin County society man square in the eye and *asked him* what would I know about that and me from a Winetavern Street tenement – sandwiched between a whorehouse and Christchurch Cathedral. That was enough to convince him of my allegiances. I was told, on the spot, that the job was mine and not to be late the following Monday morning. Then the Dublin society man cleared his throat and stuck out a hand. I shook it heartily and walked away without another word. Only for Father Murtagh – who placed a dollar in the society man's breast pocket – I would have been sacked before I had even started.

Then there was the King's County dance. Jim Gorman tagged along once he heard there was the chance of a job in it. Jim had no talent for doing voices, but entry was almost guaranteed. The King's County accent is as flat and indistinguishable as any Longfordian's brogue. It was the same as always – lots of drink flowing; two sexes eyeing each other up like they were about to go into battle; the county society men going about their business with great diligence.

It was then she appeared from a cloud of smoke – an angel puffing on a cigar. She crossed the floor in a confident strut. I was determined to get in early. I swallowed the drink and wiped my lips in a hanky – the *hanky of sophistication*. On non-public occasions I always used my sleeve. But when girls were at stake, manners were on show. She was defying the rules, heading in my direction, and getting more beautiful with every step of those long, slender, legs. Her hair was jet-black and her lips full and crimson. She continued as straight as an arrow; a determined, green-eyed, stare locked on her target. I straightened up and put on my best smile. It wasn't hard to guess her age – she was twenty at a push.

'Hi there,' I said, trying to sound as cool as I could.

'Hi yourself, daddio,' she purred, blew smoke in my direction and walked straight past.

The padre, who was tapping his foot to the music, suddenly felt a hand pulling away the bottle of water he had been sipping. Some spilt on his chin as he looked over his shoulder, expecting another fight to flare up. He was pleasantly surprised when, instead of some bear of an Offaly man, there stood what could only be described as one of the most beautiful visions a man could behold.

'Wanna shuffle,' she asked as she stamped out her cigar, not in an Offaly accent – or any other Irish voice – but the sweetest New York twang imaginable.

He told me he felt like a trapped animal, especially when he looked around to find most eyes in the hall firmly fixed on her.

In his younger days, long before his vocational calling, Father Murtagh did have a fleeting experience with the opposite sex. As with many other Irish love stories, it happened in a culvert – beside Saint Colmcille's hedge school in Aughnacliffe. Back then, he was only fifteen years old. The girl wasn't much older. But he still remembered the bliss of kissing a girl on the mouth; the bliss of kissing her on the neck; the bliss of kissing a girl. It was like heaven on earth, and something that almost cost the padre his ministry before he ever set foot in Maynooth seminary.

What the padre faced that night at the King's County dance was not entirely different to the circumstances in the culvert in Aughnacliffe. She looked incredible. She smelled like roses on a summer's day. She was giving him the full eyelash-batting treatment. And the best thing about it was that *she* had asked *him* to dance. There was some trick in it, thought Father Murtagh. This had to be the handiwork of James Gorman or, more likely, Joseph Farrell. The padre would be administering a piece of his mind and then some. But there was nothing he could do about that now. It was time to face the music and dance.

Taking his hand, she led him onto the floor. The padre felt foolish. But he couldn't resist. The dancefloor was almost vacant. His head was swimming. The feel of her skin was intoxicating. She could have led him to his death and he wouldn't have care – like a lamb skipping joyfully to its slaughter. She turned and faced him again, clenched his other hand and assumed the dance position. She tucked her free arm under his shoulder and they moved around awkwardly.

'Whatsa matte',' she asked.

'I'm just not used to it,' he replied, his tongue barely able to move with dryness. 'I haven't danced with … with anyone for years.'

'Yeah. Well, it's time to lighten up, buste'. I've seen more rhythm in some of the stiffs down at city morgue.'

The padre was doing his best to relax. Nobody had ever called him *buster* before. He was concentrating hard on his steps, trying not to stand on her toes. He hadn't a clue how a young woman danced. If he was honest, he hadn't a clue how *any* woman danced.

'You're not in construction, that's a gimme,' she said, opening her mouth to smile for the first time.

The padre swallowed hard. It's all he could do. Everyone knows America is famous for its pearly whites, but this girl took the biscuit. Her teeth were amazing. It was like every time he was about to come to terms with her gorgeousness, she would produce something new to stupefy his wits again.

'How can you tell,' he stammered, almost punch-drunk from the scent of her perfume.

'You' hands – they're as soft as any lady's. But only a peccadillo when a girl considers the whole package.'

Peccadillo, the padre told me later, was a word which had him thinking. It wasn't every day you'd hear a word like that used on a dancefloor.

'Do you work,' she asked. 'Whadya do?'

'Oh yes. I'm a pr… I'm a painter.'

'A painte',' she gasped. 'What, like an artist?'

'No. I'm a painter and decorator by trade. I do up houses and the insides of buildings for the most part. Ever feel the weight of a paintbrush?'

'No, I can't say that I have, buste'.'

'Not exactly the kind of thing to put blisters on your fingers. Who's buster,' snapped the padre, getting annoyed at the young lady's brashness.

'Ow, sorry. Getting a little querulous there, ain't ya? What's you' name then?'

'Francis Murtagh,' said the padre.

'Uh, Francis Murtagh. A little square, don't you think? It's not Fran, o' Frankie, o' nothin' like that?'

'No, it's not. It's not Fran or Frankie. And it's not square. It's Francis, thank you very much. And by the way, girls don't just break ranks, walk up to strange men, and take them out. What's going on here?'

'You think I'm working an angle,' she said, halting their dance for a moment.

Father Murtagh didn't know what *working an angle* meant. He didn't even know if she was making a statement or asking a question. So he kept quiet.

'You think I'm busting you' chops?'

Again, he hadn't a clue what she was talking about.

'I get it – my turpitude must be quite frightening, especially to an *Irish* Irishman.'

The word was out then and she couldn't retract it. And she *did* want to retract it. She was making a conscious effort to water down her vocabulary at county dances, having already lost more than her fair share of dance partners – men of a certain standard of education who were sure to be overwhelmed. But words like *turpitude* simply slipped out – it was a force of habit.

'What would an attractive American girl like you want with a scene like this?'

'A scene like what,' she asked.

'A county dance then. And me. There, are you happy?'

'I'm from King's County,' she quipped.

'You, from King's County? What kind of an eejit do you take me for?'

She stopped in her tracks, unhooked her right hand from under his shoulder and offered it.

'Hi, I'm Breda. Breda Nayle.'

He shook her hand as if it was made of precious glass.

'You're right, sortta. And I'm right too.'

'What are you talking about,' asked the padre.

'I'm not from King's County pe' se. But I've got as much King's County blood running through my veins as anybody else in here. That's one thing for sure.'

Father Murtagh felt more like a fraudster than ever when she said this. Not only was his name not Francis, he hadn't painted a thing in his whole life. And he'd never even been to Offaly – or King's County, as young Breda Nayle called it.

'You see, my mum, she was a King's County gal. So that means I've got as much right to be at this dance as you. Got that, buste'. And one more thing while we're at it – I'll break ranks any time I want. And I'll take a guy out dancing any time I want. That's the difference right there between the King's County gals you grew up with and the King's County gals I hang out with – you think we should all act like nuns just because we're of Irish Catholic stock. But this is America, dude. You may be a product of a bucolic backwate', but I'm a product of New York City. So drop this *we're all the same* routine, comprende?'

The padre's head was swimming again. He wanted to be with her, and yet he wanted to be a thousand miles away from her. He felt a little more at ease when Breda Nayle shut her beautiful mouth and let peace reign. She took his hand again, returned her other hand under his shoulder and resumed their slow waltz.

Jim Gorman consoled me in my loss. He pointed out that she was only a girl, not like some of the real women in the hall – real women who had respect for tradition and conducted themselves with self-restraint. But the men in the hall weren't looking at these real women, they were looking at Breda Nayle.

'What do you think of my dancing now,' asked Father Murtagh, feeling more confident than he had done on his first go around.

'Presentable, at best,' returned Breda Nayle. 'You're no Maste' Juba, by any means, but at least you're beginning to thaw out a little.'

'Master who?'

'Aw shaddup and keep dancing.'

The padre leaned down towards Breda's earlobe.

'By the way,' he whispered, 'your parlance is quite impressive, a paradigm shift from the type of woman usually found in here.'

Her eyes shot open in surprise.

'Fancy lingo for the product of a bucolic backwater, wouldn't you say,' continued the padre. 'You see, even those with the most heterodoxic of notions can be shocked every now and then.'

## Eleven – The Points

Ever since meeting Jonty McArthur – as a result of his house-hunting advice – I had been itching to see the Five Points. So, one Saturday not long after our first American Christmas, Mickser Burrows agreed to bring us on the grand tour. Father Murtagh declined the offer; he had to go out to the docks to see a man about a dog, as Mickser himself would say.

'A dog and a monkey,' quipped Jim, 'I wish Missus Begley was as understanding as the padre's landlady.'

We left Thompson Street nice and early – to be back in Jonty's for the evening session. As we passed through Mott Street I thought of Missus Kerinsky – the old woman from Saint Patrick's – when I saw a priest coming out of the Church of the Transfiguration. A shower of showmen – that's what she called the Italian clergy. It was then that I noticed the crowd, standing by the horse-drawn hearse. A white box was being loaded through the back door. Mickser took off his straw hat and we stood until the horses had moved on.

'Another young life,' Mickser said, as he grimaced and blessed himself. 'Solas Mhic De ar a n-anam dilis. Now, brace yourselves guys for a long walk.'

But there's no such thing as a long walk in New York – at least not the kind of long walks endured in the Irish countryside. Mickser had obviously lived too long in the city. Ten minutes later there was a sign for Cross Street. Mickser told us we were now on one of the main throughways leading to the Five Points. It wasn't exceptional from any other street – apart from the sheer volume of tenements. They were everywhere. And they were much higher than the tenement housing Abraham's shop.

'Alright bucks, take a look at the old brewery. That was my house there.'

Mickser's eyes lit up as he pointed it out. It was an imposing sight, to say the least, a bit like the workhouse in Shroid.

'We don't mind waiting if you want to have a look around,' Jim suggested.

'A look around,' replied Mickser, 'what's there to see – pimps and opium pushers. God but you've no sense, Jim Gorman. It was different when I came here first – *times* were different then. All the good guys are gone, mo chara.'

We came to a street sign with two wooden arrows. One read *Anthony Street*. The other pointed to Little Water Street.

'That's a co-incidence,' said Jim. 'There's a Little Water Street in Longford too.'

We walked a bit further, pushing through the crowd, until we came to Paradise Square.

'Don't let the name fool you,' warned Mickser.

We were getting to the nitty-gritty now – rough-looking fellas piled up against the steps of a burnt-out doorway, the ground-floor windows boarded up and the wall as black as our boots. We were met with blank stares and suspicion. A gang of boys were hunkered down by a wall. They were racing mice. It reminded me of the old fair days, when we used to race piglets. We'd tie a number to their tails. But the mice had no numbers. I wondered how the boys could tell the difference; the mice all looked the same to me.

'Keep a tight eye on yere purses, guys,' said Mickser, 'nothing but sneak-thieves around here.'

Jim felt his inside pocket. For once, I was glad I had no purse.

The sound of a thousand different accents – all mixed together and rushing towards you – takes some getting used to. I picked out a woman and her child. She had a red suitcase in one hand, a Rosary beads in the other. She was praying away. The child, a girl of about six years, stopped crying only to wipe her nose in her coat sleeve. The woman turned around to say something. I noticed that she had been crying too. And I noticed something else – that look of wonder and terror. They were fresh off the boat, the latest edition of the starving Irish.

'They stick out like a sore thumb,' I said. 'There's nothing on earth as frightening to someone who has spent all their life by the village pump.'

'They may get used to the big city,' Jim replied, 'they haven't much choice.'

Two girls, carrying baskets of clothes, crossed the cobbles in front of us.

'It must be laundry day,' Jim muttered.

'Ara, they're going off that direction,' said Mickser, pointing to an intersection away to our right, 'to do their laundry at the Collect Pond. God, it brings me back.'

'When you lived here, did you wash your clothes at Collect Pond too,' asked Jim.

This made Mickser laugh out loud.

'No. But the queer one did,' he said, before declaring that we were now entering the Old Sixth Ward.

People were everywhere, up close and personal. Irish flags were flying and posters of Ted Ireland too – the real Irish flags, the green with the gold harp.

'Anyone would think there's another election,' I remarked.

'This is one of the big voting stations. It would be a brave Republican who would venture down here, wearing the red on his sleeve,' said Mickser.

We continued to the junction and then onto Orange. It was like a fair day at home. Actually, it was like a year of fair days rolled into one. There were heaps of market stalls. Rows and rows of women sold bags of flour for five cents and tea at four cents per half-pound. One quart of milk was going for three cents even, half-pounds of sugar for a half-cent piece, and a pound of butter for one cent.

'It's cheaper here than above in Canal,' exclaimed Jim. 'A bushel of coal is only ten cents.'

Canal Street, the market area beside Thompson Street, prided itself on its low prices.

'A dime,' said Mickser. 'That's what we call ten cent – a *dime*. I'll educate you bucks in the American way if it kills me.'

'You and the padre's landlady would be well met,' quipped Jim. 'She has him well versed on the local lingo.'

An old fella in a slouch hat overheard their conversation. On his advertisement board he sold bags of timber for a trime, whatever that was supposed to be.

'I'll give yis a bag for nine cents, seeing as I haven't met yis before,' he said.

He was selling coal oil, soap, and starch as well.

'We're only having a look,' replied Mickser, slightly embarrassed. 'We haven't a whole lot.'

'Go 'way from around me,' said the old fella, 'yis have the money that was thrown into your cots.'

We continued on our way and came to a tenement with a sign on the front window. It read: *Apartments to rent. Accommodation 1 dollar 50 cents per month.*

'That can't be,' said Jim. 'We're paying a dollar a week and it's only up the road.'

'Do you know what you'd be getting for your dollar fifty,' asked Mickser. 'Come on and we'll have a look.'

We stepped inside the advertised tenement. A rat scooted across the hallway. The first three apartment doors were locked up. The fourth room in was empty. We had a glance inside; I'll never complain about the state of a house again. Missus Begley's may not have been a palace, but it was a palace compared to this place. And that's coming from a man fleeing a famine. It was exactly what Mickser had called the Points on voting day – a shithole. The windows were blacked out and a smell of something terrible came from a back room. Half the dresser was missing, and some of the floorboards were gone too. Water ran down the walls.

'They couldn't possibly be renting this out,' I said.

'It's not too bad. I stayed in worse places when I lived up here,' replied Mickser, fully in earnest.

'I wonder what that smell is?'

'You'll be wondering, Jabber,' said Mickser, 'come on, let's get out of here.'

As we were leaving, the coppers were moving in, batons drawn, to disperse a crowd of drinkers gathered in the doorway of a tenement across the way.

Beside a fruit and vegetable stall stood a man with a horse's hoof between his legs.

'Only shod last week, all four of them,' he could be heard saying. 'You can have a look in his mouth if you want.'

'I'll give you the eagle,' replied another man, inspecting the animal's mane.

'You won't,' he said, releasing the hoof. 'You'll give me the double or nothing at all. I'll tell you what, give me nineteen and we'll call it quits. It breaks my heart to part with him.'

Beside the men striking the bargain, a boy was busy tightening a wagon wheel in a vice.

'Throw in that saddle and we'll say nineteen.'

They spat on their hands and shook then.

At the end of the street was Mulberry Bend. It was a lively place too. A couple of black fellas were tap-dancing to an African shuffle. Spotting a flat-cap on the footpath – or sidewalk, as Mickser called it – I rummaged in my pockets. I checked my coins carefully because, even after three months, I still wasn't used to the money. I found a piece of silver with *Liberty 1793* inscribed beneath the head of a woman with flowing locks. To make sure, I had a quick look on the back. A laurel wreath and the bow encased in the words *United States of America*, and the half-cent sign that confirmed my belief. I tossed it into the flat-cap and kept walking. Across the street was a public house called *Benbulbin*. Outside the front door, a few white fellas started up with a fiddle and a flute. The black fellas weren't too happy. They stopped their tap-dance and glared over. The fiddle player told them to piss off back to Africa, them and their jungle noise.

'We might as well stop for one,' said Mickser, and we went into the *Benbulbin*.

There was no draught beer like there was in Jonty's, so Jim ordered three bottles of stout instead.

A hefty lady with a rag in her hair took up a pliers and uncorked the bottles.

I looked down the bar at a bunch of young women. They were busy chatting and laughing. They wore crinoline dresses, just like the leading ladies of the *Erin's Queen*. It was strange to see them in the main bar. They took no notice of us.

'Six cent flat,' the barmaid told us, breaking into a smile.

'The drink is cheaper here than in Jonty's,' I said.

'Ara, everything's cheaper in this part of town,' added Mickser.

'Do you take Spanish dollars,' asked Jim with a worried expression.

Before she could answer, Mickser produced a gold five-dollar piece and handed it across the counter.

'Leave your money where it is,' he ordered Jim, 'I had a good weekend at the cards.'

As soon as they saw the gold, the ladies down the bar perked up considerably. They were chuckling and elbowing each other.

'Break that up well for me,' said Mickser.

'Must have a game tonight as well, sweetheart,' replied the barmaid, coming back from her till with a stack of change.

The tallest of the ladies made her way across, waving a fan. She was no Marie-Claire, but she was still pretty. She wasn't as shapely as Marie-Claire either. In a bold move, she propped up a stool without being asked. She pulled out a cigar and gestured for a match. At least that's what I think she was gesturing for.

'I haven't seen you guys before,' she purred.

I followed Mickser's cue and ignored her. But I didn't want to. In fact, I was mad to chat her up. I saw in her the chance to redeem myself in the wake of the Offaly County dance debacle. The haughty little Breda had put a fair dent in my credentials as a ladies' man. I didn't want to shun her too long – in case she went away.

'I like your hoopy dress,' I said eventually, 'sorry, your *crinoline* dress.'

'It was a present,' she conceded, pursing her lips in anticipation of the lit match.

She took a pull of the cigar and let out a cough.

'Mind you don't get a chest infection,' said Mickser with a grin, suddenly coming to life.

'A present from a former lover,' she added, still on about the dress.

'A fool of a young fella,' I said.

'You don't like it then,' she inquired.

'Oh, I like the dress well enough. He's a fool for letting the dress get away from him.'

She was delighted with this. She pulled her seat a little closer. Soon enough, she'd be mine for the picking. By now, the rest of the girls were upon us too.

'Any more gold in that pocket,' asked one of them, placing a hand on Mickser's trousers.

'Leave it out now,' he grunted, and moved along the counter.

'I bet there's a small nugget somewhere,' said my woman.

Her friend sat up beside Jim and batted her eyelids. He pointed to the ring on his finger and she nodded and looked away.

A couple of hardy-looking coves came through the door. They must have been locals; the barmaid asked one of them if they were having their usual. He wanted the full bottle and she pulled out two glasses.

'You're Irish,' said my new companion.

'I am indeed, that's not a problem for you,' I replied, testing the waters.

She smiled. She had nice teeth – American teeth like Breda's.

One of the whiskey-drinking coves approached the bar. I pulled even closer to my woman. He had a dose of his shite if he thought he was going to wipe my eye. He undid his overcoat after a quick look around.

'Something for the night-time, boys,' he said, displaying an array of knives hanging on the inside of his coat.

My heart jumped – I thought it was a holdup. He took a switchblade from his pocket and showed it around. But Mickser didn't want to know, shaking his head as he gulped his stout. Then he produced a bowie.

'Put it away, Denis, or get to hell out,' shouted the barmaid. 'I told you before about this sort of thing. I get enough trouble off the coppers.'

But Denis took no notice of the barmaid, and turned the bowie so as the blade reflected the light on Mickser's face.

'He said he wasn't interested,' said my woman.

I could feel the tension in the bar.

'I wasn't talking to you,' Denis seethed, 'so go home and shave.'

She aimed a kick towards him and he pointed the blade at her. Mickser grabbed Jim's arm, wheeled around and headed for the door.

'Come on, Jabber,' he turned and said, 'show's over.'

But the show wasn't over, not as far as I was concerned.

'Hey, I was making hay there,' I said as we were leaving the Benbulbin, 'and you had to go and ruin it on me.'

'Just as well you didn't cock it then,' returned Mickser.

'You weren't making any hay,' explained Jim. 'They were prossies.'

'What do you mean by prossies?'

'Ah come on, Jabber, *prostitutes* – like the girls from Winetavern Street.'

'And your one wasn't even a *female* prossie,' added Mickser. 'Another couple of drinks and you'd be having a sausage and two puddings for tomorrow morning's breakfast.'

I was stunned. I really hadn't noticed. But I wasn't about to admit it.

'What do you take me for,' I quipped. 'I knew *she* was a *he* all along. I was just waiting to see if you fellas would cop it.'

I caught Mickser giving Jim a wink.

'Come on,' he said then, 'it's getting dark. Time to be saying goodbye to the Points. After all, nil aon tintean, mar a thintean fein.'

## Twelve – Over at Frankie's House

While Mickser was giving us a tour of the Five Points, Father Murtagh was continuing with what he referred to as his *secret ministry*. He called it secret because he wore plain clothes, not his preferred cassock. Trudging home through the cold streets, he was heartened by the biblical proverb at chapter five, verse eighteen of *Timothy:* the labourer is worthy of his wages. The padre was especially looking forward to a warm bowl of soup and a sit down with his pet monkey, Charlie. He had spent that Saturday in early February along the Hudson, talking to people about God and whatever else they were interested in. He gave money to those he thought most in need of a hot drink or some food. He lifted drunks out of harm's way. He listened to a woman's problems down by the carriage stand that reminded him of Bianconi's omnibus shelter in Mostrim's main thoroughfare. She was distraught, having been abandoned by her husband for another woman. She cried as Father Murtagh patted her hand and a couple of prostitutes tut-tutted before telling her she didn't need a creep like her husband in her life and that she was better off without him. It had certainly been an eventful day and now the padre was tired – but his work was done.

Nearing his new apartment, the padre noticed a gathering of youths. This concerned him. He hoped it wasn't a neighbourhood gang or, worse still, a non-neighbourhood gang. He quickened his step, hoping to get by without a fuss. He was never going to be so lucky.

'So, you really do live on the corne' of Thompson and Canal.

Have you nothing to say to you' girlfriend?'

The padre was startled. It was only a group of girls. He knew the voice instantly.

'Miss Nayle.'

There was tittering and laughing. Then a stout-looking teen, with a crewcut and red galluses, repeated the word *miss* – as if he was after saying something wrong. Not one to miss out on the dramatic, Breda ran over and threw her arms around the padre's shoulders.

'Enough with the *miss* already,' she chirped. 'Is that any way to receive you' new love', Francis?'

This confused Father Murtagh. What new lover was she on about? He made up his mind to return her hug, although less intimately than Breda would have preferred. She pushed her way forward, gripped his jaw, and kissed him hard on the mouth. This rendered the padre somewhat incapacitated. Before he got a chance to denounce such behaviour, she placed her finger to his lips and, grabbing his hand, told her little posse of girlfriends that she could be a while and not to wait up. Then, she led Father Murtagh to his own front door.

'Show him who's boss,' shouted the girl in the galluses, 'come on Catherine, let's split.'

Catherine – beautiful and tall, with braided hair sticking out of a woolly hat, boots to her knees, and a skirt that didn't belong to a spring day in New York – waved and said *chao*.

Once inside his apartment, Father Murtagh's confusion turned to anger.

'What, in God's name, was that all about?'

'Oh, lighten up. No need to get all stentorian on me. Don't tell me you didn't enjoy it as much as I did,' Breda returned, still beaming from her starring role and the reactions of her girl-gang.

'Not funny,' he fumed.

'Okay, take it easy, Francis. Don't get you' knickers in a twist because someone decides to kiss you in public. Geez, anyone would think you were a pederast or something, or are you being perfidious in the cold light of day? You had no complaints the othe' night, when I kissed you afte' the dance.'

Father Murtagh pulled away from her grip and walked towards the window. He rubbed his eyes and tried to keep his mind off the fact that there was a gorgeous young woman standing there – in his living room, as the Americans would say – wanting to kiss him. The Americans had it correct – a living room indeed. And this was *living* like never before. His concentration returned to his present plight. He thought about the Epistle of Saint James – verse one, paragraph twelve – and asked God's help in resisting this trial. Mentally, he prayed: *blessed is the man who endures temptation*. Then he forgot himself.

'For when he has been approved, he will receive the crown of life which the Lord has promised to those who love Him,' he continued in a low voice.

'What's that you're muttering,' said Breda, a frown taking charge of her pretty face.

'Nothing, Miss Nayle, nothing at all.'

'Oh yeah, it didn't sound like nothing. It sounded like a praye' or something. Wanna tell me why you're being so God-almighty weird? What do you want me to do, Francis Murtagh, perform a skimmington the whole way back to my gal pals because I had the courage to kiss a man I like? Is that what you gents from the old country expect of a broad?'

Breda Nayle's attitude did not sit well with Father Murtagh. He associated her forward behaviour with fear more than courage and her over-exuberant choice of words as a tool of manipulation instead of a means of expression.

Taking her by the shoulders, he sat her down by the table and swept away the hair from her face. He looked at her luscious red lips and thought about how much he wanted to massage her beautiful mouth with his.

'Blessed is the man who endures temptation. For when he has been approved, he will receive the crown of life which the Lord has promised to those who love Him,' Father Murtagh repeated, losing himself in her gorgeous green eyes.

'Have you gone mad,' she asked, before moving in for the kill.

He jolted backwards, working against every instinct he possessed.

'I can't,' he shouted despairingly. 'I just can't.'

He gripped her arms, as if pleading for his life.

'You don't know what you're doing to me. I want you so much. But I can't.'

He got up and walked back towards the window, leaving Breda confused and frustrated.

'You're married,' was the accusation that followed him across the room. 'You cowardly bastard, you're married.'

He rubbed the sides of his forehead and turned to face his accuser. She was even more beautiful than he remembered from the Arms Hotel – more beautiful in kitchen candlelight than a dimly-lit dancehall.

'I'm a priest,' he confessed, with all the desperation of a cornered animal.

She sat in silence at first, then began to laugh. The padre felt that she was mocking him.

'I *am* a priest.'

She really went over the top then, pretending to be in hysterics.

'Look, if you don't believe me …'

He took her arm and led her to a wardrobe. He swung the door open to reveal his old black cassock, hanging there in pristine condition.

Breda looked at the priest's uniform, then at Father Murtagh. She drew out and slapped him across the face.

'What's that for?'

Without answering, she swung her left hand and stung his other cheek so hard it brought tears to his eyes. As she attempted a third swing, he caught her wrist and told her to stop.

'I didn't deserve that,' he shouted, struggling to restrain her.

'Lia',' she hissed.

'That's not fair, Breda. I never lied to you. If anything, I discouraged your advances from the start. Calm down, and I will explain everything.'

Eventually Breda Nayle's wrists stopped fighting for freedom and peace descended on the apartment. She took back her chair. Father Murtagh made a pot of tea. His mind was racing. He wouldn't tell her everything, just the bits about himself. By the time the tea was fully brewed, he had come to his senses. She could have given him up as it was – along with Jim Gorman and me – any time she wanted. So, in the end, he told her everything. He started with the daring rescue orchestrated by Paddy Sugrue – the paddy-wagon crash – and finished with the Offaly County dance a few days prior.

'That's why I have to pretend I'm *not* a priest,' he concluded, 'for fear of detection. I'm wanted in relation to a robbery – worse still, a sacrilegious robbery. But my friends are in more serious trouble. If they're caught, James and Joseph will be sent back to Ireland to face British justice – the hangman's noose or a penal colony in Australia.'

'Who are these guys,' asked Breda.

'They live at the other end of Thompson Street. James, you don't know. Joseph, you've met. He's the big man you saw me with at the dance the other night.'

'The old guy with the grey hai',' she announced, and I don't thank her for the description. 'You're afraid I'm gonna rat you out?'

'Should you feel as if that is the only course of action open to you at this time, I would ask nothing for myself. But I would plead for an opportunity to alert my friends of the impending danger.'

'Would you now,' said Breda, as a strange sort of smile crept across her beautiful face.

'I'm at your mercy,' continued the chivalrous padre.

'Yes, you are,' she pointed out, clearly enjoying this new position of ascendancy which had presented itself. 'Let's get one thing straight already. Even the idea that I would rat you out is injurious to my very core. This is America, buste'. I don't know what goes on in Ireland, but here, we Irish look out for each othe'. We don't give each othe' up, especially to the British establishment. Got that, Pops?'

Father Murtagh kissed Breda's hand tenderly and said he had got it loud and clear.

'But, seriously, I'm a little disappointed – telling fibs and you a priest is not very punctilious. I'll bet you' real name isn't even Francis. No more lies, Pops, got it? No more lies and I think we could get on like a house on fire.'

Father Murtagh and Breda Nayle did get on like a house on fire. After playing with his pet monkey, she felt much more at ease. Then it was Breda's turn to bare her soul by candlelight. She told the padre how things were at home. She and her mother, Bridget, had been on a collision course with regard to Breda's friends. Their unladylike behaviour was a contributory factor, and one that her mother was unwilling to accept. So, she enrolled Breda in a finishing school. This was like a red rag to a bull, only encouraging Breda to lay siege on what she regarded as her mother's subordinated views in relation to women and their place in society. Bridget also hated the slang used by her daughter – town talk, as she called it. The latest battle in the war occurred when her mother found out that Breda had been skipping church on Sundays. Catholicism was very much pride of place in her mother's home – the Angeles and the Rosary could be heard in the evenings, and the house was full of sacred iconography.

'She'd love you, Pops,' joked Breda, 'especially in that black dress you have in you' closet.'

'It's called a cassock. And I've never heard of the word *closet* before – it's a wardrobe where I come from. Why are you calling me *Pops*?'

What Breda knew about her mother's homeland she had gleaned from school and Saint James's. Bridget Nayle hadn't talked much about it. She certainly never told her daughter just how poor most of the country was. Her mother's Ireland existed only in blank daydreams, or forays into prayer when a letter from home appeared in the mailbox. She did, however, fill Breda in on her experiences since coming to America. Because of these experiences, the one thing her mother guarded as closely as her religion was her daughter's education. She was unwavering in her determination that Breda would not follow her into domestic service. She made absolutely sure her daughter got the best of learning. Bridget Nayle also guarded her *lace curtain* image at all costs, now that she had risen to it. Her motto was: *the pen is mightier than the wooden spoon*. She had thrown off the shanty Irish tag and, through her daughter's hard work and dedication to the books, would certainly bury that view of her family forever.

Brigid O'Neill arrived in America in her late teens. A combination of her flat Midland accent and some indifferent spelling at Hudson Bay Registry Office led to the birth of her new name. She had become Bridget Nayle before she had even spent a homesick night of sleeplessness in her adopted land. From the very beginning, Breda's mother had a burning ambition to be a mill girl. She wanted to get out of New York and head north to Massachusetts. This kind of life appealed to her. She wanted to live with other mill girls in company houses, attending classes and lectures – just like Deirdre McAnaspey, a Derry girl she had befriended on the ship. Their hearts were set on Lowell, a town in somewhere called New England. It had been employing women in its textile mills since eighteen twenty, and boasted the pioneering Female Labour Reform Association – a trailblazer for women's working rights.

'Now I know where you get your feminism,' the padre said with a smile.

However, getting out of New York was easier said than done. Setting foot on dry land, Breda's mother hadn't the price of the trip north. Besides, she was under contract – like most of the girls she had shared with in steerage. To pay off her scheme debt and earn money for Lowell, Bridget took a job in the well-to-do Chamberlain household. At first, she liked it there – the work was easy and she had free time to ramble aimlessly in the leafy suburbs. She quickly became convinced that these Americans were some kind of geniuses, or perhaps even psychic. Everyone who called to the door – total strangers whom she was meeting for the very first time – all knew to call her Bridget. It was amazing. How could they possibly have known her first name. This really impressed the young Bridget – until she learned that all the Irish girls who plied their trade as housemaids were known as *Bridgets*, and her employers and their high-society friends were merely poking fun at her. Bridget's free time gradually dried up. Maid-of-all-work really meant maid of *all* work. Two free evenings per week soon became one – and only on condition that Master Chamberlain wasn't entertaining. Sixteen-hour working days were the norm and began with lighting fires at five in the morning. Some jobs had no knocking-off time, such as answering the door or fixing the young master or mistress a midnight snack. Yet despite the grind, and the horrible taunts, these homes gave the Bridget Nayles of this life a glimpse into a world they longed to be part of. They were getting a close-up of how to dress, act, and speak like a lady. From the humble beginnings of setting the table, holding a cup in the correct fashion, and chewing their food properly, they became expert in domestic etiquette. The money was small considering the work, but it was honest and it was steady.

'So, when she saved up her pennies what happened then,' asked the padre, wetting another pot of tea.

It took a long time for Breda's mother to save enough for Lowell. Despite her small outlay – she was fed in the house and board was part of her pay – putting money by was a luxury. Some was sent home to her parents in King's County. The earl had to be reimbursed for the price of the passage. And then she met a boy.

'When you say met – she began stepping out with a boyfriend?'

Thursday was usually her night off. It wasn't long before Bridget and a few colleagues from the neighbourhood sought out a bit of excitement. They didn't go to snugs. If their employers got a smell of drink, or knowledge to that effect, it wouldn't have gone well for them. Not many women back then had the nerve to enter a saloon without male company. Besides, Bridget had grown to hate alcohol. In her short life, she had witnessed too many people from respectable Offaly families being tipped into the paupers' corner of the graveyard – all because of the dreaded drink. Instead, it was at the playhouse – during a production of *Romeo and Juliet* – where Bridget met her beau.

'How romantic,' gushed the padre, the soft auld eejit.

Breda's mother's boyfriend arranged the trip for Lowell and she advanced to her employer a notice to quit. Chamberlain did not want to let her go. He told Bridget he would give her a raise and wondered where he was going to get another maid-of-all-work that he could trust. On the planned date of departure, her boyfriend came to take her away. However, they were separated by the Chamberlain family. Her boyfriend was promptly escorted to the study by the head of the household; Bridget, with her coat and luggage, was instructed to wait in the hallway. When her boyfriend reappeared, he lobbed a spit on Bridget's new shoes. He called her a slut and marched straight by her. And that was the end of Bridget's days as a mill girl in Lowell.

'She didn't go in the end,' whispered Father Murtagh.

'She made one more attempt at leaving, a few years on, afte' she learned that he' forme' boyfriend had been handsomely compensated for the loss of his trip to Lowell. Chamberlain had spun him a web of lies – about mum becoming pregnant with anothe' man's baby, and how she was using him as a stand-in dad. Mum decided enough was enough and gathered he' things togethe'. By that stage, she'd climbed the domestic ladde' and was head of the kitchen. But the young housemaids informed mum of the terrible strikes happening in Lowell. It was decided that she'd be bette' off staying putt anothe' couple of months until the commotion died down. These housemaids had also been bribed. They were unde' the diktat of the maste' to discourage mum from leaving. He was overheard complaining that he hadn't spent so much money training mum up, putting a roof ove' he' head and food in he' belly, so she could swan off to Massachusetts wheneve' the mood took he'.'

'How did your mother leave the house in the end,' asked the padre.

'She married my fathe'. His name was Florence O'Flaherty. You know where Kerry is, Pops?'

'Yes, but I've never been there. It's a couple of days away from Longford, depending on your horses and carriage.'

'Well, that's where he hailed from. He took mum out of domestic service. He wasn't obstructed. By then, they had too many cooks in the kitchen – and too many young domestics willing to twist the knife in orde' to get a leg up. Mum was surplus to requirements and, it was rumoured, she was about to be loaned out to one of Chamberlain's associates in any event.'

'Is he still alive?'

'Who, Chamberlain?'

'No, your father, Mister O'Flaherty.'

'I should be asking you that, Pops. You' hierocracy deals with the afterlife. His body is in Calvary, and soone' than it oughta be. He was a young man – forty, to be exact. The bottle. Mum loved him, but kinda fell out of love towards the end. Afte' he passed, mum started to use he' maiden name again. That's why I'm Nayle, instead of O'Flaherty.'

Father Murtagh noticed the trace of a tear on Breda's cheek.

'And your mother?'

'Oh, mum's doing okay, Pops. She resides in Manhattan's Lowe' East Side and belongs to the parish of Saint James. She's active in the church. Sixteen-thousand parishioners, think you could *first Friday* that lot in a day? Anyhow, mum would harass me about getting the best education in America. She can be a real harridan when she wants. And I fought back, saying I'd be a maid like she was. I loved to rile he' up. One day, out of nowhere, she took me to a county home down by Saint Patrick's, to visit a dying lady. So we stood there, gawping at this frail old betsy in a ward bed. Then, afte' mum had left some flowers, we went home. On the way, I remembe' asking why we'd gone there in the first place – and fell right into mum's trap. She said that dea' old lady was the hardest worke' she had eve' known. But the lack of security in domestic service meant she would soon die in a county home almshouse. Fifty years, mum said, and not one penny of a pension to show fo' any of it. I neve' again complained about school o' about working on my education. I went to the Sisters of Mercy on the Lowe' East Side. I can still see the portrait of Catherine Elizabeth McCauley in the assembly hall. Ou' convent was across the street from the Christian Brothers' De La Salle Institution, where Ted Ireland – you know the politician – once went to school.'

'Yes, I've rubbed shoulders with his right-hand man, so to speak,' said the padre.

'It was in that Mercy Convent I developed my sense of right and wrong. The sisters opposed the suffrage movement as anti-Irish and even anti-Catholic. They accused those brave ladies of being uppity, and referred to them as waspy women. But hey, Pops, if a good education teaches you anything, it's how to think for yourself. I'm a proud suffragette, a women's rights advocate foreve' more. I would like to think that one day, through me, mum will eventually have he' say – and, perhaps, she will finally reach he' Lowell. As fo' my girl-gang – all part of a women's rights mini-society. We agreed to help Ted Ireland during the election. Asking you out was my part in a dare. I got off light compared to what some of the girls had to do.'

'Oh great. And here was me thinking you asked me out for my good looks.'

'Easy Pops, you're not a bad-looking guy – for a priest.'

The laughter broke the tension in the living room.

'What do you hope to achieve from your suffragism – the vote,' asked the padre, not daring to admit that he was only a couple of hours in the country when the vote was bestowed on him – several times.

'An insistence upon the basic civil principle of free speech for all. In this country we've got three types of people. There's you guys – affectionately known as newbies. There's mum's type – the hyphenated Americans. And then there's me – a true and blue, dyed-in-the-wool, inveterate American. Why should an immigrant have more say in *my* country than me, just because of my gende'?'

Father Murtagh maintained his silence. He didn't really know what to say or whether it was an actual question directed at him.

'I also believe in the American Standard of Living fo' all,' continued Breda. 'That means highe' wages, shorte' working hours, and safe working conditions. Why shouldn't domestics and labourers enjoy the same perks as professionals and business people?'

'I wish you luck with that one,' said the padre.

'I don't believe in luck,' returned Breda. 'You make you' own good fortune in this world, Pops.'

Breda stopped and had herself a giggle.

'I was just thinking, if mum was here, she would be none too pleased.'

'What? With me? I did nothing wrong.'

'No, silly, with me. She doesn't like me using slang words – like calling a priest *Pops*. But I don't care. You see, she has this hatred of made-up words. When she came to America, the Irish were continually mocked by the natives ove' thei' thick, awkward, speech. Therefore, anything but perfect English became associated with shame and poverty. Mum ditched he' old parochial way of talking a long time ago. It had no place in the new, respectable, middle-class, America. Although sometimes, if she gets excited o' angry, you can hea' traces from the distant past – that old flat-as-a-pancake King's County palave'. And now she wants me to talk a certain way too.'

'You have the vocabulary, would you not be willing to give elocution lessons a try? They'd tune up that New York twang of yours.'

'Look, Pops, elocution had no place in the ethnically-mixed neighbourhood of my upbringing. Slang was the orde' of the day. Mum called it trashy. If she caught me using it, she'd say I sounded like someone out of Harlem o' the Jewish Quarte'. I used to have great fun winding he' up.'

'What would you say to get her going?'

Breda recoiled when the padre asked this. It was like she realised for the first time just how much she had been talking – and how much she had been enjoying his company.

'I don't know,' she replied eventually, 'a lot of wate' unde' the bridge since those days.'

'Teach me some of your American slang.'

'I can't think right now, Pops, maybe late'.'

'Ah now, you're not getting shy on me.'

Father Murtagh was beginning to figure out how to provoke a response from Breda.

'You're all talk. You probably don't know any slang words to begin with. This twenty-five-cent piece,' he said, lifting up a coin, 'says you're full of shite, as they so eloquently put it in Longford.'

'Am not, and it's called a quarte', by the way,' replied Breda. 'I can smart-mouth with the best of them. What do you wanna know?'

'Tell me – in American slang – what you and your girl-gang get up to.'

'How do you mean, get up to?'

'Get up to,' he repeated, 'at the weekend.'

'When we're hanging in the hood,' said Breda. 'From Thompson to Mulberry on the Lowe' East Side is ou' scam. All those blocks we conside' ou' turf. On a Saturday night you can find us trawling the speakeasies, hunting fo' dudes. We don't want no stool pigeons o' squealers, just you' regula' swells. Although Janey – the punky one you met outside with Catherine – she's a sucke' for phonies.'

Father Murtagh was intrigued by such language.

'What's a phony?'

'You know,' replied Breda, 'a pretentious person.'

'And what's a swell?'

'Come on Pops, what is this? A swell is a guy with a lotta class – class in his dress sense and class in his manne' – you know, the way he conducts himself.'

Breda reddened a little then.

'Someone like you, Pops,' she said shyly.

Father Murtagh allowed himself a brief smile, but said nothing more on the matter. He didn't want to ruin his moment.

'When are you bringing me to the Lower East Side to visit your mother,' he asked instead.

'I don't know if that's a good idea,' returned Breda.

'Why not? It's like as if I know her already.'

'I've gotta bette' idea. I'll bring he' ove' to visit you. But make sure and wea' you' black clothes…you' priest costume. She'll love you in it. Mum loves priests, especially fully-fledged Irish priests.'

'Good idea,' said the padre.

'Oh, and one othe' thing,' quipped Breda, 'don't let on I call you Pops.'

## Thirteen – Prize Fighting at the King's Hall

Thursday was waiting day. They were the words Jonty used in justification. Workers were waiting for their wages. Friday was not a day to be missing from the job – not because of drink, not because of sickness, not because of anything. Collecting the pay packet made for a quiet Thursday night in the saloon. It was mostly just ourselves and Mickser – if he wasn't in the Spieler. But we were getting tired of it too. We needed gainful employment, especially as my hundred pounds – the proceeds of Lady Jane Teale's benevolence – had all but dried up. It was only by chance that we found ourselves at the boxing. Father Murtagh heard about it on the docks. The padre may have hated the sight of blood, but he still loved a good old scrap. He thought it would be healthy for me and Jim to get out and about, away from a public house for at least one night in the week.

Naturally, the atmosphere was toxic inside the King's Hall on Washington Square. But it was marvellous pugilistic fun. The air was thick with smoke. Drink was something you either brought yourself or bought in a glorified broom cupboard for double its price. Gambling was all around us. You could place your bets with half-a-dozen well-dressed men in bowler hats at different points in the hall. Sectarian chanting was the order of the day. Racial abuse rang out to the rafters. The usual stuff. The cold would cut through your bones. As I already said – marvellous pugilistic fun. On the wall opposite the doorway, a huge picture of James Yankee Sullivan smiled down. He got his nickname from the American flag he wore proudly around his waist before each fight. He was wearing it in the picture. Underneath were the words: *American Heavyweight Champion.*

Despite the madness, or maybe because of it, the great people of New York really needed the King's Hall. We all needed it. Jim Gorman insisted on calling it Washington Square Hall, because he was sick of the king owning, or being associated, with everything. Our first boxing Thursday will always stay with me. The place packed out in jig time. I looked up at the large ring in the centre of the arena, remembering the old days. I would have loved the luxury of the ropes and a designated fighting area. In my day, the spectators formed the ring. It could have been any shape or size. Father Murtagh led us through the mass of bodies until we got up close to the ring ropes. He claims fight night is even better when you're so close you can smell the sweat, and the liniment leaves your eyes watering.

'He won't be smiling for too much longer,' shouted an Irish fella at Mickser Burrows, who was looking for a free space to spit a mouthful of tobacco.

'Who's that,' asked the slightly inebriated Mickser.

'What do you mean *who*,' said the fella, and he pointed at the picture of Yankee Sullivan. 'There's this new Irish strong boy on the scene, John Morrissey they call him. They say he could take Sullivan out any time he wants.'

Mickser was supping from a half-bottle of brandy and hadn't the slightest bit of interest in what the Irish fella was saying.

'There's a slew in now,' said Father Murtagh, trying to impress with the new slang words he was learning from Breda. 'It must be time for the opener.'

'*Sea, slua mor,*' answered the Irish fella, who, through all the noise, thought the padre was speaking in his native tongue.

A bare-chested man made his way through the crowd, holding aloft the blue, white, and red of the British Union flag. He was like a giant. The preliminaries had begun for the first contest of the night – a heavyweight bout. An old man, his weskit unbuttoned, walked behind the bare-chested fighter, and two others flanked him on the way to the ring. I scanned the hall for a second fighter.

'He must be shadow boxing this evening,' I joked, looking over at the empty fighters' entrance.

'Ara, I hope not,' said Mickser, 'I'm after laying a continental against him.'

'The other fighter is above already,' replied the padre, pointing to a small black boxer standing in a corner of the ring.

He was looking a bit unsure of himself. When I say small, he wasn't a pipsqueak. But he had no business in a heavyweight boxing bout either. His manager, another little black fella, stood beside him. He wore the expression of a man in line for the gallows.

The announcer jumped into the ring and proclaimed that this was to be the first bout of the evening, a contest between Mister George Harland – the pride of the Scots-Irish, representing Her Majesty Queen Victoria of Great Britain and Ireland – and Bartholomew … But Bartholomew's surname, or who he represented, was lost as the hall erupted in frenzy of boos and jeers and chants.

'That little scut of a gosuir, sure he's hardly out of short pants,' exclaimed Mickser, putting his hands on his head. 'All my money is gone.'

'Well, whoever he is, it's too bad for him,' warned Jim, 'I don't fancy your chances, Mickser.'

The ring announcer started up again, declaring that the boxing match was to be fought under the new rules as drawn up by the scientific father of self-defence himself, Mister Jack Broughton.

'Jayses, who's he,' said Mickser, and Father Murtagh reminded him about his language.

'It's a boxing match we're at, Padre, not benediction.'

'Yes, I'm well aware of that Michael, but it's still no excuse to take the name of the Lord your God in vain.'

The bell went. Bartholomew had barely got out of his corner when George Harland was across, swinging wildly with both fists. To the surprise of the large attendance baying for blood, young Bartholomew sidestepped his opponent and threw a few jabs of his own. But he couldn't get through Harland's defence.

'It's a partisan crowd,' I said to Jim Gorman, just to annoy him.

'You're at it again with the priests' education,' he replied, and I had a chuckle to myself.

There was a royal standard banner in the crowd, and the British Union flag that Harland had brought into the arena was tied to the ropes of the ring. The crowd was really playing its part for the empire, raining abuse down on Bartholomew. He searched for a place to run from his opponent's considerable bulk. Then Harland trapped him in a corner. There was nowhere left for Bartholomew to go; he was pounded to the floor.

A very English voice beside Jim Gorman wanted to know who Harland was actually fighting for – Ulster or his queen.

'He claims to be a proud Ulsterman. Ulster is in Ireland, innit,' inquired the English voice. 'Well, wot's this geezer's game then? It's the queen all the way.'

'I feel sorry for that poor little fellow,' said Father Murtagh.

'Whisht, don't be saying that too loud or we may head for the door,' whispered Jim Gorman. 'Your southern Irish accent is one thing – a bit far down for most of the crowd's liking – without rooting for the opposition into the bargain.'

While he had his man on the ground, George Harland goaded him – gesturing with his muscular arms as the crowd went into raptures. The referee pushed him away and began his count. But Bartholomew, to his credit, did get up – only to be hammered down again with a ferocious right cross. Before the referee could get to ten, the bell sounded and he helped Bartholomew back to his corner.

During the wait for the second round a skirmish broke out in the crowd. A section of George Harland's supporters attacked a number of men wearing black skull caps. The chant of *Betzemar, Betzemar* went up. Abraham was nowhere to be seen, thankfully. The hall men had to intervene, separating the two factions and restoring normal chaos to proceedings.

The bell finally sounded and everyone refocused on the shenanigans in the ring. Surprisingly, Bartholomew started this round much better. He had recovered his feet and threw a few hooks, but couldn't get through the cover. Then Harland ambled forward, hoping to trap his opponent as he had done in the first. However, Bartholomew wasn't for catching this time. He completed the round with some slick footwork, angering the strong Scots-Irish presence in the crowd.

'Come on William, get your fighter going for Christ's sake. Do it for Queen and country,' shouted a man from the northern part of Ireland at Harland's corner. 'Give 'em Woodstock while you're at it.'

The crowd surged forward and I could feel his hands pushing against my back.

'See that there boy, that cornerman,' the north man continued, trying to get Father Murtagh's attention, 'that's William Travers.'

'Who's he when he's at home,' I said, looking behind.

'Yes, who is this William Travers,' asked the padre.

'That's cracker, just cracker,' replied the north man, tugging at the back of my coat. 'Everyone knows who William Travers is, so they do – the champion of last year's Orange Green Riots. But, then again, what would southern bastards like yous know about fighting?'

I turned to get a proper look at this upstart. There he was, far away from the banks of the Lagan, still trying to bully and annoy people. I suppressed an urge to knock his block off. And he wasn't finished yet. He shouted more advice at the man who was attending George Harland, then said he hoped the nigger was a Catholic nigger. I tightened the muscles in my buttocks. It was perfect timing. The fart stung the cheeks of my arse.

'You're rotten,' said the padre.

'Good,' I replied. 'It might get rid of your man behind.'

It was hard to envisage this fight lasting much longer. Bartholomew had thrown all he could at his much bigger opponent. He sat there awaiting the bell, his delicate-looking cornerman wiping blood from his nose. They didn't speak at all. It was clear that Bartholomew's second had no idea of what he was supposed to be doing.

The hammer hit the anvil for the third. Harland sprung from his stool and launched into a series of haymakers, resembling a windmill as his trunk-like arms raked through the night air in search of their target. But Bartholomew had learned how to stay out of trouble. Harland continued to goad him. Whatever he said clearly upset Bartholomew – who lost his poise and charged headlong. As he came forward, a vicious uppercut to the midsection sent him down in a crumpled heap. Harland stood over his man yet again, talking down at him all the time. The Jewish contingent booed and called foul, causing the skirmish to start anew.

Amazingly, the referee postponed the count until after explaining to the incensed Jews that there was nothing wrong with the punch under the Jack Broughton rules. Bartholomew's cornerman didn't budge. It was like he was afraid to open his mouth. There was pandemonium in the hall. The injured fighter got to his feet – one arm outstretched, the other down protecting his private area. Harland could sense blood and was moving in for the kill. Bartholomew's jaw was left exposed and Harland sent a left-right combination to his head, forcing him to cover up. The opportunity arose for Harland to sink a second low blow, bowling his rival over again. The bell sounded once more and Harland paraded back to his corner to a chorus of cheers as *Rule Brittania* broke out in the hall.

Bartholomew sat like a trapped bird. It was almost at an end. The pain was evident on his face as he gasped for air. He looked for the referee's attention, but couldn't catch his eye. He nodded as his timid cornerman located the nearest towel. He was about to hurl it into the ring – signalling the end.

'Give me a round with him.'

When the cornerman turned I was right in his face, the cold ringside bottle in my hand. It was time to show my northern friend what this southern bastard knew about fighting.

'Take a sip and spit it out,' I instructed Bartholomew, 'then listen very carefully.'

Bartholomew didn't know whether I was real or if he was hallucinating from the punches.

'Give me that, you,' I said, taking the towel out of the cornerman's clutches, 'if you do exactly as I say, you won't be needing it tonight.'


Father Murtagh had been so busy lecturing Mickser Burrows on the evils of gambling that he didn't notice my absence. He turned back for the start of the fourth and there I was, ringside, giving Bartholomew some last-ditch instructions before returning him for battle.

'What in heaven's name is he doing,' shouted the padre.

'See that there boy,' said the north man, seizing Father Murtagh by the arm, 'that there's one of the finest examples of good-old Belfast heft, so it is. It's the way it should be – the natural order of things. That wog is no match for raw imperial power, so he isn't.'

Father Murtagh dislodged himself and made his way over to Jim.

'What's *he* doing up there? Is he trying to get us lynched, or what?'

'If he is, then he's making a good job of it,' returned Jim.

I inspected Bartholomew's eyes. He wasn't in great shape, but he was coherent and that was a start.

'What's that Harland fella been saying,' I asked the cornerman.

'He bin a whoopin' and a hollarin', callin' m'boy all sorts,' he replied.

'Listen to me now. Don't lose your temper and charge in. That's what he wants. His defence is too strong. You're not getting through. You must fluctuate instead.'

They looked at me as though I was speaking double-Dutch.

'Fluctuation is the key. It's your only chance to get Harland to drop his guard. So let him come to you. Then left jab, right cross, left hook. Is that clear? The first two at the head, and the hook to the body. Have you got that? Just concentrate hard on that combination for this round – jab, cross, hook to the body.'

The cornerman looked more confused than Bartholomew did.

'Never lose your temper. Now get out there and do your stuff.'

Bartholomew nodded as the bell went again. He was walking forward and looking back, trying to make sense of it all. George Harland snapped him out of it with a thunderbolt to the face. This shook Bartholomew, nearly putting him down again. The hall erupted as he stumbled back, almost falling through the ropes onto me and his cornerman.

'Here you go, nigger,' snarled Harland, as he readied himself for the kill.

Suddenly, as if by magic, Bartholomew regained his wits and his balance. He took a step to his left, evading a wild swing. He stuck out a left jab of his own, followed by a quick-as-lightning right cross. Harland's arms went up to block. Then Bartholomew finished his combination, sinking a heavy blow to the ribs. Harland was stunned and reeled backwards towards his corner.

'M'name's not nigger,' said Bartholomew, as surprised as anyone in the hall at this new development.

This infuriated Harland.

'You little black bastard, I'm going to kill you,' he shouted, lunging forward with his muscled arms down low to protect his body.

'Remember the combination,' I roared.

Bartholomew started anew with a jab to the head. Then the right cross, that beat Harland's rising arms, landed square on the jaw. He took his time, putting all his force in the hook to a newly-exposed midriff. Harland staggered all over the ring. Shock reverberated through the hall. A bookie, forgetting himself, threw his bowler hat in the air. *Rule Brittania* died down. Harland was breathless as blood flowed from his lips.

'It's not black bastard nether,' mouthed Bartholomew, clearly on a high.

Harland collected himself as best he could and came forward again, trying to muster some of his earlier menace.

'Nigger's cur,' he grunted.

Once again, right on cue, Bartholomew side-stepped and put everything into his combination, this time sending Harland crashing to the floor. I looked at the referee who, by this stage, was shocked as well. He didn't want to start a count for fear of inciting the crowd. But what could he do. There was no point standing with his mouth open like an imbecile. He looked across at the timekeeper, who shook his head. The bell was a long way off. He began the count. It was the longest ten seconds in the history of mankind. He gave Harland every chance to get up. As he neared nine, the bottles were already flying towards the ring. The referee was praying that George Harland would resurrect himself. But Harland's race was run. He was slumped down on the bottom rope. It was over, and a relieved Bartholomew jumped into his cornerman's arms.

'This contest is null and void, I demand my money back,' was the first comment I heard levelled at the nearest ringside bookmaker. 'That white guy is not the negro's manager.'

The bookies, overjoyed at Bartholomew's sudden change in fortune, had no chance to reflect on their considerable winnings. They knotted their cloth money bags and ran for the door of the King's Hall.

Bartholomew, who had been hoisted aloft in celebration, was now locked in battle once more. Harland's supporters guarded the door and the two windows, preventing escape. The ring announcer tried to calm the situation. But he couldn't be heard. In the end, he was glad to get away – after being seized and choked with the top ring rope.

'What'd yous expect from those southerners – the nigger-Irish. Ye'll side with the blacks, so ye will,' said a north man, before grabbing me around the neck.

Jim Gorman, who had climbed into the ring to avoid a beating, took offense with this remark and gripped the north man by the lugs.

'Who are you calling nigger-Irish,' I heard Jim shout. 'Get into the ring, Mickser.'

We were trapped! The neutrals showed their true nativist colours, joining Harland's supporters as they stormed the ring. The door was forced open and in rushed the police – batons drawn and swinging. And not a moment too soon. The last thing I saw was the ring collapsing as we beat a path for the safety of the street. Bartholomew was smuggled out beneath the padre's topcoat.

'Not so fast,' said the north man who had been guarding the doorway until the police forced him back. 'Yous are the cause of this situation in the first place, so ye are.'

I planted him with a combination of my own. I just wasn't in the humour for any more bullshite.

'Wow,' said Bartholomew's cornerman. 'Where did yo' learn to hit like that, boss?'

'At the fair in Longford Town,' I answered.

'Did yo' see that, Bert,' said the cornerman, 'this ole-timer has some purty moves goin' on.'

## Fourteen – A Blast from the Past

Every day is a school day. That's what the padre said as we headed over to the Lower East Side docks. He was trying to make me feel better after my case of mistaken identity below in the Five Points' *Benbulben* bar. If that little misunderstanding had taught me anything, it was that I needed a job more than I needed a woman. And there's where the padre stepped in. He said he knew a couple of stevedores. I thought I was a bit on the old side for such heavy lifting, but the padre said they'd be only too glad to have the likes of me – a hardy lump of a fellow with a few lines of experience in his face.

'Don't you worry, Joseph, there are plenty of agey boys working on the docks.'

What he meant by *agey* – I didn't even know it was a word, and me with the priests' education – is anybody's guess.

'But he looked so like a woman,' I explained, 'even talked and walked like a woman. Mickser said I should be counting my lucky stars I didn't find out the hard way.'

'As I said, every day is for learning. I wouldn't have much experience with regard to the opposite gender. But you couldn't be too careful nowadays, Joseph.'

'Do you hear the innocent fella. What about this Breda one? You're a dark horse, Father Murtagh, and make no mistake, a very dark horse indeed.'

'Myself and young Breda are merely on first-name terms.'

'Go on with you. And what is your first name today – Father

Gerard, Frankie, Francis? I knew Ribbonmen who hadn't as many first names.'

On reaching the docks we slotted into the line-up, facing a container. All the men were younger. So much for the padre's *agey* boys. The same expression told on every face – a look of desperation. There was hunger in their eyes. Two things I could sense – after a couple of barren, potato-failing, years on the other side of the Atlantic Ocean – were desperation and hunger. But these men's faces were different from the sickly wretches who would stagger into their jobs at Cranley House. There was a hope, however faint, hidden somewhere deep within.

'I wonder who'll be picked today,' said the padre, before blowing his white breath onto his hands.

The container door swung open. A little man in a long blue jacket with double-breasted buttons and brown leather boots came out and surveyed the crowd thoughtfully. He transferred a cane to his left hand and adjusted his black naval hat as he walked slowly towards us. The jostling had already begun in the line-up.

'Degoes for the shake-up,' he bellowed, and drew a line in the mud with his cane.

The men started for the mark. I could feel the shift of adrenalin as we jostled along the line.

'That's Nigel,' said the padre, 'they call him Napoleon – but never to his face.'

'I can see why,' I replied. 'He's not two hands higher than a duck's arse. You'd have to get down on your knees to say anything to *his* face. Charles Sherwood Stratton, eat your heart out.'

'It's nothing to do with his height,' explained the padre.

'He's French so,' I contended.

'And nothing to do with his nationality. He's of English extraction – he hates the French with a passion.'

The line-up was getting pushy. They were trying to influence Napoleon. One man began to call out in Irish.

'Don't bother,' shouted Napoleon, 'I don't understand what you're saying.'

I could hear them breathing behind me as I looked across the line. Youngsters – barely able to shave – stared longingly at Napoleon in his warm jacket, willing him to point the cane in their direction. The jostling stopped.

'You,' he said, and a tall blonde teen said something in what sounded like German before stepping out of the line-up and over the mark.

The jostling began again. Napoleon was enjoying every second of it. He had the power to make their day or send them home empty-handed. He pointed his cane again.

'You,' he repeated, and a strapping Dubliner thanked him very much and puffed out his cheeks.

But then Napoleon changed his mind.

'No, not you. You,' he said to the next man, dashing the Dubliner's delight.

I didn't like Napoleon after that. I thought it a low act to raise a man's hopes only to knock them again for fun. I also felt that I didn't really belong in this line-up. After all, these men were twenty years younger than me. Some were probably married with children, relying on the day's wages. I could see it all now – and not just on their faces, but in their body language. They were a highly motivated bunch. A single man like me, with nobody to fend for but myself, had no business in this line-up.

'Hey, nigger-lover,' said a voice from somewhere behind the padre, and I felt a hot sensation on my cheeks.

I ignored it, hoping it would go away. But then I heard it again. The padre looked around at the man who said it.

'What did you call me?'

'Not you – your pal. He wasn't as quiet the other night in the King's Hall. Do you remember me? You cost me two dollars and I want my money back.'

But this pest wasn't going away.

'I've never seen you before in my life,' I said.

'Are you sure about that, nigger-lover,' he growled.

Sugrue once told me that when your back is to the wall, try bluffing first. If bluffing doesn't work, try fighting. And if fighting doesn't work, there's a problem. I could have got myself killed – and the padre too – but I thought it best to take Sugrue's advice.

'Very sure. I'd remember an ugly bastard like you. And if you don't piss off and leave me alone, you're going to be a lot uglier,' I determined, my heart thumping.

For all I knew, every other man in the line-up might have been his friend – and ally. But I felt it was a chance I had to take. Nobody stirred. And the pest shut his mouth.

Napoleon was on the move. He patrolled his mark, adding to it by dragging his cane's shiny brass tip through the muddy ground. He looked over when he heard our voices, then held the cane behind his back and kept strolling. He looked again and swivelled on his brown bootheels.

'Good morning, Frankie,' said Napoleon.

'Good morning, Nigel,' returned Father Murtagh.

So that's what the padre was answering to on the docks. A few short months in New York and he had more names than Ted Ireland.

'You,' said Napoleon.

I didn't move. After all, *you* could be anyone. And there was enough of a choice – hardy bucks, as Mickser would say – without pointing his cane at me.

'Hey you, big man, let's go. I haven't got all day.'

So, I stepped across the mark and waited with the chosen few.

Napoleon kept pointing until he counted ten. That's when hope gave way to pent-up frustration. Voices were raised and the mark was breached. A big man came out of the container and positioned himself between Napoleon and the would-be degoes. He had a wooden bat – not a weapon that inspired a great deal of confidence when faced with such a mob. He was the dockland's security force – the driving-away man. He appealed to the men to go home, that there was nothing more for the day. But this only incited the line-up further.

'You,' said Napoleon, pointing the cane at me again, 'get over here and help out.'

That was the last thing I wanted to hear. I was quite content to stay with the other nine and do the job I was picked out for in the first place. I looked around for the padre, but he was swallowed up in the row. I could hear *nigger-lover* being aired again – by more than one voice, I might add.

My colleague on the security staff – the driving-away man – swung his bat into action, catching one of the line-up on the side of the head. Then all hell broke loose.

'The water hose,' shouted Napoleon, pushing me forward and gesturing towards the platform.

'What are you on about,' I replied.

'Under the canvas.'

There was a huge leather water hose, with a ten-inch iron nozzle, under a green canvas sheet. I found out later that it was used mostly when the ships' decks were being scrubbed. I jumped up on the platform, tore off the sheet, and let loose. It took all my strength to hold it at full blast. I didn't care where I aimed it. Water splayed across the docks, driving a man from the line-up back towards the mark. I pointed it at a couple of blagguards who were battering the driving-away man with his own bat. One was repelled immediately; the other fell and tried to get back to his feet. But I wasn't having that. I doused him until he let go of the bat and then swept him across the mark. I was beginning to enjoy myself. I spotted the man who called me nigger-lover. Well, I swept him down the street. Every time he tried to get up, I let him have it again. Then I saturated as many as I could point the hose at. That took the heart out of the row. It was over as quickly as it had started.

I eventually spotted the padre, making his way towards the platform.

'Are you alright,' I shouted.

He didn't seem best pleased.

'I'm not injured, if that's what you're asking. But I'm frozen to death, all thanks to you and that god-forsaken hose. If you had to leave well enough alone for a couple of minutes, it would have all fizzled out.'

'Only doing my job, *Frankie*, only doing my job.'

From then on, whenever Napoleon was the stevedore in charge, I was picked out of the line-up. Sometimes, I wasn't even needed. He'd pick me for the sake of it – or perhaps he felt he owed me for saving his skin.

I got to know most of the degoes over time. But that didn't stop me from using the hose on them if they misbehaved. We treated those members of the line-up who didn't get picked with respect at all times. However, respect didn't always work. There were always the few determined to cause trouble, no matter what. It was then that I reached for the lever on the water hose. A belt of the north Atlantic usually settled even the most hot-tempered degoes. And, of course, there was always the bat. But I would feel sorry for those that Napoleon left behind. If it was up to me, I'd have employed the lot of them. But the bosses were out to maximise their profits. They didn't care a jot for willing workers who were left to face another day without a penny in their pockets.

I loved the docks. I got to meet different and interesting people all the time – with crews from the Caribbean Islands or far-flung regions of Africa constantly coming and going. The smell of spices and coffee beans and tea stirred the imagination for places I would never see, and places I had already been. Sometimes, when I closed my eyes and breathed deep, it was like being back in Viscount de Bromley's basement in Cranley House.

There was no middle ground on the docks. A driving-away man wasn't allowed help out on the ships. If I wasn't protecting Napoleon, I was keeping my eyes peeled to make sure nothing went missing. It was complete boredom one minute and utter chaos the next.

One morning, after the little man had finished his selection, a fracas was in its infancy. Verbal abuse had given way to violence. Stones had been hurled at Napoleon. I received the nod and, together with the bat-wielding bruiser, faced the line-up. The pushing was over and fists began to fly, so I stepped up on the platform and pointed the hose. After a final plea, I let rip – breaking the line-up and bowling them over. And that was it – or so I thought. After a good wallop of water, the degoes would either go home and dry out or into the city to try their hand at something else. However, on this particular day, one young man – chilled to the bone – remained behind. He was still shouting and causing a fuss.

'Go home, young fella, or we'll be forced to blast you again,' warned my colleague. 'Do I have to bring down the bat?'

But the youngster kept roaring for all his worth. Napoleon gave another nod. I turned the hose on, sweeping him off his feet a second time. He spilled across the docks, his arms and legs fighting in vain. I turned off the hose and was headed for a loading bay – a goods ship from British Guyana should never be left unattended for long – when I heard what I thought was the word *workhouse*. When I turned again, my colleague had the youngster pinned to the ground. I felt like going back, but I was also anxious to get on with my morning checks. If anything went missing from that ship, heads were going to roll. Did I really hear *workhouse* or was my mind playing tricks? I don't know why I went back. I was being silly – it was a complete waste of time.

'Let him up,' I said. 'Okay sonny, what's your problem? You know the choosing's over for the day. Come back and try your luck tomorrow.'

The young man picked himself off the ground.

'It is *you*,' he chattered. 'I just knew it was *you*.'

'Listen, sonny...'

'You helped me escape from Shroid workhouse. It's me, Jeremiah. Jeremiah Figg. Do you not remember?'

The name cut me to the quick. I couldn't believe it. For sure I remembered the name Jeremiah Figg. Many a night I sat up wondering whether the boy was dead or alive, if he'd made a decent life for himself or succumbed to exhaustion in some rat-infested ditch along the way. I couldn't take this in. There, right in front of my eyes – a world away from that hellhole in Shroid – was the very same boy.

'Merciful hour,' is all I could muster.

The young man shook my hand.

'I knew it was you,' he kept on saying, 'I just knew it. You haven't changed all that much over the years – went a bit greyer, but that's all.'

'You have,' I exclaimed.

'Yeah, I'm much wetter than the last time you saw me.'

'My God, you're all grown up now.'

'I should hope so,' said Jeremiah Figg, 'it's been eight years, after all, since you released me into the wild.'

I couldn't take my eyes off him. It was hard to believe that this was the same skinny kid I had set free from the workhouse all those years ago.

'Come on,' urged my bat-wielding colleague, 'that ship is moored in the loading bay.'

'I have to go now,' I said to Jeremiah, 'but could you meet me here this evening? We'll have a chat over a couple of pints.'

'Do me a favour before you go,' he replied. 'Ask your little boss for the lend of his big coat – I'm freezing my arse off here.'

That same evening, I introduced Jeremiah Figg to Jonty McArthur's saloon. He regaled us with the story of the great workhouse escape. They were all there for this epic tale – Jim, Mickser, Abraham, and the padre. I liked Jeremiah's version of events. He made it sound so daring. They listened with bated breath – about my plan to rub crushed grass into Jeremiah's face to make out he was jaundiced with a highly-contagious disease; about Jeremiah's quarantine in the black room; about the food I sneaked in for him; about how I helped him down the planks at the black gable; about Jeremiah putting as much distance as possible between himself and Shroid workhouse during the hours of darkness, spending his days hiding out in gripes and ditches; about how the third dawn found him exhausted and staggering towards an old wooden hayshed; about how his stomach squelched and his bare feet throbbed with cuts and bruises as he wrapped himself in hay and bedded down for the day; about how he fell into a deep sleep and was awoken by the prongs of a pitchfork.

As he spoke, Jeremiah's hand reached for his left shoulder. I knew he was feeling his *LX* – hadn't I held him down during the branding. He wasn't even aware that he was touching it – maybe it was a comfort thing.

The skeletal face of a farmer looked down, poised and ready to give the deadener. Jeremiah pleaded for his life. He promised he'd be on his way. He begged the farmer not to involve the peelers, that they'd only send him back to Longford – to the workhouse. The farmer didn't move a muscle. Jeremiah was sure it was the end. Two of the prongs dug into his neck. Eventually the farmer broke his silence. He asked Jeremiah what was his business in Portroe. Jeremiah had managed to run, walk, limp, and crawl all the way from Longford to County Tipperary by the light of three moons.

'You're a good man on your feet,' said the farmer, relaxing his pitchfork. 'Can you work as good as you walk?'

And so, Jeremiah had himself a job as a farmhand. He minded the few scrawny cattle and a hen coup while the farmer did most of the work on the land. But minding animals can be a tricky business – and a dangerous one – at the height of a famine. Jeremiah got to see the blight they had talked about in the workhouse – horrible black puss, that smelled to high heaven, oozing out of potatoes the family pig wouldn't eat. Then there was the constant flow of the walking dead. Whole families – parishes even – passed on the road near the farm. The men drunkenly led the way; the women keened and carried babes in their shawls.

The Tipperary farmer was married with one child – a boy of three, who was bad with dysentery. The woman of the house was kind. Jeremiah stayed in the hayshed. On Sundays they invited him in for whatever they could offer. He made the hayshed comfortable. With Jeremiah's help, the farmer kept body and soul together. The rent was paid on time and there was just enough to eat. They reared turf as well.

But the farmer's son was a grave concern. His deterioration was swift. One day, the landlord's agent showed up and was in the house for a long time. Jeremiah was spying through a crack in the hayshed wall. Later, the farmer explained what it was all about. The agent had given him the option of a paid passage to America. The landlord wanted to clear his lands, but wouldn't force the farmer from his holding. He told Jeremiah he wasn't going, that there was no way the child would survive the crossing. Jeremiah was relieved. The last thing he wanted was to be back on the run. That very same night things took a turn for the worse. The farmer's son died. The next day, the farmer informed Jeremiah that himself and the wife had been talking. Now that their son was gone to God, there was nothing for it only to take the landlord's offer. The place held too many reminders for them – too many harsh memories. The farmer thanked Jeremiah for all his help, but that's where it had to end between them.

Therefore, Jeremiah packed up the few belongings he had lying around the hayshed and got ready for the road. As he was leaving, he went into the house to say his goodbyes and wish them well in America. It was a mournful sight, even by Jeremiah's standards. The farmer cradled his dead baby's head, and rocked him as if he was sleeping. The wife dabbed her red eyes and coughed angrily, then wrapped some bread for Jeremiah's journey into the unknown. The family pig grunted, as if he knew this was goodbye. The poor little hoor, thought Jeremiah, he wouldn't be grunting for much longer.

And then came Jeremiah's moment of freak luck – the big break he had been awaiting all his life. The farmer's wife suggested they take Jeremiah with them to America. The landlord had made provision for a party of three and he had no knowledge of their son's death. Jeremiah could travel in his stead. The farmer agreed and Jeremiah found himself on the *Hope and Glory* a week later, sailing for the new world.

'And that's the story of how I beat the system and ended up here with you good people,' said Jeremiah to his captivated audience in McArthur's Saloon.

'What about the Tipperary farmer and his wife,' asked Father

Murtagh.

'They lived and worked around this city for a couple of years – odd jobs here and there. I used to have an apartment beside them. Then they headed west to try their hand at this new panning for gold business. That's the last I heard, God bless them,' replied Jeremiah.

'The salt of the earth,' whispered the padre.

'Amen to that, Father. Here's to them,' continued Jeremiah, gesturing with his drink, 'and here's to that man over there.'

I was embarrassed as all heads turned in my direction. Sometimes you'd be as well off playing the villain.

'Fill them up again, Mister McArthur, and make mine a brandy. I need something to warm me after the wetting I got below at the docks today,' said Jeremiah, undoing the buttons of his shirt to unhook a chain.

Then he told me to close my eyes and open my hand. When I looked again, I could hardly believe it. My dear late father's compass was attached to Jeremiah's silver chain.

'Do you remember this,' he said with a smile. 'You gave it to me just before I slid down the planks of the black gable.'

I remembered only too well.

'I was always going to keep it safe for you,' he added. 'But I never thought I'd get the chance to give it back.'

'Just as well,' I retorted, 'because any fella given a compass to travel east to Dublin and who then ends up in Tipperary is obviously better off without it.'

## Fifteen – Jack Fitzgerald

After the events of the King's Hall, Jim's old insecurities returned. He went about his business with the same caution he had displayed on the *Erin's Queen*. And, when I thought about it in the cold light of day, I couldn't have faulted him. I was reckless in my actions that night. Getting involved in the fight wasn't the best move I ever made. After all, we were fugitives from the long arm of British law – an arm long enough to reach the American side of the Atlantic Ocean. Jim was extra careful. He took the odd paint job here and there, eking out a few dollars now that Lady Jane Teale's money was spent. I still had my security job down by the docks – a guarantee when Napoleon was on duty. Jeremiah got loads of work in the dockyards too, once I assured Napoleon that his standard dollar-a-week subscription would be forthcoming.

At least Father Murtagh was managing his paranoia – and trying to manage Jim's too. When he wasn't blessing people or helping them out, he was over on our porch – swinging and telling Jim he'd have to snap out of it.

'You have to let it go,' the padre advised, 'all this suspicion will eat you up.'

He also claimed the King's Hall incident was a good thing. He said it showed that there could be harmony between persons of differing race and colour.

'Harmony between persons of different race and colour is one thing,' I pointed out, 'but harmony between persons of different race and colour in the middle of a hall full of mad Ulster buggers is quite another.'

'It got you back in the ring – where you belong,' said the padre. 'What are you going to do, hide away in the shadows for the rest of your life? It's time to let go and start living again. That young black boxer needs your help, Joseph. It's high time to stand up and be counted.'

In the true spirit of harmony, the padre sought out young Bartholomew and invited him to Ina Begley's apartments on Thompson Street. His full name was Bartholomew Campbell. He said he was living in New York for five years, but was raised in Louisiana. He explained how he needed two things – a proper job to support his sister, and a proper manager. His cornerman was just a neighbour who was doing him a favour.

'Logan haint no manager,' claimed Bartholomew, 'and he be the first to say so.'

I mulled it over, but I couldn't decide – especially with the padre giving me his *please do it* stare. So, producing a pen and a piece of paper, I asked Bartholomew to jot down his address and I'd get back to him.

'T'ain't no use,' explained Bartholomew, 'canst nether read or write, boss.'

So, telling him not to worry, I scribbled it down instead.

Surprise visits were not confined to Ina Begley's apartments. Below in Jonty's saloon, a tall moustachioed man walked through the swing-doors with the poise and grace of a ballroom dancer. His pressed blue suit flowed down his long limbs. A brown leather attaché bag, tucked underneath his arm, added to his air of importance. Jim Gorman's eyes stalked him all the way, as he hung his jacket on a stool and scanned the bar for service.

'Jabber, look lively,' warned Jim, as the man in the blue suit came towards us.

'I'm after forgetting it now,' said Mickser, who was telling myself and Abraham about an incident in the Spieler the night before. 'Jim Gorman, you've my head gone astray – fussing like an auld mother hen.'

I was delighted Mickser said so, because that was exactly what Jim was like – his cautiousness was becoming intolerable.

'Excuse me,' said the tall man in the blue suit, 'would Mister McArthur be anywhere in the vicinity?'

Suddenly, I was concerned myself. The ordinary man in the street didn't come into a public house spouting words like *vicinity*. Jonty was on duty, but had gone to the kitchen for fresh glasses.

'Who's asking,' said Jim nervously, and the tall man broke into a smile.

'No need to be alarmed,' he replied, reading Jim's worried face, 'I'm not the bogie man.'

'Well, in that case, he's in the back kitchen. He won't be a minute.'

Jonty caught sight of the blue-suited man and came storming back to the bar.

'Jack Fitzgerald, how the hell are you,' he hollered.

They embraced like they'd been to school together.

'So, you got my message,' asked Jonty, pulling out his own chair for his friend.

'I did to be sure,' replied Jack Fitzgerald. 'You told Malarkey's missus, and Malarkey's missus told Ted Ireland's people, and Ted Ireland's people told my secretary, and she told me. A couple of Irish guys, is it?'

'God bless you, Sister Concepta,' said Jonty. 'It just so happens that these are the very guys in question. Guys, meet Jack Fitzgerald – the famous union leader.'

Jack Fitzgerald dropped his attache bag on the counter and went around in a ring, meeting everyone in turn.

'I know you from somewhere,' he said, shaking my hand.

As long as it wasn't from the *New York Tribune* with a one-thousand-pound sweetener under the artist's impression, I didn't mind where he thought he knew me from.

'So, they're looking for the start,' he said to Jonty, as if we weren't there. 'No problem. I'll send one of my teamsters down to have a word with one of the railway bosses. A day or two at most. No point starting 'til Monday.'

Jack assured me that work on the line would be steady – not like the docks. It also paid more money. He wanted the padre on board too. He told us we'd be working in a gang – and he liked to keep his gangs close-knit. We'd be required to work regular hours mainly. But sometimes a nightshift was unavoidable. The work would need our full care and attention, especially when blasting was in full swing.

'You've the makings of a head-ganger,' he said to me and winked.

The real reason for Jack Fitzgerald's personal visit to Jonty's saloon was soon revealed. He wanted to make sure we all joined up to his union. It was his only condition of employment. We had no problem with that.

'Are you fellas looking for a certain type of worker,' I asked, remembering how Bartholomew was job-seeking and had the handicap of illiteracy to deal with. Fitzgerald seemed to know immediately what I was getting at.

'Are you kiddin' me, son,' he declared, glancing at Abraham's skullcap. 'Just because your friend here wears a yarmulke, does not mean he has no place at my table.'

So that's what Abraham's little cap was called.

'I'm a shopkeeper, but thank you all the same,' said Abraham.

'I was in Philly in thirty-five, part of the Catholic-Protestant co-operation to achieve better pay. We won – and it was no flash in the pan. The goodwill of that co-operation lasted a full four years, until the depression put everything under stress again. You could say I know what it's like to soldier with a certain *other* type of worker.'

'What about the blacks,' I said bluntly.

'What's on your mind, son,' asked Jack Fitzgerald, leaning back thoughtfully in Jonty's comfortable chair. 'Wait a darn minute, now I know where I saw you. You were cornering for a black fighter the other night in the King's Hall.'

Jim nearly fell off his stool.

'Yes, you're spot on, Mister Fitzgerald,' I admitted. 'The boy is strong and willing. I can vouch that he will pull his weight and more.'

I hopped down from my stool and had a word in his ear.

'You see, he has no education of any sort.'

'Say no more,' whispered Jack.

He then returned to a conversation he had started with Father Murtagh.

'You see, I can pick them out of a crowd,' he boasted, pointing a long finger in my direction. 'I knew this was the man for leading a rail gang. He has a thought in him. And that's very important when you're in charge of men. Bring the black kid along, and don't take any flak from anyone. We Irish have a lot of the same experiences and grievances as the blacks, stuff that should unite rather than separate. In spite of this, there are a lot of rumours going around – fears among the white workforce – that an end to slavery would cost the majority of them their jobs. And, I'm sorry to say, the railways are in it up to their necks with this tale. But not me. Change is good, and I don't care what colour or creed a guy is if he can get the job done. Tell your young black fighting friend to take his place and not be afraid to work shoulder to shoulder with his Irish brothers.'

Father Murtagh allowed himself a smile of satisfaction when he heard this.

'Mind you,' continued Jack Fitzgerald, fidgeting with a ginger ale, 'I'll take it he won't have any objection to joining my union. I'm on a mission, guys. I'm striving to make my New York Labour Trade Union – a subsidiary of the CLU – even bigger than the Textile Spinners' Union above in River Falls, Massachusetts. And I just don't want to make it bigger, I want to make it all-inclusive.'

'You've a job on your hands there,' said Jim Gorman, 'especially if what happened in the King's Hall the other night is anything to go by.'

'Yes, it's a heck of a job, son. But we've got to start somewhere. When I was a lad, the AFL union – that's the American Federations of Labour to you boys just off the boat – used to be one of the great Irish-American moorings around here. It was up there with family, neighbourhood, and Tammany machine politics. So why shouldn't my new union be a mooring too. And not just for the Irish, but for other ethnic groups and societies within this city. If America has taught us one thing, guys, it's that there's place and opportunity for all of its many diversities.'

It was easy to see why Jack Fitzgerald was so well respected. Here was a man who was dreaming outside the box, and daring to believe in that dream. He wasn't finished yet.

'There's a belief out there that because we're white, we're above reproach. Now that's an old imperial idea. Correct me if I'm wrong, but the Irish know different. We've been treated appallingly at home, by the British, as well as here, by the nativists – much worse than the Jews or the Swedes or the Italians. Therefore, how can we discriminate against our black brethren?'

'Amen to that. Offer your back to those who strike you, and your cheek to those who tear at your beard,' proclaimed Father Murtagh, not sounding much like the layman he was pretending to be.

'Exactly,' replied Jack, 'I like a man with a bit of religion. So, guys, there you have it. My aim is to build an inclusive union based on tolerance and respect. Every man in this room has a duty. We, as Irishmen, should be front and centre in seeking the emancipation of mankind. That is what our great leader, Daniel O'Connell, told us to do and that is what we, as standard-bearers for the free world, are expected to do. Emancipation of mankind means the emancipation of *all* mankind – black as well as white, Jew as well as Christian. So when you tell me of your young black fighter's plight, this becomes my plight and your plight. We must address this plight together.'

Abraham smiled and tapped his yarmulke. But the padre had something else on his mind.

'What about the Catholic Church? Below in Saint Pat's, the priests denounce the working unions to high heaven. Are you asking us to go against our clergy – the watchdogs of our morality?'

I could tell by Jack Fitzgerald's face that the padre's question did not sit well.

'Why should the clergy be the watchdogs of your morality? Why can't you be the watchdog of your own conscience and moral behaviour? Don't you see, son, that is exactly what they want. Down through the years, too many Irish-Americans have maintained a distance from what was termed *organized radicalism of labour*. They did so because of three things – their treasured association with the Democratic Party, their hostilities with ethnic groups of socialist persuasion, and opposition from the Catholic Church – the same Catholic Church that says division is a bad thing and difference should be embraced. The church talks the talk, but does it walk the walk? I can confidently say the Central Labour Union – which is labelled super-radical in today's world – embraces division and difference in a theoretical *and* practical way.'

It was seldom Father Murtagh was at a loss for words, but this was one such occasion. Jack Fitzgerald talked quick and to the point, but he also talked a lot of sense. His union wasn't just paying lip-service to the margins in society, it was delivering by actions.

Jack went over to his stool and searched in one of his jacket pockets. Producing a number of shiny button badges with yellow and black CLU lettering, he handed them to Jim, the padre and me. He asked us to display them prominently when we received our railway coats. He gave me a second badge for Bartholomew Campbell.

'You might as well take one, Mickser,' I suggested, 'you could do with the money, seeing as you're heading out to California.'

When Jack Fitzgerald heard this, he gave out a chuckle.

'Going prospecting are we,' he inquired, but Mickser turned away to drink his pint.

'I'll take one more for safekeeping,' I said, Jeremiah Figg very much in my thoughts.

'Don't forget guys, this button is a weapon for the classes – a badge of honour. And if you don't wear it with pride, then you are against it and all it stands for. That's the long and short of it.'

He finished his ginger ale and went around shaking hands again.

'Do you think Malarkey is throwing a mixture into the missus,' asked Jonty, returning with more drink.

'Who, Sister Concepta,' exclaimed Jack. 'God bless us and save us.'

'Stranger things have happened,' said Jonty, pretending to be all concerned, 'I heard he has half the broads in Tammany Hall in the family way.'

Jack Fitzgerald's face was a study of concentration. Then he burst out laughing as he took his suit jacket from the back of the stool.

'You're some kind of guy, Jonty McArthur, some kind of guy indeed.'

Jim Gorman, a grateful Bartholomew Campbell, a reluctant and ungrateful Mickser Burrows, Jeremiah Figg and myself were all signed up to Jack Fitzgerald's union before we ever worked a day. As head-ganger, I had to meet with railway officials to get a briefing. They concentrated on the fact that there was a certain amount of danger – like when nitroglycerine was being used in an explosion. Otherwise, it was fairly run-of-the-mill stuff. If anything, the nitroglycerine would provide us with a lively distraction from wheelbarrowing debris out of a rockface or shovelling ballast onto trailers.

The boys did everything right. They took Jack Fitzgerald's advice and attended union meetings. At one such meeting, the Central Labour Union had a *No Rent Battle for Ireland* banner emblazoned across the officials' table. After adjournment, there was a collection made for the land agitation in Ireland and the Evicted Families' Trust. This new way of life – or *Ireland abroad*, as Jim Gorman termed it – certainly was an eyeopener. Through meetings like these, I saw how things were done differently in America. Finances were in perpetual motion. Money was spent more liberally for the common good, especially for what were considered home causes, to garner fellowship and favour. There was no government intervention causing major delays. In Ireland, money – what little of it there was – was mainly put aside for rents. This money ended up across the water, being spent in the British economy. The other essentials – food, thatching, clothing and the like – were mostly got through bartering or in lieu of hard graft. Collections and other charities, especially government-based, spent ages tied up in what the *Freeman's Journal* liked to call *red tape*.

I noticed new customs too, like how railway gangs left drink-money behind the counter at Jonty's for their bosses or union delegates. After enquiring into this, I was strongly advised to follow suit. Failure to do so could have resulted in extreme hardship or a premature end to our contracts.

'What do you mean by extreme hardship,' I asked another ganger, a fella from Wexford by the name of Cullen.

'You wouldn't want to lose the protection of the union's heavies, especially from the organised attacks of the nativists,' he answered.

'What union heavies?'

'Ah, that's just it,' added Cullen. 'What the eye don't see, the brain don't question.'

So, on Friday evenings, I would organise a whip-around for the union – making sure my rail gang's name was in large print on the front of the envelope.

'I wonder would Jack Fitzgerald condone this sort of practice,' asked Father Murtagh, the first time I deposited my little collection with Jonty for safekeeping.

'I'm not planning on finding out, Father,' I replied. 'When you're in a position of responsibility, as you well know, it's always better to be safe than sorry.'

## Sixteen – All in a Day's Work

Our first assignment for Central Pacific Railroad was right in the heart in the city. It was beginner's luck really. A shortage of nitroglycerine meant that we spent the first fortnight packing ballast along rows of new sleepers, not ten minutes from Thompson Street. A lovely handy opener – that's how Mickser Burrows described it.

Our gang was very small in number – I've been part of bigger meitheals drawing turf from Lacken bog – so I asked the padre to join up. He refused, at first, going into preaching mode and citing a biblical parable – and how it could apply to him in his secret ministry.

'There was a master who was leaving his household to travel. He entrusted his properties to his servants, each in proportion to their abilities. He gave to one servant five talents, to another two, and to another one. On the master's return, the servant who had received five talents produced another five from his investments. The servant who had received two came forward with four from his enterprise. But the last servant came forward with his one talent. He gave it back to his master after admitting he had buried it for fear of losing it. The master was furious and threw him out of his household.'

'And what's that got to do with taking a job on the railway,' I asked.

'I do not want to be the third servant,' answered the padre, 'who buries his talent for fear of his master's reputation. Pray for me, Joseph, pray that I shan't be put to the test.'

I told him I studied the parable – Matthew twenty-five, verses fourteen to thirty – in Maynooth seminary back in eighteen twenty-two, and I wasn't trying to put him to the test. I also suggested he preach that parable to his landlady when she comes looking for her rent the following Friday evening and see how far it gets him.

So, my gang was growing by and by. The padre joined Jim, Jeremiah, Mickser, and Bartholomew – who was overjoyed to finally get steady work. It was still small compared to other railway gangs – with most between ten and a dozen or so workers. Central Pacific had many Chinese labourers, with Union Pacific Railroad catering primarily for European settlers. But we didn't mind throwing our lot in with Central.

'A day's pay is a day's pay, no matter who you're working for,' declared Jeremiah, and he was spot on.

The night before we started, Missus Begley arrived to the apartment with a crude-looking contraption.

'What is it,' asked Jim.

'My husband's old candle clock, Lord rest his soul. You boys might as well get the use out of it, now that ye have early hours to face into.'

Jim looked at me and shrugged. I'd never seen the like of it either.

'It's nice,' he said. 'But how on earth does it work?'

Missus Begley afforded herself a little smile of triumph. She liked it when someone, especially someone from the old country, marvelled at one of her possessions.

'Look here,' she said, pointing out a steel nail in the clock. 'The candle burns so far after a certain number of hours and then this nail becomes dislodged and falls into the tin, making a rattle that'll wake ye up.'

There was a lovely simplicity to it all. She trimmed the stem of the candle, checking a gauge to make sure the nail would be dropping at around five o'clock the next morning. Then she grunted a farewell and fled into the night. I've always wondered about women like Ina Begley – why they always felt the need to hide their inherent goodness within a cold, hard, exterior.

During our first working week, a young fella came into our canteen shed, shaking hands and wishing us all the best. He was to be our safety representative.

'I heard an explosion from where my own gang is working,' he said, pointing to some invisible place in the sky. 'Someone must have gotten their hands on a bit of the black powder. Be careful of that stuff, lads, it's terrible unpredictable.'

'You're Irish,' said Mickser.

'Well spotted,' returned the fresh-faced safety representative. 'Jim Brady's the name. But my friends call me Diamond.'

'You're too young to have your own gang,' the padre reckoned. 'You couldn't be long out of school.'

'Ah, I'm not as young as you think,' chirped Diamond. 'Don't let the blonde hair fool ya. I've been working on the railway this ten year now, got the start as a messenger boy in thirty-nine.'

None of us could believe that this slip of a lad was a head-ganger in his own right. Mickser Burrows, who had been washing down a sandwich, said *fair play* and extended his bottle of beer in Diamond's direction.

'No ale for me, thank you all the same,' said Diamond. 'I aim to get ahead in this life, and alcohol is not the way to go – not for me anyway.'

'I've seen it all now,' replied Jim. 'An Irishman who doesn't drink.'

'You bet I don't,' said Diamond proudly. 'If it wasn't for the drink wouldn't the Irish rule the world.'

Mickser drained the bottle in front of him.

'Rule the world! Why would we want to do that – so we can be hated, the way the English are hated,' replied Father Murtagh.

'Now Francis, you know it's not Christian-like to hate,' said Mickser, imitating the padre's voice as best he could.

When nitroglycerine was plentiful, we were always at the tunnels. So I'm glad to say we were the first gang to try out the new railway helmet. It had a safety lamp attached.

'This is just like the miners' lamp, the type invented by William Reid Clanny – one of our very own,' Jim Diamond Brady told us, twirling it about in his hands.

'Who,' said Mickser, 'never heard of the buck, riamh in mo shaol.'

'It's designed to prevent methane gas explosions,' added Diamond. 'No more paraffin lamps in the tunnels. But we'll also be using it to prevent getting our heads bashed in by flying rocks – so wear it at *all* times.'

One day, after blasting, something was happening at the far end of our tunnel. It was another gang excavating towards us.

'They must have been sent to give us a hand,' said the padre.

We could hear their pickaxes and shovels, but we couldn't see them. Both gangs inched closer as the day wore on. Eventually, the lamplight of their helmets pierced the cracks in the rockface. Shafts of daylight arrowed their way in from the besieged wall, and shadows were visible through the smoke and dust.

Ape echoed its way through the tunnel. As I stood up for a look through the gap, it could be heard again. *Ape.*

'Nigger Irish by the sound of them,' said a voice, as laughter rang out from behind a cluster of rocks.

'Is something funny,' said Mickser, in the direction of the laughing.

Then the voice piped up again.

'Hanging around with wee smokie.'

There was another chorus of laughter. Mickser was mad.

'Is that all ye've got, ye cowardly bastards. Come over here and show yourselves.'

The padre put a reassuring hand on Bartholomew's shoulder. Mickser lifted a shovel and issued a threat that heads were about to roll. I told him to cool off, that I'd see to it.

'Who's your ganger,' I asked, approaching the shadowy figures on the far side of the rubble.

A monster of a man in a dirty shirt came forward.

'That wae be me,' he said, squaring up. 'It seems we have a problem, Irish. Me and my boys dinnae sign up to work with no smokie contraband. We have a policy. We don' share our work, nae our pay, with negros. So how will you explain that un to Fitzpatrick an' his union buddies?'

His Scottish voice reminded me of Walter Pollach.

'You tell him, Kelso. We won' work on nae job with nae monkey,' said one of his crew.

I had heard quite enough. I walked the few steps closer. I was now eyeball to eyeball with my opposite number.

'Fitzpatrick *is* the one who hired him,' I pointed out. 'And if you don't believe me, then ask him yourself. Bartholomew is staying with us. If you don't like it – tough. Now get out of my sight.'

The rest of the gang gathered around their boss, awaiting his response. I'll admit I was a bit concerned. There was at least ten of them and they all looked like they could handle themselves.

Jim Gorman, Father Murtagh, Jeremiah Figg, and Mickser

Burrows – with his shovel still hovering in mid-air – moved forward to flank myself and Bartholomew.

An anxious silence followed. We looked into each other's eyes. I held a determined stare. My opposite number wasn't concerned. Both gangs waited with pent-up adrenaline, ready to let loose at a second's notice. This was the moment of truth. There was no going back – not an inch. If we stood down now, we were finished. Then, Kelso raised his right hand.

'At ease, boys,' he said. 'We'll leave this alone, *for now*. After all, we wonnae want these newbies blottin' their copybooks so soon.'

He broke into a laugh. He was so close I could smell the liquor off his breath. Then his gang started to laugh too. I didn't move a muscle, and neither did my boys, until Kelso and his team had turned around and walked out of the tunnel.

'Good man,' whispered Father Murtagh, 'I think that's deserving of a beer.'

I didn't say it, but I was proud of my gang. They didn't take a backward step, despite being outnumbered by a crowd of bullies. There's a lot to be said for that.

That evening in Jonty's, the hottest topic of discussion was how we had faced down Kelso and his mates. Backs were slapped and hands were shaken. Jim said Kelso reminded him of the howler monkey of South America – all talk and very little balls.

But not everyone was in celebratory mood. A young Stetson-wearing Texan, whose father hailed from the old west – the Ballinasloe of the eighteen twenties – slammed down his fist and declared openly that he didn't mind most folk, and he'd stand up for pretty much anyone, apart from niggers. This was a surprise. The Texan was a regular in Jonty's and we always knew him to be quiet-spoken and pleasant. In a freak coincidence, Mickser

Burrows knew his father when they were growing up in Galway. Determined to copper-fasten his view, the Texan sized up Abraham – who wasn't long after turning the key in his shop door – and ploughed on.

'Shucks, I could even side with a Jew. Although my daddy told me they were all crooks and poisoners.'

Mickser looked up from his glass of whiskey.

'Your daddy didn't tell you much about having manners.'

'Or butting into other people's conversations,' added Jim.

'Hey, don't you guys dare round on me. After all, I'm not shootin' my gob all over the bar about how great I was at work today. No Irish tinker is going to tell me off about my manners.'

Not for the first time that day, I saw the whites of Mickser's knuckles. He placed the whiskey carefully on a napkin, alighted his stool, and headed in the direction of the young Texan.

'Easy, Mickser, we don't want no trouble,' said Jonty.

Mickser waved his hand to ease Jonty's fears, then sat down beside the Texan – taking him by his shiny bolo tie and pulling him close.

'Who told you I was a tinker? Was that your daddy too?'

The Stetson hat bobbed up and down.

'But your daddy didn't say it to my face. This isn't Ireland. Over here, it's every man for himself. Listen well, my young bucko. I'm no tinker. I'm a settled traveller who's making an honest living by the sweat of my brow. Insult me again, or any of my friends for that matter, at your own risk.'

'Okay, you asked for it,' said the Texan, attempting to get his legs under him.

Then, before the fight could get off the ground, a hand reached in and loosened Mickser's grip on the young man's necktie.

'It's like Mister McArthur said, we don't want any more trouble,' said Father Murtagh. 'Be on your way, young fellow. We've had enough drama for one day.'

The Texan had a staring match with Mickser before taking the padre's advice and calling it a night.

'He should be ashamed of himself,' barked Jim.

'Leave it so,' said the padre, 'he's not to blame.'

'I suppose,' replied Jim, 'his father has a lot to answer for.'

'No, not his father either. Society is the problem. Partiality is the problem.'

'Bullshite, Father. Partiality, my arse. Boldness, more like.'

'No, James, no. I disagree with such an assumption. It's not boldness. Chapter ten, verses thirty-four and thirty-five of Acts tells us: *God shows no partiality. But in every nation whoever fears Him and works righteousness is accepted by Him*. Humans show partiality. Every nation is partial to its own ends. We have used it as a survival technique for centuries. Even Stone Age man relied on a form of partiality as a tool for essential living – he wasn't about to let his tribe get swallowed up or lose out to another. Now, take the ordinary Irish people. We're under British rule and we resent this something awful. If we were under Irish rule, we'd be no better off. But the resentment would be easier to live with because the mistreatment would come from within our own tribe. So, with regard to the young Texan's attitude, we haven't moved on from Stone Age man's outlook all that much because, in truth, we can't. It's human nature to use partiality in order to get on and in order to suppress.'

'Merciful hour, there he goes with Stone Age man again,' I said.

'Well, I always say if you want to know the base nature of human beings,' continued the padre, 'you have to look at the way Stone Age man conducted himself.'

'How much wine have you had to drink, Francis,' said Jonty

McArthur, 'you're talking through your ass.'

'No Jonathan, that's just the thing, I'm talking facts. Take the Penal Laws as another example.'

'What are those,' asked Abraham.

'A set of seventeenth-century laws passed by the British. They criminalised the practicing of Catholicism. They also barred Catholics from holding public office, voting, or owning land. Becoming a priest was punishable by death. What do you think of that?'

'In Charleston, South Carolina – where my parents are from – they burned down our synagogue before,' said Abraham.

'Was there anybody in it at the time,' asked Jim.

'No,' replied Abraham.

'Thank God for small mercies.'

Jim Gorman winked across at me before adding his own two pence worth.

'At least Cromwell wasn't on the job.'

Just as we were about to crack open the old Cromwellian chestnut, Jonty produced a copy of the *New York Tribune*.

'Take a look at that, guys,' he said ruefully. 'The old country is gone to the dogs.'

I watched Jim's smile disappear as he read about the awful conditions and the estimated death toll in the Irish countryside. His face went blood red.

'Trevelyn,' I said.

'He's doing their work well,' whispered Jim. 'Whoever heard of exporting grain at a time like this.'

Jim went awful quiet after that. We all did. No doubt, he was thinking of his wife and daughter – consumed by the thought of having left them to face the famine and the Crown. It was time to lighten the mood.

'Okay, smart-arse,' I said to the padre. 'Seeing as you know so much about the Bible and Stone Age man, answer me this one. In the Garden of Eden, Eve wore a fig leaf to cover her modesty. What did Adam wear?'

'He obviously wore a fig leaf too,' replied the padre.

'Wrong. He wore a hole in it.'

The craic was back on – full steam ahead.

## Seventeen – California, Here I Come

Mickser going away was not something which excited me first time around. I don't say that begrudgingly – it just felt all wrong. But the padre and Jim were having great fun. And it was like a holiday to Missus Begley. She was organising among the neighbours like it was some sort of week-long carnival. I thought, by the appearance of her, that the soft-spoken Missus Burrows – who didn't look at all comfortable with any of Ina's shenanigans – was going to call the whole thing off. Abraham was down in McArthur's Saloon every night, curling his fingers through his payot and reliving the good old days. It wouldn't be like him; normally, he didn't drink during the week.

'I can't believe he's doing it. But, in fairness to the man, he said he'd do it. It was one of the first things he ever said to me.'

If I heard Abraham say those lines once, I heard them fifty times. But, I suppose, I could understand. Abraham was sad. His oldest buddy – the man who made him and the Ishmel family feel welcome when they plucked up the courage to open their own business in an Irish part of town – was going away.

'I remember the first time he entered the store – on the very first day we opened our door. He came in for a couple of woodbines and small bottle of whiskey. He was on his way to a job that morning,' lamented Abraham, shaking his head as if it was some dramatic event he was retelling. 'What am I going to do without him?'

The question on my mind was not what Abraham was going to do without Mickser, but what was I going to do without him.

My railway gang was small enough as it was. Mickser made up the half dozen. Abraham was running a shop – a grocery store, as he called it. He was his own boss. All he had to do was employ someone to work the pencil and stack the goods. I was running a finely-tuned operation. My boss was some snotty-nosed git in a suit and tie, a number-cruncher who drew red lines through names when they failed to reach his quota. He didn't care about me, or the five others I could trust to blast and load. Without Mickser, I'd be forced to seek outside help. And the last thing I wanted was a stranger in my crew.

But the jackpot had been struck. Two weeks on the railway and Mickser was already a new man. He was a regular swell – as Breda would say – with more money than Zachary Taylor. If I'm honest, I advised against it. I didn't like the idea of Mickser heading to the Spieler on a Friday after work. I told him to go home and see his wife first. Three dollars and fifty was hard earned – too hard earned to be spent all in the one turn. Three dollars and fifty would get more appreciation in Missus Burrows' bib apron than it would in Elsa's. Not that Elsa wore aprons, but the prettiest little petticoats ever to drape a pair of hips. She dealt the cards and poured the whiskey. The players got drunk on the smell of her perfume. Her touch was so light, her fingers so nimble. She could hold you in her spell all night – if you had the money to stay that long.

It had to happen sooner or later. That's just the law of averages. Mickser was a good card player. And all the ingredients were in the mix that night – money, ambition, greed, testosterone, adrenaline, and a good-sized dollop of lady-luck. Finally, she shone for Mickser and California beckoned. At long last, it was off to pan for gold with James W. Marshall in Sutter's Mill.

Missus Begley's going-away party for Missus Burrows was organised for a Saturday evening. Jim and I went in early. The padre said he would join us as soon as he got home. Because he was working on the railway, the weekends were all he had for his secret ministry. Saturdays were reserved for hearing confessions and helping out the soup-kitchen staff down in the Points. If a body received forgiveness and nourishment on the eve of the sabbath, it was more likely to nourish its soul with the Body of Christ the following day. The padre's philosophies were simple and wise.

You'd hardly think a party was about to break out. There was nobody in the bar – not even a barkeep. All the noise came from the snug. Then Jonty appeared, plonking a tray on the counter and reaching for two bottles of stout.

'All the fun is out in the lounge,' he said. 'Those are some kinda gals to tell a yarn.'

Looking through the gap in the bar, I spotted Missus Begley. She was having a whale of a time, laughing her head off. Missus Burrows was there too, hidden beneath a headscarf. Jonty said we should go around and join them.

'Merciful hour, a snug! I was never in a snug in my life,' I said, 'I'm not about to start into them now.'

'Here, guys, you've got to try these buns,' said Jonty, pointing to the tray. 'Abraham's missus made them.'

Jim picked up a triangle of pastry and had a bite.

'Where's Mickser,' I asked Jonty, 'he's hardly in the snug as well?'

'No, I haven't seen him,' answered Jonty, 'but his missus is out there.'

'I see that. There's a first for everything.'

'She's not drinking, only leaving in the trays with Missus Ishmell.'

'Is it not her party as well as Mickser's?'

'I only serve the drink, Jabber,' answered Jonty, nodding his head in agreement. 'I leave the questions to those better qualified.'

Jim devoured the bun and had another.

'They're not buns,' he muttered with his mouth full, 'they're pastries. You have to try them. They're delicious.'

'Rugelach, that's the name of them,' added Jonty, 'a Jewish delicacy. Try the fruit one, it's even better than the chocolate.'

Jim took Jonty's advice and agreed that the fruit rugelach was to die for. Then he tried to get me to have one.

'If I want a bun there's an eating-house across the road,' I answered. 'I'm thirsty, not hungry. Where on God's earth is Mickser Burrows?'

Abraham arrived in. He looked sad again.

'My compliments to your good lady wife,' gushed Jim. 'These pastries would melt in your mouth.'

'Oh, the rugelach,' said Abraham, managing a smile. 'Nice, aren't they. Try the chocolate, it's even better than the fruit.'

'God give me strength, will ye quit about the buns. Abraham, any sign of Mickser on your travels?'

Jeremiah and Bartholomew arrived in. Jeremiah made straight for the rugelach. Bartholomew ordered their drinks.

'Lemonade,' exclaimed Jonty. 'I don't sell lemonade in this bar. If it's lemonade you're after, you'd be better off in the snug.'

'Oh, give him a bottle of porter,' said Jeremiah. 'I know he's in training, but the one won't hurt him.'

Bartholomew glanced nervously in my direction as Jonty poured out two bottles of stout. He was well aware of my feelings on alcohol – how it had destroyed many a promising fighter. We were boxing again in the Arms Hotel at the end of the month. The last thing I wanted, after what happened at the Offaly County dance in the Imperial, was to leave another local hotel with my tail between my legs. I needn't have worried. Bartholomew made his way across and assured me that he would only have the one. I asked him had he seen Mickser on his way over from Rivington Street. He said he hadn't.

'Did you see any sign of him,' I asked Jeremiah.

'Who, the padre?'

'No, *Mickser*. It's that fecker's party and he's not even here yet.'

'We came straight from Rivington Street,' said Jeremiah, 'no sign of him anywhere. Hey, Bertie, try out these buns. They're delicious.'

'Rugelach,' I pointed out, 'a Jewish recipe. And you take it easy with the eating, Bartholomew. I want you nice and trim for the fight. We're not taking this Gonzalez boy for granted. He was undefeated in Mexico before he got here.'

Jonty arrived back from the snug and said that Sister Concepta was next door. She was representing Jack Muldoon, who was otherwise detained. She also wanted to know what everyone was having to drink – courtesy of Mister Ted Ireland.

'Malarkey, detained? He must be in jail,' replied Jim.

'God help the warders,' I said.

Father Murtagh arrived in.

'Ah, goodie, rugelach. Jonty, you're spoiling us.'

'How did you know that,' asked Jim.

'We studied the cuisines of other religions at the seminary,' answered the padre.

No wonder the Irish clergy are like pigs at a fair.

'Any sign of Mickser on your travels,' I asked. 'He's the only one not at his own going-away party.'

'Yes, I saw him on my way in the door,' returned the padre. 'He's gone into the Spieler to say his goodbyes. Elsa was out on the street waiting for him. She's going to treat him for old time's sake. He said he'd be over in a couple of minutes.'

'Why didn't you go in with him?'

'Not a chance, Joseph. You won't catch me in that den of iniquity.'

'Or at least wait for him outside.'

'He's not a child,' continued the padre. 'And it's not a surprise party. We'll miss him off the railway. He's a real go-getter when he's not on the sauce.'

'There you go again with your new American words – *go-getter* indeed. This concubine of yours is teaching you well.'

'I beg your pardon, Joseph Farrell. That is a scurrilous remark and one you will retract please. If you mean Breda, I haven't seen her in weeks. I'll also have you know that she is no man's concubine, least of all a man of the cloth. Just because she spurned your advances, doesn't mean you have to take it out on me.'

Three large bottles of stout and two trays of rugelach later, there was still no sign of Mickser.

'Come on Jim,' I said, 'let's get into that den of iniquity and see what's going on.'

The Spieler was quiet and tense. Elsa sat at the main poker table, looking beautiful. She brushed away her flowing blonde locks and showed her pearly whites as we entered. Then she weaved her magic with a deck of cards, skilfully shuffling and splitting it in two. She lifted her drink.

'Skol.'

On her left – closest to the bar – sat a cowboy, with hair as long as Elsa's. On her right –closest to the door – sat Mickser, a study of concentration. He lifted his shot glass.

'Slainte.'

The other tables were empty. All games had been forgotten. A crowd gathered around Elsa like moths to a beautiful lamp. There was an awful lot of money on the table, as well as an awful lot of empty shot glasses.

'There's a few nice crinoline dresses knocking about,' quipped Jim, 'mind how you go, Jabber.'

You mistake a man for a woman once in your life and you're never allowed forget it. I wouldn't dignify Jim's jibe with a response.

'That must be DP,' I whispered, nodding towards the cowboy sitting opposite Mickser.

'How do you know,' asked Jim.

'A good railway ganger is intuitively aware of his surrounds,' I said, rehashing what my young, snotty-nosed, boss told me at my briefing.

'*Intuitively*, if you don't mind. The priests' education again,' Jim grumbled.

I'd never seen this DP in my life, but I saw the initials on the saddlebag of a chestnut Arabian tied at the railings. The lady working the bar popped the corks from two bottles of stout and slid two empty glasses across the counter. She was also engrossed in the game. Elsa placed the deck face-down and beckoned the bar. Merciful hour, the whiskey was free! That meant only one thing – it was no friendly game of cards. This was a big one.

'Raise you fifty,' said DP the cowboy.

'Fifty,' whispered Jim. 'Did I hear him rightly?'

'I'll see you there,' replied Mickser. 'And I'll raise you fifty more.'

The cowboy touched his hat like he was swatting a fly. He tilted his head and threw back a shot of whiskey.

'Buttermilk,' he said, and licked his lips. 'I'll see that. But will you see this?'

He put his hand in his right trouser pocket and whipped out a handful of notes. Then he gathered whatever he'd left on the table. The count began.

'One hundred and ten, one hundred and fifteen dollars, and twenty-five cents.'

Mickser stared a long time at his cards. Then he took a sharp breath.

'Hit me,' he said to Elsa, and she poured the whiskey.

'Mickser,' cried Jim.

'Whisht,' I said.

I wouldn't have minded hitting Mickser too – a swift kick up the arse to knock a bit of sense into him. But there was nothing we could do now. And there was no point in embarrassing him from the casino floor. It was simply up to Mickser.

I didn't like it. I couldn't see DP's face, but Mickser didn't look confident. He finally nodded at Elsa.

'Ara, it'd be a shame not to see them,' he said.

All eyes were fixed on Mickser's every move. Even Elsa's gorgeous smile went unnoticed. He gathered the rest of his loot – the money he had won for California – in a heap.

'I'm all in,' he admitted.

Elsa did a quick stocktake.

'Four hundred and thirty-two dollars, fifty-five cents,' she declared in a soft Swedish accent, before piling it all into the centre of the table.

'Four hundred and thirty-two dollars,' gasped Jim.

'And fifty-five cents,' I added.

Merciful hour! Just shy of two and a half *years* pay on the railway!

'You first,' said DP, and Mickser slowly turned over his hand.

Three kings, a ten and a four.

'Three kings,' panted Jim, 'great hand, great hand.'

'It's only a great hand if the cowboy can't better it,' I whispered.

Jim was right though. It was a great hand. Well, a good enough hand at any rate. Besides the sixth of January – on the feast of the Epiphany – it was rare enough to see three kings together. But the danger was still there. Where were the aces? And there was always the slim chance of a flush or four-of-a-kind. It was the moment of truth and DP knew it. He stroked his stubble and looked slowly around the room. Finally, I caught his face. It didn't tell me much. Jim and I were fit to burst with nerves.

'Your cards, sir,' said Elsa.

You could hear a pin drop. DP arranged his cards in a neat stack, then placed them face-down.

'Show your hand, Denman.'

That's what the D stood for. So, I was probably right in thinking the chestnut Arabian, tied up at the water trough, was belonging to him. Elsa got a start. Instead of showing his hand, DP pulled out a Belgian Pinfire revolver from under the table and pointed it at her. I knew it was a Belgian Pinfire because I'd seen one in a bunker belonging to the Mostrim Ribbonmen.

'Take your purty little hands off the money,' he said, as calmly as if he was asking for another drink.

He turned around and looked at us.

'Hey, you,' he said to the bar waitress, 'git out from behind thar and bring one of those sacks with you.'

She did as she was told. He instructed her to fill the sack. He stood up slowly with the gun trained on Elsa.

'Now, anybody so much as farts and she gits it.'

He moved over to where Jim and I were seated.

'You see, I'm fixin' to think these good old boys were a scoutin'' for thar buddy,' he growled, and I was wishing the waitress would hurry up with the sack.

Then, he thrust his bristled chin in Jim's face.

'I heard you a hollerin' his name.'

Finally, the waitress had the full four hundred and thirty-two dollars and fifty-five cents stuffed inside the sack. He snapped it from her and took one last turn at pointing the gun around the room. Elsa started to cry and he told her to shut up her babblin'. He ordered the rest of us to go behind the counter. Just before he departed, he turned to Mickser and tipped his hat.

'Much obliged, Irishman. You know what they say – everybody's luck runs out in the end.'

Then he was gone. And when I looked after him, so was the chestnut Arabian with the DP saddlebag.

## Eighteen – Breakfast at Jonty's

The war cry of the summer. Long hard hours during the week, and on a Saturday – breakfast at Jonty's. Of course, breakfast at Jonty's had very little to do with the first and – some would say – most important meal of the day. It was our code for an all-night booze-up and a tequila at sunrise – a practice which Father Murtagh spoke out against vehemently.

The padre had nothing personal against alcohol, or anyone using it to have a good time. As he rightly pointed out, Jesus supplied gallon-loads of the finest wine to the wedding guests at Cana – and they already half-steamed at the time. The partaking of alcohol was a good thing, he conceded, when consumed in moderation. He admitted that he too was partial to an occasional dram of Frank Phelan's Bordeaux red. But lately, the padre argued, since Jonty McArthur introduced this new Canadian beer, moderation had gone flying out the window.

'For the last time, it's not Canadian. It was founded by John Labatt from County Laois,' Jonty pointed out.

'He was in Canada at the time,' replied the padre. 'Therefore, it's Canadian beer. Labatt's brewery is in Canada, not Ireland.'

Wherever the beer was brewed, nobody could argue that we weren't stone mad for it. The pints of stout were cast aside. This new beer transformed McArthur's Saloon from an ordinary low-brow establishment into the land of milk and honey. We spent every day of rest in Jonty's, downing Labatt's. Except for Jim Gorman. He gave Labatt's a wide berth, reminding me more than once that it was far from Labatt's we were when lapping poteen out of Micheal Mooney's still on the old boreen in Lacken. Jim stuck steadfastly to the bottle of stout, and a drop of the stiffener when the tank was getting full.

The padre made it part of his secret ministry to return myself and the rest of the crew to the practice of moderation. He was determined also that enough time would be set aside for God and Saint Pat's on a Sunday. There was even an attempt to abolish breakfast at Jonty's, and to reserve Saturday mornings for the Society of Friends in its stead. He recruited several of our compatriots to donate a half-day to the charity mission, offering it up in recognition for what the Quakers were doing in Ireland.

'The Quakers did it decent,' Father Murtagh contended, 'and they didn't hold a bowl of soup under our noses until we signed up to them either.'

Jim Gorman gave a helping hand one Saturday. He was going full pelt, spooning out hot drinks to those who wandered in off the streets. He spotted the ginger head at the back of the crowded hall. Dropping his ladle, he raced down to confront the man who had been spying on him since we sailed from Dun Leary on the *Erin's Queen*. But by the time he had reached the back of the hall, through a crowd gathered for the lunchtime rush, the ginger man was nowhere to be seen. Jim ran outside and into the adjoining street. He searched frantically in shops and behind stalls. But yet again the *ghost with the red hair* – as Father Murtagh once christened him – had eluded Jim Gorman and left him chasing shadows.

Despite his paranoia, Jim was beginning to settle into his new life. He loved America. He loved the railway – especially the security of working with Central Pacific. Take Fridays for instance. In the beginning, Fridays brought back the bitter memories of payday at Cranley House – the inconvenience of having to form a line for hours on end. And the humiliation of the counting room, with Walter Pollach and his oath of allegiance to

Victoria Regina. We had to beg for our wages. Jim had no such worries on the railway. On a Monday morning, I simply filled out our timesheets for the previous week and brought them to the booking clerks' office. The following Friday, I'd collect six neatly-folded pay packets to be distributed among my gang. Easy-peasy, japaneasy!

'Sugrue would have loved life here,' Jim once said with a rueful smile.

'Imagine the railway offering him an extra half-dollar if he'd declare his love for Brittania,' I quipped, before winking at Jonty as he lined up the bottles of Labatt's.

'This Sugrue, he must have been some kinda guy,' returned Jonty.

'In all seriousness, I'm sorry for Sugrue and his generation,' continued Jim. 'They knew nothing about a country like this, only injustice and hardship at the hands of those British bastards.'

The Hibernian box did the rounds on Friday evenings. I always thought of Sugrue – wondering where he was at that precise moment and what was he doing – as it circled the room and left for the snug.

It may have been on his secret-ministry agenda, but the padre wasn't keeping Jonty's breakfast club much of a secret. One Saturday morning, we received visitors. Breda Nayle and her mates showed up, looking for Frankie – as they called him. He came in the door behind them, so they obviously had it all arranged. I turned my back, still feeling a bit sore from Breda's snub at the dance. I heard her telling Jim that she taught English language classes at night-school, to supplement her career as a struggling actress. Actress, my arse, I remember thinking – she'd want to learn how to act like a lady, and not some scruff from Tin Pan Alley. She claimed teaching was the easiest job in the world and very much a labour of love. Her students hailed from

Germany, Poland, Sweden, Italy, and Lithuania in Russia. They were a motivated lot – English being the language of municipal employment, politics, the police, the Church, trade unions, and all sorts of other upwardly mobile work. But the Irish attended too – particularly the famine Irish from the western seaboard, those who spoke nothing but gaelic. I had heard enough.

'Who are you calling the *famine Irish*,' I snapped.

'The recent Irish immigrants,' she retorted, without so much as an idea of what I was getting at.

'Us, in other words.'

'Yes,' she said, 'why, does that offend you?'

There was no point in talking to her any further.

She wanted the padre, who was about to head for the docks, to give her students a talk on the Catholic religion. Of course, Jim felt obliged to tell her all about Pope Pius IX and his new constitution. I know what I'd have told her. And I'd have liked her to apologise for her use of the term *famine Irish*.

At first, Jonty didn't know whether to apply the daytime rule or not. They were, after all, young ladies! But they were also friends of the padre. In the end, he told them he would serve them – but preferred if all self-respecting females would retire to the comfort of the lounge to sip their sherries.

'Just as well we're not self-respecting then, Grandad,' said Janey, the one with the red galluses, 'I might just take a pee.'

The hairs on Jonty's eyebrows stood out with pure temper.

'Who are you trying to impress,' he roared.

'The *comfort* of the lounge – o' the *safety* of the lounge. I'm getting a very patriarchal vibe here,' said Breda to her mates, 'I think this bottle-washe' wants us out of sight and out of mind. Don't forget to kowtow at the doo', girls.'

Despite failing to understand half of what she was saying, that was the last straw for Jonty.

'Okay, you and your girlfriends – ye're out of here,' he shouted, waving his tea towel like a matador's cape. 'Come on, no toilets, no lounge either. Out the door with ye.'

'Can we at least have ou' drinks first,' asked Catherine, 'now that we've paid fo' them.'

'I don't give a continental – out!'

Of course, the padre had to be the knight in shining armour.

'Please, Jonathan, forgive the impudence,' he begged, positioning himself in front of Breda.

'Well, excuse me, but I must demu',' said Breda. 'I can speak fo' myself. I don't need a man to forgive me my failings, thank you very much.'

'Breda, don't do this,' implored the padre. 'Be nice now. Act like a lady in front of the gentlemen.'

'Oh, now we're getting somewhere,' she replied, egged on by Catherine and Janey. 'Now we're seeing Frankie in all his true colours. If it's a lady you want, then I'll act like a lady fo' you. I'll act just like a lady fo' the next boy who enters this establishment.'

'Be nice,' repeated the padre.

'Don't try me,' snarled Breda.

The swing-doors went again. In walked Jeremiah, fresh from a dip in the Campbells' bathtub, his blonde hair racked in the old Brutus style and his button nose shining. He was yawning as he approached the bar. Breda ambushed him from behind, planting a big, sloppy, kiss on his mouth. The poor gossan nearly fell out of his standing. He looked punch-drunk, like a man who had just gone three rounds with James Yankee Sullivan.

'How does Frankie – your ex-boyfriend – like that,' quipped Janey.

'*Ex-boyfriend*,' exclaimed Jim Gorman, astonished by this revelation.

'Ex-boyfriend,' questioned Jeremiah, who was firmly rooted to the spot. 'You must have got it wrong, miss. This man is a pr…'

I got my hand around Jeremiah's mouth in the nick of time. If I had known that Breda knew already, I wouldn't have bothered.

'What's going on,' asked Catherine, coming back from the *latrine* – as she called it. 'What's the big secret?'

'Nothing at all,' replied Jim.

'What was that young guy saying, before you so hurriedly shut him up?'

'Em, he was just saying, well… he was just talking bullshite. He's badly shook after the kiss,' I explained.

'He was just saying how Francis here is such a prized pain in the ass,' stated Breda, before gripping Jeremiah by the collar and planting another kiss on his recovering lips.

It was a passionate kiss, and it seemed to go on for ages. I, for one, was glad to take comfort in my drink. Janey pulled nervously at her galluses and Catherine bit on her bottom lip. Jim and Jonty looked on like two dummies.

But Breda wasn't concerned with Jeremiah. Instead, she looked longingly into the eyes of Father Murtagh. She searched for hope, or even a spark of jealousy. It was a look the padre couldn't bear. He turned away and faced the counter.

'Forget about it,' she sniffled, making a beeline for the door. Tomboy Janey and the statuesque Catherine trailed in her wake. Poor Jeremiah stumbled to the bar, intoxicated before a drop of the good stuff had passed his quivering lips.

Breakfast continued with a group of surveyors, who were working on a line in the Harlem district. They mistook the silence, in the wake of Breda's departure, for a falling out.

'It's too early in the morning for a row,' said one.

'Maybe, but not for a drink,' joked his buddy, overjoyed at having stumbled upon an early house.

They started poking fun when they discovered we had joined Fitzgerald's Central Labour Union.

'Why did ye go and do that,' quipped the fella from west Kerry, 'surely ye know that the only real union worth joining is the one in here – the Irish Drinkers' Union. Nobody for miles around would dare say a word against it.'

Another elderly railway surveyor – a fella they called *Old-timer* – endorsed this notion. When Bartholomew Campbell came through the swing-doors, he took a position beside Jeremiah at the other end of the bar.

'There's another railwayman,' Jonty declared. 'Ye must be having a convention in here today.'

The surveyors looked at each other when they heard this. They couldn't hide their surprise. Old-timer extended a thinly-veiled warning.

'A word to the wise for you Longford guys. Look around you. Now, tell me, what do you see?'

'A bunch of fellows who are on the drink much too early, and who are old enough to know better,' said the padre.

The railwaymen had a laugh at this.

'And two fellows drinking on their way to work who should know better,' the padre concluded.

'Yeah, besides all that,' continued Old-timer. 'I'll tell you what you should see. You guys should see a delicately-balanced operation. It's based on Irishness – types of Irishness – and it relies on a ring of trust. Once you're inside it, this ring of trust has its advantages. But be careful not to break the ring – you do not want to be on the outside, looking in. And believe me, you won't get as much as an hour's work sweeping a platform if you find yourselves on the outside. I'm not just talking about the railway.

Take the police department as another example. Since it was set up in forty-five, Tammany and its ruling-class have been reserving it for the Scots-Irish Protestants. Railway work is for the bog-standard Irishman. I strongly advise you to respect that and leave darkies out of it.'

I didn't reply. As his friend had already pointed out, it was much too early for a row. Old-timer gave another glance at Bartholomew, then swallowed his whiskey. He touched my shoulder as he got up to leave.

'My old man came to this country in his bare feet. I'm glad he's not here to see this. Take a little advice from one head-ganger to another – ditch the negro. There are plenty of young guys, fresh off the boat, only crying out for a day's work.'

I couldn't keep my silence after that. I just had to give him something to mull over on his way out to Harlem.

'That negro, as you call him, is a good friend of mine. He has done nothing wrong. On the contrary – he's always on time, hardworking, obliging, and good-humoured. He's a joy to work with,' I said out loud, so Bartholomew as well as the rest of Jonty's customers could hear.

'And he goes above and beyond the call of duty while he's at it,' added Jim, also out loud, 'and we wouldn't swap him for the world.'

'Come on Kerry Joe,' said Old-timer. 'We've more to be doing than spending our time in the company of wog-lovers.'

'He's not a wog. He's a human being like the rest of us. His name is Bartholomew Campbell,' announced Jonty, 'and his money is as good, in my bar, as anyone else's. Now, gentlemen, there's the doors. Don't let them hit ye on the way out.'

That was a breakfast at Jonty's to remember. After the surveyors had stormed off, who should stumble through the swing-doors but two young men from our neck of the woods. They were new in town, relieved to be finally set free from the *Oliver Cromwell* after three days of quarantine in the bay. There was no plan, Mel told us. He simply packed up his tools, walked off White's plantation, and took a ramble on one of Bianconi's coaches – the whole way to the ship in Queenstown.

'Don't tell me,' said Father Murtagh, who still hadn't left for the docks, 'you fellows are from south Longford – somewhere like Tashinney or Kenagh.'

The young men were astounded at the accuracy of the padre's guess. They wanted to know how he had come to such a reckoning.

'Because I heard you using the word *ramble*. It's distinctive to that part of the county. My grandmother hailed from a place called Forgney. In north Longford – where I was brought up – we don't visit our neighbours, we *ceili* with them. But in Forgney and the rest of the south, ye *ramble* with them.'

The padre's insight into the county's local dialects was all new to the south Longford men, and drove them into a tailspin of remembrance and nostalgia.

'Who mentioned Oliver Cromwell,' shouted Jonty McArthur, with two freshly-opened Labatt's beers for his newest customers to try out.

'I was just saying we came over on a ship called the *Oliver Cromwell*,' said Mel.

'My people were given Cromwell's vacation in the year of our Lord, sixteen and fifty-three,' Jonty lamented, 'the year after the Act of Settlement outlawed them from their religion.'

'What's a vacation – some sort of prize,' asked Mel.

'That's what the Yanks call a holiday,' explained the padre.

'My dear man,' said Jonty, placing the bottles on the counter napkins, 'Cromwell's vacation occurred when one was forcibly removed from one's home and sent to a labour camp to work until exhaustion or starvation put an end to one's plight. My ancestors were sent westward to ceili – excuse me, to ramble – with the Barbadians.'

Jonty's story always reminded me of Shay Gorman's transportation to Van Diemen's Land. But I'd never bring it up publicly in front of Jim. I prayed to God that Shay had not succumbed to exhaustion or starvation, as he slaved away in his prison camp for a crime he didn't commit. Thoughts of Turk also crossed my mind. I recalled his solitary grave by the peaceful lapping of water, a place specially chosen by Jim's wife. I couldn't help wondering how Turk's life would have turned out. I imagined his face when I looked at Mel, having a tequila at sunrise and a bottle of beer in a new and free land. What wonderful possibilities lay ahead for young men in a place like America.

The other south Longford man, a skinny fella called Ivan, brought me back to reality.

'My descendants emigrated too. They came over in Reverend James McGregor's boat, reaching Boston in seventeen eighteen. I intend to travel north to see them one day.'

'You'd want to get a move on or they'll all be dead,' joked Jim.

We had a good laugh at this.

'McGregor's boat,' said Jonty, closing one eye and pointing his towel, 'that makes you a left-footer.'

'Yes,' agreed Ivan, matter-of-factly. 'A Presbyterian to be exact.'

'The famine is getting worse all the time,' said Mel, changing the subject quickly. 'The failed uprisings of last year have only added to the people's misery.'

'What about the Mostrim area? Have ye any news for us,' Jim inquired.

'Where's that,' asked Ivan.

'Edgeworthstown,' whispered Mel.

'Look,' said Ivan, 'we're away from the famine now. So why don't we leave it where it belongs – on the other side of the Atlantic.'

'Mind your tongue,' warned Jim, seizing Ivan by his coat.

'Excuse my friend,' said Mel, 'he didn't mean it like that. We'll leave the horrors of the famine in Ireland – not forgotten, but in respectful silence.'

'Can we leave our shame there too,' asked Jim with a haunted look, peeling his fingers from Ivan's lapel.

'Come on guys, there's been enough aggravation for one morning,' said Jonty. 'Have another beer on me. What's it gonna be – seven bottles of Labatt's? And myself makes eight. Drink up. Breakfast time is over. Now it's time for lunch.'

Jonty leaned in for a word in my ear.

'Any sign of Mickser?'

'Not yet, Jonty. It's still a bit raw.'

'Any word about the cowboy who made off with his money,' whispered Jim.

'Not a dickybird.'

'I was out in Elsa's the other day,' said Jonty. 'She'd never seen the guy before in her life. Oh well, time I suppose – time is a good healer.'

I looked around at Jonty. I was going to say something about Elsa, but then I didn't.

'What,' he said.

'So is Labatt's, Jonty – a good healer.'

## Nineteen – Rivington Street

It wasn't long before Father Murtagh and I were heading down the Lower East Side of Manhattan again. Not to work on the docks or spread God's mission, but in preparation for the next big fight at the King's Hall. The programme had been drawn up, and now that he had disposed of a very game Italian called Kid Rossi – a knockout in the thirteenth round – Bartholomew was pencilled in to contest his next middleweight bout against a Swede called Andersson. It was on the undercard to the Morrissey-Pritchard heavyweight clash – a winner-takes-all preliminary for a title showdown with Yankee Sullivan. The new boxing board of control was putting pressure on us to choose a name, something which wasn't as easy as it seemed.

'What about Kid Chocolate,' said the padre. 'It's catchy, and captures the whole dark and exotic side of Bartholomew.'

It was a mouth-watering name, I'll give him that. But it just wasn't right.

'What happens when we reach the championship rounds and the heat comes on. Chocolate goes soft, starts to wilt, and then falls to pieces,' I pointed out. 'No, I liked your first attempt – Iron Bart Campbell. It's easy on the ear.'

Bartholomew lived in a place called Rivington Street, not far from the intersection with Pitt. It was only a ten-minute walk from Thompson Street. But as we had already found out, ten minutes of walking was a lot different in New York City than it was in some Irish hamlet. When we reached our destination, there was a smell of human waste in the air. The houses were in a bad way.

Some were boarded, others sheeted with corrugated iron and chicken wire. The faces were anything but friendly.

Bartholomew was leaning by his door, expecting us. He bowed politely before showing us inside, a gesture which always made me feel awkward. His home was clean and orderly. Father Murtagh was offered a seat while Bartholomew and I discussed tactics. A thrashing sound came from another room. In walked a young woman with a floor mat in her hand. She got a fright when she saw us in her living room.

'Boss, thissie my sister, Melanie,' explained Bartholomew.

Dropping the mat, the young woman pulled down the sleeves of her dress, covering her bare arms in a hurry.

'Melanie, thissie Mister Jabber, my manager. And over yonder, Mister Frankie.'

She nodded bashfully and fled the living room.

'Kid Chocolate,' said the padre, 'what do you think?'

Bartholomew looked confused.

'Is that the guy I gotsta fight?'

The padre laughed.

'No, it's your new name.'

'It's not his new name,' I said. 'At least it's not, until it's agreed upon. What do you think, Bartholomew? Do you like that name?'

'I suredy do, boss. But I have me a name.'

I couldn't help but admire Bartholomew's innocence.

'I know that,' I said, 'but what about a stage name – a *boxing name*?'

He looked confused again.

'Well, I never had me no boxin' name afore. P'haps I can keep my ole name. The preacher down in Lisiana, he called me Bartholomew. And I was a figurin' mayanbe it might not be so lucky to change a name a preacher gave.'

I smiled over and the padre nodded his approval. What more was there to say.

Then myself and Bartholomew got down to business. I told him I didn't want a repeat of the slugfests he had been dragged into by Harland and Rossi. I wanted Bartholomew bouncing on his feet more, sticking and moving, and working the ring right into the corners. I was demonstrating the crouch I used to protect my chin in the old days, when a jingle of delph disrupted my lesson. Father Murtagh jumped up from his seat to help Bartholomew's sister through the living-room door with a tray of cups and plates. She seemed in an awful hurry, rushing back to the kitchen to retrieve a pie. That was the first time I ever tasted banana pudding – it was like my taste buds had just gone to Heaven.

'A grand sup of coffee,' said the padre to the woman of the house. 'We'd be more used to drinking tea, but it's delicious all the same.'

She looked at him shyly and nodded, then fled again to the sanctity of her kitchen.

'Beggin' yo' pardon, Mister Frankie,' said Bartholomew, 'Scuse my sister. She hain't used to people in the house, 'part from me, that is.'

I continued with my boxing briefing and the padre sipped his coffee while wandering about the room aimlessly. He was clearly bored. He lifted the coffee pot and poured. Then he disappeared through the living-room door. Melanie was taking the ribbon from her hair as he walked in. She stopped immediately and looked set to leave, but the padre pleaded with her to relax – and save him from the boring prattle of pugilistic stratagems.

'I brought you a coffee,' he said.

This embarrassed Melanie, whose barely audible protestations included that *he* was supposed to be *her* guest.

'For who is greater, he who sits at the table, or he who serves,' replied the padre.

A twinkle of recognition appeared in Melanie's eyes.

'Yo' know yo' Bible,' she said softly, 'Luke, twenty-two, twenty-seven.'

The padre was taken aback.

'Indeed. You're a child of the Bible yourself, Miss Campbell.'

'Rever'nd Charles teached us back in Lisiana Baptist Sunday School, sir.'

'*Sunday* school - very impressive. It was hard enough to get our lot to go during the week.'

The padre's joke did not go down so well with Melanie. She recoiled to the back wall of the kitchen, as if retreating from a dangerous animal.

'There's no need to be nervous,' Father Murtagh assured her. 'You can relax and talk to me, you know, I won't bite.'

She looked at him suspiciously, wondering why this man with his strange voice had come into her kitchen to speak with her.

'I'm Francis,' he said, offering his hand. 'But I'm better known as Frankie.'

Melanie looked at it awkwardly. Not many people had ever formally introduced themselves to her, especially not many white men. Shaking his hand felt weird. She took a shawl from the back of a chair. She placed it over her shoulders, hiding her neck and upper-chest. The padre took the hint – his presence was making her too uncomfortable. He got up, bowed politely, and turned to go back to the living room.

'What's my brother doin' with that man?'

'He's talking to him about boxing,' returned the padre, surprised by her question. 'His name is Joseph Farrell – a friend of mine. He's Bartholomew's new boxing manager.'

Her brow became furrowed as she turned this information over in her mind.

'Is he stupid? Don't yo' friend know he could have a heap o' trouble for bin a manager to a black boxer?'

Realising what she had just said, Melanie held up her hand in apology. But Father Murtagh liked the honesty of her spontaneous outburst.

'Very stupid indeed. I've been telling him that for a long time.'

The padre laughed and Melanie's brow relaxed.

'But Joseph sees it as a way of breaking down fences.'

She folded her arms and announced that good fences made for good neighbours, and that her brother must have lost what little sense he had between his ears.

'It's plum crazy – Bartholomew carryin' on fightin' is bad 'nough, without gittin' yo' friend in trouble too. Folk from Lisiana would say he got feathers for brains. Lord have mercy, they both got feathers for brains.'

'Excuse me, Miss Campbell, but I think that's a risk Joseph Farrell has earned the right to take. You see, he doesn't see things the same as most men. Neither do I. Bartholomew told us that he was once a slave. We come from slavery as well – only we were slaves to the British.'

'Well mercy, mercy, me. Yo' fixin' to tell me white men can be slaves too?'

'Well, yes. Yes, I am. And some Irishmen understand – are sympathetic to – the abolitionist sentiment now existing in this country. You see, Miss Campbell, our land and our people are in bondage also.'

It was clear from the expression on her face that Melanie was having a hard time taking this in.

'Our great leader, Daniel O'Connell, was an abolitionist sympathiser.'

Melanie's face remained blank when the padre mentioned the great counsellor.

'Well, he died a few years ago. And then there's Father Theobald Mathews, another great Irish social commentator. He speaks out against the owners of slaves. The rest of us must do the same – speak out against what we know in our hearts is wrong.'

Melanie's smile was broad and beautiful as she pushed brown strands of hair behind her ears. She had never heard anyone speak like this.

'The path of the just is like the shinin' sun, that shines ever brighter unto the perfect day,' she said.

It was the padre's turn to smile and recognise.

'Proverbs, chapter four, verse eighteen,' he remarked.

'More coffee,' said Melanie softly, and she hung the kettle over the fire again.

## Twenty – Workers for the Kingdom

My little band of merry railwaymen was simply called the Slashers. Despite Malarkey's claims that Longfordians were famously known as the Far Downers, no one in Central Pacific was privy to this information. But we weren't alone – many other groups had pet-names too. There was the Leesiders and the Kingdom Comes; the Kick-the-shites were from Dublin and the Red Handers from Tyrone. The term *Connachtmen* could be confusing, as there were more than one rail gang with this name. Sometimes they were from Galway, while another time a Mayo gang turned up laying claim to the title. The Sheep Stealers were from Roscommon. Mickser Burrows reckoned it was lucky for them the Brits weren't in charge of the American railway or they'd all be sent to Van Diemen's Land. The Sheep Shearers were from Leitrim, and the Sheep Shaggers from Donegal. Sometimes the Royals worked the same stretch of line as ourselves. Jeremiah Figg thought it a good idea to sabotage their bogeys, until he found out they were a bunch of Meath men and not an English crew.

If the job was large-scale, like cutting away forestry or excavating through mountainous terrain, we'd be required to join with other gangs. We mostly worked with the Midlanders, an amalgamation of Offaly – or King's County, as Breda would say – and Westmeath men. The Midlanders had their own distinct handshake – a rather awkward thumb-pressing clench. It looked childish, but they were quite proud of it.

Indeed, the Midlanders was not the only gang noted for its traits. Dialects and sayings often denoted the original Irish whereabouts of certain groups. The Kick-the-shites would roar *go on ya bleedin' good thing* and *ger-em-inta-ya* as they cheered each other on at beer-drinking contests.

'You know, for a small country, hasn't it a world of different accents,' remarked Mickser Burrows, of Ireland's many voices.

The Dublin crews ate different foods as well. Coddle – a kind of sausage-stew dish – was a thing of wonder to us, despite Jim comparing it to a dog's dinner. The Connaught gangs also had their own grub, tried-and-trusted recipes from the old west.

Christian names were often another tell-tale sign of a railwayman's birthplace. Laurence was a big name among the Dubliners, while Carthage was to the Offaly men what Canice was to a crew from the sunny south-east in Kilkenny. There were a number of Florences working with the Kingdom Comes – a strange name to those of us who hailed from outside the Munster region.

'I had an Auntie Florence from Virginia, whom we holidayed with one summer when I was young,' the padre recalled. 'I never knew it could be a boy's name until Breda told me.'

'You went on holidays *to Virginia*,' exclaimed Mickser Burrows, after examining the bottom of another bottle.

'Not Virginia in *America*, Mickser, the Virginia in *Cavan*.'

But differences among the Irish crews working for Central Pacific Railroad were not confined to foods or names. Attitude could also be a major bone of contention. Older workers, fellas who had been years in the country, tended to be really Americanized. I suppose it was only natural. They drifted, with the passage of time, away from old Irish mentalities – like shedding a worn-out skin for a shiny new one. Politics afforded the perfect opportunity to prove themselves more American than the fellas fresh off a disease-ridden ship – fellas like myself. While we couldn't have cared less about communism – Jeremiah actually thought it was to do with how gypsies lived – these old railway veterans were smarting from a recently-published book by Karl Marx and Friedrich Engles, called *The Communist Manifesto*. Not content to rage against such an obscenity, they took every opportunity to call into question *our* loyalties to their adopted homeland. One day, a senior member of the Kingdom Comes – a man with thirty years of immigrant life under his bulging belt – asked me was I sure the Longford Slashers weren't secret supporters of Tsarist Russia.

'That's how it starts, you know,' he ranted, pointing a finger at Bartholomew filling his barrow with debris from a blast, 'mixing up your navvies is a first step on the slippery slope to mixing up your loyalties.'

Despite the obvious differences among the railway gangs, there were many universal similarities. We were bound by the never-to-be-tampered-with language of the railway. The *six foot, five foot, the cess, limited clearance, the permanent way* – all exclusive jargon and all crucial to the safe practices and procedures of the job. *Blacklegs* and *scabs* were terms to describe strikebreakers and those who sallied across the picket line in times of disagreement. *Good graft* was the name given to job bribes – usually offered by a machine politician to ensure his voters got what was promised. Jim Gorman thought *black lung* was an old Indian chief from Montana or the Santa Fe Trail. That was until a rascal from the Midlanders downed tools and refused to work alongside Bartholomew, suggesting my protégé would be better suited to the railway company's coal mines – where he could get a black lung to go with his black skin. After calling the young scallywag to order, Jim learned that black lung was a complaint miners often succumbed to.

By times, the Slashers were forced to face all sorts of abuse. We were branded nigger-lovers, potato-heads, monkey men, and Irish apes. We attracted racial jibes wherever we went, and not just from other railway gangs or the navvies who worked with subbies. Once, while laying a piece of track beside Manhattan's West Side docks, we were set upon by the longshoremen of Pier Sixty – the *most Irish pier* on the Manhattan waterfront!

'How dare you bastards bring a nigger to work 'round here. If ye don't get rid of him, we will – just like the other contraband sold down the river last week.'

The *contraband* the longshoremen spoke of were two-dozen black men and women, missing and feared well on their way to the southern states – to a life of forced labour in the cotton or sugar trades. Recent inventions had increased the demand for slave labour, which meant black people in the northern states were being snatched off the streets, restrained in ships, and sent down the Hudson. And all for a handsome turnover. Eli Whitney's cotton gin could process one-hundred-times faster than a person, resulting in a higher demand for cotton pickers. Along with this was the invention that revolutionised the sugar cane business. In 1843, Norbert Rillieux introduced his sugar works patent model. It reformed the process of extracting sugar from cane. In the intervening six years, it wasn't uncommon for black people to just vanish into thin air. In the beginning, these vanishings were treated as isolated incidents. It was thought that the missing had either died by their own hand or moved of their own accord. But, as time passed, a pattern formed which was altogether more sinister and twisted. Free black people in the northern cities were being overpowered, bound, and sent – or rather, sold – down the river to Alabama and Mississippi and Tennessee.

Being a southern boy himself, Bartholomew Campbell knew all about this lucrative business of getting sold down the river. The thought of an unexpected trip back to his native Louisiana scared the daylights out of him. The fact that he was, like many others who called New York home, a free and independent black citizen didn't come into the reckoning. Despite what the longshoremen had assumed, Bartholomew was not contraband – or, in layman's terms, an escaped slave. Even so, if an African-American was unlucky enough to be caught in the wrong place at the wrong time – free or not, male or female – they might find themselves involuntarily signed-up for a lifetime of non-profitable work in the cotton or sugar business.

I watched Bartholomew closely. I never wanted him working alone. If a job caused us to split, I usually sent Jeremiah with him. They helped each other settle into life on the railway. Father Murtagh once said that humans can get used to anything. He was spot on. The human mind is a wonderful thing – it can shield and fortify. After a while, it was almost as if Bartholomew didn't hear the cutting remarks. Even so, he wasn't complacent. He never stepped over his neighbourhood deadline alone or away from the protection of myself and the Slashers. The last thing any of us wanted was Bartholomew reliving history – in chains in the Deep South.

## Twenty-one – Saturday Night at the Playhouse

Breda hadn't been seen since her Saturday morning meltdown at Jonty's. Jeremiah Figg nursed a heavy heart. He pressed Father Murtagh continually on her whereabouts. But the padre's advice was always the same – girls like Breda were only to be found when *they* wanted to be found. He also said there was no point in wallowing over what might have been. Wasn't there plenty more fish in the sea. It was time for Jeremiah to forget about her and move on. And that's the way it remained until one day, many months later, McArthur's Saloon displayed a poster of the upcoming vaudeville performance of *Othello*. It was in aid of the Tammany Hall Fundraising Committee and was to be held at Saint Patrick's Clubhouse on Mulberry Street, not far from the cathedral. There, among the list of players, Jeremiah read the name *Breda Nayle*.

'We have to go, it's as simple as all that,' he gushed, almost knocking down our railway gazebo, 'for the education of it alone. It's not every day you get the chance to see Shakespeare.'

'Who's he,' quipped Mickser Burrows, before gulping down the remnants of his hipflask, 'does he work on the railway?'

'Now young Jeremiah, it's far from the playhouse we were reared,' said Jim Gorman, hiding a smile and winking at Bartholomew Campbell.

'Ara, what would gobshites like us know about a play,' continued Mickser. 'We'd be better off in the Spieler.'

'Now Michael, there's no more Spieler,' warned the padre.

'It's a fundraiser for Tammany Hall. It says on the notice in Jonty's that Ted Ireland is going to be there,' pleaded Jeremiah. 'Father Murtagh, it's educational – tell them.'

We all looked at the padre, who was in the middle of devouring a sandwich.

'Jeremiah, I asked you before not to call him *Father Murtagh*. Francis is his name on the job,' I said. 'Don't forget yourself in the public domain.'

'The *public domain*,' repeated Jim, 'airing the fancy priests' education this morning are we, Jabber.'

'Educational? I thought *you* said it was some sort of comedy,' said Mickser to the padre.

'A lampoon, that's what he called it,' explained Jim. 'A comedy lampoon.'

'Tell them what, Jeremiah,' said Father Murtagh, after his big swallow, 'that they have to go? I can't. That, my young friend, is entirely up to them. But, if it makes you feel any better, I'll go along with you. After all, I wouldn't want you missing out on something *educational*, or on a chance to see Ted Ireland and add to Tammany Hall's already hefty war chest.'

'How, in heaven's name, could anyone lampoon a Shakespearian play,' I asked, and Jim shook his head sarcastically once more.

'What's a lampoon, a thing for killing whales,' asked Mickser.

'Begod, I think we'll have to tip on over to the clubhouse and check this out ourselves,' I concluded, spilling the remainder of my tea out the door of the gazebo and grabbing my pickaxe. 'Are ye finished supping tay, lads? Time to go back to work.'

And so, Jeremiah got his wish. Himself, the padre, Jim, and I headed down to Mulberry Street the following weekend to see *Othello*. We went in early – and just as well. It wasn't long before

Saint Patrick's Clubhouse was bursting at the seams, sending Tammany Hall stewards scurrying to a nearby hotel for extra seating. Jeremiah looked nervous as he awaited the action. It had been put to him on more than one occasion during the week that maybe, just maybe, it wasn't the educational aspect of the play – or the financial windfall the Democratic Party was poised to receive – fuelling his determination to see it. Perhaps it was the names – *a name* – on the cast of players that drove his interest. Jeremiah denied this vehemently, pointing out that Saint Patrick's Clubhouse was not your regular Auburn Hall in Mostrim. A theatre of such magnitude, he argued, probably played host to dozens of actresses called Breda Nayle.

Eventually the curtains parted. It wasn't long before the concept of the lampoon became obvious to those schooled on the bard. Othello was a *white* man. All the other characters appeared to be black. Jeremiah's head bobbed and weaved. He was as giddy as a kid goat. Slowly, his mood changed. With the passing of each scene his hopes decreased until despair descended from the smoke-filled ceiling. There was no Breda Nayle. There were girls alright, but of a different colour. The only white player was Othello – and he was much too tall, much too muscular, and much too masculine for Jeremiah's liking. Ted Ireland hadn't even bothered to show up.

But the rest of us loved it. Even the sceptical Jim Gorman had to admit that time just whizzed by.

'Time is a precious gift from God. Why do you guys spend so much of it in the saloon, when there are productions like this to be enjoyed,' asked the padre.

'There you go again with your American talk, Padre,' said Jim. '*Guys*, indeed.'

We were having a rare old time – until the usual abuse began. The fact that the white Othello was a high-ranking member of the army was not lost on the crowd.

'The natural order of things,' shouted a voice from the back of the hall.

'Hello Mister Coon,' shouted another, causing an almighty cackle among the audience as Iago weighed up his options.

'I'm glad Bartholomew's not here. He does be embarrassed enough on the job, without getting it in his free time as well,' I whispered to Father Murtagh.

'He couldn't come even if he wanted to,' replied the padre, 'there's a *no coloured, no dogs* policy on the door. Melanie told me that the only time she gets to see inside Saint Patrick's Hall is when she's doing administrative work at elections.'

I noticed the strange way the padre looked at me as he spoke her name.

'You're spending a lot of time in Rivington Street lately, Joseph.'

'I'm Bartholomew's manager. A manager has to put in the time with his fighter.'

'Are you sure that's all it is?'

I have to say, I was surprised with Father Murtagh. Jim and Mickser, I could ignore. I wouldn't stoop to their level of childishness. But honestly, I'd expect more from the padre.

'She was asking for you the last time I was over,' he continued. 'Are you listening to me, Joseph?'

'Ssh... here come's a good part,' I replied, as if I had seen the play before.

It was gripping stuff all the same. The crowd was enthralled by this new take on *Othello*. The men guffawed at the suggestion of a white ram tupping a black ewe. The women gasped, threw their eyes skyward, and almost swooned in sheer disgust at the very notion of a mixed-race union. The happy half-time hum must have been music to the producer's ears. His experiment was working. The gamble had paid off.

The second half began and Iago went to work on Othello's confidence. The manipulation increased, obliterating Othello's self-assurance and creating a din of unrest. Iago broke the noble – white – Moor down, piece by piece, as the civil unrest intensified around us. The play was becoming something of an outrage. Catcalls and boos replaced the happy hum. Some could scarcely believe what they were witnessing. The gentleman sitting directly behind me wanted to know if this was a mockery of the white race – the portrayal of a gallant general being treated like some barbarian half-wit by a tribe of subordinate blackamores. By the end, as the ruined Othello knelt over the body of Desdemona, the audience was fit to be tied. Insult gave way to injury, as they hurled food at the actors. A rotten potato hit Desdemona square in the face as she lay on the stage. She promptly arose from her murdered state, seized the offending spud, and flung it back with interest.

'Take that, you wretched scoundrels,' she shouted, before dabbing a cloth on her bruised jaw.

'That wasn't in the script,' I said, picking up a tomato and joining in the fun.

Suddenly, Jeremiah's big blue eyes were wide with excitement.

'It can't be,' he exclaimed. *'Breda?'*

'I believe it is,' returned the padre, as we watched the cloth clear the polish from her face. 'It looks like our Desdemona is Breda Nayle in blackface.'

The food fight was the best part of the night. I got stuck in and so did everyone else. Well, almost everyone – Jim and Jeremiah sat there like two dummies as all manner of bedlam broke loose. One look at Breda was enough for Jeremiah. His heartache had returned to render him useless. Jim was a different matter. He told me later that the sight of all the wasted food flying through the air brought him back to the awful day Maisie Rourke and her child were found starved in Lisnageeragh Lane; the same day we made Soyers' soup for the people of Mostrim.

'Thank God we've left all that behind.'

As soon as I had blurted it out, I realised my mistake.

'Yeah,' replied Jim, 'pity our loved ones can't say the same.'

'What can we do,' I said, searching for words to console him.

'I'll have to go back. Let's not cod ourselves, Jabber, there's no hope for Ireland – regardless of what the papers say. There are shiploads of food leaving the ports every day of the week – and you won't read that in the *London Times*. It's downright murder – people-cleansing. The British government won't stop until the job is done – not with the likes of Wood and Trevelyn in Westminster. I'm going back for Mairead and Maggie – while they're still alive to go back to.'

That was the moment I knew my days as a railway ganger were numbered. There and then, in the middle of a food fight, I decided I was going back to a famine. I had made a promise to my mother on her deathbed – to protect my men – and I wasn't about to break that promise for anything.

## Twenty-two – An Ancient Order Says Hello

It was one of those knocks – so faint that you're not sure if it's a knock at all. It could have been the wind blowing the swing-tile on the porch. But it captures your attention anyway – the strangeness of it. I was getting ready for bed when I heard it, while quenching the oil lamp. Moving closer, I waited for another knock – just for confirmation. Jim didn't call this late on a worknight, and Father Murtagh always tapped the window to signal his arrival. I put the blame on my imagination. It was time to hit the hay. Then I heard the whisper.

'You were in the clubhouse last night.'

My throat went dry. How did the voice know that I was standing just the other side of the door.

'Who goes there,' I asked hoarsely. 'What do you want with me?'

'It's time to do your duty. Saint Pat's… after work… tomorrow evening.'

'What duty? Who are you?'

There was an eerie silence then. I was about to move when it spoke again.

'The auld Order.'

And then there was nothing.

Sure enough, the padre and Jim Gorman had received the same instruction. Jim scurried over when he thought the coast was clear. The padre was already giving his prognosis by then.

'It's one of these secret Irish societies of America – along the lines of the Fraternal Society or the Defenders. A fellow in the steerage compartment of the *Erin's Queen* was telling me all about them on the voyage over. Its full name is the Ancient Order of Hibernians and it's over a decade operating in New York. Protecting Catholic churches from nativist arson attacks – which, I suspect, is why we've been summoned – is just one of its many functions.'

'And how do they know there's going to be an arson attack on Saint Pat's Cathedral at any rate,' I asked.

'The same way they knew that you and James and I were in Saint Patrick's Clubhouse last night. Their business is knowing all things Irish in this town. It's the intelligence they work off – their lifeblood, so to speak. And that intelligence is recovered from a vast Irish network – not to mention infiltration of other groups – much like the way the secret societies at home operate.'

'So, they had us marked at Hudson Bay Registry Office,' said Jim.

The padre shook his head.

'No. Much earlier. At a guess – the moment we stepped onto the ship. These boys put the Ribbonmen in the haypenny place.'

Jim was anything but relaxed. He chewed his fingernails as he listened to the padre berating me for being *careful* with the sugar cubes.

'What if we say no,' he eventually suggested. 'I'm *not* a practising Catholic. I don't go to mass – why should I have a duty to defend the cathedral?'

'Settle,' said the padre. 'They've *asked* you. So you'll have to show up. If you don't, it could mean big trouble – and not just for you. We'd probably end up losing the protection these fellows give immigrants. We'd certainly lose our jobs and be shunned.'

'What protection,' argued Jim. 'I didn't see any protection

when that Scottish ganger and his crew kicked up a rumpus.'

'Who do you think got us the jobs – Jack Fitzgerald? Or maybe it was Malarkey? Or perhaps Ted Ireland? Don't you see, James, they're all in it together. They're all part of the machine. And they don't mind us being part of it too, as long as we do what we're told.'

'Too right,' I agreed. 'We can't take the chance on calling their bluff. We have to play along with these fellas, they're too dangerous to start messing with.'

'The police force are more dangerous to be messing with. What if the law nabs us and we end up being recognised? Then, it's a one-way ticket home to face the Crown and the hangman.'

'That's not going to happen, James,' replied the padre. 'The last time there was a donnybrook on the streets of this city, the locals – Irish, mostly – baton-charged a mob of socialists on the Lower West Side. But the police turned a blind eye and let them at it. If we fail to show tomorrow, we are putting ourselves in real danger of being dobbed-in by the Order – and then you really will be on your way home to face the hangman.'

And so, the following evening after work, the padre and I headed to Saint Pat's Cathedral. A disgruntled Jim Gorman, an excited Jeremiah Figg, a fearful Bartholomew Campbell, and a thirsty Mickser Burrows tagged along for good measure.

'Don't worry,' the padre assured Bartholomew, 'no need to look over your shoulder. The Washington Square deadline doesn't apply to anyone here to fight the good fight. You're one of us today, young man.'

We took our stand beside the Gophers, a West Side gang, whose reputation in the distribution of punishment beatings went before them.

'It's not enough that I'm a gopher on the railway, but I have to fight with them in my spare time now,' quipped Jim.

A little further along the frontline stood the Hudson Dusters, eyeballing the Gophers despite their emergency ceasefire. The International Longshoremen's Association also weighed in with its considerable bulk. There were other street gangs – or athletic clubs, as they were more sociably known – from the Five Points, vicious-looking specimens who were licking their lips at the prospect of trouble. The Tammany machine had its soldiers in place, primed and ready for war.

A well-dressed fella in a top hat sauntered through the cathedral gates. He looked like an important man – an entourage scuttling about him like mice at a crossroads. I was sure he was some middle-man or peace negotiator – the head buck cat of New York City Council, maybe. Then, a peculiar thing happened. The well-dressed man began to rouse us up.

'Not an inch, boys,' he roared, waving his arms hysterically. 'Not an inch today. It is kill or be killed, or we will end up with another Saint Michael's of Philly on our hands.'

The man may have been speaking English, but he sounded foreign.

'He must be at the wrong gig,' Jeremiah surmised. 'I think he's a guinea.'

'That's Senator Lombardi,' said Father Murtagh. 'He's what's known in the Lower East Side as a cosmopolitan.'

'I thought that was an ice cream,' quipped Mickser.

'No, a politician who adapts to the cultural mix. You'll find Lombardi has as many Irish followers as he has Italian around these parts.'

The battle cries of the nativists could be heard in the surrounding streets. The shouting got closer and soon their frontline warriors were visible. I recognised one of their foot soldiers instantly.

'Does anybody look familiar,' I asked Bartholomew, 'it seems like we're about to renew old acquaintances with our boy from the King's Hall.'

'Georgie Harland, boss,' said Bartholomew, 'I was figurin' I'd saw me the last o' hem.'

Harland and his pals walked in even strides like an army division. They were empty-handed, but that didn't mean anything. They lined up across from us. There was a strange silence. Secretly I hoped this standoff was to allow for negotiation, and that the whole thing could come to some amicable conclusion. Maybe, somewhere in all the madness, common sense could still seize the day. But I was preparing myself for battle. I looked at the padre. His lips were moving. He was probably saying a prayer – a prayer for peace, no doubt. After all, the padre was there, first and foremost, to carry out his priestly duties and heal the wounds of sin and division.

Suddenly an avalanche of bricks came hurtling towards us from a place further back from where George Harland and the frontline stood.

'Have some Irish confetti, you Irish bastards,' a voice called out.

A second wave of bricks followed. Father Murtagh took one full force to the face. He had a nasty cut to his forehead and was dazed. As the Gophers made their move to engage the enemy in hand-to-hand combat, the padre arose from his knees and marched forward. Gone were the thoughts of healing and harmony – he just wanted to get into the thick of the action. The Hudson Dusters and longshoremen swept around, attacking from the side in a pincer movement. The nativists were hemmed in. They had no path of retreat. The bricks were still flying, but to less effect. They hit as many of their own as they did us. Bartholomew was locked in battle with his old adversary. Jeremiah faced a man twice his size in fisticuffs. He dropped after a blow from behind and Jeremiah turned to look for his next challenge.

'Watch out, the knife,' I yelled.

Jeremiah wheeled around, ducking in the nick of time. Instead of the knife lodging deep in his neck, it only grazed the top of his head. After that, Jeremiah disillusioned his opponent with a flurry of blows before disarming him.

Confrontation did not come natural to Jim. He looked uneasy as he faced his foe. But that soon passed as the fighting progressed. It was good for him to let off steam. It afforded him an opportunity to work the frustrations out of his system.

Once I got started, it was like old times. All my fair-day escapades were rolled into one. I soon forgot all about the common-sense approach. I held nothing back, cutting nativists down with big lefts and rights. Father Murtagh was proving his worth, watching my back as I strode forward.

The sound of muskets pierced the air. They caused the first scattering, putting an end to the bricks. Muskets rang out again. One of the nativist leaders, who was holding a torch, fell to the ground. The other torches fled for cover. The police rushed in and a corridor for retreat presented itself once more. The nativists were backing off now.

Jim Gorman could scarcely believe his eyes. Across the battleground stood the thin man with the ginger beard. Jim fought his way against the crowd. The ginger man ran towards the cathedral. Jim got a wallop of a truncheon but continued on his way. The cathedral doors were guarded, so the ginger man raced around the back. In desperation, he made for the high garden wall and gripped the jagged rocks for dear life. Jim made a grab for his foot but was just out of reach. The race was on – the ginger man eyeing the top of the wall and his freedom. Again, Jim made a swipe for his ankles. The ginger man wrestled his leg free. Jim was gaining ground, but also running out of wall. The ginger man kicked out. Jim lost his grip and slipped back. The long thin arm searched for the top of the wall. He was there. The ginger man looked down. It had been a close-run thing – too close for comfort. Jim looked up in despair. So near and yet so far again. The ginger man swung a boot across the capping.

'Hold it right there,' said a voice.

The ginger man attempted to get his other leg over the top.

'I said hold it, or I *will* fire.'

Below on the lawn squatted the cathedral-door guardsman, his musket cocked and aimed. The ginger man looked up and thought about swinging his leg again.

'I mean it,' said the guardsman.

'Relax your weapon, I surrender,' cried the ginger man.

He spoke with an upper-class Irish accent – the very same as Viscount de Bromley, Lord of Cranley House.

The musket-wielding guard, still cocked and aiming, arrested Jim and the ginger man right there on the cathedral lawn. A crowd was gathering, now that the nativists had pulled out entirely. The musketeer ordered them face down on the grass, tying their hands behind their backs.

'What, in heaven's name, is going on here,' cried Father Murtagh, when he came on the scene.

'Stay back,' warned the musketeer, 'or you'll get the first ball.'

'That's our friend,' I pointed out, 'he's been fighting on our side, protecting Saint Pat's. Why is he being treated like this?'

'Shut your yap,' said the musketeer, 'I'll ask the questions from here on.'

He turned to Jim and the ginger man as they squirmed on the lawn.

'Well, have you anything to say for yourselves?'

Jim turned his head sideways, so he could talk more plainly.

'This red fella has been spying on me and my friends ever since we got here.'

'Here? What do you mean, *here?* Here this evening,' asked the musketeer.

'No, since we arrived in America. I caught him several times. He was even at it on the ship coming over.'

Father Murtagh looked at me and shook his head in amazement.

'So, he wasn't just a figment of James's imagination,' he whispered.

It wasn't as big a surprise to me. After all, I had seen the ginger man before – Jim even pointed him out at the registry office. But I must admit, just like the padre, I thought Jim was totally paranoid about the whole spying business. Considering it further, my heart began to thump. Maybe Jim Gorman was right all along – what if this ginger man was one of Viscount de Bromley's men. Perhaps he was reporting back to Roger Giles or the British authorities in Ireland. Was the game finally up for us. I could feel a cold sensation pass through me as though I was about to faint.

'I was not spying on the chap,' said the ginger man. 'Rather, I was ensuring that he and his comrades came to no harm.'

There was an outbreak of laughter among those looking on. The musketeer promptly restored order.

'I have enough on my plate without this sort of shite,' he growled. 'Are you two sure you weren't scaling the wall so you could get into the cathedral and burn it down?'

Then he pulled the ginger man's head back by the hair.

'You sound like you belong to those waspy bastards we've just put the run on.'

Father Murtagh intervened again, swearing on everything sacred that they were only protecting the cathedral.

'Did I tell you to be quiet,' shouted the musketeer. 'Open your mouth again and I'll plug you one.'

'He's telling lies,' said Jim, wriggling on the ground.

'I am not,' replied the padre.

'Not you, Father. I'm talking about this fella here.'

'I am not telling lies, you blighter,' said the ginger man, addressing Jim even though he was facing away.

'Someone's telling lies. A night in the cells might put manners on you pair,' said the musketeer. 'Right, on your feet. Let's go, the barracks.'

'Wait, wait,' pleaded the ginger man.

He rolled his head on the grass, attempting to make eye contact with the musketeer.

'Jim is right, I was despatched from Ireland.'

'How do you know my name,' roared Jim, causing the musketeer to caution him again.

'Because it is my business to know your name.'

This stunned Jim into silence.

'Well,' said the musketeer, 'what's it to be – a night in the clink?'

Jim tried to shake his head.

'No,' I interjected. 'There's been a misunderstanding. This little red fella – he's friend, not foe.'

After their release, the ginger man agreed to come back to Thompson Street. His real name was Charles Langley – or so he said. His instructions were to follow us wherever we went and report back through coded letters. It sounded like one of those mystery stories which were periodically published in the *New York Times*. Jeremiah and Bartholomew couldn't get enough of it.

'Coded letters,' exclaimed Jim, 'the bastard is some sort of British spy!'

'I cannot elaborate,' said Charles Langley, 'I am not at liberty to say another word.'

'You can't – or you won't,' I argued. 'How well you knew to be on the *Erin's Queen*.'

'I knew all your movements – from hiding beneath a dead man's bed to your trip into Dublin on the barge, and even your time in the bawdy house.'

Jim Gorman went white with nerves. I wasn't far off getting sick. Merciful hour, I couldn't believe my ears.

'I don't understand,' said the padre, 'how *could* you have known?'

'As I have already stated, I am not at liberty to say,' repeated Langley.

'Oh, you'll tell us,' growled Jim, taking him by the scruff of his collar. 'Who's your snitch?'

The padre told Jim to take it easy. But he only succeeded in maddening him more.

'As God is my judge, I'll beat it out of the little ginger fucker.'

Suddenly, something went off in my brain. It was like things were beginning to make sense.

'Leave him be,' I said to Jim. 'Give us space, fellas. Let me talk to Charles in private.'

Jim, prompted by the padre, backed off begrudgingly.

I knelt down beside Charles Langley. I looked him in the eye and spoke slowly. I told him that he'd have to give us answers. One way or the other, we'd get the information out of him. As a member of a secret society myself, I knew how to make him talk. I asked if he understood. He nodded.

'You say you were sent here for our protection. Charles, are you a member of the Mostrim Ribbonmen?'

'Yes.'

'Did you come here on the instructions of its leader?'

'Yes.'

I got so close then, my lips were almost touching his ear.

'Paddy Sugrue,' I whispered.

'No,' he returned.

'*No,*' I exclaimed.

'No,' he repeated, his little ginger head going from left to right and back again. 'Paddy Sugrue's superior officer – Lord Harold Teale.'

## Twenty-three – To Have and to Hold

The padre was enjoying himself. He could almost feel the old woman's stare. He took his time preparing the table, basking in her curiosity. But Missus Begley had to be put out of her misery at some stage.

'It happened a little over a decade ago – the fifth day of January, eighteen-hundred and thirty-nine. They call it the night of the big wind.'

Her face burned with anticipation. He rearranged the turnips and the cheese, as if it made a difference. The padre loved a captivated look – many a dull-natured parishioner he entranced during a good Sunday homily.

'They say it was the last great night of merrymaking among the fairy folk. The disagreement was so bad their chieftains departed Ireland amid a hurricane, with no intention ever to return.'

Father Murtagh didn't actually specify who *they* were that said all this and Ina Begley dared not ask, lest she be struck dumb on the spot by the wee folk. The padre looked out thoughtfully at Mickser swinging absentmindedly on the porch, whiling away the time before his Sunday morning retreat to McArthur's Saloon.

'Do you know what we're missing, Missus Begley, a drop of porter.'

She was up quickly for a woman of her age.

'Oh, and a couple of small glasses of whiskey if you please,' he called out, after she'd gone to the scullery.

She placed a large jug of cool beer, four small glasses, and a bottle of whiskey on the padre's table.

'The blessings of God on you, Missus, but no fairy chieftain would lift a finger against a hair on your head. They'll be mighty pleased with all you've done. There's enough on this table to feed an army. They love the bit of fruit you know.'

Missus Begley was fighting her smile of satisfaction when a black woman peered around the corner of the house.

'Are you lost, dear,' said Ina, while peeping down the street to see if the neighbours were watching.

Father Murtagh, who had been on his haunches giving the table a final touch up, looked across to see the beautiful dusky features of Melanie Campbell.

'Hello Frankie. Beggin' yo' a pardon for the intrusion but may I speak with yo' a moment?'

Father Murtagh was surprised to see Melanie so far away from her Rivington Street base. But, on the other hand, if there was a day for braving the deadlines of New York, then Sunday was definitely the best. Gangs were known to relax their attitudes on Sundays – perhaps their nod to the Man above. Besides, gangsters had to eat like the rest of us. Sunday lunchtime was a really sensible hour to make your way around the city.

'Melanie, what a lovely surprise,' returned the padre. 'Melanie, meet Missus Begley from Longwood. Missus Begley, meet Melanie Campbell from Louisiana.'

Melanie beamed a great white smile in Missus Begley's direction. Ina nodded ever so slightly back, before seeking the comfort of her bamboo porch-chair. Noticing her unease, the padre said the table was finally finished.

'You want to see me, Melanie?'

'Yessie, Bartholomew's friend showed me where to go a huntin' for yo'.'

'Ah, Jeremiah. A grand young man.'

Mickser Burrows was off the swing and taking the turn for Jonty McArthur's. The padre looked down at all the booze.

'I have a feeling the fairies will have a great feast at this table at some stage this evening, Missus Begley.'

Missus Begley's smile was fleeting, her good humour all used up.

'Probably at closing time,' he added, under his breath.

'Was that a altar yo' was prepin', Frankie,' asked Melanie, walking away with the padre.

'Well, I suppose you could call it an altar,' replied Father Murtagh, 'an altar to honour the feast of Saint Ceara.'

'She must be a hard on the drinkin', thissy Saint Ceara – mayanbe the bestest drinker in Heaven, I do declare.'

'I didn't want Missus Begley thinking like that. So I told her it was a table for the fairies, just to be on the safe side.'

Melanie told the padre – or Frankie, should I say – what was on her mind. She had become quite close to a particular individual – a white man. Their relationship had moved to a deeper level and marriage was proposed. But Melanie was hesitant in the extreme. A mixed-race marriage wasn't the only stumbling block. The issue of children had annoyed Melanie to the point of seeking out the padre's advice. While it was okay to raise children south of the Manhattan villages – where there's a mix of Irish and black communities – Melanie was petrified that her future kids would be rejected by their own in Louisiana. Besides Bartholomew, the remaining family – including her dear mother – still lived in the South. Their approval was important to Melanie. Her greatest fear was that her young ones would be classified as neither black nor white and therefore, falling between two stools, be ostracised from both communities.

'We was frever taught when we was bin growed up that white blood and black blood made for bad churnin'.'

'By whom,' asked the padre, 'actually, I don't want to know. Tell me this, Melanie, what's so wrong with mixing blood? Are we not all God's children? Is it not written: *for there is no partiality with God*?'

'Romans, chapter two, verse eleven,' said Melanie.

'Correct. The world is not about to end if you and your white gentleman-friend have children – conceived, I hasten to add, out of God's love for you both.'

'Any childern I brin' forth to thissy here world would be disadvantaged 'nough, without mixin' up the colours an' all.'

Father Murtagh was getting annoyed at such talk.

'Disadvantaged – to have two loving parents to nurture and protect them, educate and bring them up in God's ways? That's not disadvantaged. I could show you disadvantaged children in two minutes flat. If we were to take the short walk down Tenth Street, I could show you any number of disadvantaged children. Or we could go over to Union Square and I'll show you as many disadvantaged children as you want to see – children with no homes, no parents, no hopes.'

Father Murtagh stopped and composed himself, just like he had a habit of doing during his sermons.

'I'm not trying to make you feel bad, Melanie, and I understand your fears about the future. As far as this marriage proposal is concerned, it's entirely your decision. But I will give you one piece of advice. Don't base that decision on the disadvantages it could bring to your children, but on the many blessings you can offer them when they come along.'

'Mayanbe it's a shameful thought but I am all a fluster, Frankie. Where I come from, havin' dark-black skin is bad 'nough but havin' light-black is worser still.'

'Correct me if you will, or tell me to mind my own business, but you and your brother look a little on the pale side yourselves – and you both seem to have survived fairly well out of it.'

Melanie blushed when the padre said this. He was about to apologise when she spoke first.

'I've had the baddest luck with men – lost a husband already, Frankie.'

This was news to the padre.

'Yessie. I'm twenty-three years on God's green earth and a widow so soon. Yo' see, I married young. My husband's name was Tobias Trent and, not mindin' my tender years, I loved that man with all my heart. He was a driver, and we met one day while he was runnin' a errand over at master's house. We fell in love at once and, lordy me, the chances that boy a took to come over to ole George Campbell's estate house just to tarry ten minutes in my company. Master frowned on our courtship at first, sendin' word to Mister Trent whenever he found Tobias on his plantation. Never mindin' how many whuppings my man had to endure, he dusted hisself down and kept comin' back for more.'

'He sounded like a good sort,' said Father Murtagh, surprised by what he was hearing.

'Oh, he was a – what do yo' Irish brothers say – a topper.'

Father Murtagh smiled. He was anxious to hear the rest of the story.

'By and by, on the advice of Mister Trent, master was persuaded to allow us jump the broom. He only gave his blessin' on condition that Tobias would leave the Trent plantation and set up house with us at Breaux Bridge. I was not to leave my work at the big house. Anyways, we fetched a preacher to the servants' quarter of Master Campbell's plantation and boy did we have a right old… how do yo' say it, hooley.'

Father Murtagh smiled again and told Melanie that she had

been spending too much time around Irish people. She was almost fluent in the lingo already.

'It was the bestest time of my life. I moved away from Momma and Bartholomew, and into my new cabin with Tobias. He was a thinkin' man, always plottin' and plannin' out the way our lives would be. And he could read and had interest in political topics too, tellin' little ole me all about the speeches of Frederick Douglas.'

Melanie went quiet and the padre thought she was going to break down in tears.

'What happened,' he whispered.

She made a great gulp and went on.

'Oh, after a couple o' weeks of wedded bliss, I was hangin' out some washin' at the big house when a peg poked my eye and blacked it. O' course, when Master Campbell sawed it he was mad – cussin' and blamin' Tobias for hittin' me. He stormed out, even though the lady of the house pleaded for my case. That whole night I waited for Tobias to come home. It was the darkenest, lonesomest, night of my life. But he never did. He never came home, Frankie.'

Melanie began to sob uncontrollably and Father Murtagh rested her head on his shoulder. When her body had stopped shaking, she finished her woeful tale.

'His body was never saw again. Master, or mayanbe I should say George Campbell – he hain't *my* master – never admitted to nothin'. Oh, there was rumours – mostly in the servants' quarter. They set to figurin' George Campbell had no choice because Tobias, under the influences of Frederick Douglas, was plannin' a mutiny on the plantation. Another whisper was that Tobias had bin whuppin' me all along and George Campbell was onerly standin' up for one of his own. Oh Lord have mercy. He done away with my Tobias in cold blood, with not 'nough decency to leave the body so as I could set out a Christian burial.'

'What then,' asked the padre.

'I slept from then onerward with a knife under my pillow. I knewed the master would be a doin' his rounds. By and by, he lookeyed in on our cabins. I figured on gettin' my chance sooner or later. But afore I did, my momma found the knife in my bed. No matter that I denied it, she knewed what it was there for. Then she set to tellin' me the truth. If I stuck that knife into the master, it would mean the end for us all. She also told me somethin' else – that George Campbell was mine and Bartholomew's papa.'

Father Murtagh had been waiting for it. He blamed himself. Why did he have to open his mouth about the shade of her skin.

'I'm sorry Melanie, for… you know.'

'There's no needin' to apologise, Frankie, yo' didn't do nothin' out of the way. Anyways, after the shock of findin' out, I got to thinkin'. I figured things was so clear then. For one, I always wondered why me and Bartholomew was treated different to the other childern in the servants' quarter – we was allowed to the big house with the cotton-pickin' season in full swing. We often turned up to the church where the whites went and there was never a word. We could go in and out of the stables without any special permission. After Momma told me, it all made perfect sense. George Campbell was our papa and me and Bartholomew was the only fools who didn't know it.'

'What did you say when he finally showed up?'

'By then, Momma had chased the notion of a killin' him clean out of my imaginin'. So, I faced him head-on in the middle of my cabin and put my question to him directly. He admitted Tobias was dead. But he denied a killin' him. He said Tobias had bin hanged from a tree over at the Trent place and buried on the plantation. I asked him straight up if he was my papa. He admitted to it, but said he kept things hush hush because his wife and the other whites up at the big house didn't know. I stared him in the eye all the while. He didn't want me to do that, but I didn't care what he wanted. He kept lookin' away and fussin'. I packed some food. I wrapped a parcel of my Sunday clothes and demanded he drive me to the Trent place hisself. I laid some flowers on the supposed restin' place of my dear husband. Then I ordered George Campbell to give me my papers so I could come north and start my new life, away from him and his cotton plantation. The last I sawed of him, he was limpin' away from my cabin like an ole dog with a sore paw.'

'What about Bartholomew?'

'When I was good and settled in N'York, with my own work and my own money, I sent for him. I demanded the papers a provin' his freedom from George Campbell and I got them without so much as one holler.'

'I'm surprised he didn't fight you on that, Melanie. These southern men can be very obstinate.'

'I hain't surprised, Frankie. He didn't want his dirty secret gettin' out, 'though I suspect the olden servants and Momma's friends knewed already. Yo' see, he really did love me and Bartholomew, the bestest way he could. He played with us and brang us in his ridin' cart. He'd take us up to the big house durin' quiet times and give us cold lemonade and let us relax on his rockin' chair. It was all mighty fine, so long as no one asked no questions. The pure shame of it all – he could only shew his love for us while we was someone else's childern, he couldn't allow hisself to do that once we knew we was his own.'

'And that's why he had Tobias killed,' the padre said.

'His double life was his undoin' at the end. George Campbell did love me, I'm sure. And he done a terrible thin' out of his love for me. He believed Tobias was a beatin' his only daughter. So he decided on a takin' the law into his own hands. He as good as put the rope around Tobias hisself. And by and by, in his twisted sense of right and wrong, George Campbell really believed he was actin' in my bestest interest.'

Melanie looked up to find Father Murtagh pushing a tear from the corner of his eye.

'I'm a figurin' love is strange, Frankie, it makes folk do the baddest things.'

'You've had a hard time, Melanie, to say the very least. But ask yourself one question – can you be happy with this new man by your side? If you can, then take the chance. Not many people get a second shot at happiness in this life.'

'I spent my whole life a searchin'… a searchin' to belong. And I will not have that life for my childern too. I will not brin' them up between two races, in the same manner that myself and Bartholomew was reared.'

'Is it not better to bring your children up between two races than between none? You are comparing two totally different things, Melanie. You grew up in slavery. But your children will belong to a free world. Take a look around. This is New York – capital city of the free world. The sooner you realise that, the better …'

'What will I do, Frankie?'

'Hard to say – without knowing the other party. Could I assume that we're talking about an Irishman?'

Melanie's silence was good enough for the padre.

'Well then, I have a solution that might suit you both. Why not have a trial marriage?'

'A *trial marriage*. What in tarnation is that? Oh, I'm sorry for a swearin'.'

'It's quite self-explanatory. Yes, a trial marriage in the old Brehon-law style would work wonders in this case. You and Jos…er, I mean your white, Irish, gentleman-friend would receive a blessing, before a hand-fast would bind you in a trial-marriage for a year and a day. After that, if you're both agreeable, a real marriage will take place.'

Melanie thought about it, before looking at the padre and smiling.

'I'm a thinkin' it's a great idea, Frankie. Will yo' perform the ceremony?'

The padre was shocked.

'I know this trial-marriage is rooted in the pagan tradition, but – in the absence of a druid – you would still need a priestly figure or a preacher of some sort,' he stammered.

'But yo' is a priest.'

The padre was even more shocked then.

'Me, a *priest*? Have you gone mad, Melanie?'

'Fo' sure, yo' is a priest.'

There wasn't much point in the padre denying it any further.

'How did you know? Was it Joseph?'

'No, sir.'

'James?'

'No siree, wrong again. Yo' could a torture Jem, an' he'd still pucker up like a duck's backside.'

'Bartholomew or Jeremiah?'

'Wrong, wrong, wrong. I worked it out for myself, Frankie. Twas easy-peasy. Everythin' about yo' – yo' manner, the way yo' is concerned for others, even the way yo' talk – told me that yo' is a man of God. Yo' brin' to mind my dear ole Rever'nd Jackson, who preached in the white's church on the Campbell estate. But no need to worry, yo' secret's safe with me.'

And so, it was all arranged for a wedding in the Brehon-law style. I was delighted with the idea. In the beginning, the age gap did bother me. Being twenty years her senior, I was what the padre would call *apprehensive*. If we were back in Ireland, there wouldn't have been a problem. Many Irishmen were at least twenty years older than their wives. But I wasn't sure how this would work in New York. After all, I wanted to talk to Melanie, and eat with her, and have a laugh with her – things which some Irishmen considered a pure waste of good drinking time. I knew men back in Longford who wouldn't lower themselves to speak to their wives, because speaking wasn't part of their arrangement. The women were there to have babies and rear them, tend to the cooking and the indoors, and speak when they were spoken to. I wouldn't admit it to another soul, but I wanted a bit of romance in my life.

If a trial-marriage in the Brehon tradition was to work, I'd have to forget all about the age gap. And I wouldn't be going to Jonty's as much. The saloon was alright the odd time, but a married man would have to be at home more often. I'd have to forget about my mates and respect the hand-fast. Therefore, I found myself negotiating the deadlines between Soho and the Lower East Side until I became a regular fixture. Once I got familiar with the streets and the gangs, I felt like a new man. Then Melanie made another Sunday lunchtime call to Thompson Street. She was carrying some more news. I also needed to see the padre urgently. The trial-marriage would have to be scrapped.

Father Murtagh was making a Saint Bridget's cross – something he had done on the first day of every February from the time he learnt the art in Saint Colmcille's hedge school, Aughnacliffe. Since moving to the big city, rushes had become something of a rarity. In the end, he was forced to place an order with one of the local shopkeepers whose brother owned a farm out in New Jersey.

'She's pregnant, Father. What am I going to do now? Merciful hour, she's pregnant.'

Father Murtagh got such a jolt that he let go of the rushes and the cross fell apart at the seams.

'What are you... who's pregnant?'

'Missus bloody Begley. Who do you think? Melanie, that's who. What am I going to do now?'

'It sounds like you've it already done,' he said, gathering up the rushes to have another go. 'Why are you getting in such a state? She's pregnant – not dying. It's a new life – something that should be celebrated. Besides, the season of imbolc is upon us. Your timing is spot on, my good man.'

'*Imbolc?* What are you on about?'

'An ancient Irish spring festival celebrating the impregnation of cows and ewes and whatever else happens to get in the family way,' he explained.

'But Father, we're not married.'

'I'm well aware of that, Joseph. But it's me you're talking too now, not the likes of Canon Reidy. Remember, we're not in Ireland anymore – there's not as much remarks passed over here. The trial-marriage will sort you out.'

Charlie the monkey was looking for a banana, so I peeled one for him. I felt like peeling another for the padre while I was at it.

'I was thinking of ditching the trial-marriage and marrying Melanie for real.'

He was concentrating hard on his new cross.

'It'll have to be soon then,' he said.

'I thought you said there wasn't much remarks passed over here?'

'You must act with haste, Joseph, if you don't want to be rolling her up the aisle. It'll have to be on or before Shrove Tuesday.'

'*Shrove Tuesday.* That's next week!'

'I'm sorry, but it's the last available day for two whole months. The Church won't marry a couple after Shrove Tuesday until Lent is over. And besides, Shrove Tuesday is traditionally the most popular wedding day in the Church calendar. What's it to be?'

It all seemed so sudden. But, then again – as the padre pointed out – it was a shotgun wedding. Shotgun weddings, by their very nature, are supposed to be sudden. My life as a singleton was passing before my eyes – eyes that had yet to reach the tender age of fifty!

'Why has Catholicism so many rules and regulations about everything?'

'You could always leave it until after Lent,' he suggested.

'That's too late – she'll be showing too much by then.'

'Well then, bring it forward. Have it tomorrow.'

'*Tomorrow*, are you mad? I haven't even suggested a real wedding to Melanie yet.'

'Well, you'd better get a move on,' said the padre. 'Shrove Tuesday is nearly upon us. You go over to Rivington Street and do the needful. I'll stay here and load my shotgun.'

It turned out that Father Murtagh didn't need a shotgun. I explained to Melanie the Church's rules on Lent and the mandatory forty-day wait. She was all for a Shrove Tuesday union. There would be no Brehon-law trial-marriage. In the end, the padre was the only one I needed to coax to the altar.

'I didn't disguise myself as a railwayman for the fun of it,' he pointed out.

'Yeah, and we all know how that's working out,' I replied. 'Drop the act Father, because, quite *frankly*, it's not much of an act to begin with.'

I wasn't trying to ridicule him – I was trying to save him from ridicule. For a start, too many people already knew he was a priest. Melanie and Bartholomew knew. The padre had told Breda of his own free will. Jonty McArthur worked it out for himself – and admitted his suspicions had begun with the Gowna men from the *Erin's Queen*. Abraham and Mickser knew – and that meant their wives knew. And Jeremiah knew too. However, the padre wouldn't listen when I pointed this out. His paranoia knew no bounds. He simply refused to hang up his civilian clothes.

But once Missus Begley sidled up to his door, all doe-eyed and wearing her church-day expression – a kind of Mona Lisa smile – the padre knew the game was finally up for good. So, on the following Shrove Tuesday, he dusted down his vestments and waited outside Saint Pat's Cathedral, greeting a small group of arriving guests.

Missus Burrows haunted McArthur's Saloon until Mickser could take no more. He threw a glass of whiskey into the remainder of his pint, downed the lot in one go, and went off to the Spieler. She attended the ceremony with Missus Begley instead.

Abraham and his wife attended. They were celebrating also. Coincidently, it was their wedding anniversary and Missus Ishmel wore a beautiful marriage scarf. She called it a tichel. She said she had worn it on the twelfth of every February since taking the plunge. But she was afraid in case she was breaking some rule; the last thing she wanted was to show disrespect to the Church. Missus Begley told her not to be silly and that if she had kept the tradition since eighteen thirty-nine, why should eighteen fifty be any different.

Charles Langley – the newest recruit to our railway gang – turned up in a smart suit, his ginger hair slicked neatly behind his ears. He didn't burst into flames after all – a Protestant setting foot in a Catholic Church – like Mickser told him he would.

I waited at the altar in a straitjacket of nerves, Jim Gorman by my side. The padre had finally succeeded in talking him around. My mother came into my head and I checked my scapular. It's strange to say this – and maybe it was just my imagination – but I felt her presence in a peculiar sort of way.

Jeremiah strutted down the aisle, arm-in-arm with Breda. He

gave a big thumbs-up and side-stepped into a pew. Breda looked different without her girl-gang.

'She told me she wasn't coming,' whispered Jim, 'that her mother would disown her if she attended a mixed marriage.'

'I don't think she'd mind being disowned,' I said, 'she's too strong-willed for her own good.'

As the clipping of a horse's hooves sounded on the cathedral avenue, I could feel a knot in my stomach.

'Indeed and she wouldn't,' continued Jim. 'Sure hasn't she loads of black schoolmates. No, I didn't mean mixed racially – mixed as in Melanie belonging to the Baptists.'

'Isn't it great,' I remarked. 'It's only a five-minute walk to the Baptist Church on Clinton Street. That means a lie-in on Sundays from now on.'

'This is your last chance to make a run for it,' said Jim, as the carriage doors slammed outside.

Melanie shone like a beacon. I don't think I've ever seen a woman so beautiful. Bartholomew walked her up the aisle, looking embarrassed as he shook my hand and gave her over to be married.

Father Murtagh had been wary of staleness. But, once he settled in, he performed the ceremony like he had never been away. The wedding breakfast was scheduled for McArthur's. Jonty sectioned off the lounge. He placed a large table in the middle of the floor, dressed it, and hung ribbons and balloons from the doors and ceiling. He arranged an assortment of his best wines on the coldest window ledge out back. In the kitchen, his two daughters were busy. A delicious meal was had by all. Father Murtagh – a stickler for tradition – insisted on Melanie and I commencing the festivities by devouring the eggs on our plates, thus ridding ourselves of the symbol of fertility before the Lenten season was upon us.

'Mind now, Joseph. Take heed to consummate before midnight,' advised the padre, his cheeks glowing, 'otherwise, you'll have to wait until Lent is over.'

'Does that go for the rest of us too,' said Jeremiah, eating his eggs as fast as he could.

'The cheek of the guy,' quipped Breda, 'you won't be doing any consummating, so you can relax you' spoon, buste'.'

'Is young Jeremiah fixing to sleep with her,' asked Jonty, slightly alarmed.

'I wouldn't worry about him sleeping with her,' replied Jim, 'it's when the hoor's awake that he'd do the damage.'

'Such badinage as I've neve' heard,' joked Breda. 'If by *damage* you mean the act of intromission, I assure you such solecism could neve' be tolerated.'

'Jesus wouldn't be alone in fasting for forty days and forty nights – isn't that right, Jeremiah,' the padre said, laughing off his embarrassment.

'Mazel tov,' sang Abraham and Missus Ishmel in unison, holding aloft their wine glasses.

Jonty McArthur went all out. After a delicious breakfast, he laid on a fine champagne reception as we took to the bar. Then he had a fiddler in for the evening – who played slow, romantic, music to begin with. Breda was first to join us on the floor, dragging Jeremiah from his stool as the marriage dance ended. The fiddler pulled up his sleeves and let fly with a jig. The dancefloor was soon throbbing. Breda clung on for dear life, her hands gripping Jeremiah's strong arms for all she was worth. At first, she thought she had imagined it. She adjusted her fingers and felt it again. The skin was raised and rough, like a strange scar under his left shoulder. She traced the rugged lines – the scar tissue – with her fingers, first the X and then the L.

'What's that,' she asked, breaking from their clench.

'What,' he said, unable to hear properly.

'The mark on you' shoulde' – that *sca'*. How did it get there?'

Jeremiah went silent. He had put the shame of Shroid workhouse far behind him. He had left its bitter memory on the hungry plains of east Longford, never to be spoken of again. Since then, each day spent in a new, free, land had been another nail in the coffin of his past. But no matter how he tried, that XL – X for workhouse, L for Longford – would be there to haunt him until his dying day. He searched for an excuse. He thought about a lie. But, in the end, there was only one way to break the stranglehold the scar held over him.

'It's the mark of the workhouse,' said Jeremiah. 'A symbol of oppression, hatred, and fear from the old country.'

Breda was mortified for asking, but all Jeremiah felt was a huge release of pressure.

'I'll tell you all about it later. Don't let it ruin your day, Breda, because it's certainly not going to ruin mine.'

Father Murtagh waltzed by with Ina Begley.

'It'll be your turn next, darling,' he shouted at Breda over the sound of the fiddle.

Missus Begley lost her Mona Lisa smile momentarily when she heard her favourite priest referring to a young lady in such a derogatory fashion.

'Me? Get married? Are you out of you' mind, Pops? Let me elucidate something fo' you – the day they put a woman in the White House, that's the day they'll get me down the aisle.'

## Twenty-four – Dagger John

It was all anyone could talk about – in the streets, down at McArthur's Saloon, even between blasts on the railroad. Archbishop John Hughes was coming back to say mass at Saint Pat's Cathedral. Jim Gorman said that he didn't know what all the fuss was about, pointing to the confirmation on the front of the *New York Tribune* – under an advertisement for the General Relief for Ireland Lenten Appeal in the Broadway Tabernacle.

'What's all the excitement about,' he asked Father Murtagh, 'are bishops not supposed to say mass?'

'You're missing the point, James,' replied the padre, 'this is no ordinary bishop. This is Archbishop John Hughes – Dagger John himself. Over here, he's one of Ireland's most famous sons. It's a very big deal for Saint Pat's to have him.'

'Hold your horses,' said Jim. 'What do you mean by *one of Ireland's most famous sons*? I bet a pound to a penny he wouldn't find Ireland on a map.'

'No, no, no. He really is Irish – born in County Tyrone in seventeen ninety-seven.'

'And how do you know so much about him,' asked Jim.

'Everyone knows about Dagger John. He's famous – like George Washington… or Christopher Columbus.'

'He has a very rough-sounding name. I might be better off staying away from him,' said Jim.

'Come on James, now that you're back with the Church… you've got to go and listen to the Archbishop. He's a legend. You may never get another chance to see him in the flesh.'

'No offence Father, but I reckon if you've heard one priest you've pretty much heard them all.'

'Oh, get you James Gorman, with your *pretty much*. You're beginning to sound like a real Yank.'

'That young Breda lassie, she has the lot of us – including yourself Padre – astray in the head with fancy American talk.'

'The simple truth is that you haven't really heard mass at all, until you've heard it out of the mouth of Archbishop John Hughes. It's a spiritual awakening quite like no other. You can't miss it, James – I won't let you miss it.'

Everyone was waiting for Sunday mass. Missus Begley went out and bought two new headscarves, and fretted for days on which to wear with her best blue coat. In the end, Father Murtagh had to decide for her. Since finding out, Ina had hung around his porch like a spider. She harassed him every chance she got. She was so proud to have a real-life priest as one of her former lodgers.

I came back from my honeymoon – which consisted of a week bumming around the city – to all the commotion surrounding the archbishop's imminent arrival. I didn't care much for all the fussing, but I was glad to hear that Jim was going to attend. His self-enforced church ban had only annoyed him.

'I'm going and I'm bringing Melanie with me,' I told him. 'A baptism of fire won't do her a bit of harm.'

Even Mickser Burrows declared his intention to be there, claiming he was at Dagger John's inauguration in forty-two.

'That was a quick eight years,' said Mickser, shaking his head, 'where does the time go? We'll be auld men before we get to Californey.'

Mickser's wife was busy trying to keep him off the drink in the run up to the big event, afraid that a smell of alcohol in the cathedral would let them down.

'Won't the Dagger be sousing it into him,' replied Mickser. 'Listen to this, Padre, I've a great joke for you. Here's an Irishman's four favourite pastimes – *ol, feoil, ceol…and hole!*'

'I'm afraid you'll have to explain that one to me, Michael.'

'Well, ol,' began Mickser, 'is the Irish word for drink. Feoil is meat. Ceol is music. And then…'

Mickser pointed to his good lady's backside.

'And then there's …hole. Do you not get it, Padre? Of course you don't, you're a priest.'

'Michael Burrows, shame on you,' shouted his mortified wife. 'You will apologise to Father Murtagh immediately.'

'I didn't think we'd be having you along to the cathedral. Are you not a Protestant man, Michael,' asked the padre.

'Protestant? Catholic? It's all the same to me, Padre.'

We set out from Thompson Street an hour before the archbishop's mass. With the massive crowd expected, we thought it best to go early. Besides, as Missus Burrows pointed out, Missus Begley could hardly be expected to stand with her bunions. It was a sensible call – the cathedral was three-quarters full when we got there. Irish-America had gathered to welcome Dagger John home.

'We Irish are among God's chosen ones – we look after our own people and mind our own business. We do not rely on others for the necessities to live and move and have our being. We are peace-loving and fair. We believe in the old adage of audi alteram partem.'

Dagger John had come out like a wounded bull, determined to shield his flock from what he described as the pack of savage, nativist, wolves. He looked down on a heaving Saint Pat's, as if searching for somebody to put the whole blame on.

'And what President James Polk said last week from the steps of the White House is nothing short of an outrage – another example of the anti-Irish sentiment that has taken root in this supposed free land. How dare he threaten to veto a governmental bill granting American aid to a starving Ireland. How dare Senator John Niles label any such bill as disrespectful towards England – by the implication of inadequacy on her part. The inadequacy of England is staring him straight in the face. The Irish famine is England's inadequacy and England's indifference. The famine is England's shame. How come Ireland is the only country within her Act of Union suffering such hardships at this time of plenty? Because of Westminster and her politicians. Well, I have only one thing to say to President Polk and Senator Niles and it is this – nemo judex in causa sua. And the iudices in the case I am referring to is England and her nativist offspring.'

Dagger John was nothing like I had envisaged. On the way to the cathedral, I imagined an old cleric – balding and overweight and aloof from the troubles of his congregation. But I was surprised to find the archbishop slim and handsome, with a fine head of curly brown hair. From the side, he reminded me a little of Jonty McArthur. He spoke eloquently for the most part, until a rage took hold. Then he'd roar like a lion and bang his fists. He also had an annoying habit of inserting Latin phrases – not the usual Latin of the mass back home – into his sentences. The archbishop moved seamlessly from the famine to the changing of the school curriculum, a hot topic in recent newspapers.

'We will not be sharing Protestant catechisms, or those of any other kind. The Catholic schoolchildren of America have a right to their own version of the Bible. And the schoolteachers of America have an obligation to teach it. Failing this, we will be left with no choice but to propose the establishment our own separate schools.'

He held up the Eucharistic Host.

'Et Verbum caro factum est. Corpus Christi.'

He returned the Host to the table, then once more scanned the crowd with his blame stare.

'What or who is Corpus Christi? I know what you think it is – the Body of Christ. But it is more than this. It is more than the Sanctissimi Corporis et Sanguinis Domini Iesu Christi. We belong to this host. We belong to Corpus Christi. With this in mind, I am charging each one of you. I am charging your family and friends, praesenti et in absentia. I am charging all Catholic New Yorkers to defend Saint Patrick's Cathedral, *by whatever means necessary*, and to extirpate this nativist fire. By *whatever means*, I say, in nomine Patris, et Filii et Spiritus Sancti. We belong to the fellowship of God's kingdom, and now is the time to stand up and fight for that kingdom.'

Archbishop Hughes returned to the high altar, rummaged among some old books, and produced a newspaper. He held it above his head for the benefit of the massive congregation. It was a copy of the *Liberator*. Jim Gorman was forever reading it below in the saloon. Jonty always prided himself on having the latest edition behind the counter.

'This is what they think of us in Boston,' said the archbishop, a strange little smile creeping across his lips.

The headline read: *Irish Heroes Save St. Pat's*.

'This is not a heroic tale of the Fianna and Fionn MacCumhaill, of Oisin or Diarmaid. Oh no, this is Patrick Ford telling it as it is,' he added. 'When I reflect on this headline, my heart soars with pride. It tells of the bravery and conviction of those defending their own. It is a modern tale of heroism, of the ordinary and the poor – heroes who defended this very church from tyranny and terror. Heroes who are in this very church right now, in nobis. Ordinary men and women, just like those who defended this cathedral against the orange raid of thirty-six. And for the bravery you have shown, I thank you sincerely. Now I know that in our time of need we will not be found wanting. Gratias tibi.'

Dagger John folded the newspaper and replaced it among the old books. He was going through one of his quiet spells. Once he went quiet it felt awkward. Mickser fiddled with the shiny buttons of his railway coat. Melanie placed her new gloves on her knee. Jim Gorman inspected the soles of his new shoes. Missus Burrows whispered away to herself and Missus Begley practiced her Mona Lisa smile.

'Love thy neighbour – the second Joyful Mystery of the Holy Rosary. This leads to the age-old question: *who is my neighbour?* Sure, it's the person who lives beside us – in our neighbourhood, and in the surrounding streets. But *neighbour*, in the biblical sense, has a more far-reaching notion than this. Our neighbour is all mankind – regardless of colour and creed, especially those who are weak or in pain and want. I'm sure you are all aware of the recent attacks on the Jewish synagogues in this city. Well, let me guarantee, we will not stand by and allow this to continue. The Catholic hierarchy and Tammany Hall condemn these attacks. We must defend our Jewish brethren, the same way we have defended our own Saint Patrick's against the perpetration of violence. I stand here before you and speak in the interest of justice. I believe in a fair hearing. My dear people, I pray for the day when the pen will be mightier than the sword. But until that day comes, pugnare ignibus ignes.'

The mighty crowd left Saint Pat's in a hush. Thompson Street was upon us before a word was spoken.

'What did you think of him,' asked Father Murtagh.

'A very impressive man, God bless him,' returned Missus Burrows.

'A living saint if ever I saw one,' added Missus Begley.

'He reminded me of ole Revern'd Leroy Jackson, back at the Bridge,' said Melanie.

'Well, what did you boys think of him,' asked the padre. 'Did I not say you'd be moved?'

'Moved – or scared shitless,' I answered, 'he has a tongue on him that'd clip a hedge.'

Ina Begley almost fainted when she heard this.

'A grand auld topper,' said Mickser, before pretending to drink an invisible pint as a sign for us to go to McArthur's, 'hasn't aged a day since the last time I saw him.'

'I couldn't understand some of the Latin he was going on with – stuff that isn't part of the mass we knew in Ireland,' Jim admitted. 'But I have to agree with Jabber, he's sharp – very sharp. And very to the point. No wonder they call him Dagger John.'

## Twenty-five – The Gangs of New York

I took to married life like a duck to water. That surprised me. Gone were the long leisurely evenings in the saloon. But I didn't mind. I much preferred to be at home, giving a helping hand in the kitchen. We decorated the house in preparation for the new arrival. But I put in an odd appearance at Jonty's – I didn't want them thinking I had gone soft.

'It'll be the makings of you,' Jim remarked.

'You'll be getting all paternal,' added Jeremiah, 'now that you're under the thumb.'

'*Paternal!* No need to ask where you got that big word,' I replied. 'You're even beginning to sound like Breda – now who's under the thumb.'

'This man wanted to make a baby too,' announced Jonty, patting Jeremiah on the back, 'the night of your wedding.'

'He wouldn't make a good shite,' said Jim.

'I've seen the roughest and toughest of them reduced to lumps of butter at the sight of a little baba – especially men who came to the game late in life,' continued Jonty, rubbing his hands in his bar towel.

'What game is that,' asked Jeremiah.

'Fatherhood,' said Jonty. 'I don't give a continental what any of you guys say, Jabber is no spring chicken at this stage.'

'Hang about, Jonty,' quipped Charles Langley, 'I am of a similar vintage and I would not class myself as over the hill. On the contrary, my dear fellow, I would consider mid-forties to be the prime of life. The very prime of life, I say.'

No matter how Charles Langley tried, he just couldn't sound like your bog-standard Irishman. God knows, we worked hard on him. We even gave him elocution lessons. His voice was too grand, as Jim put it, for McArthur's. He would have been much more suited to the upmarket hotels of Chelsea and Central Manhattan. Charles tried to fit in with the pints of stout, but he winced with every mouthful. In the end, Jonty got fed up of him making faces and introduced Charles to a white chardonnay – all the way from South Africa.

'No fault to the rest of you guys,' said Jonty, 'but that man is of different breeding. And it's not his own fault. He's too refined for bottles of stout or pongers of ale, even though he can't be blamed for effort.'

Indeed, Jonty McArthur was spot on. Despite a generous allowance from Lord Teale, all Charles wanted to do was blend in and enjoy the simple things. The high life held nothing for him. He took a job on the railroad. He rented an apartment from Missus Ina Begley. And, despite being a Presbyterian, he attended Saint Patrick's Cathedral every Sunday.

Charles was what Breda would call a *consummate* professional. He never let his guard down, not even for a minute. He was fearful. He used his fear to keep him focused – even three-thousand miles away from those he feared most. Charles understood men like Viscount de Bromley and Walter Pollach a lot better than he understood us. He knew that they would never accept defeat. He also knew their capabilities, if not their limits, because he was brought up in and belonged to their world.

I asked Jonty to leave word for Malarkey. Then I got a letter from Jack Fitzgerald. Charles was to fill the position vacated by Father Murtagh – who had decided to retire from the railway, come out of hiding, and take up open ministry. But the railroad is no respecter of an Oxford tuition, and Charles soon found that out the hard way. Lugging rocks and twisting spanners soon turned his baby-soft hands into a mass of welts and sores. And then, as if by magic, they transformed into a leathery hardness that he found wonder and comfort in. As long as his highbrow tone was kept in check, Charles eventually found a way to masquerade as one of a motley rail crew known as the Longford Slashers.

After my big move to Rivington Street, I helped Bartholomew convert an outhouse into a training room – with weights and a punching bag. When we weren't pounding the dirt roads of the Points, we trained there for our fights. Since the shock win over Harland, we had fought and won five times in the King's Hall on Washington Square, twice at the Imperial Hotel and once at the Arms Hotel. Bartholomew Campbell was the new name in pugilistic circles. The *New York Tribune* called him the up-and-coming coloured challenger. I preferred the description in the *Times*, referring to him as the new Tom Molineaux. Offers flooded in from New Jersey, Philadelphia, and even Boston.

At first, Melanie was worried about me moving to a black neighbourhood. A white man stepping across a black deadline could be just as dangerous as the other way about. But her anxiety was unwarranted. The local gangs didn't cause me any bother at all. Word on the streets had circulated that I was Bartholomew's manager.

Father Murtagh always said it's an ill wind that doesn't blow some good. When we had the training room up and running, some of the neighbourhood kids – fledgling gang members and future bosses – would exercise with us. I found out a lot about city gang life from chatting with them – some of which surprised me. Despite their negative press, the gangs of New York didn't simply exist to intimidate, loot, and fight for territory. They actually did a power of good in the community. I listened with admiration to how local gangsters had helped the poor of the Rivington Street neighbourhood, organised children's parties, and policed Fourth of July picnics.

It was much the same with the boxing training – these miniature mobsters really surprised me. Once their young minds were focused in a positive fashion, it was amazing to witness their development. I was so impressed by their application that I floated the idea of them joining the railway. But this is where the line was drawn. I was quickly informed that if a budding enforcer should find himself lugging sleepers up and down the railway tracks then, inevitably, some other budding enforcer was sure to be prowling his turf. While the cat is away the other cats will play, so to speak.

So my workforce gained but one new member. Charles Langley, for a slight man, certainly knew how to handle himself. He was a useful asset when things got out of hand. And, when it came to other rail gangs, things could always get out of hand. Sometimes it was hello and how are you. But far more often we were just a pack of nigger-loving papists. One never knew when the working day would just explode into a fight. One angry exchange and then we were off. Fists were only a last resort. Shovels, chains, spanners, bits of sleepers – I've seen them all used in the heat of the moment.

'Always bring your shovel to work,' an old railway veteran once told me.

'Even on days when you know there's no blasting?'

'Especially on days when you know there's no blasting,' he advised. 'It's better to have your shovel and not need it, than need your shovel and not have it.'

On one occasion, I had to answer before head office. An allegation was doing the rounds that we had locked another gang in a steel container overnight. I stuck to my guns and denied all knowledge. It didn't matter how much I denied it, the waspy managers were determined to give us the heave-ho. And we would have got the sack too, if it wasn't for Jack Fitzgerald.

Shortly after the charges were dropped, I was ordered to report to the bosses' canteen again.

'I wonder what it'll be this time,' said Jim. 'They won't be satisfied until they've got their pound of flesh over the lock-in.'

But I didn't mind. Once we had Jack Fitzgerald on our side, they couldn't sack us. And if the supervisor known as Jonjo was on duty, we were elected. He was a balding man with spectacles – an agreeable sort. He was of Irish descent too – his mother came from County Waterford. Some of the others were not so pleasant, especially an Italian supervisor named Borgine. There was a tense atmosphere when he was in the room. He despised me. But I didn't hold it against him, because he was the sort who despised everyone. He was always on the warpath. I arrived at lunchtime. There was no sign of Jonjo. Borgine was nowhere to be seen either. Instead, a man they called Helmet-head stood in the doorway of the canteen. He was known as Helmet-head because of the way he kept his hair – squarely-cut like a riding helmet.

'Are you Farrell the ganger man,' he asked, his suspicious eyes twinkling.

'Yeah,' I replied. 'I'm here to see an area manager.'

'You're not. You're here to see me.'

He looked over both shoulders.

'You're on duty tonight,' he whispered, and spat a lump of tobacco back into the canteen.

'What do you mean, *on duty?* Is this to do with the cathedral?'

'What cathedral,' asked Helmet-head.

'Saint Patrick's. Is this to do with what Dagger, I mean, Archbishop Hughes was on about?'

The first thing to come into my head was Dagger John, his speech on defending Catholicism and the cathedral. But I knew by his face that Helmet-head had no idea what I was on about.

'Union Square and Tenth at eight o'clock,' he muttered through gritted teeth. 'The name is Briody Regan. You'll be making sure no harm comes to her.'

Helmet-head really had me going then. I wanted to draw out and hit him.

'Piss off with yourself and get some other mick to be your skivvy. I thought this was something to do with the archbishop.'

'If you know what's good for you, you'll do exactly as you're told,' said Helmet-head.

'Oh yeah. And what if I don't? What are you going to do about it?'

'It would be a shame if any harm was to come to your nice new wife. What's this is her name – Melanie.'

His eyes darted around the place again and he gave out another tobacco spit.

'Less of your shit and just be there.'

Back at work, I mulled it over and over. I had to hand it to him, Helmet-head was vague – and dangerous too, I suspected.

'What is ailing you,' asked Charles Langley, 'bad news from the pen-pushers?'

'No, just a bit of shop talk. Pure nonsense.'

I smiled as best I could and asked if the welders were finished.

'Well, if it was that innocuous, why did they bring you all the way over to the canteen,' continued Charles, his ginger chin twitching.

'That's the trouble with you, Langley, everything has to be scrutinised. You're the most suspicious little bastard I've ever met.'

'Steady on,' said Jim, 'the man is only showing an interest. And yes, Jabber, I agree with him. It was a bloody big deal bringing you over to the canteen for *pure nonsense*.'

'Don't you start as well,' I snapped. 'If it was concerning you fellas do ye not think I'd have let ye know.'

That evening, I told Melanie I was heading over to Jonty's for a railway meeting. I didn't like having to say that, but it was only a white lie so she wouldn't be worried. On leaving Rivington Street, I didn't go left for Jonty's. Instead, I turned right into Union Square. The questions kept coming – what was going to happen on the corner with Tenth Street? What was so special about this Briody Regan? Why did I have to be there? I watched the faces of the people as they passed. It was hard to read them. I thought a young fella with a newspaper gave me a suspicious glance. I gave him a nod, but all he did was quicken his step. I was getting paranoid in my old age.

I didn't walk too slow. I did my best to look natural. I felt I was being watched, especially as I neared Tenth. But it was probably just nerves. I reached the corner and stopped, then fumbled in my coat pocket. There was a crowd of men in the doorway of a saloon across the road. They were just chatting. One was smoking a pipe. Another was drinking something. There were four of them. But they seemed passive enough – enough to convince me that they were on the level, as Breda would say. They didn't look in my direction – not once. Two others approached. I straightened up in anticipation. But they walked on by. Then, one of the four men – the one who had been smoking – put the pipe in his pocket and headed towards me.

'You're wanted in the snug,' he said sharply, nodding at the side door where his friends were.

'Are you in the An…'

But he was already heading for Union Square, emptying the bowl of his pipe as he walked.

My mouth was bone dry with fear – even though I had no reason to suspect I was in any sort of trouble. The strangeness of it all was worrying. These American micks could be scary – and I don't say that lightly. At least I thought they were American micks. When you got them in the mood, they were great fun. But they had a dark side too – a side that could bring out the shivers in a man as big and strong as me; a dark side that was usually shrouded in secrecy.

I walked into the saloon as coolly as I could. Catching sight of myself in a mirror, I even looked nervous. I felt the tension in the backs of my legs. I stood at the bar and peered over at the bartender, who was polishing a glass. Before I could attract his attention, the saloon's side door opened again and in came Helmet-head. As he walked towards me, two men seated by the fireplace decided to take themselves and their drinks out to the big bar.

'Can I help you guys,' the bartender asked eventually.

'Two of malt,' said Helmet-head, directing me over to the corner of the snug.

'I'll bring them down to you,' shouted the bartender, but Helmet-head wasn't listening.

Instead, he was focusing on what he had come in for – briefing me on whatever was about to take place.

'When you have your drink, go outside and wait. A girl will pass on the far sidewalk. Let her walk ahead. Then follow her. Make sure nobody talks with her, walks with her, or interferes with her in any way. Have you got that?'

'Yes. What is this all about? Why am I following her?'

'She will be wearing a dance costume. You don't have to know anything more. Do what you're told.'

'Answer me one thing, Helmet-head, are you AOH?'

'The last man who called me that is six foot under in Calvary. Don't do it again.'

He obviously didn't like his pet-name.

'You know all you need to know for your end of it. Now get out and do your stuff.'

Helmet-head downed his whiskey. Then he pointed towards the door and I found myself back on the street, being blinded by the early summer sunshine.

Union Square wasn't empty. There were a few pedestrians knocking around. I took note of what they were wearing. I was certain there was no girl in a dance costume. The seconds ticked by like minutes. The men who had been standing outside the saloon were gone. There was nobody there now. I took up position across from the saloon. One minute, the street would be empty. All of a sudden, a glut of people would gather from nowhere and my heart would skip a beat. Then Tenth Street would be empty again. Brian Boru's – that was the name of the saloon.

The questions came flooding back to my mind. Before I could think of plausible answers the street was full again. I was concentrating hard on what people were wearing. Time ticked on. At one stage, I considered walking straight back down Union Square and going home to Melanie. Why should I do their dirty work. The Ancient Order of Hibernians had enough saps they could call on, fellas who were actually *in* their organisation. Then I started to think awful things. I couldn't abandon my post. What if something was to happen to Melanie. Or what if something happened to the men I patrolled – Helmet-head was a railwayman too.

Suddenly, there she was – a girl in a green dancing dress – walking in the direction of Brian Boru's. She had red hair, pleated at the sides. She was hesitant as she walked past me, as nervous-looking as myself. I waited until she was a distance ahead, then took off after her in the direction of the Points. Briody Regan picked up the pace as she negotiated the bridge that ran adjacent to my old stomping ground of Thompson Street. I lengthened my stride, every now and then gauging the distance between us. I went through the full range of emotions. Why in God's name was I following a teenager to the Five Points. It made no sense. We pressed on through a narrow alley. I could hear her steps, quickening all the time – the steel of her tap shoes against the pavement. She was out of the alleyway. I could see her silhouette against the evening light. I got to the end of the alley. And then I heard the voices. There were bushes and a park. Then a scream. Briody Regan looked behind and started into a trot. The bushes were moving – and then more voices. I didn't know whether to continue after Briody or stay where I was. I decided to investigate the commotion, turning quickly into the public park separating Tenth Street from Union Lane.

The four men from the Brian Boru doorway were there, one with his arm locked around the neck of an old cove in a trench coat.

'Cut the bastard up.'

The pipe smoker – the fella who had ordered me into Brian Boru's – didn't reply to this, just sprang into life with a flurry of punches to the old cove's body. He was set free from his head-lock and howled with pain. He was arrested again. This time his arms were pinned behind his back. The tallest of the four aggressors, a thin man with wax in his hair and a woollen-collared frock coat, took a few steps forward and eyeballed their captive.

'You like her? Does she get you off?'

'Put a smoke in his eye, Johnsie,' said a small fella, who wore a similar Herringbone tweed to Mickser's.

'Shut it, Tiger. Remember what Barnsie said in Boru's,' growled Johnsie, shining the blade of the knife in his captive's eyes.

Barnsie must have been Helmet-head's real name. The old cove nearly passed out at the sight of the blade.

'Do it, Johnsie, do it,' said Tiger excitedly. 'Serves the old pervert right for spying on a thirteen-year-old girl.'

'What were you planning to do,' asked Johnsie.

'Please,' muttered the old cove from behind a restraining arm, 'I was never going to harm her.'

'Oh yeah, a likely story. He'd say anything to get out of it,' gushed Tiger.

'Easy Tiger,' said Johnsie. 'Keep your voice down. Barnsie wants this done clean.'

The old cove begged for mercy and repeated that he never meant the girl any harm.

'Why were you hiding in the bushes – leering at her – and following her home every night,' snarled Johnsie.

With all that was going on behind the bushes, I had completely forgotten about the girl. I got up from my haunches. I went back through the park entrance and looked down Tenth Street. Briody Regan stopped outside a dilapidated dancehall, looked around her one last time, before disappearing through the half-open door.

The situation had deteriorated upon my return to the park. Tiger and the pipe smoker had the old cove on the grass. Johnsie had the knife in one hand and a bag in the other, which he handed to the fourth member of their gang.

'Put it on him,' instructed Johnsie, 'I don't want to have to look at the bastard's face.'

'Please,' cried the old cove, 'I have a wife and children.'

'Well, you should have thought of that before you started harassing young Regan,' said Johnsie.

'I wasn't harassing her. I never meant her any harm. Please, I'm begging you.'

'Give him a dog's beating and leave it at that,' said the pipe smoker.

'No. Barnsie calls the shots. He wants us to give him the

Sicilian. Cover his face with the bag.'

'Please,' the old cove whimpered. 'My brother's a police officer.'

He didn't mean to be funny, but Barnsie's gang shrieked with laughter all the same.

'Maybe you know him, Larry,' said Johnsie.

'Yeah, where's he stationed? Perhaps I'll get to partner him some day – and tell him all about his pervert brother,' joked Larry.

I could feel my heart in my mouth as the bag went on the old cove's head. Was this really happening before my eyes. Johnsie got the knife and ran the point of it down his captive's face. I knew it was now or never. I jumped out from behind the bushes and crashed straight into Johnsie, shouldering him out of the way.

Tiger let go of the cove's ankles and sprang at me. I received a blow to the jaw. But I was more than a match for little Tiger, kicking him into the bushes. My attention was fixed on Johnsie – on the knife in his hand.

'Drop it. We can all walk away.'

Johnsie had no intention of granting my request. I felt a sharp pain in the back of my knee. I dropped to the ground. Larry bombarded me with punches. Tiger returned from the bushes. The pipe smoker had a choice to make. In order to take me down, he loosened his grip. Seizing the opportunity, the old cove raced for Brian Boru's – the bag still clung to his face.

Barnsie's gang was now minus its target, but had me in his place. I was hauled to my feet, my hands restrained. The pipe smoker laid into me some more – just to soften me up, as Tiger put it. Catching my breath, I saw the glint of steel once more.

'You're in big trouble, punk,' said Johnsie, this time running the knife down *my face*. 'You cost us our man. For payback, you take his punishment.'

Tiger got excited on hearing this.

'You're not gonna cut *him*? What about Barnsie,' asked Larry.

'And what about him?'

'He mightn't like it if we do this guy. After all, it was Barnsie who recruited him in the first place,' the pipe smoker argued.

'Yeah, well, if he minded his own business he wouldn't be in this mess. All this punk had to do was follow the girl. Barnsie wants blood and that's what he's gonna get.'

I tried to struggle free. It was no use. I felt the cold steel against my windpipe. Then I closed my eyes and braced myself.

'Okay, you blighters. No sudden movements and you shan't be hurt.'

I thought I was hearing things. I opened my eyes to the ginger head of Charles Langley. He stood there, as bold as brass, with a pistol cocked.

'My dear chap, you will retract your weapon ever so carefully,' advised Charles, and Johnsie lowered the knife.

'Now, untie this man and assemble by yonder tree.'

He pointed to the spot where he wanted the line-up.

'He's spoofing,' said Tiger, struggling to break away.

'Not a good idea,' warned Charles, turning the gun on Tiger, 'do you really want to call my bluff?'

Tiger thought better of it and was compliant with Mister Langley's wishes.

'Now tie them up, starting with Violet Pomatum here,' quipped Charles, poking Johnsie with the gun. 'Back on back, if you please.'

I secured Barnsie's gang with their own chord. Charles tucked the gun into his trousers, covering it with his weskit.

'How did you know,' I asked, as we headed away from the park.

'By jingo, have I not already stated, I was sent here to make sure you chaps came to no harm,' he replied. 'Lucky for you I showed up when I did.'

'I had the situation under control.'

'Oh yes, indeed. It looked all of that.'

'Where did you get the gun, Charlie?'

'From the Right Honourable Lord Longford – otherwise known as Harold Teale.'

'Any more,' I asked.

'No, regrettably. One could do with an arsenal of cannons to keep you blighters out of harm's way.'

## Twenty-six – A Prayer for the Fallen

Jeremiah noticed the bright blue from a distance. Shuffling on the doorstep, he realised it was part of an altar. The Blessed Virgin, the centrepiece of a magnificent shrine, was flanked by a standing picture of Saint Martha of Bethany. Flowers adorned Our Lady's feet, freshly cut in a glittering vase. Pictures of James and Anthony hung close by. Jeremiah was no expert on Christian theology – and it wasn't as if he knew what they looked like. The inscriptions were etched at the bottom of each picture: *Saint James, pray for us; Saint Anthony of Padua, Protect Us.* There was a woman, dressed in green, brandishing a sword. And there was a man, in a brown nightie, looking up towards his halo. On a separate white marble top lay a Rosary beads, a family Bible, and two newspaper cuttings – of Leo XIII and Pius X.

'Can I help you, sonny,' said a creaky voice from down the hallway.

Jeremiah looked in through the open door at a glamourous old lady.

'Hello, madam. I'm sorry to trouble you. I'm looking for Breda, if you please.'

He was nervous, having already been warned in Jonty's – by a neighbour of Breda's – to be careful around Missus Nayle. She could be awkward at the best of times.

'I don't *please*, as a matter of fact. I don't please at all. Especially when she's out wandering the streets with all sorts of tomboys and chorus girls. God give me strength but that young one will be the death of me.'

The old lady ran her long, twisted, fingers through her perfectly-groomed hair. The rings sparkled in the sunlit porch as she travelled through her thoughts, forgetting all about Jeremiah. He felt like an eejit as he stood there, picking at his fingernail.

'Stop that dirty habit,' she barked, returning to the real world.

This was a waste of Jeremiah's time.

'Could you just tell her Jer...'

'I know, I'm not senile. You're looking for her. Great, now she's hanging around street corners with the latest edition of the famine Irish.'

Jeremiah took a deep breath and counted to five.

'That's fine, madam. I'm Jerem....'

'Don't get cute with me, sonny. With your *that's fine, madam*. I'm not madam, I'm Missus Nayle to the likes of you.'

He waited until she had stopped giving out.

'Tell her Jeremiah called,' he said hastily, while turning on his heel.

How right Breda's neighbour was in McArthur's Saloon. To be forewarned was one thing, but you'd need to be forearmed for the auld bat. Not only *could* Missus Nayle be awkward, she *was* awkward – if not impossible. No wonder Breda was rebellious; you couldn't but rage against such a woman. He stomped down the impeccable garden path. As he was turning to close the gate, her head popped up from behind a hedge.

'Jeremiah? Did you say your name is Jeremiah? At least have the manners to answer me, sonny.'

He looked back and nodded.

'I didn't know *you* were Jeremiah. The last I heard, Breda was stepping out with an older man. Come in and wait, if you like. I wouldn't have her saying that I ran you.'

Jeremiah was confused. Had she invited him in or not. He

didn't particularly want to spend any more time in her company. But if she was going to be half-civil, he wasn't about to throw it back in her face. Besides, he hadn't seen Breda in days – and it was anybody's guess as to where she and her friends were hanging out in the city. So he wandered into the living room, where a fire was roaring beneath a marble mantel.

'An older man? Ah, that'll be Father Murtagh,' said Jeremiah.

'*A priest?* Don't say she's shaming me in the sight of God Almighty,' shrieked Missus Nayle.

'No, not nearly. Breda's not *stepping out* with him – well, not anymore.'

Missus Nayle didn't know what to make of it all.

'You have a lovely altar inside the porch door,' he said.

She did her best to hide her delight, complaining that if it was left to the youngsters there wouldn't be an altar standing in the country.

'Will you drink coffee,' she asked.

Jeremiah had never tasted coffee quite like it. Missus Nayle made it with sugar and cream and he told me it was like something from Heaven.

'I'll never drink tea again,' he vowed.

Missus Nayle couldn't be faulted as a host. Her cups and saucers were the best of sparkling bone china, the like you'd see at Cranley House. The very best in stainless steel cutlery too. And small handkerchiefs – napkins, as she called them – all folded neatly on a brilliant-white tablecloth.

Between the coffee and the roaring fire, Jeremiah was overheating. So he removed his outer garment while he waited.

'God between us all and harm,' Missus Nayle prayed, before a trembling took hold of her.

'Sorry,' said Jeremiah, 'I'm too warm.'

He didn't want to embarrass the old lady, but it wasn't as if he was stripped to the waist. Jeremiah still had his vest on – his Malarkey vest, as Jim used to call it.

'I hope my presence isn't unsettling. I could always come back some other time.'

But it wasn't Jeremiah's presence – or his vest – that had unnerved Missus Nayle. She gazed in awe at the scar on his shoulder.

'Are you alright,' he asked.

Missus Nayle didn't answer, just paced the length of the living-room floor. Her face was deathly pale, as if she had just seen a ghost. Jeremiah noticed a tear dropping on the patterned mat. He said nothing, because he really didn't know what to say. She eventually broke her silence, as she gazed out the window in a trance.

'I once knew a girl from County Offaly who came to America on the Earl of Charlemont Scheme.'

Jeremiah was puzzled by this sudden outburst. Perhaps it was her way of apologising for calling him the famine Irish.

'She boarded the *Mary Tudor* on the third day of September, eighteen twenty-five.'

Missus Nayle placed a hand inside her cardigan, rubbing her left shoulder and gritting her teeth. Jeremiah wondered what was wrong. Before he could ask, the old lady was away again.

'She was told different things by different people. The directors of the scheme told her she was a slattern, an ungrateful wench who had been bought and paid for. But her father had a different view. He told her it was for her own good, that she was going to America to fulfil her life's purpose as a woman – to marry and breed. And that's what her father told the men he drank with in the pub in Mucklagh – saving his reputation, as their beards twitched to hide their smirks. It was all a front. Despite being considered in the strong-farmer bracket, her father could only afford one dowry. That was already spent on the eldest daughter's marriage. Dowry or not, the younger girl wanted to stay put in Ireland. But family pride was at stake. Then the bad harvest of twenty-five drove the final nail in the coffin of her hopes to remain at home.'

'Why are you telling me these things,' asked Jeremiah.

'Because she bore a similar mark on *her* shoulder, sonny – bears it still.'

'Well then, Missus Nayle, she must have tried to escape a workhouse. That's what they do in the land of saints and scholars to runaway girls.'

She was still in her trance, still rubbing her shoulder.

'I know that, sonny, only too well,' she whispered.

'But there was no workhouse back then – in twenty-five, I mean.'

'There wasn't, sonny. But punishments weren't invented in the workhouse. The girl I knew was disciplined for trying to escape the directors of the Charlemont scheme. She didn't mind going bald; her hair was always going to grow back. But the mark on her shoulder is permanent.'

There was a blurred image on the mantlepiece.

'Is that Breda's father,' asked Jeremiah, in an effort to lighten the mood.

'His name was Florence,' Missus Nayle recalled, 'from Kerry. He was a hotel porter in Chelsea. He lost his job when Breda was small. Inactivity gave way to the drink, until desperation set in. He tried upstate in Albany for a while, but fell in with a bad crowd. He returned and started running around the city, doing errands for one of the big Irish gangs at the time – the Dockers. He ended up in Calvary, where we'll all end up one day. But he ended up in Calvary far too young – just another hard-luck story. It wasn't always a sad tale between him and me. Florence had a good nature. When we met in twenty-eight, we were so in love. He saved me from a lonely servants' quarters and mouldy biscuits. Some of my friends reckoned I was wasting my time. They slated me for trading domestic service for a two-bit run-around and a slum in the Five Points. But I didn't see it that way. In the world of service, I was treated as backward and stupid – by people who should have known better. It didn't matter how good I became at my job, all I ever amounted to was a skivvy to be used at will. And I was an all-rounder, the best of the best. I rose quickly through the ranks – maid-of-all-work, cook, valet, head-lady. I would often light the fires, cook the dinners, and organise an evening reception all in the same day – and all with equal efficiency. If I met Florence tomorrow for the first time, I wouldn't change a thing – despite how it turned out. One lesson you'll learn with the passing of time, sonny, is that everyone has their faults. My husband had a kind soul and he gave me Breda – a blessing, even though she breaks my heart.'

Missus Nayle was crying again, so Jeremiah produced a hanky. He didn't offer it directly, just placed it on the table beside her.

'We left the Points behind for Breda's sake. I'm used to roughing it with the best of them, but you couldn't bring a child up in such squalor. It's different up here. Saint James's is a lovely parish – warm and neighbourly. The schools are top of the range – the Mercy Sisters and De La Salle, where Ted Ireland was educated. But, no matter how he tried to leave them behind, the Points kept drawing Florence back. The last time I saw him alive was above in Saint Anthony's Ward. His face was yellow, his hands were trembling. He tried to hide his blood-shod eyes. He was at the end of the road and he knew it. He was ashamed. But I still loved him. I never stopped loving him through it all.'

Jeremiah could feel himself getting emotional too. He searched his pockets. He found another hanky. He folded it into her hand. Then he left her there, rubbing her shoulder and whispering a prayer, as she gazed into space.

## Twenty-seven – A Shot at the Title

Another roar went up as a perfectly-timed combination met its mark. The tall blonde-haired fighter groaned yet again and threatened to capsize. The ropes had already collapsed, now it was about to be his turn. I looked around anxiously at the timekeeper.

'Call it, call it,' I remember shouting, praying that he'd ring the bell.

Eventually he did. Bartholomew turned and walked back towards me with the strut of a champion.

'We have him now,' panted a delirious Jim Gorman from somewhere behind me, 'he's only hanging on.'

Bartholomew winked at a supporter in the crowd before taking a sip from the bottle. Up on the large cemented steps at the back of the hall – what were termed *the cheap seats* – a black gentleman in a white hat forgot himself and hugged his friend. Across the ring, the blonde fighter – the gallant Swedish hopeful, Ingemar Andersson – swayed in his manager's arms, half way to oblivion.

'How's I doin' boss,' said a smiling Bartholomew, not the least bit worried about his progress but fishing entirely for compliments.

I wasn't listening to my prodigiously-talented wonderkid – as the *New York Tribune* had described him that morning. My attention was fixed on Ingemar Andersson's manager, who was slapping his man in the face and checking his eyes. But for the untimely collapse of the makeshift ropes, the young pretender would have been long tucked up in the land of nod. Bartholomew and the championship belt, a thought that earlier in the evening would have sent my heart soaring, now scared the living daylights out of me. The ring collapse bought Ingemar Andersson at least thirty seconds of recovery time. It had got him to the end of another round. Four rounds in – but I knew there was no way the Scandinavian Thunderbolt was going to hear the end of the fifth.

A night which had started with such promise was slowly turning sour. I was informed before the contest that it was an official final eliminator. The winner was guaranteed a crack at Battling James Evans – the Boston Strong Boy. Evans, from the backbreaking coalmines of south Wales, was unbeaten on the east coast. Just like Bartholomew, James Evans wasn't the biggest of fighters – especially for a heavyweight. But his slender shoulders belied an amazing strength, garnered from the dark recesses of the Pembrokeshire mine shafts. I knew what a victory over the Boston Strong Boy would mean – a big-money match-up against the man in the picture on the wall behind us. James Yankee Sullivan had just showcased his heavy hands by clobbering John Morrissey into submission inside two minutes in Philadelphia a week earlier.

Unfortunately, I was also informed about something else before the contest. While leading Bartholomew through the smoke and the smell, a man in a white trench jacket took the large cigar from his mouth and leaned in for a word as I passed.

'Win and you're dead – *you* along with the nigger,' he said, grabbing with his pudgy diamond-ringed fingers to halt my progress.

I put a hand across and pawed him out to one side. I'd seen it all and heard it all before – some Arthur de Gobineau-type spokesman for an Aryan race, or some desperado bluffing his way back from a losing streak in an attempt to pay off his bookie. Was there nothing these King's Hall chancers wouldn't clutch at to steal a march on the men with the pencils.

I had another anxious look. Ingemar Andersson's eyes were

drooped. I couldn't tell if they were fully closed. A strange feeling came over me – for a man in the opposite corner. I felt a mixture of sorrow and regret. In all my many jousts as a fighter and a manager – whether on the backstreets of County Longford or in the luxury of New York's Imperial Hotel – I have rarely encountered such courage and fairness in an opponent. Ingemar was both gutsy and well-spoken. He was the ultimate gentleman, and I was sorry to see such a honourable pugilist reduced to his present condition. Facing him had been a privilege in itself. Ingemar not only refused to engage in racial mudslinging, he even rebuked one of his own followers who was shouting obscenities in Bartholomew's direction at the handshake. He put no stock in low blows, rabbit punching or after-the-bell antics. The long count, enabling Ingemar to continue in the second round, was not of his doing. It was the fault of the referee. Now the end was near. Ingemar's manager was busy splaying water at his bloodied face, while a cornerman clung to his shoulders and held him upright.

'Almos' there, boss,' said Bartholomew, smiling as he examined his new Broughton gloves, clean again after being wiped down by the blood-stained towel.

I faked a smile and rubbed some goose grease above his eyes. I then looked over at Mickser Burrows, who tipped his hipflask against his lips and saluted. He held up a piece of paper to let me know he would be collecting his winnings soon.

'Have hem now, boss.'

Despite being my brother-in-law, Bartholomew didn't call me by any other name – I was the boss of his working life on the railway and the boss of his sporting life in the ring. It sometimes irritated me when he called me *boss* in McArthur's Saloon, or in front of Melanie at home. But I never let on.

Bartholomew's prediction was a sound one. He *did* have him now. In fact, he had Ingemar Andersson from the second bell – or whatever else the timekeeper was banging his hammer against. In round one, the capacity attendance in the King's Hall thought they were in for a classic. Blows were hard, and traded evenly. But once Bartholomew got his footwork going – an area he had improved on – he could pick off the honest Ingemar at will. The third round was a procession, with the Swede stumbling into a flurry of combinations and body shots. The crowd hissed with contrariness. The black men on the cold steps tried hard to hide their smiley faces.

And then the fourth and latest round – that's when I saw the man in the white trench jacket again. He approached the ring as the ropes were being tested. He made sure to catch my eye. He held my attention with a wincing stare, puffed on a cigar, and swept his jacket open. I got the barest glimpse of the pistol. But a glimpse was all that was needed to set my heart racing. Suddenly, everything had changed. No longer was this just another desperado down on his luck. Now the tables had very much turned. The threat was no longer a hallow bluff, but loaded and menacing – like the gun inside his white trench jacket.

I had heard all the diagnoses in the week leading up to the bout. They'll let you fight no problem, but will they let you win. Not on your life. There's no way they'll tolerate your black fighter whupping all these white guys in the King's Hall. Not a hope. It's bad for business. It's bad for image. The Ingemar Anderssons and John Morrisseys of this world – perfect physical specimens of manliness – weren't designed to be shamed by black fighters. The sport of boxing won't have it. You can win all the Empire State Championships you want – as Bartholomew had done at the Park House Hotel in Albany – but the American Heavyweight Championship is a different matter. Ye should thank yere lucky stars just to be let into the King's Hall. The very suggestion that Yankee Sullivan should have to face a black man is an insult to the fighter and to the sport alike.

Yet, despite all this, I had dared to dream. I imagined a world where Bartholomew could run the gauntlet against all the odds – bigger men, hostile crowds, dodgy referees determined to keep a brave black boxer down-at-heel – and come out the other side. John Yankee Sullivan was a powerhouse in the ring. That much, nobody could deny. But I would have dearly loved to see how Bartholomew, now that I had him at the peak of physical fitness, might have fared against the greatest boxer of them all.

Another look into the opposite corner and suddenly that dream was fading before my very eyes. Ingemar Andersson's manager had the expression of a man about to be guillotined. He gripped a towel and nodded. Here was the moment I had been dreading ever since witnessing a pistol at rest beneath a white trench jacket. It would be a bitter pill. But the choice was plain and simple – get Bartholomew out of the King's Hall alive, or celebrate a victory below in the city morgue.

I wiped his face one last time before flinging the towel towards the centre of the ring. The crowd went silent. The referee stopped in his tracks, not knowing whether to go over and raise Ingemar Andersson's limp arm in triumph or shower my boots with kisses. My opposite number looked confused, retracting his own towel hastily. Ingemar slumped to his stool, before collapsing altogether. Bartholomew was confused as well. He must have thought I had gone mad. As I put my arms around him, tears ran down his cheeks.

'Why boss, why,' he shouted over the euphoria of the hall.

Having got over the initial shock, the crowd danced and cheered and chanted Ingemar's name. They accosted the bookmakers at ringside, who guarded their purses with all their might.

'I'm sorry Bartholomew,' I whispered. 'I had to do it.'

I felt a tug on my jersey. It was Jim.

'What's wrong with you,' he barked, 'we had him.'

I told him that I'd explain later. Then I scanned the crowd for the man in the white trench jacket. He stood by the cold steps, next to the black men. Their hangdog faces said it all. He was waiting for me to seek him out, staring back without emotion. Before his departure he made a salute, bringing his stubby index finger up to his forehead.

'You bastard,' I mouthed.

He watched me as I said it, lit a new cigar, turned and walked off.

## Twenty-eight – Tales from Home

Charlie was looking for more nuts. Jim Gorman delayed for as long as possible, just to test the monkey's nerve. I had a habit of doing the same thing, of keeping them to myself until I absolutely had to part with them. You'd think he was going to go out of his mind with excitement – Charlie that is.

'Come on Jim, let's get down to business.'

He was testing *my* nerve now.

'Patience is one of the truly great virtues.'

'Well spoken, Father,' said Jim with a smug puss, before drawing the pages closer once more. '*You, Jabber and Sugrue are the talk of the parish. The suspense is unbearable. They're saying one of de Bromley's servant-girls has gone to the police. They say she has news concerning Shay's transportation and the disappearance of Constance Ryan. Others think it's all a cod. Lord Teale said he will spare no expense in taking this new evidence to whatever court is necessary to exonerate the Sugrue Gang and bring Shay home. He's also stepping up his efforts in the search for Constance.*'

Jim stopped for another breather. I looked at the padre. He was deep in thought. I should have been jumping out of my skin at this news. Yet all I could think about was Turk. There could be no justice for him. Strangely, nobody wanted to say anything – so Jim continued reading.

'*There has been a slight improvement in Mostrim's fortunes since black forty-seven. But the countryside, where the worst of the famine can be seen, is still full of evicted families. They rely on hovels to get them through the winter. The Cranley cluster is no more, with Viscount de Bromley sold up and living on his English estate.'*

'Black forty-seven,' said Jeremiah.

'That's what they call it in Ireland. Imagine, three whole years ago already – where does time get to. It got so bad that some of the newspapers, including the *Longford Journal*, referred to the year as *black forty-seven*,' Father Murtagh pointed out, 'and the name seems to have stuck.'

Jim straightened out the pages of his wife's letter before ploughing on.

*'There have been many noble contributions of charity to relieve the distress. Father Reidy even mentioned the Choctaw Indian Tribe of Oklahoma at mass last Sunday.'*

I was astonished to hear this. A tribe of American Indians sending money to Ireland – poor people who wouldn't have it for themselves.

'Things like that remind me of the goodness of God and how near He is in our lives,' said Father Murtagh.

'I wonder did the old girl, Victoria, send anything,' quipped Mickser, under his breath.

'Or Pope Pius the Ninth,' Charles Langley contended.

*'Ireland's new tricolour of green, white and orange...'* declared Jim, pressing on with his reading, *'....is now flying proudly outside Shay's cabin. Lord Teale hung it there himself. The cabin remains empty. I have no news of Paddy Sugrue. I hope, wherever he is, that he has heard the latest regarding Cranley and the above....'*

'Hey, nice writing – if a little abstruse,' said Breda, having a peep. 'Pity she can't spell. There's no *u* in tricolo'.'

'It's bad manners to read over someone's shoulder – or is that another thing they forgot to teach you at that fancy convent school of yours,' snapped Jim.

'Hey, watch you' mouth,' replied Breda, 'only fo' me you'

precious lette' would be half way to Palookaville already.'

It was Breda who had taken the envelope from a confused postman, who wanted to know why a letter for a Mister John Brown would be addressed to Jim Gorman's apartment.

Seizing his opportunity, Jeremiah called her a nosey parker and then stole a kiss. Jim looked to the heavens before resuming.

'The Journal reported that Longford people were drowned in the Royal Canal when disaster struck a packet-boat bringing locals from Clondra harbour to Dun Leary port, for a sailing to Britain. Some of the large crowd, gathered by the water's edge to shout and wave their farewells, were accidently pushed into the canal. Lord have mercy on their souls.'

We blessed ourselves and Father Murtagh said we'd all stay on after the reading of the letter and offer up a Rosary for the drowned victims and their families. Jim then continued on.

'Bishop Higgins is very happy with his parishioners in the forty-one parishes of Ardagh and Clonmacnoise. He said he was proud of their efforts in response to his call to do their civic duty and that the recent census would give future generations vital information about the times we live in. The results of the census show that County Longford has a population of one hundred and fifteen thousand, four hundred and ninety-five people.'

'They were as well to have evened it out at one hundred and fifteen thousand, *five hundred*,' suggested Charles Langley.

'We're the missing five,' said Jeremiah, looking around at the padre, Jim, Charles, and myself.

'The county is coming to terms with the results of the recent election. There was cause for celebration among the Catholic poor at the return of Samuel Blackall of Coolamber Manor and Richard Maxwell Fox of Foxhall, who received four hundred and forty-seven and four hundred and thirty-three votes respectively. Father McGaver, secretary of the Longford Repeal Club, said it was great for Mostrim and County

*Longford in general. They defeated Anthony Lefroy, three hundred and fifty-two votes, and Harman King-Harman, three hundred and twenty-three. Both Blackall and Fox agree to support Repeal. They were returned as Liberal/Repeal candidates, even though they had proposed and supported the extreme Tory, Lefroy, at earlier hustings.'*

'What a shower of bastards,' I shouted, 'I cannot believe the people of Mostrim would fall for such a pack of lies. Once a Tory, always a Tory – that's what I say. They're not called the robbers for nothing.'

'Language, please – a degree of respect for the padre's house,' said Charles Langley.

'Don't be so negative, Joseph,' Father Murtagh advised. 'People can change. Time will tell if they can be trusted or not. We must give them a chance and respect the wishes of the democratic majority.'

'Are you serious,' I said, continuing to raise my voice. 'The wishes of the democratic majority my arse. There's no democracy in Ireland. The only way a tenant can vote is on the wishes of his landlord. Until secret ballot is used, Ireland will never change. The whole thing stinks to high heaven. Blackall and Fox are just as conservative as Lefroy and King-Harman. They were clever enough to know that they would never have got elected on anything other than the Liberal-Repeal ticket. Only in a country so rotten to its core could so little be done by so many of them for so few of us.'

Charles Langley's ginger beard began to twitch. He had to have known how contrary the subject would be, but he asked the question anyway.

'*Them* and *us* – I take it you mean by so many *Protestants* for so few *Catholics?*'

'I mean the Anglo-Irish – so, in a manner of speaking, yes,' I agreed. 'Why do we insist on bending the knee to the wealthy Anglo-Irish, *Protestant*, ruling class?'

'You see, that is the difference between us right there,' explained Charles, a crackle of emotion evident in his voice. 'There is always going to be a *them* and *us*, is there not, Jabber? It is easier that way. But there was no *them* and *us* for Theobald Wolfe Tone or the men who led the rebellion in ninety-eight. Many of the leaders – and the fighters – were Protestant, but there was no *them* and *us* back then.'

The atmosphere in Father Murtagh's living room was charged. Even Charlie the monkey looked on nervously. Attempting to ease the tension, Breda made a silly face at Jeremiah.

'That's all very well for you to say, Charles. You come from the side of the winners – the privileged. Why should you rock the boat – in case you were to fall in and get wet.'

'That is a scurrilous accusation and you will take it back,' Charles demanded. 'May I remind you who saved your behind in the first place. Lady Jane Teale, that is who, a member of the so-called *them* – an Anglo-Irish, Protestant, ruling-class lady.'

I rose to my feet and Charles did likewise. When we squared up, things were really beginning to get out of hand.

'Calm down, gentlemen. Take a breather,' said the padre, stepping between us. 'Jeremiah, Bartholomew ...'

Jeremiah brought Charles away to cool down; Bartholomew led me back to my seat.

'Good. Now, let common sense prevail,' concluded the padre.

Then Jim cleared his throat and proceeded with news from the old country.

*'After Peter Hogan's escape and recapture, he was detained at Mostrim's new police barracks while awaiting the court magistrate. Instead of charging him with burglary – carrying a sentence of transportation – the authorities were pushing for the more serious charge of treason against the Crown. They wanted to hang him as an example, especially as raids on food depots were becoming so widespread.*

*However, the night before the court, the Ribbonmen set fire to one side of the barracks in an attempt to lure the policemen out into the open.'*

'Yahoo,' shouted Mickser, and he punched the air. 'Up the Ribbonmen, they'll never be bested. Up the Longford rebels.'

Mickser's elation was short-lived as Jim Gorman's face began to sour.

'What's wrong? They rescued Peter, didn't they?'

Jim shook his head ruefully at my question.

'I'm afraid not,' he muttered, before returning his attention to the letter.

*'The policemen were heavily armed and, after a fierce struggle, they succeeded in repelling the Ribbonmen. Peter Hogan was trapped inside as the fire spread throughout the barracks. He was found dead in his cell a short time later. His body was taken and dumped in the main street of Mostrim. The sign around his neck read: TRAITOR TO THE CROWN.'*

The room was charged again, this time with a different energy. Father Murtagh was slumped in a chair, his face red with anger. I was stunned. All I could do was open my hipflask, take a gulp, and hand it across to Charles Langley. Jeremiah and Bartholomew didn't really know what to do except observe a respectful silence. Breda put the kettle on and said she'd make coffee.

Jim Gorman squeezed the pages of the letter in his white-knuckled fist. It felt like we'd been cheated, as if a great victory had been snatched away at the last moment and replaced with utter despair.

'No coffee for me,' said Mickser, as he grabbed his coat. 'Ara, I need something a little stronger after all that.'

'Nor I,' replied Charles, who came across to return my hipflask and shake my hand.

'Nor any of us for that matter,' added Jim, accepting the padre's condolences. 'We'll all go down to Jonty's instead, and celebrate the life of Peter Hogan – one of Ireland's bravest ever traitors to the Crown.'

## Twenty-nine – The Saddlebag

After the trouble with Helmet-head, things changed on the railway. I had a constant feeling that we were being watched.

'You're paranoid,' joked Jim – at least I assumed he was joking.

'Well Charlie,' said Mickser, 'are you spying again?'

Charles had a good laugh and said it was nothing to do with him.

'It's all in your skull, me bucko,' Mickser contended.

But this was no laughing matter. It wasn't all in my skull. Helmet-head was no figment of my imagination. He was real. His gang was real. And their threat was very real. I had a black eye and a sore jaw to prove it.

'In all seriousness, you blighters were not present,' said Charles in my defence. 'Therefore, you cannot appreciate the gravity of the situation we faced.'

'All anyone can do is keep the head up, the mouth shut, and the eyes open,' Mickser concluded. 'This Peter Hogan news gave you a start, Jabber. In a week or two, when everything is calm again, you'll feel a good deal better. Beidh tu ar ais chugat fein.'

A week or two went by, but I didn't feel better. If anything, I felt even worse. I knew I was driving the other fellas mad, but there was nothing I could do. Everything had to be double-checked and triple-checked, even the little things. I gave all my workmates an individual briefing, including a stern warning to do nothing and go nowhere unless instructed by me – and me only. Likewise, I took no order from anything or anyone except my railway circulars – officially-typed week-on-week lists of instructions, setting out in detail the manoeuvres for the upcoming seven days.

And it was while I was picking up my weekly circular, one Monday morning at the clerks' office, that I acted on my cunning plan. After signing for the circular, I turned to the booking clerk and asked if Barnsie had left a drum of kerosene oil in the parcel office for me.

'Barnsie? What are you talking about?'

'I'm talking about kerosene oil I've been promised,' I replied. 'It's getting on in the year and I need to start lighting my lamps before knocking-off time.'

He looked all confused, then mouthed the word *Barnsie* to himself as he thought. He got up, put away his ticket book, and searched the adjoining parcel office.

'Are you sure it was *this* office,' he asked on his re-emergence.

'Come on,' I said, all in a hurry, 'don't be holding me up. Barnsie said he'd leave it here.'

He shook his head.

'Barnsie? As in Thomas Barnes,' he asked.

'And what other Barnsie would I be talking about?'

'Well, none,' he confirmed. 'But Thomas Barnes works way out in Brooklyn. Why would he come all this way just to leave a drum of kerosene?'

'Ah, forget it,' I said. 'I need to get back to my men. I'll sort it out with Barnsie myself.'

I was thinking of Auguste Dupin as I passed the stables outside the booking clerks' office. As detectives go, he wasn't a patch on me. I now had a name – a full name – and the place where Helmethead worked. And that's when I saw it again. Right in front of my eyes, where the railwaymen kept their horses – the saddlebag!

I got such a fright that I sought cover immediately. Kneeling behind a wall, I gathered my thoughts. I looked back towards the booking clerks' office. Then I pulled my black railway coat up around my ears and walk over to the stables. There were lots of horses – there must have been fifty of them – but nobody else around. I made my way over to the chestnut Arabian. There it was, as plain as day, on the saddlebag – the DP. The horse whinnied and I sought refuge again. I hunched down and thought about my next move.

Jim Gorman looked at Bartholomew and Charles and then shrugged his shoulders.

'Usually, he would be back by now,' said Charles. 'I wonder what is keeping the blighter?'

'Come down to the tent and drink a mug of coffee,' Mickser suggested, 'or would you prefer something to take the edge off a Monday morning?'

He produced his hipflask. But the man in the hard hat told Mickser to cop himself on, that he had more to be doing than drinking on the job.

'This is a load of crap, guys,' said Steve, taking his hard hat off impatiently. 'I don't give a shit who calls the shots. I was sent out to tell you guys to get your asses down to three-nought-eight bridge immediately. That means now, gentlemen – not when your ganger returns, and not after coffee. Now!'

'And who sent you again,' asked Jim.

'I told you already, the area manager. Look, this is a waste of time. I'll just go back and tell him you won't do it. He can come out here and get you himself.'

'And what is going on that requires such swift attention,' inquired Charles.

'I really don't know – and I don't care. My instructions are simply to tell you guys to go to the bridge with three-hundred and eight written on it with your equipment, then wait there for further instructions. That's three-nought-eight bridge at milepost thirty-seven.'

'Okay,' said Mickser, 'close off the tent.'

'No,' replied Charles, 'on the contrary. Close off no tent. Jabber told us to stay *here* until he gets back.'

'What are you, a baby,' asked Steve. 'Why do you need this Jabber guy to hold your hand?'

'He's right,' said Jim. 'Let's get going. Jeremiah can stay behind and fill Jabber in on where we are. It's hard lines if we can't show a bit of initiative every once in a while.'


I decided not to go back to the booking clerks' office. It would have aroused too much suspicion. And besides, what if this Denman fella had been hanging around – I certainly didn't want to bump into him. He might have remembered me from the Spieler. There was only one thing for it – sit tight. Hide and wait, no matter how long it took. Then follow him. Because beating Denman up wasn't the answer. That wouldn't get Mickser his money back.

So, I dug in and waited. I saw a stable hand – a boy of no more than twelve or thirteen. He only came by once, checked the trough for water, spread some hay on the ground, and left again. After an hour or so, there was an almighty blast. The horses were upset and reared. Then it went quite again.

After another while, a gang of men approached. I spotted Denman's long hair among them. At least he had the manners to leave off his cowboy hat while working. I could hear them talking as they drew nearer. One was saying how delighted he was to be coming off the night-shift. Another said he wouldn't go near the bed until he got a few things done around the house. Then they went their separate ways. I watched Denman mount his Arab and stride away. Finally, the moment to act was upon me.

The only thought going through my head was whether or not the horse would gallop. After all, I wouldn't want a total stranger up on my back and me at my wits' end from the sound of explosives. But I picked a good one. She didn't cause a bit of trouble. I took off after Denman like the wind. I slowed her as we headed east across the Harlem River and into the Bronx. Denman never once looked back. He stopped at a house on the edge of a wooded area. I gave him lots of space as he unloaded the Arab, tying her up before flinging the DP saddlebag over his shoulder and trudging inside.

I waited a while. I was so nervous. I almost talked myself out of it. But I had come too far to turn back now. I took a deep breath and went inside. The kitchen was empty. The cowboy hat hung from its string on a coat hanger. I kept walking. I opened the door to one of the bedrooms. He was in the bed already – and who could blame him. For the beautiful blonde head of Elsa lay next to him – Elsa from the Spieler. They were blissfully unaware of my presence. That was, until the door creaked. Elsa was first to notice. She shrieked and pulled the covers up to her neck. Denman turned his head slowly on the pillow. Then what did the cheeky fecker do only make a go for the saddlebag which was hanging from the headboard of the bed.

'Looking for this,' I said calmly, producing his Belgian Pinfire revolver from the hand behind my back.

The eyes nearly popped out of his head.

Elsa started to cry. I told her to shut her trap but she wouldn't.

'You have a go, Denman. Tell her to stop her whinging.'

He did, to be fair to him.

'It's a bit late in the day for bawling your eyes out,' I said to her.

'What do you want,' asked Denman.

'Two things. Firstly, what does the P stand for?'

He looked confused when I asked this – but, then again, he had just finished a gruelling night-shift on the railroad.

'What P,' he asked.

'Poe,' sobbed Elsa, with an expression that said *now that you know his name could you put away the gun and let us all be friends.*

'Thank you, Elsa. Secondly – four-hundred and thirty-two dollars, fifty-five cents.'

Even Elsa was confused by this.

'You heard me, Elsa. You will get yourself up, get yourself decent, and then get me the money you stole from Mickser Burrows. And that amounts to four-hundred and thirty-two dollars, fifty-five cents.'

I told her to tie up her boyfriend before she went anywhere, and to make sure he didn't slip his binds.

'Because you wouldn't want to be responsible for anybody getting shot now, would you, Elsa?'

Then I told her to take the saddlebag from around the headboard and fill the specified amount into it. She tried to pull one last stroke.

'We don't have that kind of money.'

All I did was cock the trigger. Then she wasn't too long about finding that kind of money. She opened a drawer full of it. You wouldn't see as much in the Mellon Financial Corporation. I watched her count four-hundred and thirty-two dollars into the saddlebag, while keeping the Belgian Pinfire firmly trained on Denman Poe.

'And the rest,' I said, and she looked at me as if I had fifty heads.

I knew what she was thinking – that I wanted her to clear out as much of the drawer as would fit in the saddlebag.

'The other fifty-five cents, please. The rest of your money is none of my business. I don't steal – just take back what is rightfully owed.'

She fastened the saddlebag and handed it over.

'What now,' she said sheepishly.

'What now,' I repeated. 'I'll tell you *what now*. You two have enough money in that drawer to last a very long time. So, here's the deal. I'm going to walk out of here now, but remember this gun. If I ever see either one of you again, I'll shoot first and ask questions later. Yere last swindle in this city is done. Ye've lost the right to live among the good people of New York.'

'But I can't just drop all and go,' said Elsa, her lip beginning to quiver again.

'Yes, you can. Because if you don't...'

I pointed the Belgian at her for dramatic effect. It seemed to do the trick.

'And that includes your apartment on Sullivan Street,' I added. 'Yes, I know all about it. I followed you home from the Spieler one night. Very handy actually, not far from Thompson Street at all. I searched your house the next day – found nothing though. You almost got away with it, little lady. Only, the day you robbed Mickser, you mentioned Denman's name by mistake. And you two were supposed to be perfect strangers.'

Poe pulled at his binds to no avail. Elsa had taken my advice and fastened him tight.

'Goodbye, Elsa. So long, Mister Poe,' I said, and winked in his direction. 'You know what they say – everybody's luck runs out in the end.'

## Thirty – The Big Bang

They were wondering about the limited-clearance sign. Mickser reckoned there was no need for one, as long as they had a lookout. The irony of the whole thing was that Bartholomew had always been our lookout. And if I was in charge of possession that day, he'd have been at least fifty yards up the track. All ifs, buts and maybes.

Charles said he remembered everything, Mickser remembers nothing. Jim remembers some things, especially the white dust. The white dust was everywhere – in his eyes and ears, in his throat, all over his clothes, and all over everybody else. He was the one who pulled Mickser out of the rubble. But Jim doesn't remember that. Mickser had a broken nose, a fractured cheekbone, and an open wound across his hairline. There was so much blood that it mixed with the dust, turning it like cement on Jim's black railway coat. Bartholomew was thrown onto the embankment. He was moving, or so Jim said. He was wriggling. But by the time Jim got over, he was stone dead. Jim shook him. He said Bartholomew lay there with his eyes open and what looked like a smile on his face. Jim closed his eyes and made a sign of the Cross on his forehead. Then he went to say an Act of Contrition into Bartholomew's ear, but he couldn't remember the words. The wound was as big as a fist on the back of Bartholomew's skull. A halo of blood surrounded his head.

Charles said he didn't get scared. And he knew exactly where he was – under a pile of rocks that used to be part of the three-zero-eight bridge. He said it was the strangest feeling he had ever experienced. It was like time stood still. He wasn't in bad form. Then he moved the fingers. No problem. He moved his feet. Again, no pain and he could feel every toe. What he remembered most was the quiet. That, and the feeling of helplessness at being trapped.

Jim left Bartholomew lying on the embankment and went over to Mickser again. He sat down on a rail and stared into space. When the rescuers came, that's what they saw first – Jim sitting in silence by the side of the track.

'Charles,' said Jim to one of the rescuers.

Then he kept saying *Charles* while looking at the ground. But Jim doesn't remember it. Luckily for Charles, the toe of his boot was sticking out of the ballast. They dug the stones from around it. They were afraid to touch him. They wanted to wait for assistance. But Charles wasn't for waiting. He got to his feet as soon as he could and walked away. He had barely a scratch on him.

Jack Fitzgerald showed up to the funeral. His little grey moustache made his mouth look even sadder. He told me that he had heard the bang out in Staten Island, where he was attending a safety meeting.

'All the blasting around the Battery can be heard on the island,' he said.

Diamond Brady took it hard. He apologised to me as he paid his respects. I told him he had nothing to be sorry for. But he shook his youthful head as he walked away, muttering something about being the safety representative and the buck stopping with him.

Malarkey showed up as well. He was also standing in for Ted Ireland and the Democratic Party. I nearly didn't know him. Finally, he had got rid of the dirty vest. He looked well in his black suit.

Father Murtagh concelebrated the funeral service with Reverend John Dowling, senior pastor of Calvary Baptist Church. The padre spoke about the Way of the Cross, and how it wasn't an easy road. He said Bartholomew had followed that road to the best of his ability all the days of his life. The reverend gave a beautiful rendition of *Amazing Grace*. He told us all about John Newton the slaver, how he had been saved from a storm at sea to reform and become a man of God. Just like John Newton, Bartholomew Campbell had cast aside a life in the slave trade – albeit at the other end of the business – to serve God and His people.

'And we must all do the same,' urged the reverend.

Bartholomew's old boxing second – the man I replaced as his manager – whose name is Logan Rowntree, then got up and regaled us with some fond memories from George Campbell's plantation in Breaux Bridge, Louisiana.

'Mayanbe he cudda made it big in the boxin' world,' concluded Logan, placing Bartholomew's gloves on top of his coffin, 'Bert had the skills, the heart, and, in Jabber, the bestest bossman a fighter cudda hoped for.'

Logan's kind words were of little consolation. I was supposed to protect Bartholomew – both inside *and* outside the ring. If I was that good of a boss man then why was he dead. Melanie sobbed and put her arm around me after Logan had mentioned my name. I wanted to hug her back. But I couldn't do it. I was just too ashamed.

Later in Jonty's, as we reminisced about some of Bartholomew's outstanding boxing performances, Charles Langley took me aside and apologised. He said he should have waited for my return – no matter what. I told him it wasn't his fault.

'Who, pray tell, is at fault then? Did not Lord Teale send me to watch your back? I should not have agreed to go to that bridge.

Neither Mickser nor Jim knew the extent of the danger we were in.'

'The danger we *are* in,' I whispered, as I shook his hand. 'This Barnsie and his boys will stop at nothing until we're all six feet under.'

'What will we do,' he asked.

Just then, Jonty beckoned me across to his counter. It was getting worse than a meeting of the Mostrim Ribbonmen, the way we were all whispering in corners.

'Look what arrived in my mailbox this morning,' he said, handing me an envelope. 'No forwarding name or address.'

Inside the envelope was a page from the *Boston Pilot*. It contained a crude sketch of Paddy Sugrue, Jim Gorman and myself, with our particulars and a warning to the public.

'Three ugly bastards, ain't they,' quipped Jonty.

'An artist's impression only, Jonty. But beauty is in the eye of the beholder.'

'So they say,' he replied.

'All the way from New England to my local public house,' I remarked, and puffed my cheeks out. 'The net is certainly closing in.'

'They know where you drink,' said Jonty, 'but that doesn't mean they know where you live.'

'They know,' I whispered, and tapped Jonty on the back of his hand.

I turned around and showed the page to Charles.

'What will we do, you ask me. We'll have to leave, Charlie. It's time to get out of New York – while we still have the choice.'

## Thirty-one – Decision Time

Father Murtagh plucked a large bottle of Californian wine from his living-room cabinet.

'Especially for the night that's in it,' he said with a smile.

Jim popped the cork and handed around the glasses.

'None fo' us,' said Breda. 'There's somewhere we gotta be.'

Her nervousness showed on her face.

'Come on,' urged Jeremiah, 'let's get it over with.'

Going to see her mother was something that could not be avoided. But she dreaded the thought nonetheless. Jeremiah squeezed her hand. He could feel her slipping away already.

'As you'd say yourself, Michael, here's a wallop of the good stuff,' quipped Father Murtagh, 'it's not every day we get to wet our lips with a fancy champagne.'

Mickser wasn't himself. He was all at sea. Every now and then he'd soak a napkin and dab the cut on his forehead.

'Well, I never knew you to be shy around drink. Is that cut still annoying you?'

'Ara, I'm alright Father, I'm just not in the mood,' returned Mickser, and it was plain that something was troubling him.

'Would you like a little whiskey instead,' asked the padre.

'No, I think I'll take a walk – I need the fresh air. It might clear my head.'

I didn't think I'd see the day when Mickser Burrows refused a whiskey. I was sitting on the floor, playing with Charlie the monkey. I was shocked to say the least. Mickser got up and, muttering something about being back in an hour, stepped across myself and Charlie.

'What's got into Mickser,' I asked the padre, 'you'd think he was waiting for the gallows with the gimp of him.'

'He's missing us already. He told me life won't be the same once we're gone. New York is going to be a different place for Michael,' said the padre. 'And he's not the only one. Jeremiah's holding onto Breda like the ground is about to open up and swallow her. This is their last night together too. Any wonder I went in for the priesthood; young love can be so cruel.'

'Settle now, Father, and get this down you,' said Charles Langley, handing him a glass of bubbles.

'Thank you, Charles. Are you not having one yourself?'

'No, Father, not right now. I have some business to attend. I shall be back anon.'

And with that, Charles Langley had vacated the premises also.

'I'm beginning to think there's a bad smell in here,' I joked, 'nobody wants to stay and have a drink.'

'Let them do their bits and pieces, they've little enough time as it is,' said Jim.

'The world will be after us,' I returned. 'There's no need to be buzzing about like blue-arse flies.'

'Oh yes there is,' the padre argued. 'Every minute we stay here, we're putting our lives in danger. This Barnsie fellow wants you dead – not to mention Denman Poe and the Scotsmen. Could you have made any more enemies if you tried, Joseph? And railwaymen the lot of them.'

'Don't worry your head one little bit about any of them, Father. Justice will catch up with that lot. Put your sword in its place, for all who take the sword will perish by the sword. They're your words, not mine.'

'Begging your pardon, they're not my words. They're the words of Holy Scripture – Matthew, chapter twenty-six, verse fifty-two.'

Jim Gorman offered the bottle of bubbly. The padre declined, placing his hand across the rim of his glass. I told him to have another sup, that a bird never flew on one wing.

'We must act post-haste,' stated the padre, as Jim topped him up. 'Whoever loaded that bridge – Kelso, or Barnsie, or whoever – did not want you and your boys frightened or injured, but dead. They still want you dead. You've got to get out of New York at once.'

'I have to agree with Father Murtagh on this one,' Jim added.

I would have liked to punch holes in this theory. Because, no more than anybody else, I didn't enjoy the feeling of looking over my shoulder wherever I went. But I knew it was spot on – sure hadn't I made the same assumption to Charles after Bartholomew's funeral. Still, getting out would have been a whole lot easier if we were all going together. I was going to miss everyone too, especially Mickser. But there was Shay to think about – and Constance. And there was the vow I took when I signed up to Ribbonism – to never desist from attaining, or seeking to attain, freedom for all Irish men and women. Now that I was no longer a fugitive from the law – a telegram having just arrived from Ireland with the happy news that the conviction against the Sugrue Gang had been quashed – I had to honour that vow. So, I let the padre and Jim in on what I was planning.

'I'm taking Melanie to Ireland.'

'You can't do that,' said the padre.

'I have a choice, Father, and I choose to help. Were you not listening to the words Mairead Gorman wrote in her letter? Shay, her only son, is still imprisoned in a penal colony in Tazmania. Young Constance Ryan is still missing since the day she was drugged and abducted. What good would I be to her while panning a river in Sutter's Mill?'

'We have already talked about this, Joseph. Yes, I agree, you *do* have a choice. You could choose to take your new wife – your new *pregnant* wife, I may add – back to a country ravaged by hunger and disease. Or you could swallow your pride and do what's right by your new and forthcoming family. I implore you to get out of this city – but stay in America. Stay in a country where you have some chance of a half-decent future together,' said Father Murtagh.

Jim held up the bottle and the padre shook his head. Then he thought better of it and offered his glass.

'Ah sure, I suppose I may as well. Didn't our Lord drink a sup of wine the night He and His friends went their separate ways. Permit me to raise a toast to Joseph Farrell – his health and happiness in the new world.'

'Here, here,' added Jim, 'to Jabber.'

I reluctantly thanked them and said no more on the matter.

Breda entered her mother's house on the Lower East Side in her usual barnstorming fashion. She was steeled for confrontation. As Jeremiah followed, he stopped to touch the hem of the Virgin Mary's blue robe. He blessed himself. He wasn't an overly religious person. It just felt like the right thing to do at that particular moment. Bridget Nayle was on her knees in the living room.

'Come on, we'll wait in the kitchen,' said Breda. 'Once mum starts he' Rosary, she won't procrastinate fo' nothing.'

Jeremiah hated squabbling of this sort – a domestic dispute. He also hated the tension of waiting. Every minute seemed to drag. Eventually the doorknob turned. The mother's face looked menacing and she went straight on the attack.

'To what do I owe the honour of your esteemed presence?'

Breda leapt up and made for the door.

'I knew this was a bad idea. There's no talking to he' when she's like this. Come on, Jeremiah, we're leaving.'

'Wait,' ordered Jeremiah, refusing to be pulled along. 'Cool down and wait. You came here for a reason. Now stay put.'

Breda was taken aback by the assertiveness of her newly betrothed. If she wasn't so wound up, this unexpected – dominant – side to him could have really appealled to her.

'I break my back cotton-chopping to bring her up the best,' Bridget raged, 'and she comes in here, bold as brass, and refers to her own mother as *she*. Well madame, *she* is the cat's mother.'

'Will ye both calm down for a minute. Ye're as bad as each other,' said Jeremiah. 'Missus Nayle, please. Breda has something important to say.'

'I knew it,' cried Bridget, looking up at the picture of the Sacred Heart and blessing herself. 'I knew she'd end up getting herself in trouble. It wasn't bad enough her hanging out with those other degenerates, like she had nobody belonging to her. But now she has to go and get herself in the family way. That's it, I'm done in Saint James's. My name will be mud.'

'She's *not* pregnant,' shouted Jeremiah. 'Will you listen and stop interrupting? Breda, you go first. Missus Nayle, you stay quiet. Then, Breda, you shut up and let your mother speak. Fair is fair.'

After Jeremiah had restored peace in the house, Breda spilled her guts about everything that had been happening – about Mairead Gorman's letters and how her son Shay had been set up for a crime he didn't commit and transported to Australia; about the plight of Constance Ryan and how she had been drugged, abducted, and remained missing. She also spoke of Jeremiah's imminent return to Ireland, to help Jim Gorman in his search, and how this was their last night together.

'I know I could help out too, and would love to accompany them. But then you'd be left all alone. I won't do it to you. No mum deserves that, no matte' what ou' differences may be.'

It was Bridget Nayle's turn to speak. Jeremiah was waiting for the floodgates to open, to be swept away on a torrent of abuse. But she remained calm. What her daughter had just said must have touched a nerve. Instead of going on the attack again, Bridget sat down in her old wicker chair – her comfortable chair – and began to cry.

'What are you doing, Mum? Here, come on, stop that.'

She offered her mother a handkerchief.

'There's no need fo' lacrimation,' sobbed Breda, as Bridget took her in her arms.

The floodgates opened alright, but instead of a torrent of abuse there was a torrent of teardrops and tenderness. Jeremiah felt awkward in the middle of them. It was almost worse than the fighting and bickering.

'Come on,' he said to Breda. 'Dry your eyes. Melanie will be waiting for us.'

Missus Burrows was shocked to see her husband back so soon. Secretly, she had been glad to get rid of him – so she could gossip with Missus Begley. Now he was back, moping around in the kitchen.

'I thought you were spending the night in the pub with Jabber and the boys? Wild horses couldn't drag you home if I wanted you here.'

'I didn't go to the pub. Besides, Father Murtagh has invited Jonty around to his house for the night that's in it.'

Ina Begley nearly had a fit when she heard this.

'God bless us, Missus Burrows,' she gasped, 'what is this world coming to? Imagine showing up at a priest's house and expecting to desecrate the place with drink.'

'Scandalous, Missus Begley, absolutely scandalous.'

'I have a good mind to go around there and give that Jonty McArthur a right telling off. Heaven forbid but he'd turn poor Father Murtagh out on the wrong path,' continued Missus Begley.

Missus Burrows waited for some derogatory remark from her husband to stoke a good argument. He liked nothing better than to get Missus Begley all riled up. But no such remark was forthcoming. The kitchen remained in perfect silence. On further investigation, there was Mickser, sitting in the dark, slumped and staring at the blank wall.

'Okay, what's wrong? It's not like you to pass up a good drinking session,' his wife correctly pointed out.

'Leave me alone. Go back in and talk to Ina,' he whispered. 'It's bad manners to leave a guest waiting.'

Missus Burrows didn't know what to do when she heard this. Being weirdly quiet was one thing, but calling Missus Begley a *guest* was something else again.

'I said go on. I'll bring coffee into ye.'

Now she was really worried. Mickser Burrows had never offered to make coffee in his life – not even for himself.

'Are you feeling alright,' she asked.

'Go on, before I change my mind.'

'Cut the wick on that lamp and light it,' she said, 'or you'll scald yourself with the kettle.'

Mickser brewed the coffee as a million thoughts ran around in his brain. What was he going to do when everyone was gone? Who would he work for – now that he couldn't go back to the railway? When would his luck change or was California always going to be just a pipe-dream? Would his life still be in danger if he continued living in Thompson Street? If that was to be the case, so be it. He had no choice but to keep renting from Missus Begley. He thought about Jim Gorman and Father Murtagh and myself. What a splendid three years it had been. A great sadness came over him. He tried to block it out. He put sugar in the coffees. As he made for the living room, there was a knock at the door. It gave Mickser a start. Some of the coffee spilled out on the floor.

'Will you be careful, you're worse than a child,' barked his wife, hoping to impress Missus Begley.

I stood on the step and stared back at Missus Burrows.

'Jabber. Can I help you?'

'Hello, Missus. I'm looking for Mickser. Is he in?'

'I thought for a moment you were one of those trick or treaters,' said Missus Burrows with a smile. 'Come on in, Michael's in the kitchen. It's not often he makes coffee – or drinks it for that matter. Please stay and have a cup.'

'You're training him well,' I replied. 'No, I won't disturb ye. Will you give him this?'

I took out a chunky envelope with Mickser's name printed on it. I was about to hand it to Missus Burrows when the man himself appeared.

'Will you come in, you big eejit, and don't be standing out there in the cold.'

'Michael, that's nice language in front of Missus Begley.'

Missus Burrows went back to the living room. Mickser and I stayed in the kitchen – with the door firmly shut.

'Here you go,' I said, slapping the fat envelope into the palm of his hand.

'A Dhia shabhail sinn. What's this,' he asked.

'Four-hundred and thirty-two dollars, fifty-five cents.'

'Have you gone mad or something, Jabber?'

'Take it. It's yours,' I said. 'It's the money from the Spieler – the money DP stole from you in the card game.'

Mickser didn't know what to make of this.

'Did I give you a fright? Well, here's another one, Mickser – Elsa was in on the heist too.'

'Elsa,' he exclaimed, not able for all this fantastic news at once.

'Yes, Elsa. Elsa the owner. Put on the kettle and I'll tell you everything.'

As dusk was setting, Melanie trimmed the wick of her lantern. She gave sweets to passers-by – kids dressed in Halloween costumes. She had a quick look. There was nobody else as far as Allen Street. She went back inside and checked her luggage. There was one last picture, purposely left on the mantel, to pack away. It was a drawing of her own face, small enough to place in her pocket. Bartholomew had sketched it when he was a kid. She treasured it, holding it close to her chest as she lay back in the chair. A last look around the old house brought back a flood of memories.

She had come to Rivington Street as Melanie Campbell and now, five and a half years later, she would be leaving as Melanie Farrell. Cradling her stomach, she waited patiently and whispered a little prayer. She prayed for our unborn child, for me, and for Bartholomew. It was Melanie's way of bringing the three people closest to her – the future, the present, and the past – all together at once.

She had another look outside. There they were, coming around the corner of Eldridge, Breda and Jeremiah and an elderly lady in a fur coat – a sight to behold on the Lower East Side of Manhattan.

By the time Jonty McArthur showed up at the padre's, the party was already in full swing. Jim and Charles were extremely merry. Father Murtagh wasn't far behind – for all his talk of moderation.

'You blackguards got a start on me. Well, I have something here that'll take the smiles off your faces,' said Jonty, producing a large bottle from a brown paper bag.

'That's not Canadian beer, Jonathan,' sighed the padre.

The Colmcille cleric had grown partial to more than the odd bottle of Labatt's since Jonty introduced him to it.

'Ah will you stop,' quipped Jonty. 'Canadian beer is only like spring water compared to this stuff – the finest moonshine in the American Union. Trust me, Father, once you get a taste of this you won't give a continental for Mister Labatt or any of his inventions.'

'*Moonshine*,' exclaimed Jim, tipping a clay pipe before filling its bowl again. 'Poteen, in other words?'

'This indeed takes me back to the old country,' I lamented.

'Well it might,' said the padre, as the door opened again. 'As long as it's the only thing that takes you back.'

'I'll certainly miss you guys,' admitted Jonty, taking a pipe for himself, 'the saloon won't be the same without you.'

'Come on Jonty,' said Jim, uncorking the bottle, 'enough with the soppiness. Let's have a mouthful of the good old mountain dew.'

Father Murtagh's living room was beginning to resemble the King's Hall on fight night – with plumes of smoke and not enough room to swing a cat. Abraham came over, accompanied by his wife. Missus Ishmel was treating us again – this time to delicious potato latkes.

'It's a traditional Jewish Thanksgiving dish,' she told me. 'Even though it's only Halloween, I think it's appropriate – to build up your strength after the little accident.'

The *little accident* Missus Ishmel was referring to was the deliberate attempt on my rail gang's lives by filling the inside of a bridge full of nitroglycerine and blowing it to smithereens. Then she asked how Jim's arm was and I told her it seemed to be improving every day.

In walked Missus Begley and Missus Burrows, escorted by the bold Mickser. Mickser's face was a beacon of happiness. And I was happy for him.

'Well fair play to this buck,' he slurred, 'four-hundred and thirty-two dollars. My good God, I'm made up.'

The last thing I told Mickser in his kitchen was not to talk about the money in public. He promised that he wouldn't.

'What's this all about,' asked the padre.

I tried to dodge the question as best I could. But then Charles and Jim became interested as well.

'I heard someone robbed the Emigrant Savings Bank this morning. I think I know now who did it,' I joked, hoping to get out of it in this way.

'*A Thiarna dean trocaire*,' said Mickser, 'but you're a queer detail, Jabber Farrell, a bloody queer detail.'

He beat the back of me to emphasise his point.

'Michael,' snapped Missus Burrows, as Ina's eyebrows began to twitch. 'Get over here at once, and stop making a show of me.'

She pulled him into line and I breathed a sigh of relief.

'What was that all about,' probed Jim.

'Remember DP, it has to do with him. I'll tell you later,' I whispered.

'Thank you so much,' Missus Burrows turned and said.

'I'm glad I could help,' I replied, 'say no more.'

'Help! You did more than help. You saved the day for myself and the queer one, I mean, the missus. Now, for the first time in my entire life, I have enough money to follow the dream. I'm heading out west with you, partner, out to pan for gold in Sutter's

Mill,' shouted Mickser, taking a hold of my arm. 'Padre, you'll come with us and we'll strike colour in Californie.'

'I'm afraid not,' said the padre. 'It wouldn't fit the job description. Render to Caesar the things that are Caesar's, and to God the things that are God's.'

'You mean, for the *second* time in your entire life you have enough money to follow your dream,' Jim pointed out. 'Stay away from the Spieler, Mickser.'

'Oh, I have a feeling we'll all be staying away from it,' I prophesied, 'I could safely wager that the Spieler is closed for business.'

'He's been on about heading out west since we came over from Ireland twenty years ago,' said Missus Burrows.

'Sure, what's the point of having a dream if it can't come true,' I returned.

'Here ladies, have a Labatt's,' said Jonty, Ina Begley eyeing him like he was uncorking two bottles of poison.

'I don't drink in the company of holy men,' she declared, leaving her bottle down where Charlie the monkey could get at it.

The door opened again and in walked Breda, Melanie, and a lady in a fur coat.

'Who is the uptown girl,' asked Charles, smoothing out his ginger hair, 'her style is enchanting. I am guessing she is at the wrong party.'

'Hello again, Missus,' said the padre.

'Hello, Father Murtagh. I told you already, call me Bridget.'

Melanie gave me a kiss and I got embarrassed. I had already pleaded with her not to do that in front of other people. But she looked lovely – if I did say so myself. Some women look great when they're pregnant.

'Where's Jeremiah got to,' I asked her.

It was coming near the moment I had been dreading – when I finally told my wife that I was going back to Ireland to help out Jim Gorman. I looked down at her swollen belly. What could I do – my first duty was to the oath of the Ribbonmen.

'He's a takin' in the last of m'luggage. He insisted on carryin' the wholly all and wouldn't let another soul lend a hand. He's a great boy.'

My mind returned to the Shroid workhouse, where Jeremiah was imprisoned all those years ago. It had certainly been worth the risk to set him free of that place. What a blessing he became to all of us. Some people, those who enrich our lives most, just aren't meant to be caged – that's like something Sugrue or the padre would say. It would surely break Jeremiah's heart to have to swap Breda for the chaos of Ireland. But he insisted on going back with Jim. He looked on it as some weird sense of duty which he owed since getting his own second chance.

Then a strange thing happened. My mother's scapular – the one she had given to me on her deathbed – began to itch my chest. I put my hand inside my shirt and scratched. But instead of easing, the itch got worse and the scapular seemed to burn my skin.

'Not just a great boy. He's the best kid in the world,' I said, as I gazed into Melanie's beautiful dark eyes.

And that was the moment I reviewed my own sense of duty. Just then I realised I couldn't go back to Ireland.

'I'm mighty glad the way it churned out with the butter,' said Melanie, 'now that Breda is a headin' to Ireland with hem.'

'What? No,' I answered, 'you must have got it wrong, Darling. Breda is staying here with her mother.'

'That's not the whisper I a heard. While the lovebirds were a walkin' over here ahead of us, Breda's mother told me somethin' different,' gushed Melanie, waving the glamourous lady with whom she had walked in over before I could stop her.

'Which one of you guys is going home to Ireland,' asked the lady, as Father Murtagh took her fur coat.

'That would be me,' said Jim.

'My name is Bridget Nayle – Breda's mother. I would be much obliged if you would look out for her in my absence. It can get pretty rough in the Emerald Isle at the best of times.'

'But Breda's not going to the Emerald Isle. She's staying here to look after you,' Jim pointed out, a confused look on his face.

'Listen to me for a moment, sonny. I came to America thirty years ago in an oversized coat and my Auntie Mary's sandals cutting the heels of me. I was sent here out of embarrassment – the Earl of Charlemont girls were the sweepings of the street, or so they told us. But I have been hiding, for far too long I may add, under the veil of the fake-respectability they made us put on.'

Bridget loosened the top of her dress and pulled her left arm through the sleeve of her cardigan.

'*Mum*! What are you doing,' gasped Breda.

'Leave me girl,' said Bridget, turning around so everyone could see the branded red marks below her shoulder blade. 'Ever since my youth I've been ashamed. I've carried the guilt every day. But meeting young Jeremiah Figg has taught me one thing – it wasn't *my guilt* or *my shame* in the first place. The guilt and shame belong to the animals who held down a frightened girl, all those years ago, and burned an X and an O in her skin.'

Bridget Nayle put back on her cardigan. There wasn't a sound in Father Murtagh's living room until she spoke again.

'Now somebody told me there's a Constance girl gone missing. Breda wishes to charge off and help in her rescue. Well, I'm not going to stand in her way. What was the point in educating and preparing her for life in the first place, if I'm going to be a stumbling block when one of God's children needs her most? I'll be alright. I don't need anyone to look after me. You see, I *was* that servant girl. And how I wished, back then, someone would have come to save me. I'm proud that I raised a child who would find it in her heart to do something so beautiful for a total stranger.'

Breda brushed away a tear and kissed her mother's cheek. I watched Jeremiah's face light up as the realisation dawned on him.

'What did I miss,' said Mickser, coming back after taking a pee.

Everyone turned and stared at him.

'I didn't piss in the flower beds, honest.'

There was a mighty cheer, as Missus Burrows tut-tutted and Ina Begley threw her sad eyes skyward.

'Well, it looks like you'll be having company on your trip to Sutter's Mill,' Jim said to me, nodding in the direction of Mickser.

'Who said I'm going to Sutter's Mill,' I replied.

'Ah, Jabber, forget about Ireland,' begged the padre.

'I'm not going to Ireland neither.'

'Father, it's a shame yo' won't be around to baptize the child,' said Melanie.

'It is indeed. But duty calls. I won't rest until we find young Constance. Just as a matter of interest, what names would you go for?'

We looked blankly at each other.

'Well, if it's a girl I'd like to call her Constance,' said Melanie, 'so when yo' go home and find Missie Ryan, yo' can tell her there's a little un somewhere in America named for her.'

'And if it's a boy, his name will be Bartholomew,' I added, 'Bartholomew Shay Farrell.'

Melanie mouthed the word *thankee* and squeezed my hand.

'Amen to those names,' sang the padre, holding aloft his glass.

'Father Murtagh has just given me an idea,' said Jim. 'Do you remember the night in Jeb Turling's loft and the toast he made with Sugrue? Let's do a toast now.'

'Not here,' I whispered, embarrassed with everyone gawking at us.

'Go on,' urged Melanie, and the others joined in.

Suddenly, Charles Langley cleared his throat and raised a drink: 'God bless New York...'

'The city and its people...' continued Jim.

'To Sutter's Mill in California – health, wealth, and happiness...' added Jeremiah.

'To America, may she always be free...' said Father Murtagh.

'To the people of Ireland, may ye one day be free...' declared Mickser, removing his straw hat and cradling it in his arms.

I could feel a lump in my throat. I tried to hide the emotion in my voice.

'To those we have left behind and to those we have yet to meet; to my beloved Melanie; to Jonty McArthur and Missus Begley; to Abraham and Missus Ishmel; to Mickser and Missus Burrows – otherwise known as *the queer one*; to Jeremiah Figg and his lovely fiancée, Breda; to Charles Langley and Missus Bridget Nayle. Finally, to my old and dear friend, Jim Gorman, and his quest for Shay and Constance – may the road rise to meet you; may the wind be always at your back; may the sun shine warm upon your face; may the rains fall soft upon your fields; and, until we meet again, may God hold you in the palm of His Hand.'

# Acknowledgements

I would like to extend my gratitude to my mother, Mary, and family. To my wife, Petrina, and brother, Johnny. To my brothers, Glen and Daniel, for all their help with the computer technology and for all the advice with the design.

Thank you also to Eamonn Morgan, for your dedicated and diligent proofreading.

I would like to thank The Jeanie Johnston: An Irish Famine Story and Jeanie Johnston Tall Ship Tours, Custom House Quay, North Dock, Dublin 1.

I would also like to say a big thank you to EPIC: The Irish Emigration Museum, Custom House Quay, North Dock, Dublin 1.

I also extend my appreciation to all at Strokestown House Famine Museum, Strokestown, Co. Roscommon.

Thank you also to Mr. Martin Morris and the staff at Longford County Library for all your kind assistance.

To the staff at Rapid Print Printing Shop, Sealtec House, Athlone Road, Longford.

To Mary Fleming, a massive thank you for your expertise and work on the cover design.

Thank you to Kevin Cassidy and Damien Clyne for your work in the promotion of this book.

Finally, and once again, I could not have completed this work without the help of Deirdre Devine and Michelle Bradley at Choice Publishing and Book Services, Barlow House, Narrow West Street, Drogheda, County Louth. Your hard work and attention to detail is amazing and much appreciated.

# References

*Box Like the Pros*, Joe Frazier with William Dettloff, Harper Collins Publishers, 2005.

*Early Irish Myths and Sagas*, Betty Radice (ed.), Penguin Books, 1981.

*Edgeworthstown, Myths and Memories: Seo is Siud*, Mostrim Heritage and Historical Society, self-published, 2007.

*Edgeworthstown, Parish of Mostrim: O Theach Go Teach*, Mostrim Heritage and Historical Society, self-published, 2003.

*Ireland's Own*, Channing House, multiple writers and editions.

*Life on a Famine Ship: A Journal of the Irish Famine 1845-1850*, Duncan Crosbie, Tony Potter Publishing Ltd., 2005.

*Longford, History and Society*, Martin Morris and Fergus O'Ferrall (eds.), Geography Publications, 2010.

*Making the Irish American: History and Heritage of the Irish in the United States*, J.J. Lee and Marion R. Casey (eds.), New York University Press, 2007.

*Othello*, William Shakespeare, Cambridge University Press, 2014.

*The Elements of Style*, William Strunk jr. and E.B. White, Pearson Longman, 2009.

*The Irish Way: Becoming American in the Multi-ethnic City*, James R. Barrett, Penguin Books, 2012.

*The Kerry Girls: Emigration and the Earl Grey Scheme*, Kay Moloney Caball, The History Press Ireland, 2014.

*The New Testament of Our Lord and Saviour Jesus Christ*, The Gideons International, 1987 Edition.

*The Story We Carry in Our Bones: Irish History for Americans*, Juilene Osborne-McKnight, Pelican Publishings Company, 2015.

*To Kill A Mocking-bird*, Harper Lee, Arrow Books, 1960.

*500 Words You Should Know*, Caroline Taggart, Michael O'Mara Books Ltd., 2014.